DAUNTLESS

DAUNTLESS

A NOVEL OF MIDWAY AND GUADALCANAL

●———●———●———●———●

BARRETT TILLMAN

BANTAM BOOKS NEW YORK TORONTO LONDON SYDNEY AUCKLAND

DAUNTLESS
A BANTAM BOOK / JUNE 1992

Grateful acknowledgment is made for permission to reproduce the drawing of
the aircraft that appears on the title page and on the chapter opening pages.
This drawing originally appeared in the *Encyclopedia of Military Aircraft: 1914
to the Present*. Copyright © 1980, 1990 Arnoldo Mondadori Editore S.p.A.,
Milan. Reprinted by permission of the publisher. The American edition of
the work is published by Outlet Book Company, Inc.

Library of Congress Cataloging-in-Publication Data

Tillman, Barrett.
    Dauntless : a novel of Midway and Guadalcanal / Barrett Tillman.
        p.   cm.
    Includes bibliographical references.
    ISBN 0-553-07528-4
    1. World War, 1939–1945—Fiction. I. Title.
PS3570.I39D3   1992
813'.54–dc20   91-40602
                                                                         CIP

Published simultaneously in the United States and Canada

Bantam Books are published by Bantam Books, a division of Bantam
Doubleday Dell Publishing Group, Inc. Its trademark, consisting of the
words "Bantam Books" and the portrayal of a rooster, is Registered in U.S.
Patent and Trademark Office and in other countries. Marca Registrada.
Bantam Books, 666 Fifth Avenue, New York, New York 10103.

PRINTED IN THE UNITED STATES OF AMERICA

BVG   0 9 8 7 6 5 4 3 2 1

Dedicated to:

Edward H. Heinemann:—

The designer who gave the world the Dauntless dive-bomber
when the need was greatest.

And to the eternal memory of

Ensign Frank W. O'Flaherty, A-V(N)
and Bruno P. Gaido, AMM1/c, USNR

The Dauntless crew who,
cast upon the mercy of a merciless enemy,
resisted interrogation that can only be imagined;
whose heroism went unwitnessed by friends,
and unknown to their countrymen.

They exemplified the naval airmen of their generation.
May their souls find everlasting peace.

Acknowledgments

This is a novel about people I have known and about people who never lived. Mixing them has been a pleasant task, but not always an easy one. For it is one thing to know the personalities and mannerisms of historic figures, and quite another to make fictional characters relate to them.

For the American viewpoint of the Battle of Midway, I felt confident in portraying the perspective of USS *Yorktown* (CV-5). In the course of researching previous nonfiction books I came to know all of the carrier's three squadron commanders who survived the pivotal naval engagement. Without realizing it at the time, I received a personal view of the era as well as the event from Rear Admirals Max

Leslie and Wally Short, and from Admiral Jimmy Thach. All are gone now, having taken "the last cut," and are, I'm certain, rejoined in what Max called "the Great Beyond."

But others remain, and I owe them much. Captains Bob Elder and the late Syd Bottomley, formerly of Bombing Squadron Three, and Rear Admiral Bill Leonard from "Fighting 42" were my resident experts on naval air operations in general and *Yorktown* in particular. Captain Ben Preston of Bombing Five provided useful details of the Midway preparation period, while Commander Bill Henry of Scouting Three was a fine source of *Saratoga* specifics. A marine survivor of Midway—and a survivor in every other sense—is Major General Marion Carl, who described conditions on Eastern Island. Another notable marine, Major John Elliot, lent his intimate knowledge of World War II aviation ordnance.

Two other contributors weren't there, but might as well have been. "Mr. Yorktown," aka Bob Cressman, provided details of "that gallant ship" as well as the definitive biography of the same name. And John Lundstrom, who knows everything about Midway and a lot more, was splendid. Both gentlemen proved again that they are generous, supportive colleagues.

Japanese sources largely are from Yasuho Izawa and Masahiro Mitsuda, via Henry Sakaida. Records of Bombing Squadron Three were obtained from the voluminous files of *The Hook* magazine at San Diego, California, and from Roy Grossnick's ever-helpful Naval Aviation History Office in Washington, D.C. Additional details were provided by Glenn Helm of the Navy Department Library and W. Hays Parks.

Sally Dewey of the Arlington, Virginia, Public Library again proved her research expertise with data on the Library of Hawaii in 1942 as well as publications and popular culture of the era. She is a jewel.

"Bad Chas" Harral of Mesa, Arizona, provided computer expertise above and beyond the call of friendship.

Special mention goes to my agent, Rob Gottlieb, who suggested such a splendid topic. And Bantam's ace editor, Greg Tobin, got us through our third consecutive "war" together in fine shape. We are, therefore, proud co-founders of VFW Post Number One: the Veterans of Fictional Warfare.

Not all the events described here actually occurred—but all of the major ones are factual, as are several minor episodes. In cases where memories differ or documentation is lacking, usually I have chosen the more dramatic course, tempered by considerations of what logically could have occurred.

Even for historical fiction, there is no substitute for cockpit experience. My Dauntless flight time was logged twenty years ago, but the five or six hours I flew with my father in our restored "Sail Six" were golden. Though we neither dropped any bombs nor landed aboard a carrier, that experience inspired my first book and proved strong enough to pull me through this, my tenth. The fondness lingers, and on rare occasions I visit the old warbird, kept in operational status at the Marine Corps Museum in Quantico, Virginia.

Someday I might write a third book on the subject, and I will call it *Dauntless: The Heartwarming Story of a Boy and his Dive-Bomber.*

Barrett Tillman
August 1991

DAUNTLESS

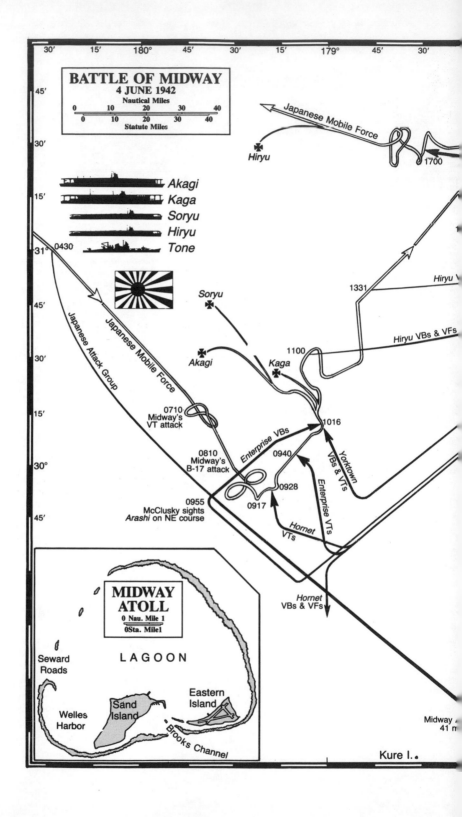

BATTLE OF MIDWAY
4 JUNE 1942

Nautical Miles
0   10   20   30   40

Statute Miles
0   10   20   30   40

Japanese Mobile Force

Hiryu ✠

1700

━━━ *Akagi*
━━━ *Kaga*
━━━ *Soryu*
━━━ *Hiryu*
━━━ *Tone*

0430

Soryu ✠

1331

Hiryu V

Japanese Attack Group

Japanese Mobile Force

Hiryu VBs & VFs

✠ *Akagi*

1100

Kaga ✠

0710
Midway's
VT attack

Enterprise VBs

1016

0940

Yorktown
VBs & VTs

0810
Midway's
B-17 attack

0928

0917

Enterprise VTs

0955
McClusky sights
Arashi on NE course

Hornet
VTs

Hornet
VBs & VFs

MIDWAY ATOLL

0 Nau. Mile 1

0 Sta. Mile 1

Seward
Roads

LAGOON

Welles
Harbor

Sand
Island

Eastern
Island

Brooks Channel

Midway
41 n

Kure I.

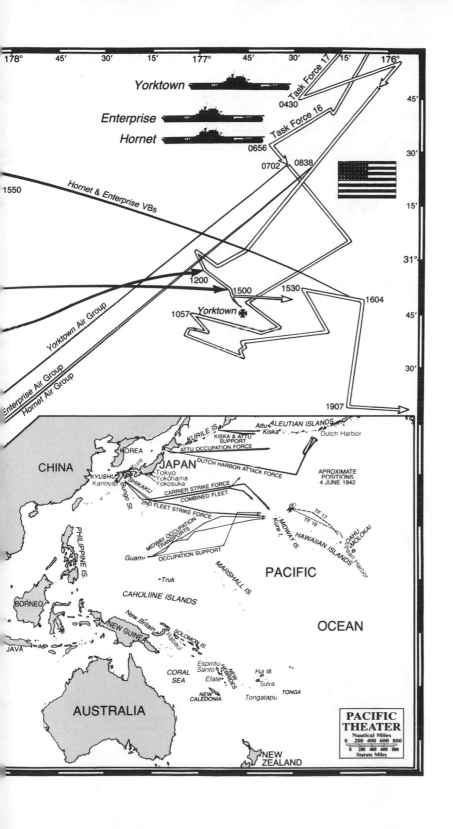

178° 45' 30' 15' 177° 45' 30' 15' 176°

45'

Yorktown   Task Force 17
             0430

Enterprise   Task Force 16

Hornet
       0656   0838

30'

1550 Hornet & Enterprise VBs 0702

15'

31°

          1200 1500 1530   1604

45'

1057 Yorktown

Yorktown Air Group

30'

Enterprise Air Group

Hornet Air Group

             1907

Attu ALEUTIAN ISLANDS
KURILE IS. KISKA & ATTU Kiska Dutch Harbor
    SUPPORT
  ATTU OCCUPATION FORCE
KOREA

CHINA   JAPAN DUTCH HARBOR ATTACK FORCE APROXIMATE
    Kure Tokyo   POSITIONS
KYUSHU Yokohama   4 JUNE 1942
Kanoya SHIKAKU Yokosuka
   Bungo St. CARRIER STRIKE FORCE
      COMBINED FLEET
   2ND FLEET STRIKE FORCE   TF 17
            TF 16 OAHU
PHILIPPINE IS.   Kure I. MOLOKAI
    MIDWAY OCCUPATION MIDWAY IS. HAWAIIAN ISLANDS Pearl Harbor
    TRANSPORTS
  Guam OCCUPATION SUPPORT

BORNEO   MARSHALL IS. PACIFIC
    Truk
  CAROLIINE ISLANDS

             OCEAN
JAVA New Britain
  NEW GUINEA Rabaul SOLOMON IS.

     Espiritu NEW
     Santo HEBRIDES FIJI IS.
   CORAL Efate   Suva
   SEA NEW   TONGA
AUSTRALIA CALEDONIA Tongatapu

**PACIFIC
THEATER**
Nautical Miles
0 200 400 600 800
0 200 400 600 800
Statute Miles

NEW
ZEALAND

BATTLE OF THE EASTERN SOLOMONS
23–24 AUGUST 1942

Nautical Miles
0 20 40 60 80 100

Statute Miles
0 20 40 60 80 100

Lord Howe Islands

Roncador Reef

155
23 August

Bougainville

Buin

Shortland Is.

Choiseul

Vella Lavella

THE SLOT

Vaghena I.

Rekata Bay

SOLOMON

New Georgia

(NEW GEORGIA SOUND)

Santa Isabel

Flor

Savo I.
Cape Esperance   Tulagi

ISLAND

Lung
Poir

Guadalcana

FLORIDA ISLANDS

Florida

Tulagi

SAVO I.

IRON BOTTOM SOUND

Cape Esperance

Tenamba R.

Doma Cove

Tassafaronga

Bonegi R.

Kokumbona

Pt. Cruz

Matanikau R.

Lunga Point

Lunga R.

Henderson Field
Fighter Strip

Tenaru R.

Rennell

GUADALCANAL ISLAND

LUNGA POINT

Nautical Miles
0 5 10

Statute Miles
0 5 10

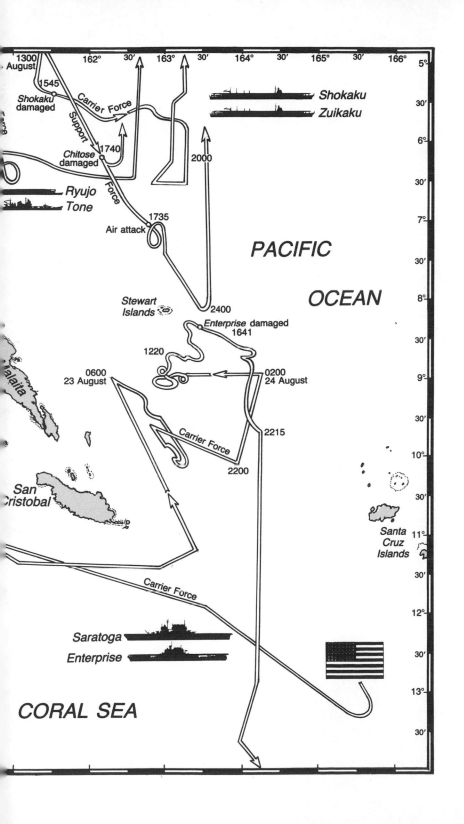

Prologue

The Pacific Ocean is the dominant feature of Planet Earth. At 64,000,000 square miles, it covers more area than all the continents and nearly as much as the other oceans and seas combined. Yet half a century ago, a tiny coral atoll totaling two square miles of land area became the focus of the greatest oceanic struggle in human history.

Midway Island (a misnomer, as it comprises two islands) is nonetheless well-named. Tokyo bears 2,250 nautical miles to the west and San Diego 3,097 to the east. Midway, therefore, occupies a place of geographic importance far beyond its size.

Geographers place Midway's precise center—in the channel between Sand and Eastern islands—at latitude 28 degrees 12 minutes north, longitude 177 degrees 22 minutes west. Near the northwestern end of the Hawaiian chain, it sits 1,140 miles from Pearl Harbor, and therein lay its interest to the naval general staff of Japan. Following six months of uninterrupted victories after Pearl Harbor, the Imperial Navy sought the decisive battle toward which all its efforts had been directed. Midway was the obvious choice: The remnants of the U.S. Pacific Fleet had to contest the occupation of an island air base so close to Oahu.

When Admiral Isoroku Yamamoto's fleet departed Hashirajima in late May 1942, it sailed with far more than a string of victories dating from December 1941. Highly professional, brutally competent, imbued with a victorious tradition three centuries old, the Imperial Navy expected a military triumph at small cost, leading to a negotiated settlement of the Pacific war on terms wholly favorable to Japan.

But the outnumbered Americans possessed the most precious of all military advantages—knowledge of the enemy's plans. Working in isolation, fighting to unravel a complex code that could reduce mathematicians to tears, the Combat Intelligence Unit's junior officers and civilians proceeded with a demonic dedication bordering on obsession. And they gave Admiral Chester Nimitz what he needed.

The Pacific Fleet committed its full strength to the defense of Midway, reinforcing the garrison with Navy, Marine Corps and Army personnel. But the primary defense lay in Task Forces Sixteen and Seventeen with a total of three aircraft carriers. The twenty-five ships of these two units embarked some 17,000 men, including about 300 aviators and aircrewmen who would conduct nearly all the fighting. Yet among even that small number, the battle turned on the one dozen dive-bomber pilots who sank all four enemy carriers.

The weapon that won the most stunning naval victory in American history had a name. It was called Dauntless.

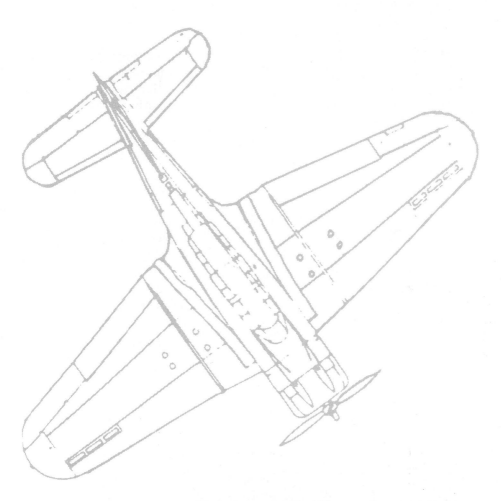

PART ONE

"We won't win the war unless we make hits."

LT. CDR. MAXWELL F. LESLIE, USN

Bombing Squadron Three

1.

WEDNESDAY, 27 MAY 1942

OFF MOLOKAI ISLAND, HAWAII

The target sled resembled a water bug flitting across a glass slide under a high-power microscope. From its current perspective, the sled was arcing in a twenty-knot port turn, forcing a slight leftward correction to continue tracking.

"Three thousand feet, sir." The warning crackled in his earphones.

Not yet, he thought. A moment ago the optical sight had been well-positioned—slightly ahead of the sled to allow for lead. But the port turn had temporarily spoiled his tracking. He made small movements with his hands and feet, felt the aerodynamic forces on his control surfaces, brought the sight picture back into alignment.

"Twenty-five hundred." Normal release altitude.

Looking better. *The sled's not turning as much now.* As he hurtled toward the Pacific Ocean at an indicated 240 knots—403 feet per second—he began seeing the sled in greater detail. The wake of the tow ship, the smaller wake of the sled itself. Tracking smoothly again . . .

Damn! I forgot the wind. As the sled turned from upwind to crosswind, the aimpoint necessarily changed accordingly. He had not cranked that factor into his mental computer. *Got to hold more lead to compensate* . . .

"Fifteen hundred, sir!" Minimum release altitude. Barnes's voice betrayed concern over the intercom.

He rolled in more aileron, felt the SBD's beautifully balanced controls bite the air, then nudged back a bit on the stick, slackening his seventy-degree dive.

Sight picture looking better. *There, coming back on target.*

"Twelve hundred!" *Barnes is getting nervous. Just a second* . . .

He reached down toward the manual bomb release with his left hand while rudder-feet and stick-hand held steady. His right eye, pressed to the rubber end of the tubular sight, shifted to the ball in its arced receptacle. *Still centered, time to drop* . . .

"One thousand, Mr. Rogers! You better . . ."

"Pull out! Baker Eighteen, pull out! You're too low!" The division leader's voice on the radio. A warning tone now, not angry. Not yet.

His heart leapt. The sled looked huge in the sight—bigger than he had ever seen it from directly overhead. He leaned back against his seat, put both hands on the molded black-plastic stick grip and pulled.

"Eight hundred feet, sir!"

At terminal velocity of 240 knots with dive brakes extended, the 10,000-pound dive bomber took a lot of manhandling. Ensign Philip Rogers tugged the stick back into his lap, loading onto himself, his gunner and his aircraft more than five times normal gravity. The world bleached out to gray as the blood drained from his head and the fuzzy channeling of his vision narrowed. His control input to the elevators took effect, changing the vector of four million foot-pounds of energy.

He sensed as much as saw the horizon seemingly dropping to meet the nose of his Dauntless, eased some of the back pressure. Color returned. The aircraft was now slightly nose-high, 450 feet over the ocean. Engine noise was falling off. Rogers remembered to shove up the power, running throttle, mixture and prop controls forward. The Wright Cyclone responded and airspeed stabilized, but only temporarily. *Dive flaps are still open.* He recalled the checkout warning: "The SBD-3 airplane will not maintain level flight with dive brakes fully extended."

Rogers reached to his right, grasped the diamond-shaped dive-flap lever, moved it rearward to the "closed" position and activated the power pack. At the trailing edge of his wings, speed brakes perforated with holes the size of tennis balls closed top and bottom under hydraulic pressure. He felt the Dauntless accelerate as the drag-inducing flaps retracted together. He was flying again. He slid back the canopy and inhaled salt air.

Now, where is everybody? What'll they say? Worse, he wondered what he would say to Barnes. His radioman-gunner depended on him for everything—for his very life. Nothing you can say at a time like that. "Ah, Barnes, I guess I sure screwed that up."

In the slight delay that followed, Rogers wondered if Barnes was being considerate of a dumbass ensign or if he was sulking. The division leader solved the quandary. "Baker Eighteen, rejoin on me." The tone of Lieutenant Shumway's voice bespoke infinite weariness—and an end of patience. Rogers looked around.

"Uh, they're above us at eight o'clock, sir."

Rogers swiveled his head left and craned his neck. The slipstream whipped at his goggles. *There they are.* Five other blue-gray SBDs, turning on course to base. Rogers added throttle and retrimmed the little bomber for best climb speed. As he slowly overtook them in a rendezvous turn, he bitterly noted that all their bomb racks were empty. He still had his remaining 100-pound practice bomb under one wing. Another embarrassment. Rogers began to think that was an ensign's lot.

The dive bomber known as Three Baker Eighteen joined on its section leader and flew home in silence.

USS YORKTOWN, PEARL HARBOR NAVY YARD

As the 20,000-ton aircraft carrier entered the repair basin, dockside greeters and the crews of other ships cheered and waved. A band played valiantly, sending the refrain of "Anchors Aweigh" across the basin. The battle-tested crew—veterans of raids on the Marshalls and

New Guinea, Tulagi and most recently the Coral Sea—felt the fanfare was nothing less than their due. Captain Elliott Buckmaster had ordered ship's company to muster in whites, and it made an impressive sight. But there were constant reminders of how the war had progressed. Approaching the dock, Yorktowners nudged one another, pointing to starboard. There, poking up from oil-fouled water, was the mainmast of the battleship *Arizona*, sunk at her berth nearly six months ago. *Yorktown* herself was a warship bearing serious battle damage, with a crew and air group badly in need of rest.

Standing portside on the flight deck with his engineering division, Lieutenant CJ Callaway felt a mixture of pride, sadness and fatigue. With a curious sense of detachment he watched the tug *Hoga* nudge the big carrier into berth sixteen, feeling the throbbing of her hard-working engines through the soles of his feet. He inhaled deeply and expelled a breath. "One hundred and one days," he said to himself.

The chief petty officer standing nearby leaned closer. "Excuse me, Mr. Callaway?"

"Ah, I was just countin' the time to myself, Chief." Callaway felt embarrassed at his lapse, but he was tired. "I figured it out comin' up the channel. We left here sixteen February. That means we've been away from Pearl for a hundred and one days."

CJ Callaway was a big, rawboned Texan without a given name. His parents, Clydia and Jimmie, had been unable to decide upon a proper name for the baby, born in 1914, so they compromised on their own initials. For his first eighteen years the tall, skinny youngster had merely been "CJ" to friends and family. Then he enrolled in Navy ROTC at college, where he collided with the granite wall of official-dom.

The United States Navy provided a blank space on its personnel forms, indicating where an individual had no middle initial—NMI. But CJ Callaway had two first initials with no names to back them up. That bureaucratic impossibility nearly scuttled his career before it was launched.

Fortunately, a sympathetic instructor in the department overruled the ultraregulation chief petty officer who wanted to deny young Callaway's application. In desperation, CJ printed his given name as Clyde James, filling the formal requirement while earnestly hoping nobody would begin calling him Clyde. Nobody did. From then on, he was "Cactus Jack," after another Texan—Vice President John Nance Garner. Eventually Callaway became simply "Jack."

As an engineering major, Callaway was a natural for NROTC.

After all, Annapolis graduates received engineering degrees, and CJ reckoned he was at least as much an engineer as any of them. Thus had he found himself assigned to America's fifth aircraft carrier, USS *Yorktown* (CV-5), in the spring of 1941.

Damage control was in the realm of engineering, and CJ Callaway served as DCA, the damage-control assistant. Even before the carrier was fully secured dockside, inspectors from the navy yard scrambled aboard to survey the ship. Callaway escorted one group, explaining the extent of the Coral Sea damage. "On eight May, the second day of the engagement, we were subjected to repeated carrier-launched air attacks," he began. "We took three armor-piercing bombs, including two near-misses. The first went through the flight deck, penetrated the bombing squadron ready room down into the hangar deck and killed three members of Repair Seven." He thought for a moment about Palumbo, Krupinski and Josen. None of the ship's company had been lost to enemy action before Coral Sea. "Then it penetrated three more levels and exploded on the fourth deck in an aviation parts storeroom."

Callaway felt a curious sense of ambivalence in his task. He wanted to demonstrate his professionalism to fellow engineers, but he felt vaguely uneasy. They were, no doubt, competent officers. But they had not been at sea in this war, had not been under fire, had not been here, in this ship. Like every man who has been shot at, CJ Callaway felt an ill-defined superiority over those who had not. *It ain't their fault*, he told himself. *They do their jobs, go where they're ordered like me. But not like me.* He swept a big hand toward blackened, twisted frames, pockmarks in bulkheads from flying steel splinters, blood-stains throughout the compartment. In a way he and many Yorktown-ers felt almost a perverse pride in their battle damage.

"What about the other bombs, Lieutenant?" A shipfitter looked around.

"Ah, I'm afraid I'm not finished yet." Callaway couldn't chase the image from his mind. The third-deck compartment had contained the fifty-four men of Repair Party Five. The blast of the 550-pound bomb had blown upward from the fourth deck, causing widespread carnage. Callaway breathed deeply, steadied himself. *Don't want to look like a sissy.* He swallowed hard. "We, uh, lost forty-two men there."

A three-striper murmured softly. "My God, forty-two men at one shot."

Callaway said, "Yessir. The officer in charge was one of 'em. Lieutenant Ricketts. Apparently he got blasted into a fireplug.

Smashed his skull. Helped pay out a hose and turned on the water 'fore he died. Survivors say he prob'ly saved the others." Callaway pulled a handkerchief from his hip pocket, dabbed at his mouth.

"Jesus," somebody whispered.

"Yeah. Cap'n Buckmaster's gonna put him in for a posthumous Medal of Honor, I hear tell." Jack Callaway had been a friend of Milton Ricketts.

The commander asked, "Any casualties from the other bombs?"

Callaway shook his head. "No, sir. But concussion damaged the exhaust uptakes in fire rooms seven, eight and nine and cut our speed to about twenty-four knots. The most damage came from two near-misses to port. The fuel tanks on that side were sprung open and we began trailing oil. We made temp'rary repairs by caulking and welding."

The navy yard officers asked a few more technical questions, then departed. Callaway showed them topside, where a lieutenant commander placed a solicitous hand on the Texan's shoulder. "Don't worry, Lieutenant. We'll get 'er into dry dock right away."

But the engineers looked at *Yorktown* and saw a damaged ship, a patchup job screaming to be done. Jack Callaway kept seeing ghosts. He ambled back down to the galley and passed sick bay. Saw again the charnel-house remnants of Repair Five. Remembered the midnight service with forty-some bodies stuffed into mattress covers, each weighted with a five-inch shell. Recalled the miserable job, performed by corpsmen and pharmacist's mates. Even when the last white sack slid over the side into the gray-black sea, there remained a ghastly assortment of "spare human parts," according to one corpsman. Somebody finally had the stomach to put them in a bag and drop it overboard.

IJNS ARASHI
SOUTH OF THE SHIKOKU COAST

Lieutenant Takeo Fuji expertly balanced himself against the rolling motion of his ship. A destroyerman soon grew sealegs under him, and Fuji had never served in any other type of naval vessel. Like most of the 240 men aboard Imperial Japanese Navy Ship *Arashi*, he had long since passed the point where he gave conscious thought to keeping his balance. It was, he thought, like riding a bicycle—you shifted your weight instinctively. For even in relatively calm seas, destroyers were lively ships with an animal quality about them, unlike cruisers or battleships.

The 2,033-ton *Arashi*, like her seventeen sisters of the *Kagero* class, was considered the ultimate expression in Japanese destroyer design. Even the Imperial Navy's follow-on *Yugumo* class, ordered in 1939 and hardly begun building, offered few refinements over the *Kageros*. Fuji's pride in *Arashi* was, he knew, shared by everyone aboard. Barely a year had passed since launching at Maizuru Navy Yard when she became the thirteenth of her class, boasting a top speed over thirty-five knots. Armed with six five-inch dual-purpose guns and eight torpedo tubes, she was as capable as any destroyer afloat.

"Navigator! Your attention, please."

Fuji's reverie disintegrated like a cherry blossom in a tornado. Commander Yasumasa Watanabe's voice carried that all-too-familiar bite across the bridge, spiking Fuji's adrenaline. He paced five steps to his master, bowed deeply and responded, *"Hai!"*

Ever stiff, ever formal, Watanabe braced himself for his pronouncement. "Navigator, I am leaving the bridge temporarily for my stateroom. Make certain that we maintain position on the flagship." With that, he spun on his heel and was gone. White-gloved salutes from all hands marked his exit.

Fuji glanced to starboard and again took in the sight of IJNS *Akagi*, flagship of *Kido Butai*—Vice Admiral Chuichi Nagumo's carrier striking force. To be at sea with such a force on Navy Day was surely a good omen. Whatever the upcoming battle may bring, it would probably be a carrier engagement. Not for the first time in his eleven-year career, Fuji pondered the wisdom of his decision to pass up a chance for flight training. Some of his Etajima classmates were making good names for themselves in naval aviation.

Fuji glanced at the chronometer. Nine hours since *Kido Butai* had sortied from Hashirajima in the Inland Sea. He wanted to go to his own bunk and close his eyes—0400 had come damnably early, and the tedious process of threading twenty-nine ships through Bungo Strait between Kyushu and Shikoku had been a trying one. Yet Fuji took encouragement at the sight around him: four big carriers—all veterans of Pearl Harbor—plus two battleships, three cruisers and eleven other destroyers, not to mention eight tankers of the fleet train. Just to be part of such an armada! To sail for the glory of Japan . . . Ouch!

It wasn't so much a pain as a surprise. The unexpected roll had caught a signalman in midstride, upsetting his sense of balance. The pressure of the sailor's foot on Fuji's toe injured the navigator's pride more than the mirror shine on his shoe. Instinct took over as Fuji saw his gloved hand snake out to deliver an open-fisted slap on the offender's face. The petty-officer signalman instantly froze in a Pavlovian response of discipline and terror. Glances were exchanged among the men behind Fuji's back—they'd seen the navigator in his moods before. They also knew that the captain never objected.

Fuji regained his composure in two heartbeats. Sometimes he regretted his vindictive tantrums, but for the moment he stared at the signalman as if the man were a specimen under a microscope. Yes, the signs were there. The onset of perspiration, tensed neck muscles, pupils dilated in fear. The officer stared down the enlisted rating for a few more seconds, quietly enjoying the oaf's discomfort. Then Fuji leaned close enough to smell the fish on the man's breath. "Idiot! Get off my bridge!"

The submissive behavior ingrained by a brutally efficient training system played itself out. A step back, an extra-deep bow, careful avoidance of eye contact, and the man was gone.

Fuji cursed under his breath. He made a show of checking the compass, assuring that *Arashi* maintained the fleet heading to the southwest. *Damn it to hades*, he fumed to himself. *Everything was going so well*. Lieutenant Fuji shivered involuntarily in the sunlight. Suddenly he had an uneasy feeling, an indefinable sixth sense. Something bad was going to happen.

SAND ISLAND, MIDWAY ATOLL

"Well, I'll be damned. Somebody in Hawaii loves us." First Lieutenant James Carpenter shook his head in wonderment. Standing at the dock with some other personnel of Marine Fighting Squadron 221, he watched seven Grumman F4F-3 Wildcats being unloaded from the ungainly aircraft transport USS *Kitty Hawk*. The forlorn pilots of Midway's garrison fighter squadron had long since abandoned hope of "new" aircraft. The fact that these were navy castoffs mattered not at all.

"Wonder who's going to get 'em." Second Lieutenant Griffin Ambruster voiced the concern of every pilot in the squadron.

"Griff, don't you ever get the word?" Carpenter stood with arms akimbo as if examining a retarded child. "Major Parks already said the Grummans will go to Captain Carey's fifth division. The rest of us keep our Brewsters."

Nobody responded to that bit of information. Floyd Parks, the squadron commander, was too good a leader to take the newer aircraft for himself, even though Midway had been alerted that a Japanese invasion force was on the way. The Brewster F2A-3, better known as the Buffalo, had once been the hottest aircraft in carrier aviation. But that was back in 1938, when it became the fleet's first monoplane fighter. Since then it had earned an unenviable reputation for poor carrier suitability. A byword in marine air held that the corps got the navy's rejects, but what else was new?

Major Parks walked up to the group, which greeted him with an informality atypical of the U.S. Marine Corps. The skipper of VMF-221 took in the scene and grunted his approval. "About time we got some new birds," he observed. A dozen ex-navy SBD-2s also had arrived for VMSB-241, Midway's resident scout-bomber squadron. Parks turned to Carpenter, whose blond California good looks had earned him the nickname "Sunny Jim." The CO said, "Carpenter, I didn't bring you over here because of your handsome face. I want your detachment to help Carey's get these Grummans assembled. Soon as they're ready, his flight will ferry them over to Eastern." He nodded toward Eastern Island with the atoll's airfield, less than a mile and a half away.

Carpenter saluted perfunctorily. "Yes, sir." As the CO stalked off, Sunny Jim turned to his wingman. "You know, Griff, in a perfect world a great-looking aviator like myself wouldn't have to fetch and carry for somebody else's flying machines."

Ambruster, trying to sound salty, snarled the conventional reply. "See the chaplain, mac."

Carpenter thought of his Pensacola classmate Buck Rogers, at last word soaking up the sun and living a beachcomber's life on Oahu. According to Phil's last letter, he'd even found a girlfriend. The marine considered that astonishing fact the most remarkable of all. At Pensacola girls had flocked around Sunny Jim Carpenter, who gallantly pointed a few castoffs toward his less-handsome friends. For the last six months the only creatures that had flocked around Carpenter were Midway's famous "gooney birds," the comical, migratory Laysan albatross. "Ain't no justice," he murmured to himself.

2.

THURSDAY, 28 MAY

DRY DOCK NUMBER ONE, PEARL HARBOR NAVY YARD

Jack Callaway sloshed around *Yorktown*'s bow, treading his way through knee-deep water. His hipboots were barely high enough to keep his trousers dry, but that was the least of his concerns. Tugs had pushed the wounded ship into the dry dock at 0720 and it had taken a while to drain the water so the carrier could settle onto the blocks. But even that relatively short time had seemed interminable. The crying need was for speed: everybody from the yard commander to Captain Buckmaster to the ship's chief engineer said so. By now the word was out—Old Yorky was sailing again, very soon.

Callaway had almost completed his personal walkaround inspection when he saw a cluster of khaki amid the drab clothing of civilian and navy dockworkers. A path opened among the repair parties, allowing the officers to pass through. *Like Moses parting the Red Sea*, Callaway thought. He slopped through the water toward the group to see if he could offer assistance.

The visitors had stopped amidships, inspecting the carrier's dished-in plating on the starboard side, below the waterline. Two or three officers seemed to be explaining something to an older man, who spoke little and listened closely. Callaway was about to join them when he noticed the four stars on the senior man's collar.

"Ah, Mr. Callaway," called the yard inspector from the day before. "We'd like to hear your thoughts." The three-striper waved to him, and CJ Callaway approached reluctantly. He was conscious of his undignified appearance, but sloshed grandly to attention and saluted. He found himself staring into the blue eyes of Chester A. Nimitz, Commander-in-Chief, United States Pacific Fleet.

Callaway was taken aback. He'd never seen Nimitz before, nor anybody with more than two stars—let alone standing around in hipboots. In a navy where captains ruled like seagoing kings, admirals were damn near deities. But Nimitz returned the salute and CJ relaxed a little. "Admiral, this is Lieutenant Callaway, *Yorktown*'s own damage-control assistant."

Chester Nimitz nodded in greeting as the DCA studied the great man. Sixtyish, ruddy complexion, lined face, white hair. *Gosh, he looks like anybody's granddaddy*, Callaway thought. But the lieutenant also knew that Nimitz had graduated seventh in the Annapolis class of '05, and had come up through surface ships and submarines. The admiral's son was in pigboats, so rumor had it.

"Well, son, what do you think?" The voice had the flat tones of Texas. *That's right, I'd forgotten*, Callaway remembered with a start. "Admiral Fletcher says the battle damage is moderate but will take ninety days to effect full repairs," Nimitz prompted.

Callaway shifted inside his waders. CinCPacFleet was asking a lieutenant whether he agreed with the task-force commander. *Well, in for a penny, in for a pound, I guess.* "Adm'ral, I'd sure like to have ninety days, 'specially after more'n three months at sea." He shook his head. "But nosir. This is a number-one ship. We can be ready in a lot less than that. Maybe a week."

Nimitz's blue eyes narrowed slightly, the white-maned head cocked a bit. "Son, I figure you for an East Texas boy. That right?" A smile threatened to escape the stern Germanic visage.

Callaway shifted his feet underwater in an aw-shucks gesture. "Jacksonville in Cherokee County, sir. South of Tyler."

Nimitz extended his right hand. "Fredericksburg here. Gillespie County." They shook. "Gentlemen, Mr. Callaway and I are practically neighbors from back home." Polite responses came from the inspection team. "Isn't that right, Lieutenant?"

"Ah, yes, sir! Only a coupla hundred miles or so." Callaway recognized the down-home angle as a leadership technique to establish ties with the common folk. And he loved the old man for it. Only a Texan could appreciate what the place names meant, especially in a state with 254 counties. Callaway knew the German-settled area north and east of San Antonio: Weimar, Schulenburg, New Braunfels. Hard-working Lutheran folk; wide dirt streets for ox teams to turn around without backing up; *Schützen* contests fired with custom-made muzzle-loaders just like in the old country. Yes, Chet Nimitz was a hell of a long way from home. And so was CJ Callaway.

CinCPacFleet looked up at the rust-streaked sides of USS *Yorktown*, noted again the dished-in plating. "Well, with a top-notch Texas engineer like yourself helping the repair yard, this doesn't seem too big a job. I'd say it's relatively minor." He turned to the other officers. "Gentlemen, we must have this ship back in three days."

Callaway's prominent Adam's apple bobbed up and down. There were some wide-eyed responses among the repair-yard supervisors, but the final reaction was as expected: "Aye, aye, sir."

Nimitz turned to go, then stopped and looked over his shoulder. "Lieutenant, bring this gallant ship back, then come look me up. We'll talk some more. Maybe do some shooting together."

CJ nodded and beamed a smile. Only as CinCPacFleet walked away in the waders did Callaway notice the admiral's left hand. Part of one finger was missing. *Submarines*, Callaway thought. *Diesel engines. The admiral used to be a by-god, hands-on engineer.* Cactus Jack Callaway figured he would do damn near anything for a man like that.

KANEOHE NAVAL AIR STATION

Ensign Phil Rogers leaned back in his ready-room chair and fidgeted at the inactivity. The skipper had called an all-officers meeting which was scheduled to begin in a few minutes and everyone else was there: eleven ensigns, three lieutenants junior grade and two "bull" lieutenants.

Rogers looked around for something to occupy himself. His scan returned to Bombing Three's squadron insignia at the head of the room—a black panther leaping onto its prey. Rogers didn't know how the emblem had been chosen, but it seemed appropriate. A dive-bomber operated much the same way, dropping onto its target from above. He supposed VB-3 had always sported the panther, from the time the unit was established at NAS Norfolk eight years before. In 1934 the squadron, then called VB-3B of the Atlantic Battle Fleet, had flown Martin BM-1 biplanes.

Phil Rogers allowed himself a touch of nostalgia. He too had been a biplane pilot when he first joined the squadron the previous spring. At that time VB-3 flew the big, noisy Curtiss SBC-4 Helldiver from NAS San Diego. Those had been good days: the excitement of joining your first fleet squadron, of making your qualifying landings aboard *Saratoga*. He grinned as he shook his head at the memory.

"What's funny?" Bernie's voice surprised Rogers.

"Oh, I was just thinking about our first carrier landings in the SBCs." He turned toward his friend and fellow ensign, Barnard Burnett, who had experienced the same rigors: flying solo the first time to the ship with a sandbag strapped in the gunner's seat because nobody trusted a fresh-caught nugget aviator.

Bernie Burnett chuckled. "Hey, do you remember Bob's first landing? He had engine trouble when the rest of us taxied out, and stayed behind to have it fixed . . ."

"And when he landed aboard, he found an army colonel in his back seat!" The two pilots laughed aloud. The colonel, a guest of Lieutenant Commander Max Leslie, had arrived late and climbed into the gunner's cockpit without informing the pilot, Ensign Elder. After landing and taxiing forward to park his SBC, Elder had been astonished to see the rear canopy slide open and a pair of eagles on the occupant's collar. "Well done, lad," the army man intoned. "My first experience in landing aboard a carrier."

Elder had been unable to resist. "Mine, too, sir!" Bombing Three was fond of noting that Mr. Leslie's friend had pointedly *walked* off the ship upon return to port.

"Atten-shun!" somebody called. Sixteen men scrambled to their feet as the CO entered the room and strode down the aisle. He made a casual gesture. "Be seated, please."

Lieutenant Commander Maxwell F. Leslie was the fifth commanding officer of Bombing Squadron Three. Short and stout, with a round
face and thinning hair, he was a "trade school" professional from the
first Annapolis class to receive aviation indoctrination.

The squadron "number watchers" knew that he had graduated
454th of 456 in the class of '26, but it mattered little. Like most young
aviators, Phil Rogers idealized his first CO. When another Annapolis
man mentioned Leslie's scholastic standing, Rogers had barged in.
"That's bullshit! Academics got nothing to do with leadership. Back in
December Frank Bolles was flying the skipper's wing on a search
mission and went in the water with engine failure. Mr. Leslie was
ordered to return to the ship before dusk, but he kept circling Frank
and his radioman until a tin can arrived. The skipper landed after
sunset, and nobody enjoys that! As far as I'm concerned, Max Leslie's
the best skipper in this navy, and I don't want to go to war behind
anybody else."

The regular officer had backed down, knowing he was out of line,
but Buck Rogers's attitude was duly noted. The navy had swelled with
reservists, whose numbers were essential to conducting a global war.
But ex-NavCads, products of the Naval Aviation Cadet program, were
expected by some Annapolis grads to know their place.

Leslie scanned the room with his blue eyes and began to speak. As
usual, he chose his words carefully, employing them with a precision
comparable to his dive-bombing. "Some of you already know that
Task Force Sixteen, with *Enterprise* and *Hornet*, sortied today. I have
just been notified that this squadron will embark in the *Yorktown* day
after tomorrow." A murmur ran through the room—half enthusiasm,
half concern.

"I am sure you all have questions, and I'll tell you what I know." He
inhaled, glanced at the deck and continued. "We are to replace
Scouting Five, which took some losses during the Coral Sea engagement of some three weeks ago. The same applies to Torpedo Three,
which will relieve Torpedo Five. Our fighter squadron will absorb
most of the *Yorktown*'s F4F pilots, but only Bombing Five is staying
aboard from the previous deployment."

"It's about time *Saratoga* Air Group got some action," Burnett
exclaimed. Assents came from the room, and Leslie understood the
sentiment. *Saratoga*, VB-3's parent carrier, had been torpedoed by a
Japanese submarine in mid-January. She had sustained minor damage
but her four squadrons—Bombing, Scouting, Fighting and Torpedo
Three—had been deposited in Hawaii while she was repaired. Since

then only Lieutenant Commander Jimmy Thach's Wildcats had seen any genuine combat, temporarily assigned to "Sara's" sister ship, the 33,000-ton *Lexington*.

Leslie consulted his notepad. "All right, gentlemen. We have a lot to do. Now here's how we'll proceed . . ."

IJNS TONE

WESTERN PACIFIC OCEAN

Flight Petty Officer Second Class Hiroyoshi Sakaida thought that *Tone* must be the most beautiful ship in the Imperial Navy—or any other. Her clipper bow and rakish funnel imparted grace and an impression of speed to her silhouette. "A flier's cruiser" was how her air officer, Lieutenant Naito, described the three-and-a-half-year-old warship, and Sakaida agreed. Forty percent of her 661-foot length was devoted to stowing and operating five floatplanes, which Sakaida flew on scouting missions.

With her entire stern reserved for aircraft, all four of *Tone*'s dual eight-inch gun turrets were mounted forward. The distinctive A-B-C-D armament layout made her unmistakable for anything else in the Pacific, except her younger sister *Chikuma*, launched in 1938.

Sakaida sat down by the port catapult and inhaled deeply. His gaze took in the armada deployed seemingly from horizon to horizon—the four carriers and the escorts comprising *Kido Butai*. At times like these, 600 miles at sea and bound on another urgent mission, the former rice farmer was prone to atypical moments of reflection.

The Eighth Cruiser Division—*Tone* and *Chikuma*—had sailed with the carrier striking force from the first day of the war. They had escorted Vice Admiral Nagumo's six carriers in the Hawaii operation, and had kept pace with them ever since. Now, however, *Shokaku* and *Zuikaku* of Carrier Division Five were absent. Word had it that the ships or their air groups had been mauled by the Americans in the Coral Sea. Well, no bother. Sakaida was an airplane pilot; he did not concern himself with strategy.

An officer's uniform entered Sakaida's peripheral vision and he sprang to attention. "Ah, there you are, Sakaida." Lieutenant (junior grade) Toshiki Azumano, second-in-command of *Tone*'s air department, strode toward the catapult. With a junior aircrewman, Azumano and Sakaida frequently flew together in one of the Aichi E13A1 floatplanes. Theirs was a relationship based on mutual trust as much as rank. Sakaida knew that Azumano had graduated from the Etajima Naval Academy in 1939 and finished at the top of his aerial observer's course. He found Azumano friendlier than most officers, while Azumano held the enlisted pilot in bemusement. The observer knew Sakaida as a first-class aviator, and a tragedy as an imperial warrior— everybody said so. His unmilitary bearing was bad enough, but his zest for Western culture was considered appalling in some circles. That any Japanese fighting man would adore the Brazilian entertainer, Carmen Miranda, was beyond comprehension.

"Have you finished your inspection of our Type Zero?" Azumano asked.

"Yes, sir. I checked with the mechanics as well. It's all in order. We can fly anytime." A pair of E13A1s, three-seat monoplanes also called Type Zero Reconnaissance Floatplanes, were the most capable aircraft embarked. The other three were older E8N2 Type 95s, two-place biplanes. Japanese military aircraft were given type numbers according to their year of entering service. The E8N series, for instance, joined the fleet in 1935, or 2595 in Japanese history. The E13A came five years later, *Showa* 2600. There was, therefore, also a Type Zero fighter—the most coveted assignment an Imperial Navy pilot could gain. Sakaida realized that his proficiency kept him on the edge of acceptability, but his unconventional ways would deny him one of the Zero-Sens aboard *Akagi* or *Kaga*, *Soryu* or *Hiryu*.

Azumano sat down and motioned for Sakaida to join him. The gesture was not entirely unknown, but rare enough to put Sakaida on guard. He nurtured a sailor's healthy mistrust of officers. "Sakaida, tell me. What do you know about our destination?"

The flier shrugged. "Sir, I only know what I have been told. That we are part of a larger force going to engage the Americans."

Azumano studied the younger man's face. *Sakaida, you're an accomplished liar*, he thought. *No doubt protecting a well-placed comrade in the communication division or captain's staff.* Hiroyoshi Sakaida was famous in CruDivEight for his contacts—most of whom owed substantial sums of money from gambling.

"Well, I can tell you a little more," Azumano declared. "Our destination is Midway Island, which we will capture with a five-thousand-man special naval landing force. We expect to take the Americans by surprise, but once they know we're there, they will be forced into battle. Midway is barely a thousand miles from Pearl Harbor. We will crush them in a decisive battle, and then they can only sue for peace." He smiled. "Then you can return to your mountains."

Sakaida returned the smile. He hailed from the village of Yamanuki, which meant "In the midst of the mountains." It lay among the Japanese Alps on the Great Holy Road North—the fabled Pilgrimage Road—to the Three Sacred Mountains across the wide Mogami River.

"I would like that, sir. You know, I was home on leave last fall. The women collected mushrooms and mountain vegetables in the forests, and green grasshoppers from the paddies. They are delicious, especially the grasshoppers. They turn red from cooking."

Azumano closed his eyes and licked his lips. "Mmmm. Rice, vegetables and mushrooms. It does sound delicious." Then he scowled. "But you can eat all the damned grasshoppers. Their legs stick in my teeth."

"Lieutenant, why have you told me of our plans?"

The officer leaned forward, hands on his knees. "Sakaida, I believe this will be the decisive battle of the war. I tell you in confidence that we have more than a hundred ships in this operation, spread over a great expanse of the Pacific. Besides our own force, there is the main body directly under Admiral Yamamoto, a transport force, and . . . another, diversionary force." He decided not to mention the deception part of the plan, aimed at the Aleutians.

"You are one of the two best pilots in this division, Sakaida. That is why I choose to fly with you. But your reckless ways cause others to doubt your ability. I just need to know that I can count on you to pay close attention to the military aspects of our mission—not just flying well."

Hiroyoshi Sakaida rose to his feet. "Lieutenant, I will honor your confidence in me. You may rely on it." And then, as if afraid of seeming too serious, he added, "If not, you can eat all those delicious grasshoppers yourself!"

FRIDAY, 29 MAY

DRY DOCK NUMBER ONE, PEARL HARBOR NAVY YARD

Yorktown was a madhouse that assaulted the senses. Shipfitters and engineers swarmed everywhere with welders, rivet guns, power lines, structural material. The ship reeked with the pungent tang of acetylene torches that showered continuous streams of sparks on almost every level. The high-pitched staccato pounding of riveters never abated. Yet, despite unremitting fatigue, CJ Callaway was unable to stay away from the noise and organized chaos.

He noticed an ungodly number of watertight doors stacked ready for use. Each measured twenty-six by sixty-six inches, weighing a hundred pounds or more. Where blast and water pressure had sprung doors or hatches, each was repaired or replaced and tested for watertightness.

After several hours of consulting, cajoling and inspecting, Callaway went topside and walked the gangway connecting the ship with the dock. In the predawn he found his way across the railroad tracks lined with boxcars bearing supplies for the carrier. Marines with loaded Springfields patrolled the tops of the freight cars, and giant gantries loomed in the dark, eerily lit by numerous floodlights.

"This ship really is gonna be ready for sea day after t'morrow," ventured a supervisor. His voice carried a mixture of awe and amazement, but Callaway's face creased into a smile. "Admiral Nimitz oughtn't be too surprised at what an ol' Texas boy can git done." He looked around, jerking a big thumb over his shoulder at the shipfitters. "With a bit of help, a'course."

BACHELOR OFFICER'S QUARTERS, NAS KANEOHE

The pile of duffel bags and sea chests threatened to become a small mountain beside the curb. Rogers and Burnett stepped back, having made their own contribution to the assemblage, and regarded the monolith of luggage. "Holy smokes," Burnett exclaimed. "I'd have never thought just sixteen guys could carry this much stuff."

Rogers tipped back his visored cap. "And the skipper's junk isn't even here yet." He glanced around. "Hey, XO, where's the skipper?"

Lieutenant Dewitt "Dave" Shumway, the darkly handsome executive officer, expressively spread his hands and hunched his shoulders.

"Here I am, fellows." Heads turned as Max Leslie ambled up to the pile. Grins and chuckles greeted his arrival as the commanding officer of VB-3 unburdened himself. He dropped his B-4 bag, slid a garment bag off one shoulder and carefully eased a bulging golf bag off the other. A sailor gratefully eased the CO's cruise box to the ground.

"Hey, Skipper," Ensign Johnny Butler chirped, "what's your handicap on the flight deck?" A few other junior officers laughed.

As always, Leslie took the ribbing in stride. "I'm too old a seadog to get separated from my gear," he explained earnestly. "Besides, you never know where we might drop anchor. Then Jimmy Thach and I'll be ready for a round or two." In fact, Phil Rogers and a few others knew that Commander Leslie was a near-scratch golfer who had won some junior tournaments in his native Spokane, Washington. The skipper's handicap bobbed up and down in single digits while Rogers, relatively new to the game, struggled to get below fifteen.

As gray-painted navy trucks squealed to a stop in front of BOQ, officers and men alike began tossing luggage aboard for transport to *Yorktown*. Rogers had just heaved his last bag up to a whitehat when he felt a nudge in the ribs. "My good man," the voice said, "when you're done here I have approximately a quarter-ton I need carried from my quarters. Just a half-mile or so."

Rogers turned and feinted a right hook at the face of Ensign Wayne W. Wik, a flight-school classmate now in Torpedo Three. The two twenty-four-year-olds sparred like high-school kids for a few seconds. "How you doing, Wayne?"

Wik shrugged. "Pretty good, I guess. We loaded our gear early this morning and now we're just marking time."

Rogers said, "Yeah, it'll be good to have most of the old air group together again." *Saratoga*'s squadrons had been land-based or operating apart for the last six months. "Say, I hear you got a new CO."

"Yeah, Lieutenant Commander Massey. He's good people. Class of '30. A quiet type, you know, leads by example. He was exec of Torpedo Six and has some combat experience from the *Enterprise*."

Rogers conspiratorially tossed his head, walked a few steps away from his squadronmates, and Wik followed. When Rogers turned around again, all levity was gone from his face. "Wayne, tell me something. How do you feel about taking those crates of yours to war?"

"Well, we'd all like to have new TBFs, but we'll do okay with the TBDs." Wik paused, gathering his thoughts. "Buck, I don't mind telling you I'm scared. Shoot, who wouldn't be? I think I'd feel better if I knew what we're going to do. But Torpedo Three is real solid, with a lot of experience. Hell, some of our enlisted pilots have been in the squadron four years or more."

Not for the first time, Phil Rogers thanked the fates that he'd been assigned to dive-bombers rather than torpedo planes. The Douglas TBD-1, though only five years in the fleet, was past its prime—slow, sluggish, armed with marginal torpedoes. Grumman's big, promising TBF-1 Avenger looked much better but only *Hornet*'s Torpedo Eight had received any to date.

Wik shifted his feet. He didn't like the course of this conversation so he changed the subject. "Seen Sally lately? She was going to fix me up with one of her girlfriends, remember?"

Rogers slapped his forehead with an open hand—what sailors called the marine salute. "Oh, no, Sally! I forgot to call her." He turned to go, stopped and turned back to his friend. "Wayne, I gotta run. See you on board, buddy." Then he sprinted back into the BOQ.

Phil Rogers had met Sallyann Downey under very peculiar circumstances for a naval aviator. On a whim he swung into the Library of Hawaii one February afternoon. He never would have stopped there with anybody from the squadron—he'd never hear the end of it. But he had read and reread the few books he could stuff in his cruise box, and he wanted something new.

A U.S. Navy scout-bomber pilot knew all about expanding box searches, and Phil methodically made his way through the fiction shelves, looking for a target of opportunity. He was in the *Hs*— Haliburton, Hawthorne, Hemingway. Then he caught something in his peripheral vision and altered course thirty degrees starboard. *Send the contact report*, he thought. Then, *Belay that. Will amplify later.*

Viewed from astern, she was worth a closer look. A cute behind, tanned legs under the knee-length print dress, and short, lustrous black hair. Phil swung wide to port, slowing to cruise speed, and passed close aboard. *No ring, that's good.* She turned toward him—dark eyes behind wire-rimmed glasses—and instinctively he averted his gaze. An attractive face with delicate features. *Too bad about the glasses, but still . . .* He wondered if she was an employee or a patron. He decided to wait and see.

Rogers sat down at a periodical table and picked up the previous day's newspaper. He hardly noticed the litany of gloom contained therein: two German battle cruisers had romped through the English Channel en route to Brest; a Russian advance slowed to a crawl; Japanese encircling Singapore; U-boat depredations in the Caribbean. Peeking over the top of the local news, he tracked his objective for a moment. She picked up three volumes and placed them on a carriage which she pushed toward a shelf. *So, she works here. That simplifies things.* She turned her head toward him and again, reflexively, he looked down. Instantly he regretted his action. *Maybe if I just look back at her she'll know I'm interested. Or maybe she'll call a cop.*

Rogers scanned the sports section without reading a word. Why, he wondered, do human males and females play this game? Why can't a man just walk up to an attractive woman and say, "Pardon me, miss. It occurs to me that we have not met before. May I introduce myself?" He risked another peek over the paper. She was looking directly at him. This time he forced himself to hold her gaze. *Jeez, she's walking this way!*

There was no pretending now. Rogers was trapped. He lowered the paper as she approached. "Excuse me," she said. "May I help you with something?"

Nice, soft voice. Good diction. Slim figure. "Ah, well, I was just . . ."

"I thought you might have been trying to get my attention. I'm here to help." She extended her hand. "I'm Sallyann Downey."

He took her hand and noted the firm grip. "I'm Buck Rogers."

A tight little smile. "Of course you are." She released his hand.

Rogers finally remembered to stand. "Oh, no, honest. I mean, my real name is Phil. Phil Rogers. But my friends call me Buck." He hoped he wasn't tripping over his words. Whatever composure he felt had evaporated.

"I see. It's traditional in the navy. All Rogers are Buck."

She's smart. She catches on fast. "Yes, that's right. Rhodes are always Dusty, Lanes are Shady and Gibsons are Hoot."

Fifteen minutes later Phil and Sallyann had a dinner date for the next evening. When the guys in the squadron heard that Buck Rogers got himself a date—alone and unassisted—they demanded to know where and how.

He smiled and said, "Ask Ming."

IJNS ARASHI, WESTERN PACIFIC

"We are here, Captain, 240 miles east of our noon position yesterday." Lieutenant Fuji's gloved index finger tapped a position on the track chart.

Commander Yasumasa Watanabe nodded curtly and grunted. The navigator reflected that sometimes it was as expressive as the destroyer skipper allowed himself to be. Both men studied the chart again, tracing the dogleg course of *Kido Butai* from its original southeasterly heading to due east yesterday, and now east-northeasterly. Fuji had sketched in the parallel track of Admiral Yamamoto's main body with three battleships, a light carrier and ten escorts, and the more easterly track of Vice Admiral Kondo's Second Fleet strike force of two battleships, a light carrier, four cruisers and eight destroyers.

"This is fine, Fuji," Watanabe allowed, "but it still does not show the Midway occupation force. I want full information at all times!" His tone was, as usual, bullying and demanding.

"Captain, I beg to explain," he wanted to add *again*, "that I cannot provide information I do not have. That is the problem with enforced radio silence." Privately, Fuji was concerned about the entire strategy of Operation MI, the occupation of Midway. Typically Japanese, it spread numerous fleet units over a vast expanse of ocean, each operating independently without radio communication.

Watanabe capitulated. "But I want you to keep me fully informed of everything you learn. I am appointing you this ship's intelligence officer since you speak English. Any American radio broadcasts that we pick up, anything at all, tell me immediately!"

"Of course, Captain." Fuji saluted as Watanabe left the charthouse. But Takeo Fuji had served under him long enough to know what the man had in mind. A navy social-climber, *Arashi*'s captain would spare no effort to impress his superior, Captain Kosaku Ariga, commanding Destroyer Division Four. That reference to Fuji's speaking English was merely further proof of Watanabe's desperation. Fuji could read and write some English—mostly nautical terms—and barely pronounced them properly. He owed his limited foreign-language skill to association with a former naval attaché to London.

Fuji pondered Watanabe's chances of impressing ComDesDivFour. He knew Captain Ariga as an ambitious, almost brutal leader himself. Commander Watanabe stood little chance against a perfect bastard like Ariga.

EASTERN ISLAND, MIDWAY

Sunny Jim Carpenter and some other off-duty marines were drawn to the newcomers. "They're off their track, don't you think?" asked a VMSB-241 flier.

"My lad, if there's anything more lost than an army pilot at a marine base, I don't know what it is." The dive-bomber pilot chuckled at Carpenter's professorial tone. "Still, that's one good-looking machine," the 241 officer admitted.

Even a confirmed fighter pilot like Jim Carpenter had to agree. The Martin B-26 Marauder, one of four that had just landed, sat low to the ground with speed and power in its lines. Carpenter called up to the copilot, standing in the right seat with the hatch thrown open. "Hey, Army. What the hell you doing here—we don't even have an officer's club yet."

"Ah, balls. We-all heard you jarheads needed some help hereabouts.

Y'all kin relax. Th' Red Raiders have landed and the situation is well in hand." The hayseed in the Marauder laughed aloud at his own humor. *Georgia,* Carpenter thought. *Maybe Alabama.*

No marine was going to allow an army flier to get away with that. After all, the navy and marines produced aviators; everybody else turned out mere pilots. Carpenter kicked the nosewheel. "Yup, I've heard about this bird. 'The Baltimore Whore—no visible means of support.'" He pointedly glanced up at the short, thin wings. "Is it true what they say about one a day in Tampa Bay?" McDill Field, Florida, was already notorious for its appalling B-26 accident rate.

Ignoring the taunts, the copilot tossed down a valise to one of the crewmen. "Ac-chu'lly, son, we're here to show the navy how to torpedo Jap ships. We got damn near three-hundred-mile-an-hour speed on the deck. Won't nobody catch us, you wait an' see."

The scout-bomber pilot spoke up. "Tell you the truth, Army, I'm glad to see you. Our squadron has SB2Us, and I wouldn't give you two bits for our chances in a Wind Indicator." The marine fighter pilots regarded their companion evenly. The Vought Vindicator, a fabric-covered relic from the late 1930s, was no source of envy.

Leaning on the canopy, the copilot surveyed the men standing below him. He took in the nonregulation uniforms—a mixture of dungarees and khakis, leather flight jackets and assorted headwear. He also cast a professional glance at their shopworn aircraft down the flight line. *These boys got no more chance than a nigger at a Klan meeting.* He pointed to his right, toward a B-17 Flying Fortress that had landed ahead of him. "Now, you want to pity somebody, pity those poor fellas that gotta fly them thangs. Four-motor barges, straight and level bomb runs through flak and fighters. An' they think they gonna hit a maneuverin' warship from twenty thousand feet? No, thank yew." He patted his windscreen affectionately. "You and me, we can dodge an' weave, climb an' dive. Hell's fire, son, we got it easy compared to them multiengine fellers."

The marines laughed and one or two even shouted, "Damn right." Not a one of them believed it.

LIBRARY OF HAWAII, HONOLULU

Phil Rogers stepped into the foyer off Punchbowl Street, removed his cap and strode to the reference desk. He recognized the librarian on duty, Mary Tanaka, who smiled at him. At first he hadn't known what to make of Miss Tanaka, but like most servicemen in the islands following Pearl Harbor, he quickly adjusted. He'd met her just once before, and the memory pained him. *Sally trusts her, and I can trust Sally.* He could have behaved less formally, and he vowed to make it up to Mary.

"Hi, Phil," she greeted him. "I don't suppose you're here to check out a book." Her dark eyes gleamed and he felt a shudder. The specter of after-hours girl talk loomed before him.

Trying to look casual, Rogers leaned on the counter, cupping his chin in one hand. "Well, maybe I'm here to check *you* out, Miss Tanaka." He looked around as if seeking confidentiality. "Say I brought you back Monday. Would there be a fine for a late return?"

Mary Tanaka's pretty head nodded gravely. "Oh, yes. It is a serious offense to return an overdue librarian." She smiled again and touched his arm. "I'll tell Sally you're here."

Moments later Rogers heard the evenly paced steps that belonged to Sallyann Downey. It occurred to him that now he knew her that well. He turned and she met him face-to-face, leaning forward to give him a quick kiss on the cheek. He was surprised. She'd never done that during business hours. "I was getting worried," she said without preamble. "I tried to call for the past two days."

Rogers took her hand and led her toward the rear of the room where they would have some privacy in the fiction stacks. "Sally, I've been awfully busy. I just couldn't get away, and I had hardly no chance to call."

He saw the realization growing in her face, the concern in her eyes. *My God, she knows. How do women know?* He started to speak.

"You're sailing?" It was more a statement than a question.

He looked over her shoulder. "I can't tell you anything, Sally. I don't know very much myself." His gaze returned to her face. "But how did . . ."

She touched his lips. "Some *Yorktown* sailors offered us a trade. They said that every book on that ship was almost worn out. I heard one of them say there wouldn't be time to read anything before they left again."

He rested his hands on her shoulders. "Sally, I've got to go. I just bummed a ride with one of the guys to deliver a load to Ford Island. He's waiting outside."

She leaned into him and he wrapped his arms around her. He

squeezed hard. They could feel one another's heartbeats and he held her for what seemed a long time.

When she looked up, the corners of her eyes were moist behind her lenses. "Phil, I'm not religious but I'm going to pray for you."

With difficulty, he controlled his voice. "Say one for Wayne and Torpedo Three. They'll need it."

"I will. I promise." She backed away, one hand caressing his golden wings. "Can I ask when you might be back?"

"I wish I knew, honey." She had asked the same thing in April, when Bombing Three relieved Scouting Six in *Enterprise*. But that had been a short cruise—out and back in less than three weeks, escorting *Hornet* for the Doolittle raid on Japan. "All I can say is that I'll call just as soon as I can. Meanwhile, I want you to have this." He pulled his garrison cap from his belt and removed the nonregulation miniature wings. He forced himself to concentrate as he pinned the wings to her collar. "Actually, I think this is against regs," he explained. "But maybe it'll keep some marines from bothering you." He tried to smile, and failed.

She touched the wings. "I won't see anyone else while you're gone."

They stared at one another for a moment, then he kissed her softly. She squeezed his neck and whispered, "I love you." Then he walked away.

Only during the ride to Ford Island did it occur to Phil Rogers that nobody had ever said that to him.

NAS FORD ISLAND OFFICER'S CLUB

"I think we're too late, Bernie. Looks like the joint's closed." The two officers had hoped for a quick snort at the O-club after unloading the squadron's gear alongside *Yorktown*, but the bar was empty except for a lonely attendant cleaning glasses.

"Well, I wasn't thirsty anyway," Burnett said unconvincingly. "Guess we'd better head back to Kaneohe." Both fliers turned to go when a small group of cheerfully noisy officers entered the bar. Grease- or oil-spotted khakis, open collars without ties. Most unregulation. "Who're those guys?" Rogers asked.

Burnett waved to one of the intruders, who returned the greeting en route to the bar. "Bombing Five," he replied. "Off the *Yorktown*. They're just back from the Coral Sea."

"The ones who're going out with us?"

"You got it backwards, buddy. We're going out with them. It's their ship."

Rogers was about to reply when voices were raised at the bar. The odds decidedly favored the visiting team.

The Filipino bartender sputtered, up against a situation never dreamt of by writers of *The Bluejacket's Manual*. The Bombing Three pilots overheard snatches of dialogue. "I beg your pardon, Lieutenant, but we are closing . . ."

"No pardon required, son. You just pour and we'll drink."

"I am sor—"

"Scotch and water for me, if you please. I'm buying the first round for my boys."

"Who's the short fella?" Rogers asked.

Burnett laughed. "You just named him. Wally Short, the CO." Rogers looked the VB-5 skipper up and down. Slim build, dark hair, angular features, take-charge attitude. But now he was getting agitated.

"Now, hear this! My men have been working round the clock to get our planes ready. We are tired and we are dirty, but mostly we are thirsty, so if you don't mind . . ."

The barman resumed sputtering. "So sorry, sir. I just cannot serve you." A helpless gesture. Everyone present knew what he meant. Standing orders. Naval regulations. Customs of the service.

"Hey, Ben," ventured a pilot with Scandinavian blond looks, "why don't you do the honors?" There were chuckles and go-ahead pats on the back, prompting a VB-5 ensign to displace the bartender. But the crowd of thirsty aviators soon overwhelmed the new server, who called for help. He was immediately joined by Lieutenant Short, who made shooing gestures to the Filipino. Rogers was reminded of W. C. Fields. *Go 'way, boy, ya bother me.*

Aghast, the barman hastened from his station; a few whistles and some applause trailed him from the room. When Phil looked back to the bar, Lieutenant Short and the ensign were pouring for all hands. Rogers and Burnett traded grins and conspiratorial winks. The message was obvious. *If we're going to war, these are the guys to sail with.*

It was turning into a pleasant evening—even memorable. Then the bartender reappeared. *Oh, oh,* Rogers thought, expecting the shore patrol or maybe the duty officer. He looked again. *Heavy artillery.* The air station officer of the day raged into the bar, gunbelt on his hip and brassard on his sleeve proclaiming his authority. The lieutenant commander even had a marine orderly in tow. Merriment died as levity fled that place.

All hands rose to attention, riveted motionless. The OOD asked a sharp question of the barman, who pointed a damning finger at the Bombing Five table. Rogers thought that the gesture resembled James Montgomery Flagg's famous Uncle Sam recruiting poster from World War I: *I want you.*

The duty officer stalked toward the *Yorktown* pilots, hissed loudly about breach of decorum, took their names and hinted darkly at dire consequences. Rogers tried, with difficulty, to follow the exchange. Lieutenant Short responded briefly, and the commander's ruddy face got redder. *"Out!"* he screamed. "Get the hell out of my club!" He pointed at the exit.

Rogers looked around the table. "Do you feel like I do?" Wordlessly, the two VB-3 aviators rose from their table and followed VB-5 outside. Over his shoulder, Burnett chanted, "Some people just don't know there's a war on."

4.

SATURDAY, 30 MAY

PEARL HARBOR NAVY YARD

Jack Callaway could feel the throbbing, pulsing power of *Yorktown*'s geared turbines driving four screws. The latent propulsion of her 120,000 horsepower became evident as the huge bronze propellers under the stern bit into the water. At his special sea and anchor detail station, Callaway felt his ship start to move. He looked at Chief Granville Riker, who grinned widely and gave a thumbs-up signal.

"Wish now I'da taken some of that two-fer-one money that we wouldn't make our departure date," Callaway said.

Riker laughed. "Mr. Callaway, I ain't sure Admiral Nimitz himself would have given you even odds."

The engineer leveled a knowing gaze at the older man. "Well, Chief, I happen to know that the admiral was betting on us. He said so, day b'fore yesterday." Callaway decided not to mention his down-home conversation with Nimitz. Folks might get the wrong impression.

Riker shifted the plug of tobacco from his port cheek to starboard. "Hell, Mr. Callaway, didn't you hear? The admiral was aboard just a while ago. Told the captain that when we're done with this cruise, we'll go to the West Coast for some real liberty! That's official."

Callaway turned away, concealing his disappointment. Ordinarily when a mere captain arrives or departs a U. S. Navy ship, there is an announcement over the loudspeaker, let alone an admiral. But Callaway had heard nothing like "Pacific Fleet arriving." Then he remembered—he'd spent most of the morning in the cacophonous din of repair parties on the third and fourth decks. The noise was deafening and unceasing; he wondered if his hearing would be permanently impaired. Several score civilian workers had only barely scooped up their tools and equipment in time to scramble ashore before *Yorktown* cast off.

Fellow Texan or not, Callaway told himself that Chester Nimitz had far more to do than pass the time of day with a bull lieutenant. *Shee-it, can't blame CinCPacFleet for not comin' to see me down here.* But the knowledge tugged at CJ Callaway's heartstrings just the same. "You got it, Chief," he said. "I'm goin' topside for a little while."

Climbing the ladders leading to the flight deck, Callaway cast a professional eye at the hurry-up patch jobs on almost every level. Generally, he approved. Few of the structural members that now replaced the originals had been painted, and the welds often were crude—evidence of haste. But United States Ship *Yorktown* had recovered from significant battle damage in less than three days.

Callaway took a transverse passageway and emerged into daylight on the port catwalk, amidships. He heard the ship's band playing "California, Here I Come," and shook his head at the irony. He wondered briefly if the music was intended to mislead any Japanese agents lingering at Pearl Harbor. But he appreciated the clear sky and promise of fair seas—wherever the carrier was bound.

The 20,000-ton carrier was slowly heading down the channel, creating a pleasant breeze on deck. Looking forward, Callaway saw two eight-inch cruisers—the ten-year-old *Portland*, and ahead of her the blue-gray shape of *Astoria*. An officer of the deck division, whom

Callaway knew slightly, said that five destroyers had led the procession. "Any idea where we're headed?" the officer asked.

Callaway said, "I reckon the cap'n will tell us pretty soon."

Jim Carpenter stood on the left rudder pedal, shoved up the power with his left hand and pivoted his Brewster Buffalo in a half circle. Abruptly he depressed his right toe brake and retarded the red-knobbed mixture control on his throttle quadrant. The fuel-starved Wright Cyclone engine sputtered into silence and the three-bladed propeller began winding down.

Carpenter rotated his magneto switch to the off position, secured the cockpit and began to climb out. His plane captain, Corporal Jacob Pankratz, climbed atop the midwing monoplane and helped the lieutenant shuck his parachute harness. Sunny Jim stretched his six-one frame out of the cockpit. He pulled off his cloth helmet with Fischer "bugeye" goggles—all the hot aviators were reputed to have them instead of the conventional navy-issue variety.

"I see we've got more company," Carpenter observed. Looking down the runway, he saw seven new B-17Es of the Army Air Force's Eleventh Bombardment Group. "Those weren't here when we took off."

"No, sir," replied Pankratz. "Things seem to be heating up. Word over at the operations center is that a coupla PBYs crossed paths with some Jap bombers."

Carpenter perked up. Some action would be a welcome diversion from the endless routine of combat air patrols like the four-hour hop he had just flown. "Jap bombers, eh?" He stood motionless on the wing for a moment, pondering the prospects. In all the six miserable months he'd been on this rock, there had only been one interception of an enemy aircraft. Back in March, Captain Jim Neefus's flight had tied into a big Kawanishi flying boat and shot it down. Though one marine had been wounded, everybody involved had been decorated. Aside from occasional shellings by enemy submarines, Midway was distressingly peaceful. So far in this war, James Carpenter was entitled to wear the American Defense Ribbon—period.

The blond Californian slid off the wing, landing with catlike grace. The other three pilots from the CAP were approaching him to initiate the inevitable postflight discussion. *Shouldn't take long*, Carpenter thought bitterly. *Absolutely nothing happened.*

He turned to watch four of VMF-221's new Grumman Wildcats taxi past. Rocking awkwardly on their narrow landing gear, they resembled beer barrels on roller skates, Carpenter thought. Closest to him was the F4F with a black number twenty-four painted on its fuselage. The pilot glanced over, waved and continued on his way. "Carey's division," Griff Ambruster remarked. "Lucky stiffs."

Carpenter looked after the number twenty-four fighter. If he had a greater ambition than winning a combat decoration, it was besting the pilot of Mike-Fox Twenty-four in a mock dogfight, just once. Marion Eugene Carl—what a name for a marine! However, the lanky Oregonian was just as handsome as Sunny Jim; was taller, had a new set of captain's bars and was a superior aviator. *Hell*, Carpenter admitted, *he's the best pilot in this squadron. Maybe in the whole damn Marine Corps.*

Ambruster sensed his friend's mood. "What's the matter, Jim? Something eating you?"

Sunny Jim flashed a sunny smile. "Hell no. What could be the matter? C'mon. Let's grab some chow."

OVERHEAD USS YORKTOWN

The squadrons had flown out from NAS Kaneohe, climbing away from the air station on Oahu's east coast. Behind them they left the Mokapu Peninsula overlooking beautiful Kaneohe Bay. In the front cockpit of Three Baker Eighteen, Phil Rogers checked his spacing in the third division of Bombing Three, anticipating his first carrier landing in several weeks. Mr. Leslie had kept the squadron sharp with "bounce drill" at Kaneohe, practicing field carrier landings, but it was never quite the same. Nothing on earth was quite like landing on a ship—even a big one like the 910-foot *Saratoga*.

Rogers looked forward and, from 8,000 feet, saw the familiar disposition of a carrier task group. He noted that the ships were already into the wind, trailing serene white wakes in the afternoon sunshine. At the center of the disposition was *Yorktown*, ready to receive her four squadrons. She was trailed by a single-stack plane-guard destroyer that Rogers identified as one of the twelve *Sims* class of 1936.

As per the briefing, Lieutenant Commander Thach's fighters

descended to land first. Rogers glimpsed them: four six-plane divisions peeling off into the racetrack pattern; tailhooks extended from the stubby Grumman tails like stingers of portly, oversized bumblebees. Rogers knew little about the makeshift F4F-4 outfit; leadership provided by Thach's *Saratoga* squadron, Fighting Three, with most of the pilots from *Yorktown*'s resident VF-42. Max Leslie led Bombing Three into a patient turn, awaiting its own time to land aboard.

Coming around the circle, Rogers glanced down again to check the progress of the recovery. Fighting Three's first division was aboard, but no other Wildcats were in the pattern. Rogers's gaze returned to his own formation.

"Mr. Rogers, somethin's wrong down there." Barnes's voice carried a mixture of uncertainty and concern. An SBD radioman, in his rotating gunner's seat, had a better downward view than the pilot.

Rogers reached up with his left hand, pulled the canopy release and with both hands shoved the hatch back. Then he slid his amber-lensed goggles down over his eyes and poked his head into the 130-knot slipstream. Squinting, he discerned an unfamiliar shape on the flight deck, an indefinable something that did not belong. *Barnes is right. There's some foul-up.*

Lieutenant CJ Callaway was not an aviator. In fact, he had only been off the ground three times in his life. But from his vantage point on the port side of the carrier's island structure, even he could tell something was terribly wrong.

The first F4F of the third division had landed safely. Snagging an arresting wire, it was brought up short; the deckhands disengaged the tailhook and the Wildcat marked F-13 taxied forward over the lowered barricades. Immediately, the steel barriers had been raised as the next fighter turned into the groove over the carrier's wake. Looking aft, Callaway had seen the landing signal officer slash his colored flags down and across his chest in the "cut" signal.

Immediately the F4F's nose dropped as the pilot made an undirected play for the deck. The little fighter accelerated briefly, overshot the arresting wires and contacted the deck. There it rebounded into the air and Callaway heard the engine growl as the frightened aviator crammed on power. *Too late*, Callaway thought to himself. He resisted the impulse to duck, watching in fascination as he grasped the railing with whitened knuckles.

Fox-Fourteen bounced over the five-foot-high barriers and, out of flying speed, crashed onto the back of Fox-Thirteen. The noise of the impact was accompanied by shreds of aluminum and steel as Fox-Fourteen's propeller sliced into the airframe of its unintended victim. Instinctively averting his face from the flying debris, Callaway glanced back at the carnage. He gasped aloud. "Ohhh, no."

Looking almost directly down on the tangled aircraft, Callaway saw a large gash through the cockpit of unlucky Fox-Thirteen. A medical corpsman scrambled into view from the island, scaled the intertwined fighters and hoisted himself onto the wing. Callaway clearly saw the medic lean into the shattered cockpit and grasp the pilot's neck, pinching off a severed artery.

Moments later both F4F pilots were helped down from the tangled metal. Callaway noticed that the pilot of Fox-Fourteen looked very young and very shocked but otherwise he seemed unhurt. The unconscious form of the other pilot was carefully lowered into a litter, which became soaked in blood. A flight surgeon bent over the form, then shook his head and pulled a blanket over the aviator's body.

Rogers checked his instrument-panel clock again. About ten minutes had passed since the recovery had stopped, but the last F4F's were landing once more. He called over the intercom to alert his radioman-gunner. "Stand by, Barnes. We're about ready."

Four feet behind his pilot, Aviation Radioman Second Class William E. Barnes double-checked his cockpit: two .30-caliber guns stowed, seat locked facing forward, lap belt fastened and canopy pushed forward and locked. "All set, Mr. Rogers."

Trailing Bombing Five, Max Leslie led Bombing Three around the pattern again, descending as he did so. Glancing back, Rogers saw the ungainly forms of Torpedo Three's Devastators well astern. Flying down *Yorktown*'s starboard side at 800 feet, Rogers ran through his landing checklist again. *GUMP*, he thought. The old litany for landing a modern aircraft: gas, undercarriage, mixture, prop. *And tailhook!* he reminded himself. He reached down with his left hand and activated the hook release. It wouldn't do to arrive at the groove and get a waveoff first time aboard a new carrier. Following his section leader through the left-hand pattern, he was careful to maintain his interval.

Lining up with the deck, coordinating throttle, stick and rudder to conform to the LSO's esoteric pantomime, Ensign Philip Rogers prepared for his first landing aboard USS *Yorktown*. Ten seconds later he saw the cut-the-gun signal. He retarded the throttle, brought the stick back and felt his Dauntless connect with the Douglas fir decking. The impact tossed him forward against his seatbelt.

Number-four wire, he thought, *not bad*. Then the coincidence hit him: *My fourth carrier*. First had been his parent ship, *Saratoga*, then refresher quals aboard *Lexington* before the war. Next had been *Enterprise* during the Doolittle raid, and now her sister *Yorktown*. As he added power and taxied forward over the barriers, Rogers grinned to himself. *I'm getting to be an old hand. Can't be many ensigns with landings on four carriers. Especially in a navy with seven flattops.*

Then the thought struck him. Nobody would ever log another landing on the Lex. She'd gone down at Coral Sea. Distracted, Rogers almost missed the crossed-arm "stop" signal from the plane director. He looked around for some sign of the deck foul-up that had delayed the landing. He wondered if anybody had been hurt.

5.

SUNDAY, 31 MAY

USS YORKTOWN

Bernie Burnett and Phil Rogers were like any other two ensigns on a new ship—trying to settle in and not appear conspicuously out of place. Their stateroom was a small cubicle with bunk beds, a locker and a writing table for each, and not much more. They had stowed their gear the day before, but some overage constantly was shifted from their bunks to the deck and back. With one toe, Bernie nudged a dog-eared parachute bag that served both men as combination laundry hamper and portable dresser.

"Damn," Burnett exclaimed. "I wonder where somebody like the skipper puts his golf bag. We're stuffed to the gunwales here." Bernie always tried to sound salty.

Rogers looked down from the top berth. At five eleven, he had a height advantage on his roommate. "Haven't you heard, Mr. Burnett? Lieutenant commanders get more space than us peons."

"Yeah, yeah. I know. There's three kinds of naval officers."

"Young studs," Rogers began the litany.

"Old fuds," countered Burnett.

"And lieutenant commanders!" They hooted in unison.

"Well, I guess we're as squared away as we're going to be," Burnett offered. "Want to take a look around this tub? See what we can learn?"

Burnett's natural curiosity was one of the things that appealed to Rogers. While other junior officers spent much of their time trying to give the impression they already knew it all, Bernie Burnett openly admitted that he didn't. "Well, what's wrong with that?" he asked. "Nobody expects an ensign to know anything. So I figure I'll astonish the hell out of people when I come up with something I learned on my own."

Rogers swung his brown shoes over the edge of his bunk and dropped to the deck. "Might as well, I guess. But I doubt there's much new to see. This ship is *Enterprise*'s older sister, and we got to know her pretty well." Eighteen days on the Doolittle raid, without much flying to break the routine, had meant plenty of time to learn the Big E's layout.

Burnett slid into his leather G-1 flight jacket. "Yeah, I know, but every ship's bound to be a little different. I've noticed one thing—this one's not as clean as the *Enterprise*."

"Well, hell, Bernie, I guess not! *Yorktown* took a couple of hits at Coral Sea." Rogers set his visored cap on his head at a killing angle. It had a trace of green on the braided gold band, indicating exposure to saltwater. In truth, both ensigns had "keelhauled" their hats to hasten the effect. He grinned. "How would you look if you'd been hit by an armor-piercing bomb that exploded somewhere around your liver?"

"Then I'd be as ugly as you!" Burnett pulled Rogers's visor down over his eyes. While Rogers readjusted his hat, Bernie continued. "You know, I still miss the Sara. Scuttlebutt says she's leaving the West Coast to join us."

Rogers shrugged. "Well, I don't imagine she's got much of an air group. Scouting Three and maybe a stray fighter outfit." He shrugged. "But you're right. I sure wish she was with us." Both men stood silent for an awkward moment, recalling Captain Buckmaster's announcement of the task force's objective the day the air group had flown aboard. This time wouldn't be like the Doolittle trip—that was certain.

"You know," Rogers continued, "I have a friend on Midway. Jim Carpenter, a marine type. We were classmates at Pensacola."

"Yeah? What's he fly?"

"Brewsters." Rogers's voice was low and flat.

Burnett's face turned solemn. "Damn. And I wanted to be a fighter pilot."

"I've thought about that, too, Bernie. But I tell you what. This war is going to be won or lost by who sinks the most ships. That means the dive-bombers and torpeckers will haul the mail for Uncle Sugar. Now, I sure as hell don't want to go to war in a TBD, do you?" Burnett earnestly shook his head. "So I figure we're in the right place at the right time to do the most good. I wouldn't trade in my SBD for anything else."

"I would," Burnett replied. He savored the expression on Rogers's face. "I'd like to fly a DC-3."

"Whaaat?"

"Sure. Then I could go home anytime I wanted!"

Shaking his head, Rogers stepped into the passageway. Abruptly he turned around and, in a level tone, asked, "Bernie—you need a good copilot?"

IJNS TONE

At one end of the cruiser's large hangar bay was a map of the Central Pacific. Multiple tracks showing various Combined Fleet units were depicted in different colors, but all converged at a point in midocean.

"We are currently here," said Lieutenant Masatake Naito. The ship's air-operations officer pointed to a hash mark along the blue track, indicating a position 700 nautical miles off Japan. His audience, composed of the aircrews who would fly the reconnaissance planes, paid strict attention. After four days at sea, they were about to learn their mysterious destination.

Naito continued. "At dawn four days from now, this force will launch powerful air attacks on the American base at Midway." He tapped the two specks indicating Sand and Eastern islands, object of the multi-pronged assault.

Sitting in the second row, Flight Petty Officer Hiroyoshi Sakaida studied the map. With the information already at hand, he could surmise his role in the upcoming operation. He looked at the converging arrows: *Kido Butai* and the trailing main body from northwest of Midway; the occupation and support force from the west and southwest. It all amounted to one thing: plenty of flight time for Sakaida, Lieutenant (junior grade) Azumano and their Number Four scout plane.

That is well, Sakaida thought. *Better than sitting on this ship without much to do.* He shifted on his hardwood bench, knowing that the Imperial Navy placed heavy emphasis on reconnaissance floatplanes and leaving most of the Type 97 attack planes and Type 99 carrier bombers for strike missions.

"We will take the enemy by surprise," Naito continued, "as we have evidence that their remaining fleet units arc still in Pearl Harbor." He paused for emphasis, a confident look on his face. "The Americans will be unable to resist coming out to meet us. They must defend Midway or risk leaving Hawaii open to invasion. When they sail to defend Midway, our submarines and fleet units will destroy them in one decisive battle."

The aviators and maintenance personnel stirred, and Sakaida felt the enthusiasm spreading through his shipmates. Encouraged, Naito pressed on. "I am coordinating our air searches in accordance with Commander Genda's operations plan from the flagship. We will have two scouts airborne through most daylight hours beginning day after tomorrow, which means heavy maintenance demands on both our Type 95s and Type Zeros.

"Our equipment must function perfectly if this plan is to succeed," Naito continued. "That means not only our aircraft, but the catapults and recovery equipment as well. You division commanders—make certain everything is in order. Take nothing for granted." He stood with his hands on his hips, chin jutting forward. "I am counting on each of you. And so is the emperor!" Naito decided against a rousing series of "Banzai" cheers. He would save that emotional moment for later—at the inevitable victory celebration.

LIBRARY OF HAWAII

Mary Tanaka ghosted alongside Sallyann Downey, who was concentrating on logging in returned books at the end of the day. Mary touched her friend's arm and Sally jumped.

"Oh, I am sorry," Mary purred. "I did not mean to frighten you." Her diction was always precise.

Sally inhaled and placed a hand on her chest. "I didn't see you, Mary." She managed a smile. "But I almost jumped out of my skin!"

Mary looked at her closely—saw the signs and knew their meaning. "You have been on edge for two days now. It's Phil, isn't it? Everybody knows that a large task force sailed on Saturday."

For a moment Sally smiled inwardly. *How quickly we become accustomed to the words of war*. They seemed even more incongruous coming from so delicate and refined a young woman as Mary Tanaka. "Yes. It's Phil. I think about him constantly."

"You need to relax just a little. Mabel is hosting a social for some servicemen this evening. Why don't you come? It will be over early, of course." The ten P.M. curfew had been in effect since December; islanders accepted it as a necessary inconvenience.

Sally shook her head and her short black hair bobbed around her ears. "No thanks, Mary. I think I'll stay home and write some letters."

"Well, all right." The disappointment was evident in Mary's voice. "Let's you and I do something this week, though. Maybe go to a movie or have a picnic."

She really won't give up, Sally thought. *Thank goodness*. "Okay, you win."

Sallyann stamped another book-return card, harder than necessary. Somehow it felt good to hit something.

6.

MONDAY, 1 JUNE

USS YORKTOWN

"Quite a sight, isn't it?" Phil Rogers turned around and found himself looking over the head of a well-built lieutenant. Rogers recognized the red-haired officer as one of the culprits from the revelry in the Ford Island officer's club. They exchanged salutes and the senior man extended his hand. "Sam Adams, Bombing Five."

"Phil Rogers, Bombing Three." He tilted his head toward the underway replenishment in progress. "Yes, sir. It's kind of interesting to me. I haven't seen it done very often."

"You know, it reminds me of formation flying," Adams said, leaning on the catwalk railing. "Keeping station, matching one ship's speed to another."

"Yeah, I hadn't thought of it that way." He regarded the smaller man, shorter by half a head. *This guy's been around*, Rogers thought.

Perhaps 150 feet away USS *Cimarron* steamed through the Pacific swells, with no apparent difference in relative motion. The 18,000-ton oiler was linked to the larger carrier by a series of support lines. Suspended from the lines were thick black hoses pumping fuel oil into *Yorktown*'s bunkers. Steaming nearby was *Cimarron*'s sister ship, *Platte*, ready to contribute her share to the enterprise.

Other men occupied the catwalk, taking in the refueling. Some of the older hands, like Adams, offered comments. Most of the new men had sense enough to keep their opinions to themselves, or at least to ask polite questions.

Rogers sized up Sam Adams as a decent guy, and decided to risk a question of his own. "Lieutenant, I was just wondering something." Adams turned his square, handsome face to the ensign. "Sure thing. Shoot."

Rogers straightened up from the railing. "Well, I was in the Ford Island O-club the other night when you fellows were, uh, asked to leave." He swallowed hard, having intended to ask one of VB-5's ensigns or jaygees about the episode. "Well, I couldn't quite hear what your skipper said to the OOD to make him so damn mad."

Adams unzipped a knowing grin. "Ha! That guy climbed all over us. Took our names and threatened Wally with a court-martial for our appearance and conduct. And the skipper just faced him down and said, 'Well, Commander, one of my pilots has just been recommended for a posthumuous Medal of Honor. Will that even things up?'" The lieutenant laughed aloud.

"No kidding?" Rogers gave a low whistle.

"Yeah, no kidding." Adams leaned on the railing again, hands folded, staring at the oiler. "Jo-Jo Powers, class of '35. He was a real good guy. The night before we attacked the main Jap force at Coral Sea, he got up in the ready room and made a little speech. Said how the folks at home were counting on us, and how he intended to lay one right on the deck if he had to."

Adams looked at Rogers, speaking slowly. "Next day, he did just that. He pressed his dive so low he could hardly miss, and planted a thousand-pounder on what we think was the *Shokaku*. But he was all shot up, and he went right into the water, alongside the target." The redhead shrugged his shoulders. "It's hard to believe that was less than three weeks ago."

Phil Rogers didn't know what to say. As yet he had lost no friends in this war. At least, not from enemy action. Suddenly he imagined that was about to change. But he also sensed that Adams may not have told the story before. It seemed important to listen.

"The thing about Joe Powers," Adams continued, "he was a good man. And I don't mean he was just a good aviator. I mean he was a damn good friend, a good shipmate. Always cheerful—a real cutup. But you know, when his ship called at Shanghai in 1937, he organized a show to raise funds for Chinese refugees."

Adams straightened up again, and this time he seemed taller to the VB-3 pilot. "Good to meet you, Rogers. Good luck to you and your squadron."

Rogers watched the little man amble down the catwalk, then turned back toward the oiler. The salt spray felt good on his face because it hid the moisture at the corners of his eyes.

EASTERN ISLAND, MIDWAY

Freckle-faced Major Floyd Parks faced the pilots of Fighting 221, crowded into the squadron command post. The only ones not present were airborne on scheduled patrols or sitting cockpit alert.

"I want you to know the situation," Parks began, "because you've heard rumors on top of rumors the past few days." He glanced around the dugout, lancing the biggest rumormongers with a commanding-officer gaze. "We've been told that a Japanese task force is headed this way, and it's supposed to hit us sometime Thursday." He folded his arms, as if to ward off the impending blow.

"Now, it's all over the island that Jap aircraft intercepted two PBYs this morning. That's true." A few murmured comments greeted Parks's announcement as he held up a clipboard with a map. Taking a pen from his left pocket, he pointed to a grid coordinate. "At 0940, the first P-boat was about here, about five hundred miles out, bearing two-three-one. He reported two Jap bombers." Parks's pen indicated a spot well southwest of Midway. "There was some shooting, and the PBY returned with three wounded aboard."

Jim Carpenter, standing in the rear of the audience, leaned over to Griff Ambruster. "Man, am I glad I'm a fighter pilot. Can you imagine tangling with the Japs in a PBY?" The big Catalina flying boat, though possessed of exceptional range and endurance, was never built for a shootout. Carpenter was acquainted with a couple of pilots from Patrol Wings One and Two, flying Midway's thirty-two PBY-5s. He envied them not at all.

"Now," Parks concluded, his freckled face tight with concentration, "an hour later another PBY also reported being attacked by Japs. But the damn fool didn't amplify the contact, and we won't know anything until he lands in a couple of hours.

"We've got more help on the way, though. Nine more B-17s arrived yesterday, which means we'll have a hundred or more planes crammed onto this island by the time the Japs show up. We also got our last scheduled fuel shipment yesterday. It should be enough to last us, if the B-17s and PBYs don't guzzle it all." There were chuckles from the fighter pilots, concerned about the multiengine aircraft that used two to four times as much aviation gasoline as the fighters and scout-bombers.

Parks returned his pen to his pocket. "Now, there's one more thing. It's confirmed that the Japs bombed Dutch Harbor this morning. That's about all I know. Information is sketchy, so I can't tell you how much damage they did. Whether it's a diversion to draw us off or they really mean to do something in Alaska is hard to say."

The CO looked around the room, privately ticking off the human assets and liabilities at his command. With twenty-five Brewsters or Grummans in commission, he felt he could put up a decent defense of the atoll. But he knew that the equipment was aged and many of his pilots were green. Some of them didn't even relish flying fighters. He looked at Marion Carl, the gangly young captain with the bill of his ballcap turned up, and Sunny Jim Carpenter, the golden boy. *I need more tigers like them*, Parks thought. *I need all the tigers I can get.*

7.

TUESDAY, 2 JUNE

IJNS ARASHI

On the wing of the bridge the doubled lookout watch shivered in the open air. A thick, enveloping mist wrapped itself around human flesh and ship's steel, settling like a moist gray pall on everything.

Inside the bridge, it was warmer but no more cheerful. Navigator Takeo Fuji wiped a gloved fist on the starboard window, removing more condensation from the glass. He cast a furtive glance across the destroyer's bridge where Commander Watanabe lowered his binoculars. *Who but a fool would try to use glasses in fog like this?*

"I estimate visibility at no more than five hundred meters,"

Watanabe said. "We still cannot make out signal flags from *Akagi*." The signal officer, Lieutenant Kakuji Takagawa, nodded his agreement beside the captain. "Can we try the searchlights again?" Watanabe asked.

"Sir! My chief signalman has tried repeatedly," Takagawa replied. "The fog is too thick. It disperses the light beam beyond just a few meters."

Watanabe dropped his glasses to his chest and let them dangle by the white strap. He looked at his watch again for the fourth time in six minutes. "We should be changing fleet course any minute, according to plan."

Fuji looked at the bridge chronometer, set to Japanese time. When he first sailed from home waters he thought it peculiar that the Imperial Navy always kept its clocks synchronized with Tokyo. The ship's clock said 0730 Wednesday, but it was 0930 in the local time zone and 1030 Tuesday on Midway, across the International Date Line. *Not that it matters*, Fuji thought bitterly. *It might as well be midnight outside.*

Watanabe turned toward the officers of the bridge watch. "This is bad, very bad. Not only can we not communicate, we certainly cannot refuel from the tankers in this mess. I fear the entire fleet schedule will be thrown off . . ."

"All ships, all ships. This is Red Castle." Watanabe was cut off short by the unexpected voice on the command radio net. Wide-eyed stares greeted the warning order. *My God*, Fuji thought, *Nagumo is breaking radio silence! We'll be heard by enemy submarines.* Then, placing himself in Chuichi Nagumo's position, he reasoned, *What else can he do?*

"Prepare to execute turn to new base course as scheduled. Stand by . . . execute!"

Watanabe recovered his composure and shouted at the helmsman. "Right standard rudder, come to course one-three-five, and keep your wits about you!" He stood silent for a moment, then added in an uncharacteristic whisper, "We do not want a collision."

Fuji leaned into the turn as *Arashi* heeled to port. Moments later the destroyer was steadied up to the southeast, beginning her 700-mile run to Midway.

O V E R H E A D   M I D W A Y

Sunny Jim Carpenter looked down at the coral reef surrounding the atoll, almost six miles across. *How many times have I seen this view?* he wondered. A quick computation skittered through his mind. He welcomed the brief diversion. *Let's see, average one patrol a day for six months, minus maybe one day a week. That's easy. Just about 160 times.*

Carpenter had to ponder how many glimpses of paradise a man could endure before the freshness eroded. Strictly from a sight-seeing viewpoint, Midway was spectacular. Varying shades of blue and blue-green water, startling white breakers along the reef, purple-shaded cloud shadows on a sunlit sea.

"Mike-Fox Nineteen from Midway Radar." The radio call crackled in Jim Carpenter's earphones, stirring him from his ennui. Though the call was directed at his division leader, he perked up as if hearing a hotel bellman hailing a friend. "Mike-Fox Nineteen, come in," the controller on Sand Island called again.

Curt must not be receiving, Carpenter thought, reaching for his microphone. As leader of the six-plane division's second section, Sunny Jim was next senior to Captain Curtis Roberts. But Roberts's laconic drawl rasped back, "Midway from Fox-Nineteen, over." If Carpenter didn't know better, he'd have said Roberts sounded just like a man who had been awakened.

"Ahh, Fox-Nineteen. There is a flight of six friendlies inbound, thirty miles out. Bearing one-one-zero. Over." Carpenter realized, *That has to be the Torpedo Eight detachment they told us about.*

Roberts acknowledged and turned his six Buffalos in a lazy orbit to port. Carpenter's competitive instincts were aroused. *Everybody will be trying to spot 'em first*, he told himself. Then, *Belay that. Some of these jokers just don't care.*

Moments later Carpenter grasped his microphone. "Tallyho! Six aircraft, two o'clock slightly low."

A few seconds silence, then Roberts's voice. "Yeah, I see 'em. We'll keep our distance."

Pleased with his minor triumph, Carpenter tracked the dark spots suspended in midair. He estimated they were between three and four miles east, and heard their leader contact Midway. A few minutes later the newcomers passed within recognition range. Carpenter noted their angular wings and tails, their prominent bellies and sun glinting off the long greenhouses. *Big sons a' bitches*, he thought. He had never seen a TBF before, but the family resemblance to the F4F Wildcat was unmistakable.

Descending toward Eastern Island, the Avenger torpedo planes were lost to the marines' sight. Carpenter checked his RPM, manifold pressure and cylinder-head temperature again. Then the thought hit him: *Where the hell are we gonna park six more airplanes on that sandpile?*

Phil Rogers and Bernie Burnett fidgeted in their chairs as the wardroom buzzed with two dozen conversations. Rogers glanced around, looking for familiar faces. He noticed the pilots of what was officially Fighting Three, more than half being old hands of VF-42. Word had gotten around pretty quickly that Lieutenant Commander Thach's exec, a well-regarded pilot named Lovelace, had been killed in the deck crash. The new fighter XO was a good-looking jaygee named Leonard, a swimmer out of the class of '38.

Rogers made eye contact with Wayne Wik, sitting among the Torpedo Three contingent, and glimpsed the veterans of the "Battle of Ford Island"—Lieutenant Short and his Bombing Five pilots.

Whoops, Scouting Five, Rogers reminded himself. With two bombing squadrons aboard, VB-5 had been redesignated VS-5 to avoid confusion with VB-3. Rogers thought it was just one more indication of the cobbled-up nature of *Yorktown*'s air group going into the upcoming battle—a fleet engagement. He felt Burnett nudge him and turned toward the head of the room.

The ship's air-operations officer, Commander Murr Arnold, strode to the front of the room. With him was Lieutenant Commander Oscar Pederson, leader of *Yorktown* Air Group. Arnold's appearance—stern, astute, professional—marked him as a no-nonsense leader. Rogers thought he was the type of officer whom ensigns did best to salute smartly and keep on moving. Pete Pederson, on the other hand, seemed a pretty regular guy.

"Gentlemen," Arnold began. "I wish to acquaint you with the disposition of our forces as we near Midway." His metallic voice cut through the crowded room, precise and clear. "We have rendezvoused with Task Force Sixteen, built around the *Enterprise* and *Hornet* under Rear Admiral Spruance. As some of you may know, Vice Admiral Halsey was stricken with dermatitis and is beached. That means that Rear Admiral Fletcher is officer in tactical command of this force."

A murmur of assent skittered through the veteran Yorktowners; Rogers knew its significance. Neither Raymond Spruance nor Frank Jack Fletcher were aviators, but Fletcher, from the academy class of

'06, was a year senior to Spruance and had been running *Yorktown*'s Task Force Seventeen since January. In its brief time aboard, Bombing Three had discerned an approximately friendly rivalry between Old Yorky and the Big E. Some Yorktowners resented Task Force Sixteen's splashy headlines, and while there was no doubt that the colorful Bill Halsey made better copy than the workmanlike Jacky Fletcher, Rogers had twice heard the sentiment, "Rather fight with Fletch than haul ass with Halsey!"

Arnold stared down the vocal offenders. "Our course is designed to take us well north of the Hawaiian chain and arrive northeast of Midway day after tomorrow. If we remain undetected by the Japanese, we'll be in excellent position to launch surprise air strikes from their flank. We know they're coming, but apparently they don't know that we know."

Arnold then described the Japanese armada steaming toward Midway: the transport group, the main body and supporting force, but he emphasized the striking force of four veteran carriers. As he did so, Burnett leaned into Rogers and whispered, "I tell you, Buck, that man of ours in Tokyo is worth every dime we pay him."

Rogers stifled a giggle but his mind registered one thought: *cryptanalysis*. A mathematics minor at Florida State, he had briefly pondered applying for the navy's codebreaking program. Just as quickly he had rejected the idea. Too secretive, too confining, too repetitive. Breaking a high-powered cipher paled in comparison to putting a half-ton bomb in the middle of the bull's-eye. Nothing could compete with carrier aviation, though Rogers secretly was pleased at the change in the daily air plan. Lowering ceilings and high seas had canceled the afternoon's scheduled scouting flights.

"Admiral Nimitz has given us a great deal of latitude in the conduct of this engagement," Arnold continued. "We will be guided by the principle of calculated risk, employing maximum attrition tactics, but actual conduct of the battle rests with us." He paused briefly, sweeping the room with his cobra gaze. "There's just one more thing, gentlemen. I have copied a message from Admiral Spruance to Task Force Sixteen, and I want to share it with you. He says, and I quote, 'The successful conclusion of the operations now commencing will be of great value to our country.'" Arnold looked up from the message flimsy. "I cannot add anything to that."

8.

WEDNESDAY, 3 JUNE

EASTERN ISLAND, MIDWAY

First Lieutenant Jim Carpenter sat strapped into his Brewster Buffalo, scribbling a letter to his parents in San Diego. His division had the duty for cockpit alert, starting engines once an hour in case a scramble was necessary. But despite the impending threat of invasion, he felt bored and restless, hardly daring to believe that combat would deliver him from a six-month purgatory.

Intent on his correspondence, Carpenter failed to notice a dusty olive-green pickup racing toward his revetment until its brakes squealed. He looked up to see his plane captain trot over to the driver's side.

Seconds later Corporal Jake Pankratz was sprinting toward the F2A. Carpenter's pulse revved and he began stuffing pen and paper into the mapcase.

Pankratz bounded up the port tire, elevated himself onto the shoulder-high wing with both hands and poked his head into the cockpit. "PBYs have reported the Japs' main body! Seven hundred miles out, bearing west-northwest." Carpenter pulled on his cloth helmet and Fischer goggles, but Pankratz waved a placating hand. "No takeoff, Lieutenant. Just a warning, that's all."

Carpenter yanked off his helmet and mussed his blond hair. Then he pulled his writing pad from the mapcase and unscrewed his pen. He sat staring at the partially filled paper, his mind a blank.

IJNS TONE

Lieutenant Masatake Naito looked at his aircrews scheduled to fly the dawn searches. He had already satisfied himself that the big cruiser's five floatplanes were ready, and his engineering officer reported catapult number one fully operational. Number two was still being checked.

Again seated along one bulkhead of the cavernous hangar, the dozen fliers under Naito's command paid close attention. They knew the Etajima graduate to be personable at times, but now he was all business.

"This is our scouting plan." Naito pointed to a chart of the sector search legs allotted *Tone*. Each leg resembled a long, thin piece of pie cut from a circular plate. Lieutenant (junior grade) Azumano leaned forward and pushed his summer-weight white cap back on his head. He and his pilot, Petty Officer Sakaida, had drawn the easternmost slice of the pie. Outbound three hundred miles along the 100-degree radial, then a dogleg turn sixty miles north before returning on a course of 260. Examining the chart, Naito saw that they would fly well north of Midway. North and slightly east.

The officer observer leaned toward his enlisted pilot. "That looks like the best sector, Sakaida." The only reaction was a silent nod. Most unlike Sakaida, the perennial clown. Still, Azumano felt optimistic. *If I were the enemy commander, that is where I would position my ships*, he thought.

Naito's businesslike voice brought Azumano back to the matter at hand. "The striking-force schedule calls for the first searches to launch at 0130," the air officer stated. "We, with *Chikuma* and battleship *Haruna*, will provide five Type 95s or Type Zeros. At the same time the carriers will send off their first attack wave against Midway itself, some 240 miles northwest of the target. We do not expect to find enemy carriers in the area for about two days, but surface units will probably be present. Your mission is to find them."

Azumano quickly computed the time difference and what it meant to his crew. *Midway is twenty-one hours behind Tokyo. We will be in Midway's zone—that means takeoff at 0430 local time.* He glanced at Sakaida, who knew the meaning of the gesture. A predawn catapult shot, a thump in the back and a slingshot ride down a twenty-meter rail into an inkwell of darkness with no horizon. Sakaida slumped forward, resting his elbows on his knees, chin in his hands. He thought again of the mushrooms and grasshoppers that women gathered in the mountains overlooking the Tokyo Plain.

USS YORKTOWN

Phil Rogers stepped into the hangar bay from portside amidships. Somehow the knowledge that the morning would bring battle had sharpened rather than dulled his appetite, and he had taken an extra helping of dessert. Now he decided on a last-minute inspection of his dive-bomber. He didn't know what else to do.

Rogers made his way through the cavernous, brightly lit hangar bay, ducking under wings, nearly tripping over inspection panels laid on the deck, avoiding mechanics' toolboxes. He noticed that several scouts were armed with 500-pound bombs for the morning search.

Arriving at 3-B-18, Rogers walked around the wingtip—and bumped into his gunner. "Oh, 'scuse me, sir. I didn't see you." Barnes was the soul of industry, working on a wad of chewing gum, wiping greasy hands on an oil-stained rag.

"That's all right, Barnes. I couldn't stay away myself." Rogers smiled. "I guess everybody's double-checking their planes tonight."

Barnes returned the smile, his blue eyes as bright as his native Montana sky. "Triple-checking, sir. You can bet we'll be ready. I been working with the plane captain, checking the guns and topping off the oil and hydraulic fluid. I also took a look at the new electrical arming system but couldn't make much of it." The gunner laid down the rag and rolled down his blue dungaree sleeves. "Mr. Rogers, what's going on? Nobody seems to know what to expect tomorrow morning."

"All I know is that we've been getting regular reports from Midway. The PBYs and B-17s are tracking the Jap main body and transports, and apparently there have been some attacks. But far as I know, the carriers haven't been spotted yet. Midway's expecting a raid at dawn, and I imagine we'll launch as soon as there's a solid contact." The pilot noticed that his gunner eagerly followed each word, the blue eyes never leaving Rogers's face. *He's sizing me up*, Rogers realized. *Looking for signs of strain.*

Rogers casually placed a hand on the round wingtip, adopting a relaxed stance. "How do you feel, Barnes? Any jitters?" Rogers was tempted to address him as "son," but remembered the radioman was a year and a half older.

Barnes masticated his gum some more, concentrating on his thoughts. "Well, sir, I . . ." He shook his head. "No, sir. I know I should be, and maybe I'm not normal. But I just keep thinking that there's a Jap plane out there and tomorrow I'm going to have it in my sights. That's what's on my mind, sir." His words came faster as he sought to express himself. "It's like this, Mr. Rogers. If I never do another thing, I'll be satisfied if I get one Jap—just one Jap that I *know* I shot." The jaws stopped working. "Know what I mean, sir?"

Rogers democratically laid a hand on Barnes's shoulder. "I know exactly what you mean, Barnes." *I haven't a clue what you mean, but I'd give anything if I could feel that way.* "See you early tomorrow. Reveille's at 0330."

On the way back to his stateroom, Rogers swung by the torpedo squadron spaces. He asked a lieutenant (junior grade) whom he knew only as Weissenborn where Ensign Wik might be found and was directed three spaces down the passageway. Rogers stopped to knock at the entry and found the door open.

"Hey, come on in, Buck." Wayne Wik looked up from his bunk, where he was sitting with three other VT-3 ensigns. Rogers recognized them but didn't recall their names until Wik introduced them: Roche, Osberg and Powers.

"Looks like the Ensigns' Benevolent Association in here," Rogers offered.

"Oh, this is just the second division branch," Osberg offered. "Everybody in the first division is senior to us, except Smith." Rogers politely laughed, then glanced around. Suddenly he had nothing to say.

Wik looked up and ran a hand through his brown hair. He had an oval face, the kind that turns jowly in older age. He finally broke the awkward silence. "What do you say, Buck? Everything all set for tomorrow?"

Rogers said enthusiastically, "Yeah, real fine. I was just down to look at my plane. I've got a good gunner, and he's putting in overtime on it."

Wik perked up. "We were just talking about the way this air group's come together. I mean, considering that all the squadrons have never operated together before, things seem to be damn near four-oh." He looked around the room, as if for encouragement. "Don't you think?"

"Yeah, mighty fine," Rogers replied. *How the hell can we tell after four days at sea?* "The air department looks plenty sharp. Arnold and Pederson seem to know their stuff, all right."

Suddenly Rogers regretted coming here. Despite his friendship with his Pensacola classmate, he realized he was out of place. This was torpedo country; he didn't quite belong. He felt worms in his belly. Best get back to his own stateroom. "Well, I'll mosey along. Just wanted to say good luck to you, Wayne." He looked around the room again. "Good luck to all you fellows."

"Thanks, Rogers," one of the ensigns replied.

At the end of the passageway, Phil Rogers ducked into a head just in time to vomit up his dinner.

In a compartment on the second deck, one level below the hangar deck, Lieutenant CJ Callaway lay in his bunk and checked his clock. *Twenty-hundred. The second dogwatch will be coming off duty.* He had time for another four hours' sleep, but he knew it was useless. That only meant four more hours to lay in the rack and ponder another battle morning. It had been that way at Coral Sea. Why should this be different?

It is different, though. Before Coral Sea we didn't know what to expect. Now we do. Some comfort. We know what Japanese bombs and torpedoes can do to ships, and we've seen how fragile human bodies are when exposed to blast and steel splinters. He wondered what his friend Chet Nimitz was doing this night.

His thoughts turned to engineers and engineering. After fifteen months aboard, he was able to tune out unwanted noise, but now he cocked an ear for the familiar sounds. The steady thrumming of the carrier's plant, the subtle creaks of expansion joints, the whoosh of water or fuel oil in their pipes.

Callaway turned on his reading light and reached a bony hand toward a photo taped to the bulkhead. He traced a long finger around the left-hand image—a plumpish, thirtyish woman with a mildly attractive face. She held the hand of an eight-year-old boy with his father's straight, dark hair and prominent nose. "Vernon," Callaway said aloud. Then he turned out the light.

The stateroom was dark when Phil Rogers entered. He assumed Bernie Burnett was asleep, so he quietly undressed and climbed into his bunk. He still felt queasy, despite thoroughly rinsing his mouth, and his body had a faintly wet, clammy feel. He lay on the blanket, clad in skivvy shirt and shorts, hands behind his head, staring at nothing. He tried to will himself to think of nothing. *The plane will be fine. Barnes will be fine. Even if he is scared, he's got it under control.* Rogers found himself running down the squadron roster, matching names and faces and personalities to aircraft numbers. *3-B-1: the skipper will take us to the target. He's tops. Baker Two: Swede, a jaygee out of Annapolis, class of '39. He's good, too.* Baker Three through Six, the rest of the first division: ensigns like himself, good guys.

Other ensigns, let's see: in the second division there's Roy Isaman. Shortest pilot in the squadron, but solid. Lieutenant Bottomley in 3-B-10 leading the second section. A strong pilot and leader with two good ensigns on his wing—Charlie Lane and Johnny Butler.

Third division: the exec, Dave Shumway, another academy man. Knows his stuff. His wingmen, Bob Elder—already one of the hottest pilots around—and Randy Cooner, he's good, too. Second section under Obie Wiseman . . .

Rogers turned in his bunk and curled into a fetal position. He imagined a demon peeking out from under a manhole cover—the demon being the thought that Philip Rogers might be the weakest pilot in the squadron. He closed his eyes and imagined himself stomping the demon back underground, where it belonged. In that moment, Rogers uttered a fervent prayer. "Please, God. Don't let me fu— screw up."

"You say something?" Bernie's voice rose from the lower berth, with a wisp of cigarette smoke.

Rogers leaned over the edge of his bunk. "I'm sorry if I woke you." He paused. "I was just . . ."

"Naw, I've been awake since I turned in. I heard you come in, too. Just didn't want to talk."

"Bernie, gimme a cigarette, will you?"

There was a surprised silence. "I didn't know you smoked." He handed up a Lucky Strike and some matches.

"I don't, usually." Rogers put the cigarette in his mouth, crushing one end with his teeth while inexpertly trying to light it. On the fourth effort he succeeded. *Damn, why'd I do that? My mouth already tastes like the bottom of a birdcage.* He pinched the ember into extinction. "What do you think will happen tomorrow?"

Burnett responded slowly, deliberately. "I think some guys we know are going to die. That's what I think."

Rogers exhaled. "Yeah, I know. Are you very scared?"

"Me? Hell, I'm scared all the time. You know that." The flippant tone had returned, and Rogers felt a little better. "How about you, Buck?"

Rogers ran a sweaty palm across his forehead. "Sure, sure I'm scared. But . . . it's not just fear of dying, you know? I mean, of course I don't want to die. But I'll tell you something, Bernie. I'm a whole lot more scared of fouling up. God, I can't stand the thought that I might let you guys down, or get somebody killed."

Burnett emitted a soft, low chuckle. "So that's what you were praying about. I couldn't quite make it out."

Rogers might have been embarrassed in other circumstances. But he knew this conversation would stay in their compartment. "Yeah, in an Episcopalian sort of way."

They lay in the dark for what might have been seconds or minutes. At length the low, even tone was back from the lower bunk. "Phil, in case you don't know, let me tell you something. Every single one of us would rather die than look bad. I mean it. Every one of us."

Rogers nodded—as if Burnett could see him.

"Phil, have you gone to bed with Sally yet?"

Rogers was stunned into silence. *Where the hell did that come from?* He didn't know whether to feel insulted at the intrusion or grateful for a friend's concern. Finally he replied, "No. Not yet. She's just not that kind of girl . . ."

"I'm sorry if that came out the wrong way. I know she's a swell kid. What I meant was, you two have been going together for several months . . ."

Rogers suddenly realized that his roommate had paid him a backward compliment. *He means, he hopes we've hit the sack so at least I'll have that experience in case I get killed tomorrow.* In a roundabout way, it was a charming sentiment.

"Well, sure I've thought about it. Who wouldn't? But Sally's already said she doesn't think she wants to get married until . . . after the war. And I just don't think she'd . . . do anything . . . before getting married. She's from a good family."

Rogers wanted to turn the conversation around. No, that wasn't quite true. He wanted to turn it off. He knew that if he got Burnett talking about women there'd be no end to it.

Philip Rogers lay back on his pillow, arms folded on his chest. He thought about families—his, hers, maybe the one they could call theirs. *You have to work for what's worth having,* he thought. That's what his father always said. It started early in life. You worked around the yard for your allowance—twenty-five cents a week—then maybe got a paper route. You worked hard in school so you could get into a good college. Then you worked waiting tables or managing a rooming house to put yourself through college. Most of the kids did it—there was no other way in the Depression years. Those who couldn't work, you pitied and maybe helped a little. The few who wouldn't work, you despised; that wasn't how Americans behaved in the first four decades of the twentieth century.

And then after college, you busted your butt studying for acceptance to the Naval Aviation Cadet program. Everything that had gone before was merely preparation, to get you to the starting line just so you could enter the damn race. Wash out and you went straight to the fleet as a whitehat. Then you worked and studied and maybe cheated some along the way. Rogers was grateful for his First Class Scout rank, since it had given him a leg up on that damn Morse code—the biggest nonflying stumbling block in training. He'd taken the test for Wik and purposely got a low passing score.

Then even after you pinned on those beautifully elegant wings of gold, you worked some more. You vied with the other pilots in the eternal competition for best bombing score, best carrier-landing grades. And now, after twenty-four years of living, your devotion and hard work had placed you squarely in line to die violently forty or fifty years before your time.

Rogers rolled over, facing the bulkhead. *Sally. She's worth working for, too.* And at length, he dreamed.

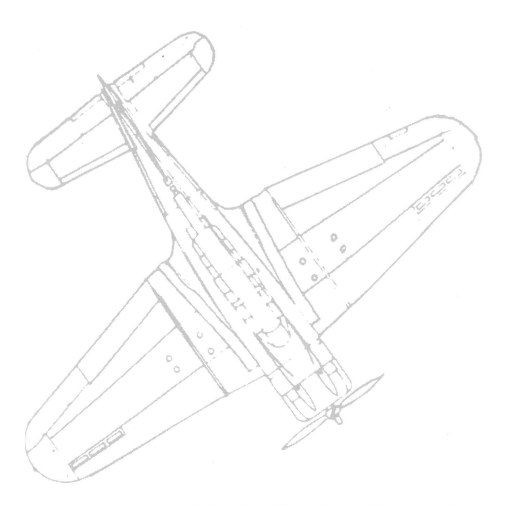

PART TWO

"I'd rather be lucky than good."

NAVAL AVIATION MAXIM

9.

0400–0600 THURSDAY, 4 JUNE

Damn all mechanical inventions and their miserable inventors! Lieutenant (junior grade) Toshiki Azumano raged in the second cockpit of the Number Four scout. The aircraft commander slumped lower in his seat, folding his arms about him. He looked downward but his view was obscured by the reconnaissance floatplane's wing—not to mention the predawn darkness. He had an impression of the catapult crew scurrying about. *And damn the idiots who work on such contrivances,* he muttered. Azumano considered himself above swearing, as befitted a graduate of the Etajima Naval Academy, but his private ravings seemed to help. He looked at the luminous dial of his instrument-panel clock yet again.

Nearly thirty minutes late, he fumed. The only consolation available to the aircrew was the knowledge that the catapult malfunction was not of their doing. Azumano could just imagine how Lieutenant Naito was dealing with the situation. The cruiser's air officer had assured the captain last night that all was in order, and now . . . delay, embarrassment and the morning search plan already shot to hell. *Tone's* Number Three Scout had launched nearly fifteen minutes before and even now was swinging toward the dawn, probing the ocean to the northeast.

Azumano felt somebody climbing the Type Zero floatplane's ladder; the extra weight canted the aircraft slightly to port as it sat on the catapult. "We're ready," Lieutenant Naito said. "We had to replace the black-powder charge. It must have got soaked somehow." Aside from the fact that Naito outranked him, Azumano merely nodded. He'd served under less understanding officers and did not wish to add to the man's misery. "We'll swing you into the wind in a couple of minutes," Naito added. "You can start the engine anytime." His white cap disappeared below the cockpit rail, then surfaced again. "Good luck!" Then he was gone.

Azumano picked up the interphone and alerted Petty Officer Sakaida in the front cockpit. "Aircraft commander to pilot. You are cleared to start engine." There was no response, but Azumano could see Sakaida squirming, busy with preflight business. The familiar motions and sensations were transmitted back through the airframe. Electrical system coming on, priming the engine; whirring, clicking sounds; instruments flicking into life. In moments Sakaida had the fourteen-cylinder engine rattling in a cloud of oil-rich haze. The pilot allowed the Kinsei 43 to settle down as he adjusted mixture and throttle setting.

"Prepared for launch," Sakaida called at length.

Azumano and the radioman, Aviation Seaman Kenji Hara, acknowledged their readiness. Then, waving from the cockpit, Azumano saw the launch officer return the gesture. In seconds the sixty-foot catapult rotated outboard, placing the nose of Number Four scout squarely into the wind. Sakaida ran up full throttle, pulling 1,060 horsepower from the air-cooled engine with the three-bladed propeller in low pitch. Satisfied with his instrument readings and with what his educated ears told him, he signaled he was ready.

Seconds later the crew felt the abrupt, unpleasant kick in the small of the back as the powder charge fired. Released from its tension on the rail, Number Four scout overcame elemental forces as thrust and lift overcame drag and weight. Sakaida, like Azumano and Hara, was merely a passenger for the first few seconds. But when he felt the big cantilever wing take the aircraft's weight, he relaxed his death grip on the throttle and firmly grasped the control stick. He allowed the Aichi to accelerate a bit more, then eased back the throttle for cruise-climb. Only then did he breathe more easily. It was good to ascend from the darkness of the sea toward the overcast and the reddening eastern sky.

EASTERN ISLAND, MIDWAY, 0502

By ones and twos and fours, high-performance engines lapsed into silence all over Eastern Island. With little to do but sit in his cockpit and watch his temperature-pressure gauges, Jim Carpenter had run another mind game: calculating just how many radial engines had been running for the past half hour or so. Discounting the six F4Fs returning from dawn patrol, and estimating the number of multiengine aircraft tracking or attacking the Japanese, left some sixty-five planes. Call it seventy-six Wright or Pratt and Whitney engines of about 90,000 horsepower. *Hell, that should be enough to propel this sandpile to San Diego.* Carpenter double-checked his cylinder-head temperature gauge: in the green. He climbed out of his Brewster, glad of the silence returning to Midway. With a thumbs-up to Corporal Pankratz, he headed for VMF-221's line shack.

As usual, Griff Ambruster dogged Carpenter's heels. The low morning light tinted the wingman's pinkish complexion with a gentle orange-yellow glow that somehow accented the baby fat around the cheeks. The sound of multiple engines turned heads all over the island. "Fifth division returning," Ambruster observed. He touched Carpenter's arm. "Hey, Jim, they're two short."

The section leader glanced upward at four angular shapes dropping into the landing pattern. "We'd have heard if anything was wrong. You know the saying, Griff. There's always somebody who doesn't get the word."

Ambruster resumed pacing, shifting stride to stay in step. "Well, I just wish *we'd* get the word. Anything's better than waiting."

Carpenter rolled his shoulders to relieve the strain in his upper back—a lifelong sign of nervous tension. "Ah, you get used to it."

TONE NUMBER FOUR SCOUT, 0525

Hiroyoshi Sakaida nudged his right rudder pedal. *The wind is picking up a little*, he realized. His compass had crept a few degrees left of his outbound course of 100 degrees, indicating a stronger southeasterly wind at medium altitude. So far there had been nothing remarkable about the search, other than the half-hour delay. He knew there would be hell to pay over that fiasco. But meanwhile, he enjoyed the sunrise—ample reward for the heart-pounding evolution of a predawn catapult shot.

The ceiling lifted as the Type Zero floatplane flew east, and Sakaida interrupted his scan of the instruments and the sea to enjoy the red-tinted clouds resembling pink cotton candy suspended in space. He slid back his canopy for a moment, inhaling the cool, crisp air.

"It's a beautiful sight, is it not?" Azumano's voice carried a lilting quality over the intercom. Sakaida realized the lieutenant must have read his thoughts. The floatplane's nose bobbed up and down in agreement as Sakaida pumped the stick. It was difficult to believe that a battle would be fought this morning.

USS YORKTOWN, 0530

In the squadron ready rooms on the O2 level, just below the flight deck, the aviators sat in their comfortable leather-bound chairs. Phil Rogers thought that Bombing Three, occupying Scouting Five's old spaces, was well-situated—just aft of the admiral and captain's galley. There was no evidence of the previous occupants, Lieutenant Commander Bill Burch's squadron. Just gray-painted deck and bulkheads with ducting and pipes in the low overhead. A blackboard and teleprinter stood at the head of the compartment—not even VB-3's pouncing-panther insignia.

Looking around, Rogers saw little activity. Reveille at 0330, a good breakfast without much banter or even conversation, then the waiting. The interminable, damnable waiting. Some of his friends feigned sleep while others read or swapped stories. *Everybody's working at looking casual*, he thought.

Rogers was thankful for his collateral duty as assistant navigation officer. Updating weather and position data gave him something to do; on the blackboard the "Nearest Land" column said "Midway, 200 miles, bearing 195." The folding armrest of his chair held his plotting board with the latest meteorological info: a weakening warm front over the two American task forces with unlimited ceiling above high, broken clouds. Scattered low clouds meant declining ceilings down to 1,000 feet toward the west.

Bernie Burnett walked up to Rogers, coffee cup in hand. "How goes it, Buck?"

Rogers looked up, glad of a break in the boredom. "Just updating my updates on the weather, that's all." He tapped his plotting board with a grease pencil. "Wind's supposed to be southeasterly all day. Bad news for us, good news for the Japs."

Burnett sipped some coffee. "Yeah, I know. We have to turn into the wind to launch or recover. They just keep coming straight on. And they're still under cloud cover from that cold front to the west, right?"

"Yeah, I guess so. No more word since the report of the PBYs attacking some Jap transports last night. Maybe our scouts will turn up something."

"How many did we launch?"

"Ten, I think. They're supposed to search the northern hundred-and-eighty-degree sector out to a hundred miles or so."

Burnett drained the last of his coffee. "This is really good, you know. I bribed a steward in the admiral's galley. Want some? It's better than ours."

Rogers said, "Gosh, no, Bernie. The last thing I want is for my teeth to be floating in java while I'm trying to bomb a Jap ship!"

"Ha! That's how much you know, Ensign. Why do you think they put relief tubes in airplanes?"

"I know that the one time I tried to use one, I peed all over my legs and the cockpit floor. No thanks."

Burnett's face revealed an evil grin. "Hell, Rogers, you don't piss any better than you bomb!" Instantly he regretted the jest. Two years ago he'd read an article about RAF pilots in the Battle of Britain; how some of them became overly polite, even solicitous of people they didn't particularly like. *They were afraid their last words to some poor bastard would haunt them*, Burnett realized. *I should tell Buck . . .*

The teletype printer clattered at the head of the room, chopping off Burnett's thoughts. PBY REPORTS ENEMY CARRIERS.

A roomful of expectant young men sat poised in their seats, leaning forward as if awaiting the punchline to a joke or the moral of a fable. Pilots turned to look at one another, seeking understanding. "Well?" somebody asked at last. Another exclaimed, "For Christ sake, where?"

Lieutenant Shumway turned in his first-row seat. "Relax. That P-boat's probably got fighters crawling all over it. We'll hear more."

Burnett punched Rogers's arm and stalked from the room, making for the nearest head.

IJNS TONE, 0550

It really was inexcusable, Lieutenant Naito admitted to himself. He had no excuse to offer. Standing on the port wing of the big cruiser's bridge, he much preferred to be alone. His stormy session with the captain had gone much as he predicted—he had listened far more than he talked. A thirty-minute delay in launching the Number Four Scout reflected poorly not only on the whole air department, but upon the ship—and, Naito knew, its commanding officer.

"Unidentified aircraft!" The lookout's cry caught everyone by surprise.

"Where?" screamed the skipper, hastening to the wing. Instantly he was answered, "Forty-five degrees to port, high elevation."

Naito looked in the direction indicated and saw nothing—clouds, just clouds. He held out his hand to the sailor. "Your glasses, please." *Why did I say, 'please'?* Following the lookout's finger, Naito slowly scanned the quadrant. A dark shape stood out against the overcast. "I see it!" Naito shouted. He studied the silhouette for five or six heartbeats before it was lost to view.

The captain looked at his air officer, expecting a reply. Naito handed the binoculars back to the lookout. "Captain, it is an American flying boat of the Consolidated type. We have definitely been sighted."

Heavyset, jowly, always businesslike, the captain lowered his gaze to the deck. Finally he said, "It may not matter. Our air attack should reach Midway very shortly."

USS YORKTOWN, 0553

Phil Rogers was earnestly printing updated position data on his plotting board when again he heard the clatter of the teletype. The exec's voice cut through the chatter: "Here we go, people."

Rogers looked up from his chair and saw the printout on the screen. RADIO INTERCEPT FROM 3V58. "MANY PLANES HEADING MIDWAY. BEARING 320

DEGREES, DISTANCE 150." Rogers held his breath. Nothing more clattered across the screen, so he plotted the contact on his chartboard. Looking across the aisle at Burnett, he said, "That doesn't do us much good, Bernie. It still doesn't tell us where their carriers are."

"Yeah, but it tells Midway what it needs to know."

EASTERN ISLAND, MIDWAY, 0556

"Scramble—squadron scramble! Japs are inbound, sir!" Corporal Pankratz's shout into Jim Carpenter's ear was unnecessary. Fighting 221's aircraft had been turning up for several minutes following a radar contact to the northwest. The frantic activity was proof that takeoff was imminent: the duty officer's pickup speeding past, marines scurrying to gun pits. Carpenter nodded to his plane captain, gave him a confident thumbs-up and watched Pankratz drop off the wing.

According to the briefing, Carpenter recalled, the skipper's division would take off first. But nobody seemed to be following the plan. On each side Brewsters and Grummans were leaving their revetments, taxiing out in no particular order. Carpenter glanced to his right and saw Griff Ambruster signaling him from the adjacent F2A. An indefinable gesture, a pumping movement of one hand. Then he recognized it—the old infantry hurry-up signal. Carpenter gave an exaggerated nod of his head, advanced his throttle and tapped the left brake.

In a high-speed taxi, Carpenter ran a quick magneto check. Left mag, rpms holding steady. Right mag, fifty revs drop. Acceptable. Fuel and oil pressure in the green. *So's engine temp. Good enough. Here we go.*

One last glance to check his wingman in position and Carpenter smoothly shoved the throttle forward, running prop and mixture controls to their stops. He saw a slight twitch in the round nose's tracking down the runway, a bauble to port. *Forgot to kick in enough opposite rudder.* He corrected easily and accelerated straight ahead. The staccato engine sound mixed with the slipstream whistling past his open canopy. Another quick look back and right. *Griff's tucked in tight. Good section takeoff.* Carpenter reached down to retract his wheels, glancing briefly into the cockpit.

Looking up, he saw several planes ahead of him. Two blunt shapes flashed overhead, right to left. He felt their slipstreams gently rock his

Buffalo. *Holy Christ! What was that?* For a panic-filled instant he feared
the worst—Japanese fighters arriving unannounced. But the shapes
were Buffalos. Carpenter realized that one or more sections had taken
off from an intersecting runway, nearly causing a collision. He
straightened in his seat, inhaled a deep breath and let it out. Then he
closed the canopy.

The Brewster climbed slowly, straining under full throttle with low
propeller pitch and high rpm. Carpenter looked back, estimating
Midway was some twenty miles astern as a straggling line of Buffalos
and Wildcats clawed for altitude. The squadron scramble had been a
mess, and he wondered how anybody avoided colliding at the runway
intersection. But apparently everyone except the two patrolling Wildcats had made it off. No, one F2A had passed underneath a moment
ago, apparently from Major Parks's division. *Must be about twenty-five,*
he calculated. *Well, that ought to be enough to handle the Japs.* For a
moment he allowed himself to imagine how sharp Mike-Fox Twenty-
one would look after Pankratz painted two or three miniature Japanese
flags beneath the cockpit.

10.

0601–0800, 4 JUNE

USS YORKTOWN, 0603

The ready-room teletype rattled off the message Bombing Three most earnestly wished for: TWO CARRIERS AND BATTLESHIPS, BEARING 320 DEGREES, DISTANCE 180, COURSE 135, SPEED 25. Phil Rogers quickly copied the data, noting that the date/time group showed the information was eleven minutes old. He plotted the contact relative to Midway, then measured the range from the task force's present position.

"Mr. Shumway, I make it bearing two-four-seven from us, distance almost a hundred and eighty miles." Rogers looked up. "But we were told there's at least four Jap carriers. What about the other two?"

The exec shook his head. "Don't know right now. The skipper's conferring with the air department. We should know more when he gets back down here."

Rogers sat back in his chair. He interlaced his fingers and stretched both arms in front of him. *It's true what they say about war,* he realized with a start. *It's ninety percent waiting to act upon incomplete information.* He looked across the aisle at Burnett. "Bernie, maybe I'll have some of the admiral's coffee after all."

NORTHWEST OF MIDWAY, 0612

"Hawks! Angels twelve." Carpenter's consciousness absorbed the radio transmission and he felt the adrenaline rush. Shifting his scan upward and forward, he unwittingly gasped. A long line of strange aircraft in impeccable formation swam into view. For an instant Carpenter wondered who they were. Then he knew.

There was a babble of other radio calls, mostly indecipherable. But the division leader kept climbing and Carpenter grimly hung on. He realized the intent: gain enough altitude for an overhead gunnery run at the enemy bombers. Carpenter performed another precombat check: power settings, guns charged, gunsight rheostat turned up. He remembered to pull his green-tinted goggles down over his eyes as a precaution.

The Japanese came straight on. Carpenter was fascinated with the scene. He took in each part individually, almost like Brownie snap-shots. The Japs' wonderful air discipline. The sea 20,000 feet below, illuminated in bright sunlight with beautiful white clouds. Well ahead, he glimpsed Major Parks diving on the lead bombers. Then the third division leader. Then it was Carpenter's turn.

He was tempted to clamp down on the trigger and flock-shoot the whole formation. There were so many, he could hardly miss. *Screw that, I'm a good gunner.* He selected a dark-green shape on the far side and, rolling inverted, pulled his Brewster's blunt nose through the horizon in an overhead run. Throttle, mixture and prop controls against the stops. *Approaching boresight range, give him plenty of lead.* Not yet, not yet . . .

Carpenter heard a high-pitched, pinging whine. Then several more. Startled, he turned in his seat and saw a strange aircraft to his left rear. Bright flashes burst from its nose and wings. More pings. "Fighters overhead!" in the earphones. Canopy glass shattering, a sting on the face. *Where's Griff? He should have warned me . . .*

Carpenter continued his headlong dive, hoping to outdistance his pursuer. He shot a glance at the altimeter but it wasn't there—just an ugly gouge in the lacquered black panel. The shooting had stopped, so he hauled back on the stick, felt the G forces building that funneled his vision. He looked back to check his tail. *Damn it to hell! He's still there . . . maybe 500 yards back.*

This time the marine let the Zero fighter commit to its attack before reacting. *If he's like us, he'll open fire at 300 yards, about . . . now!* Carpenter stomped left rudder and slashed the stick back and left. Tracers briefly sparkled over his fractured canopy, then stopped. Carpenter felt a surge of elation. *Foxed him! Now it's my turn.* He rolled hard right, reversing his turn to line up for a shot at the Japanese, who was bound to overshoot.

Carpenter leveled his wings, slightly nose-high, searching for the Zero after forty degrees of turn. Nothing. He glanced up to his right and got the most unpleasant surprise of his life since 1936, when Candice Mulvaney's parents returned early from a concert in Balboa Park. There, well above the horizon, climbing at an impossible angle, the gray-painted fighter had regained its perch above and behind the Brewster.

Recognizing a no-win setup, aghast at the enemy's performance advantage, Carpenter buried the nose of his F2A and pushed throttle, prop and mixture controls to the firewall. The murderous Zero threw a repositioning roll over the top and dived after the Brewster, almost directly from astern. Several seconds later Carpenter heard 7.7mm rounds pinging through his airframe, then felt the heavier *thumps* of one or two 20mm cannon shells.

Looking back, Carpenter saw the Zero disappear under his tail. His flesh crawled at the thought of an unseen assailant climbing up beneath his belly. He was about to turn again when the Japanese fighter abruptly appeared dead ahead, maybe 150 yards. *He overshot me!* Carpenter realized. *Misjudged his pullout and parked right in front of me.*

Carpenter pulled his nose up slightly, got a quick sight picture with the Zero's wings extending beyond the 100-mil circle of his reflector sight, and pressed the trigger. His two wing guns and both nose guns hammered out a long burst—longer than he intended. He saw the briefest glimmer of aluminum pieces chopped out of the Mitsubishi, then it was gone, wriggling away in that same incredible climb.

When he looked around again, Jim Carpenter was alone. He was aware of his engine's drone, of the nuisance pain in his left cheek, and of smoke in the cockpit. It was good to be alive.

Lieutenant Naito felt a curious sense of ambivalence. Not two hours previously he had absorbed the captain's wrath over the poor showing on the scout-plane launch. Now the captain kept him on the bridge, close at hand. *It's only because of my aircraft recognition*, Naito told himself. Still, he felt better.

"Air Officer, the flagship reports unidentified aircraft bearing one-five-zero, distance twenty-five thousand meters," the captain croaked. Shifting his binoculars southward, Naito scanned for several seconds. *No altitude given*, he mused. Not for the first time he earnestly wished for shipboard radar. The British and Americans apparently had it—why not the Imperial Navy? He wondered if Japan would ever match Western electronic technology.

Assume the aircraft are bombers rather than torpedo planes, he told himself. *Look to medium or high altitude*. He swept left to right again. And found what he sought. "Captain, approximately ten hostile aircraft, medium height." He strained his eyes to identify the types. They seemed too large for carrier planes—probably twin-engine. He hazarded a guess. "Sir, these must be land-based aircraft from Midway."

The cruiser's skipper seemed unperturbed. "Engineering, give me battle speed," he said evenly. Then, to the helmsman, "Come right to course one-five-zero. We will present as narrow a target as possible."

Naito felt a secret little thrill as four sets of geared turbines wound up, their 152,000-shaft horsepower pushing 11,200 tons through the water at thirty-five knots.

Next the captain called the gunnery officer, telling him to prepare for action with the four midships dual-purpose mounts—two five-inchers apiece. Naito glanced aft from the bridge but could see little. However, he knew the drill. The gun captains would be straining just as he had, looking for the black dots that would be pointed out by the white cane in each officer's hand.

Moments later the starboard five-inchers opened fire, erupting into blackish brown smoke and sharp concussion. Again Naito lifted his glasses, and this time he had little difficulty seeing the unwelcomed visitors. Yes, clearly twin-engine aircraft. Martin type, army land-attack bombers, evidently carrying torpedoes. He tried to recall the specifications. Five- or six-man crew, and fast—about 500 kilometers per hour. *But not fast enough!* he exulted. A rippling pattern of flak bursts crackled across the path of one Marauder, which lurched downward from less than 100 meters and went into the sea.

"They're going for the flagship!" somebody shouted. Naito regarded it as a superfluous statement. He looked toward *Akagi*, now partially obscured by her own gunsmoke with muzzle flashes intermittently visible around the edge of her flight deck. Another plane splashed between the carrier and *Tone*. Naito turned toward the captain, who atypically bounced on the balls of his feet. "The Americans are committing folly, throwing their planes at the fleet piecemeal," he declared. "Another group of torpedo planes also has been dealt with." He pounded his left hand with his right fist. "We are winning this battle."

NORTH OF MIDWAY, 0719

Sunlight. Engine sound not quite right. High-speed wind shrieking past the canopy. *No, through the canopy. I'm still alive*, Carpenter realized. *But tired. So tired, can hardly stay awake.* He forced himself to concentrate and opened his eyes. There was blood on his jacket.

He checked his gauges. Oil pressure was low, cylinder-head temp was high. Belatedly, Carpenter remembered that he should keep checking his tail. He found it easier to skid the aircraft than to turn it, and ruddered the F2A through clearing turns left and right. As nearly as he could tell, he was still alone.

Something scratching at his ears now, a radio's carrier wave. "Attention, all aircraft from Midway Radio. All clear. Repeat, all clear. Fighters, land and refuel by divisions, fifth division first." *At least my radio's still working.* But he heard only a few responses. Turning southward, he had no trouble finding the atoll. Large, black fires rose from Sand and Eastern islands, partly obscuring the lagoon. With those dreadful beacons, he began a letdown.

Moments later the radio squawked again. "All fighters land and reservice." After a few more minutes, Carpenter realized that no intact division had responded to the first call.

Corporal Jake Pankratz stood atop the revetment and watched his plane manage a shaky, barely controlled landing. As it taxied nearer he scanned the fuselage nose to tail. "Holy Christ."

The Brewster lurched to a halt as Carpenter trod on the toe brakes. Pankratz scrambled up the wing, noting a dozen or more 7.7mm and

20mm holes in the airframe, took in the shattered canopy and the dried bloodstains on the pilot's face. "Hey, you guys! Bear a hand! We got a wounded man here." Three armorers sprinted toward the F2A as Pankratz brought the red-knobbed mixture handle back to idle-cutoff.

Carpenter looked up dully, belatedly remembering to lift his goggles. "I'm hit, Jake. They got me." His voice was a croak.

"Yes, sir, I know. Just sit tight, Lieutenant. We'll get you out right away." Two of the other marines climbed on the starboard wing and gently helped the pilot from the cockpit, onto the ground. One of them applied a gauze dressing while the third man bawled for a corpsman or an ambulance.

Carpenter pulled off his cloth helmet and slumped onto the sand. Pankratz thought his pilot looked ten years older than he had barely an hour before. "How many, Jake?"

The plane captain already had counted. "Ten including you, sir. You're the last one back. That's counting three more wounded pilots that I know of." He looked at Carpenter's F2A again, and noted the oil-streaked cowling. *This one won't fly for a while.* "We got two planes still in commission, including Captain Carl's F4F. But it's got holes in it."

Ten! Carpenter thought. *If we launched twenty-five, then* . . . He groaned aloud, and not from pain. *Fifteen missing?* He looked up at Pankratz. "Griff? Lieutenant Ambruster?"

Jake Pankratz looked over the top of his pilot's head. "No, sir. Nobody knows about him."

"Major Parks?"

Pankratz felt he had to look Carpenter in the face this time. "Sir, 'cept one that came back with engine trouble, the whole first division is missing."

NUMBER FOUR SCOUT, 0725

"There they are." Sakaida thought that Azumano's voice was surprisingly calm over the intercom. The Type Zero floatplane had just turned ninety degrees port, making the short dogleg on its search pattern before returning to *Tone.* Sakaida lowered his starboard wing for a better view and at first saw only scattered clouds. Then multiple wakes appeared.

"Let's get closer," Azumano said. "I need to confirm enemy composition, course and speed."

The pilot raised his microphone and ran his tongue over lips suddenly dry. The Latin tunes he liked to whistle no longer would come, and Hiroyoshi Sakaida, the clown of CruDivEight, became a serious young man. "Sir, I think we should double back, stay above the clouds and drop down for a brief look. Then we can climb back up to send the contact report."

Azumano thought for a moment. *That makes sense.* But speed was important. And there could be enemy aircraft about. He pressed the mike button. "All right, Sakaida. As you suggest." Then, to the radioman-gunner, "Hara, remain vigilant for interceptors."

Sakaida stood the ungainly floatplane on one wingtip, allowing the nose to drop slightly in the turn. He came back on the throttle, descended into the fleecy wisps of the cloud tops and resumed cruise power. Two minutes later he turned again, focused his attention on the instrument panel and let down through the thin layer. He barely had time for a quick correction, leveling the wings, before breaking out beneath the cloud layer.

In the second seat Azumano had his binoculars ready. From 2,500 feet and eight miles he scanned the American force. It was too far for positive ship identification, but he made a quick count and estimated their base course and speed—white wakes carving graceful arcs on the azure surface of the sea. In thirty seconds he had enough. "Take us up. Climb!"

Sakaida needed no extra prompting. He pushed the throttle against the stop and raised the nose an exciting forty degrees. The Aichi was through the scattered cloud layer in several more seconds, continuing its climb. Once leveled off, Azumano ensured that Hara's radio was tuned to fleet frequency and told him to send the message:

"Scout number four. Sight what appears to be ten enemy surface ships, in position ten degrees, distance two hundred forty miles from Midway. Course one-five-zero degrees, speed over twenty knots." *Now that we've done our job, we can return to the ship.*

Two minutes later came the response. "Ascertain ship types and maintain contact." Azumano shivered. *That is not what I hoped to hear.*

USS YORKTOWN, 0745

Max Leslie ambled down the aisle of Bombing Three's ready room, a few papers in one hand. His appearance trailed both encouragement and concern in his wake. "What's the word, Skipper?" Bernie Burnett's question, though shared by everyone, betrayed his edginess. *Too much coffee*, Rogers thought.

At the front of the compartment, Leslie turned to face his pilots. He raised both hands for quiet and the room instantly fell silent. "Task Force Sixteen has been detached and is steaming to the southwest, closing the range to the Japanese carriers," he began. "*Enterprise* and *Hornet* started launching aircraft about forty minutes ago. We are waiting to recover our scouts before following Admiral Spruance's force."

A murmur ran through the steel-enclosed space. Leslie read the sentiment as part relief, part anxiousness to get going. "We probably will not launch for almost another hour. But I have just conferred with the air department and the other squadron commanders. Here is our plan." Leslie referred to his notes.

"Commander Arnold explained that last month in the Coral Sea battle, this ship used a running rendezvous. Unlike the *Lexington* Air Group, which remained overhead for a deferred departure, *Yorktown* squadrons joined up en route. The advantages are obvious: greater fuel efficiency and faster departure.

"The torpedo planes will take off first and they will form the base element, flying at about fifteen hundred feet. Commander Massey will navigate for us by watching the waves for any wind change. We will follow, climb to altitude overhead the task force and set course about fifteen minutes later. The fighters will be last off, but because of their greater speed they should overtake us well before reaching the target area."

Rogers raised a hand. "Skipper, do we have an update on the Japs' location? I need that dope if I'm going to back up the torpeckers' navigation."

Leslie said, "We'll have the latest position report just before launch. The main consideration now is distance to the enemy fleet. The F4Fs will be short on fuel, but Lieutenant Commander Thach said he's willing to go as far as a hundred seventy-five miles. Lieutenant Commander Massey feels that's giving quite a lot, and I agree. But we should be able to keep group cohesion going into the attack."

Lieutenant Shumway stretched an arm from the front row. "What about strike-group composition, sir?"

"I'm coming to that, Dave. Massey has twelve TBDs and of course we'll launch seventeen bombers. The air staff has allowed just six fighters—two fewer than Jimmy Thach wants. I suggested that he put his flight of four as close escort to the TBDs with the other pair stacked between us. We'll have the advantage of greater altitude."

Muttered comments crisscrossed the ready room. But nobody in VB-3 begrudged the bulk of the skimpy fighter cover going to Lance Massey's 130-knot Devastators. Like Rogers, many of the dive-bomber pilots had friends in Torpedo Three.

Leslie continued. "We agreed that I'll have a better view of the situation than the low squadrons, so I will be the strike leader and target coordinator. Lieutenant Commander Pederson is the air-group commander, and senior to me, but Pete is remaining aboard to handle fighter direction."

The number counters in the audience knew that Leslie and Pederson were classmates from Annapolis—the class of '26, which had graduated exactly twenty years ago this day. Privately, Rogers felt good about the plan. It was pragmatic; choice of the strike leader was proof. He knew that some air groups never would run contrary to pure seniority, regardless of ability or experience. *But then*, he thought, *no other carrier has as much experience as this one.* Rogers recalled his argument with the ring-knocker who had derided Max Leslie's academic record at the academy. Rogers's reply echoed now in his mind. *There's not a better skipper in this navy. I don't want to go to war behind anybody else.*

In an hour—maybe less—he would have his chance.

11.

0801–1000, 4 JUNE

NUMBER FOUR SCOUT, 0803

Toshiki Azumano could hardly believe his luck. *We have been tracking the Americans for nearly forty minutes,* he realized, *and still they have not noticed us.* He felt that he and his crew were doing all that the emperor could ask—let alone what Vice Admiral Nagumo wanted. Eleven minutes ago he had radioed word of the enemy's course change—now steaming 240 degrees, still making more than twenty knots. But as yet Sakaida had not felt confident enough to get the observer close enough for ship identification. And that was what *Kido Butai* needed to know.

"Commander to pilot," Azumano called on the intercom. He felt the need to make himself more forceful. "Take us below the clouds again. I must determine the types of enemy ships before we return to *Tone*." The prospect of going home surely would enhance Sakaida's mood.

Azumano and Hara felt the floatplane drop again through the low, scattered cloud base. They broke out south of the American force, which Azumano scanned with his binoculars. *Must be thirty sea miles*, he thought. Yes, still ten wakes. He peered hard and counted yet again. *All apparently surface ships. Make it . . . five cruisers and four . . . no, five, destroyers. Definitely no battleships.* He told Hara to make the call, but there was no immediate response. That concerned Azumano. Unless he received a reply, the importance of this information would require him to break contact and return to the ship immediately.

USS YORKTOWN, 0813

The thirty-knot wind across the deck was refreshing, especially after spending all morning cooped up in the ready room. Chartboard tucked under one arm, Phil Rogers walked aft and found 3-B-18 armed and ready. He knelt under the nose, examining the Mark XIII demolition bomb suspended from the belly rack by twin shackles. He noted the nose and tail fuses with safety wires properly installed, and traced them to the arming-wire attachment on the bottom of the fuselage. When he released the half-ton weapon, its own weight would strip the wires from the fuses, allowing their vanes to spin freely and arm the bomb.

"She's all set, Mr. Rogers." The pilot looked up to see Barnes standing with one of the ordnancemen. The latter, wearing a red-dyed jersey and cloth helmet, seemed torn between pride in his handiwork and concern over appearing too familiar with an officer. *Hell, like Bernie says. Ensigns aren't really officers. More like apprentices.* Rogers swiveled in his crouch and made a point of smiling. "Yes, I know it's ready. You men always have 'em ready to go."

The ordie relaxed a little and bent down to the aviator. "The tail fuse is one–twenty-five-thousandth of a second, sir. The nose fuse is one-tenth." Rogers indicated his comprehension. The former would detonate the heavy bomb almost instantly on contact with whatever it hit; if it failed, the latter would allow the Mark XIII to penetrate one deck of a ship before exploding. Bombing Three's ordnance today had mixed fusing to inflict a variety of contact and delay destruction upon enemy ships.

Rogers patted the dark-green weapon fondly and let his bare hand linger on the cool, streamlined shape. After the scores of practice bombs he had dropped, this was the one that counted—his first live ordnance meant for an enemy target. A 453-pound steel forging filled with 537 pounds of TNT. Rogers stood up and stepped back, still regarding his bomb. He thought its proportion fit the Dauntless perfectly—seventy-six inches overall, seventeen and one-half inches case diameter. If the others had not been watching, Rogers would have touched a kiss to the weapon or at least affixed a wad of gum for luck, like the movie aviators did.

"Well," he said to his gunner, "let's climb aboard. We got us a carrier to sink today!" Phil Rogers never knew that Bill Barnes saw the tic at the corner of the mouth, belying the confident tone of his voice.

NUMBER FOUR SCOUT, 0815

Flight Petty Officer Sakaida had not forgotten his promise to Lieutenant (junior grade) Azumano. The enlisted pilot was bending every effort—and not a little will—to concentrate on the military aspects of his job. But his gaze was more frequently drawn to his fuel gauge. They still had ample fuel, but unless they heard from the ship fairly soon, he was not at all certain they could reach *Tone*, even with the southeasterly tailwind.

In the middle cockpit, Azumano had the canopy open again. He had scanned the American ships several times, and there seemed little point in continuing the process. Sakaida was doing an artful job of cloud-hopping, making maximum use of the scattered low layer to shield the floatplane from American view. *But they have shipboard radar*, Azumano reminded himself. *We have no way of telling if they have detected us.* Still, no Grummans had descended on them with 12.7mm guns shredding the Type Zero's vulnerable fuel tanks. *One last look*, he thought.

Passing through an open space in the airy arena, Azumano peered down again. He was drawn to a wake astern of the others, and something about it looked different. He raised his binoculars again and settled on the spot. Twenty-five or more miles was a long way for positive identification, but this one appeared . . . flat. Azumano sucked in his breath, and the cold upper air stabbed at his lungs. He looked again. Then he listened as Hara sent:

"The enemy is accompanied by what appears to be a carrier in a position to the rear of the others." *I can just imagine how this report will be received on the flagship* . . .

"Enemy aircraft above us!" Hara's cry from the rear seat sent shivers down Sakaida's spine in the pilot's seat and caused Azumano to wrench himself around in the middle cockpit. He saw only sun and scattered clouds.

"Where, you fool?" The gunner should have given a position or bearing with his first call.

"They were crossing behind us, sir," Hara explained. He knew he had not followed procedure, but he had never seen Grumman Wildcats before, either. "They disappeared behind clouds, crossing from starboard to port."

Azumano was not convinced. "How many, gunner?"

Hara thought for a moment, concentrating with all the ability of a frightened nineteen-year-old fisherman's son. "Two or three, sir."

Azumano visualized the geometry. The floatplane had just turned westward, en route back to *Tone*, when the fighters appeared from the north. If Hara was correct, they were following a southerly vector, undoubtedly under radar control from their carrier. *Good. We will open the range on them.*

USS YORKTOWN, 0840

Well back in the pack, Phil Rogers had a poor view of the launch process. Strapped into his cockpit, his forward view was obscured by the nose of the Dauntless. He dared not try to maneuver the aircraft on the deck, lest his ten-foot propeller chew up the tail of the SBD ahead of him.

However, he glimpsed the awkward shapes of two TBDs angling away from the bow, fearfully low to the water. He realized that one of them must be piloted by Wayne Wik, who flew in the last section of Torpedo Three. All twelve Devastators had gotten off safely, and immediately turned right to take up their southwesterly base course.

In a few minutes Rogers got the signal from a flight-deck director as the dive-bombers began launching. The white-jerseyed petty officer made emphatic come-on motions to the pilot, who released his toe brakes and gingerly nudged the throttle, setting Baker Eighteen into motion. With more deck room to maneuver, Rogers saw that only two more SBDs remained ahead of him. *Skipper's and Syd's divisions are off okay*, he thought. He chuckled aloud at the thought of Lieutenant Syd Bottomley, the squadron flight officer. When the word came to man aircraft, Bottomley had just emerged from the wardroom with a peanut-butter sandwich. The big, gregarious flier had grumbled, "Here I go to war, with peanut butter stuck between my teeth."

Rogers glanced up at the sailors and officers lining "vulture's row," the gun tubs and railings along the ship's island. As always, the knowledge that so many men's attention was focused upon him left a sense of importance and self-consciousness. He took a quick look at the mainmast, saw the battle ensign snapping from its halyard above the red-diamond Foxtrot flag indicating flight operations underway, and felt a tiny thrill. *Quite a sight—something to remember.*

The next plane director was competing for Rogers's attention now. Raised clenched fists, bell-bottom dungarees flapping around the bosun's ankles in the relative wind and prop blast. Rogers depressed his toe brakes and moved the flap-selection lever on his right console, then activated the power pack. He got a nod and a thumbs-up from the deckhand, confirming that his lower set of flaps was extended thirty degrees. *Every bit of lift helps with a heavy load.*

He grasped his microphone and called his gunner. "All set, Barnes?" The response came back, clear and eager. "Yes, sir!"

The pilot advanced throttle and propeller control, then checked his gauges. Fuel and oil pressure in the green; supercharger in low blower; cowl flaps open to maintain cylinder-head temperature of 260 degrees centigrade. *Oh, yeah. Canopy locked open.* Satisfied, he nodded to the launch officer standing by the starboard wingtip.

The officer gave the two-finger turnup signal and Rogers advanced his throttle to thirty inches of manifold pressure. The black-and-white checkered flag raised briefly, then slashed down and forward. Rogers released the brakes, shoved on forty-five inches and 2,600 rpm while keeping a neutral stick position with five degrees right rudder trim to offset the Cyclone engine's power factor. The Dauntless rolled forward, straining against the wind, overcoming inertia as the airframe took the aerodynamic load and the tail came up. In 550 feet the NACA 2415–2409 airfoil generated enough lift to raise five tons of aircraft, fuel, ordnance and living flesh. Rogers felt the dive-bomber settle a little off the bow—*That's okay, it's normal*, he told himself—and he was flying.

Bombing Three was airborne.

Sakaida saw them first. He might have missed them except for the cluster of shadows creeping across the rippled blue-gray sea. *Their camouflage is quite good,* he noticed. Then, mindful of Azumano's snit at Hara, Sakaida cleared his throat and raised his microphone. "Pilot to commander. A group of enemy aircraft, below to port."

From the tone of Sakaida's voice, Azumano knew this latest sighting posed no threat. Again he slid his canopy back and peered over the side. Sakaida obligingly rolled the left wing downward, affording a better view. Azumano counted them off—at least three vics of three. "Carrier attack planes," he replied. "Obviously from the same ship we just found."

Not for over a decade would Toshiki Azumano learn how wrong he had been in that assessment. Comparing track charts with a historian of the Self-Defense Force, he would determine that the Grummans that overlooked him had been from *Enterprise;* the torpedo planes were from *Hornet.* Not that it mattered at the time, but Azumano was a precise individual who liked to put events into perspective.

At that moment, something did not fit. *At least one enemy carrier is out here,* he thought. *We were told they were all in Pearl Harbor, that we have surprised them.* Obviously that was not so. Equally obviously, something was very, very wrong.

OVERHEAD USS YORKTOWN, 0902

Phil Rogers thought that VB-3 had seldom looked better. Formed up by sections and divisions, the seventeen SBDs came out of one last orbit over Task Force Seventeen and fell in behind Max Leslie on course 240. Rogers checked his instruments again, confirming his power setting for cruise climb. Two thousand rpm at thirty-four inches manifold pressure, yielding a 120-knot airspeed.

Rogers reviewed the navigation problem. Commander Arnold's directions to the squadron leaders were clear enough: hunt east of the enemy's expected track, which seemed directly toward Midway from the northeast. But the air officer did not think the Japanese would hold that heading indefinitely. If they did, they would be less than 100 miles from the atoll by the projected interception time of around 1000. Rogers pulled his plotting board from beneath the instrument panel.

The penciled dot on the grid indicated the expected point of contact: 30 degrees north latitude, 179 degrees 30 minutes east longitude.

"Mr. Rogers, we're clear of the task force."

Barnes's voice brought Rogers back to immediate matters at hand. The pilot shoved his plotting board back under the panel and glanced backward. He knew the import of his gunner's call—they were far enough from friendly ships to arm their bomb.

"Okay, Barnes. Thanks." Rogers reached his gloved right hand down to the electrical panel and flipped the plastic safety cover over the master armament switch. He depressed the toggle, and his reason for flying, even for living, was lost in the upward surge of his Dauntless.

Rogers and Barnes felt the abrupt, unexpected lurch. For a panic-stricken moment Rogers thought that somehow he had collided with a wingman. *What the hell was that?*

An electric circuit closing had caused the bomb shackles to open, allowing the thousand-pound Mark XIII to fall away and, freed of a half-ton of weight, the SBD had lifted briefly. With the bomb went Philip Rogers's spirits, accelerating toward the Pacific Ocean at thirty-two feet per second.

Then the realization came. Despair replaced panic. Rogers was aware of his heart beating an accusatory tattoo in his chest. *You screwed up! You dropped your bomb almost 200 miles short of the target* . . .

"Mr. Rogers, did we lose our bomb?" Barnes's voice transmitted fear and concern, but no accusation. *Not yet.*

Slowly, Rogers brought the mike to his mouth. "Uhh, yeah. I don't know what happened, Barnes. I just flicked the arming switch and she went." The memory returned. Last night, the chance meeting on the hangar deck. Barnes, looking grimy and cheerful, saying he had double- and triple-checked everything. *Except the new electrical arming system. I couldn't make much of it.*

Sickened, Rogers looked around. He saw Baker Seventeen's gunner gesturing animatedly. Pointing beneath 3-B-18, the man pantomimed an object dropping away, then exploding far below. The universal two hands in the air, fingers splayed, mouthing the universal word. Boom.

"Sir, there's another explosion down there! Maybe two."

Whaaat? "You mean there's others?" Rogers grabbed hold of the thought, clinging to it like an emotional life preserver for a man drowning in a sea of remorse. *If somebody else dropped early, that means I didn't screw up.* Then reality caught up with pride and overcame fear of accusation. *God, how many bombs have we lost?*

Max Leslie's voice came across the air. "Baker One here. Do not use electrical arming. Revert to manual arming only. Repeat, do not use electrical arming. Out."

Rogers realized, *If the skipper's breaking radio silence, it's bad.* He noticed that the formation had opened up, as if some pilots were afraid an electrical glitch would detonate their neighbor's bomb in midair. Other calls came through, and Rogers knew that three others had lost their ordnance, including Leslie.

Barnes was back on the intercom. "Sir, I guess somebody mixed up the arming and release circuits." A pained lull followed, then, "I guess I should have checked them better."

Rogers pushed aside his own self-pity. "I don't know what else you could have done, Bill." Pilots seldom addressed aircrew by their given names; he hoped the familiarity would ease the radioman's sense of guilt.

"Well, can we go back and rearm, sir? We're barely five minutes from the ship."

Rogers sat motionless for a moment, watching for some indication from 3-B-1. The formation was closing up again, reestablishing confidence and pride. *We've lost a quarter of our striking power, but we're sticking to the mission.* He pressed the mike button. "I guess not. Mr. Leslie probably figures they wouldn't let us take off again."

"Yeah, I guess so. Uh, sir."

Bombing Three flew on in silence, climbing higher into the morning sky.

IJNS ARASHI, 0908

"Commander, sonar reports a submarine contact bearing two-six-zero. Estimated range at least two thousand meters."

Watanabe spun on his heel at the unexpected warning. He looked at Captain Ariga, who understood the implication. "There are no friendly submarines in this area," the division commander stated evenly. He watched Watanabe impassively, curious whether the man would make the correct choice on his own.

For a moment *Arashi*'s skipper hesitated. *The worst possible timing,* he thought. *First air attacks, now this. Which poses the greater threat?* Ariga's shark-dull eyes bored into Watanabe's. After another second's reflection Watanabe barked to the helmsman. "Come right to new course. Two-six-zero."

The petty officer had barely acknowledged, *"Hai!"* when Watanabe was on the circuit to the sonar room. "Antisubmarine officer! The contact is considered hostile and we are not currently under air attack. Prepare to engage with depth charges."

Privately, Ariga congratulated himself on giving the ambitious skipper a chance to act independently. As the destroyer heeled hard over in her high-speed turn, Ariga grasped a stanchion to steady himself. "This attack will take us out of position to defend *Akagi*," he said. "But you are correct, Commander. The submarine poses the greater danger at present. I suggest you make quick work of it."

Watanabe tried to ignore the implicit threat and concentrated on setting up his run. Not hearing an update, he screamed into the intercom. "Sonar officer! Keep ranges and bearings coming until I order you to stop!" A meek reply chirped back, immediately followed by a new plot. "Bearing now two-six-five, range under two thousand meters."

"Steady on this course," Watanabe shouted. "Prepare to drop a full pattern of depth charges." He thought a moment. "And be sure to vary your depth settings." *Must I think of everything myself?* He answered his own question. *Yes, that is why I am in command.* Two minutes later, twenty depth charges rolled off the destroyer's stern racks.

Ariga stepped onto the wing of the bridge and looked aft, curious as to the ship's depth-charge pattern. He watched the roiling, white circles of foam erupt in parallel lines to either side of the twenty-five-knot wake. There was little sound to accompany the explosions. He turned back into the bridge. "A good pattern, Commander."

"Thank you, Captain." Watanabe bowed and screwed up his courage. *This is too good an opportunity to waste.* "I only hope the enemy is not too deep to avoid our weapons, sir. We should have more powerful depth charges to use against deep-diving submarines."

Ariga raised a hand. "Yes, yes, Watanabe. I read the same reports as you. And I agree—we need more than a hundred-kilogram explosive charge, and there is evidence that they do not detonate at all much below fifty meters." He compressed his lips, deep in thought. "I shall forward a report to the antisubmarine division."

Watanabe bowed crisply in gratitude. *We still have to deal with this American.* He called his soundman again and heard the breathless reply. "Captain, we will not be able to track the enemy again until the explosive noises subside."

"Yes, of course." To the helmsman he said, "Come quickly about. We will be in position for another attack when sonar regains contact . . ."

"Torpedo track, Captain! About six hundred meters to port!"

The lookout's cry came like a belch at a tea ceremony: unexpected and completely out of place. *We are supposed to be hunting him!* Watanabe thought. He strode to the port side of the bridge, took a few seconds to sight the wake and called, "Hard to port, now!"

Arashi's pointed bow swung through the first fifteen degrees of turn, and Watanabe relaxed an increment. "It is going to miss ahead of us," he called to Ariga. "If he fired from periscope depth, we can destroy him on our next run."

Meanwhile, Watanabe realized he was being drawn farther yet from *Kido Butai*.

THREE BAKER EIGHTEEN, 0945

"Mr. Rogers, there's our fighters down there."

Phil looked down and aft, under his port horizontal stabilizer. Some 10,000 feet below, through a break in the low clouds, he found the objects of Barnes's comment—four of Jimmy Thach's six Wildcats, keeping formation on Torpedo Three. Rogers assumed the other pair were down low with the TBDs. *Yorktown* Air Group's rendezvous was complete.

Rogers picked up his mike. "I see 'em, Barnes. Looks like Commander Arnold's plan really works." Rogers was impressed. *Yorktown*'s air staff had chosen the running rendezvous as the most efficient way of getting three squadrons with diverse aircraft types out on course. Wally Short's scouts were not evident, but nobody knew whether they had launched as long as radio silence remained in effect.

Rogers scanned his instruments again. *Oil pressure sixty-five, fuel pressure five. Everything's okay.* He rolled his shoulders and felt again the emptiness in his stomach. *Except I don't have a damn bomb to drop.*

To fight off the resurgent self-pity, Rogers pulled out his plotting board. He spun the circular grid to correspond with the squadron's base course, 240 true, and looked again at the expected contact point. Allowing for the 130-knot climb speed, he calculated his present position along the search track—about 110 miles out. *Another fifteen minutes*, he thought. *Maybe twenty.*

He shoved the chartboard back and raised his hands to his earphones. The Dauntless, an extraordinarily stable aircraft anyway, was trimmed to fly hands-off. Rogers tugged at his helmet to relieve some of the pressure on his ears, then lightly gripped the controls again. He thought of his primary instructor, Lieutenant Luke, who insisted, "Mister, an airplane is smarter than most pilots. It knows how to fly straight and level because that's how it's built. People aren't built to fly straight and level. So treat your airplane like a smart horse. Keep a light rein except when you need to show it who's in charge."

Rogers wondered what Lieutenant Luke was doing now. *Probably got back to the fleet after serving his time in Training Command purgatory.* Rogers then thought of his parents in West Palm Beach. *Let's see, it must be about three o'clock there.* Were they thinking of him right this minute, speculating on whether he was thinking of them?

Sallyann. She must be going to work about now. He pondered what a twenty-three-year-old librarian would be doing on a Thursday morning in June. *Thinking of me, I hope.*

IJNS ARASHI, 0955

Lieutenant Fuji moved from the navigator's station on the bridge and picked up a set of binoculars. The lookout's uncertain statement of a few moments ago had most officers scanning the cloud-flecked sky.

Commander Watanabe was not pleased with the lookout's performance. Presumably the sailor was selected for the work because of superior vigilance and visual acuity. "Well, seaman, did you see aircraft or not?" The skipper's voice told everyone that his anger was barely beneath the skin.

The boy stuttered a response. "Sor—sorry, sir. I just s-saw a few dark spots . . ."

"There! High elevation, starboard beam." Captain Ariga himself called the sighting.

Fuji raised his glasses and studied the quadrant indicated. "Yes, sir, I see them," he said. "Twenty-five or more—probably dive-bombers." The clouds opened and revealed echeloned formations of many aircraft, crossing *Arashi's* path at right angles.

"They cannot be ours," Ariga said. "The attack groups against Midway should have landed aboard by now . . ."

Fuji's mind whirled. The ship was headed northeast at thirty knots after an apparently fruitless cat-and-mouse game with that damnable American submarine. "Captain, these could be more American aircraft from Midway, but I doubt it."

Ariga turned to the navigator. "Explain."

Fuji braced himself, fearful of appearing lax before the division commander. "Sir, we have already repulsed several land-based attacks from the island. It is most unlikely that two more squadrons of American aircraft could come from so small a base."

ComDesRonFour encouraged the navigator to continue while *Arashi*'s skipper silently fumed in the background. "Sir, we copied a message from one of *Tone*'s scouts, reporting at least one enemy carrier northeast of Midway. That was almost one hour ago. I believe these aircraft must be from such a ship."

"Enemy aircraft changing course!" cried the lookout. Watanabe was about to abuse the lout for assuming they were hostile, but Fuji's assessment seemed to impress Ariga. And Watanabe was not going to argue the point.

Fuji glassed the orderly formations again. He caught the faint glint of sunlight on canopies as the leading part of the procession turned starboard, paralleling *Arashi*'s course. *My God*, he thought. Looking aft, he saw the destroyer's prominent white wake pointing like a line on a dark-blue chalkboard. *We may be showing the way for them to our striking force.*

12.

1001–1200, 4 JUNE

THREE TARE THIRTEEN, 1002

Ensign Wayne Wik glanced at his instrument-panel clock for the fourth time in as many minutes. He was painfully aware of the time-distance equation, and if Torpedo Three did not find something soon, the squadron would have to turn back. Almost twenty minutes had passed since rendezvous with the fighters and dive-bombers, so the air group was assembled and intact. *But where are the Japs?* Wik fidgeted uneasily in his seat.

Flying tail-end charlie in the last section of the second division, Wik had a view of everything that happened ahead. Lieutenant Commander Massey held the squadron at 1,500 feet, just below the scattered clouds, to preclude easy fighter attack from above. Wik looked for the two Wildcat escorts detached from Commander Thach's division, but could not see them.

Then Wik noticed the front of the echeloned formation—four arrowheads of three planes each—slowly nose upward. *The skipper's onto something*, Wik realized. He called over the intercom, "Dowd, it looks like Mr. Massey's climbing for altitude. Stay sharp back there."

"Ah'm lookin' all the time, suh," Dowd's Carolina drawl rasped back.

From 2,600 feet Lance Massey had a view that extended his vision more than twenty miles. And he had found what he wanted. Off to the right, to the northwest, was smoke on the horizon. He led his squadron thirty degrees to starboard, accelerating toward the suspected enemy fleet. Even a TBD's slow, easy-banked turn could be troublesome when the leader turned into eleven planes behind him. In the twelfth aircraft, Wayne Wik could have been at the end of an aerial game of crack-the-whip, but TorpRon Three rolled out on course without a hitch.

The TBDs assumed attack formation, each section's two wingmen stepped down on the leader with sections stepped down on divisions. The field of defensive gunfire was thus relatively unobstructed, and best of all for the rearmost aircraft. But neither did that plane have anyone guarding its tail.

Then Wik saw it. *Oh, my God . . .*

Beneath the scattered, broken clouds, white wakes scarred the azure surface of the ocean, and distant flak bursts rippled across the sky. Wik estimated that Torpedo Three was perhaps fifteen miles from the nearest ships—Japanese ships. He thumbed the interphone button to warn Dowd, who read his mind. "I see 'em, Mr. Wik."

And they see us. Wik flinched as large explosions erupted in midair a mile or so ahead. Any hope of a surprise attack died with those bursts—spotter rounds from a *Tone*-class cruiser. Japanese fighter direction was crude but effective, as the Zero pilots on combat air patrol were alerted to the presence of Torpedo Three.

Knowing he had little time, Lance Massey led his squadron down through the cloud deck. Trading altitude for speed, he hoped to initiate his attack before the enemy fighters intercepted.

Wik temporarily lost sight of Tare Ten and Eleven as the formation descended through the low, broken clouds.

Phil Rogers noticed the tail of Lieutenant Shumway's SBD wiggle in a fishtailing motion. *Something's up*, Rogers realized. He straightened in his seat, wriggling under his harness and easing the strain on his buttocks from the hard seat-pack parachute. "Heads up, Barnes. Looks like we're on to something."

"Yes, sir. I'm unshipping my guns now." Rogers sensed Barnes unlocking his rotating seat, swiveling aft and depressing the foot pedal that opened the fuselage bay where his twin .30-caliber mount was stowed. A tug up and backward, and the weapons were deployed. A pull on each charging handle and they were ready to fire.

Rogers noted the banked wings of the division leader's aircraft and eased the controls to follow in a right-hand turn. Then he began hearing disconcerting snatches of radio calls. The skipper trying to establish contact with Lieutenant Commander Massey. For an instant of clarity in a babble of confusion, Rogers heard a cry from three miles below: "Jimmy, there are fighters attacking my squadron!" But mostly Bombing Three heard high-pitched warnings from some torpedo pilots—and just plain screams from others. The consistent phrase was "Fighters!" closely followed by "Watch out!"

Then, belatedly, Phil Rogers raised his view from almost directly below to up near the horizon. He saw writhing wakes, clearly evident of high-speed maneuvering. At length he realized he was looking at the Japanese carrier striking force, perhaps forty miles away.

Emerging below the cloud base, Wik regained sight of the rest of the squadron. And more. Churning wakes, even more flak bursts and occasional splashes or explosions in the water. *Somebody's working over the Japs*, Wik realized with a start. *We're not alone.* He wondered who it was.

Torpedo Six knew. The *Enterprise* TBD squadron also was alone and unsupported. And it died as Torpedo Eight had died, attacking alone against an aroused, alerted enemy. Lieutenant Commander Lindsey took fourteen Devastators into *Kido Butai*. The senior survivor took three other planes home to *Enterprise*.

"Up ahead! Twelve o'clock!" Dowd's warning snapped Wik back to awareness. Glancing up and forward, the pilot made out a dozen or more dark spots in the sky. With astonishing speed they grew wings, then tails. Then flashes sparkled from the dark silhouettes. Large, lazy red golf balls corkscrewed through the atmosphere. Wik watched, entranced. He was almost mesmerized by the seemingly slow-motion spirals tracing past his cockpit. He heard something strange, alien. A metallic noise, somewhere between a *thump* and a *ping*. Then one or two more.

"Christ! They're shooting at us," he exclaimed over the intercom. Somehow that realization usually is met with a mixture of astonishment and anger. *Why do they want to hurt ME?* An instant later Wik felt foolishly ashamed. He considered masking his confusion and fear with some flippant remark, but then he heard Dowd open fire from the rear cockpit.

With a start, Wik realized he was lagging behind. He pushed the throttle full ahead, trying to catch his section leader. The skipper was taking the squadron down toward the wavetops, and the TBDs bucked along at an unaccustomed 160 knots, nose down with their big torpedoes protruding from light-gray bellies. Wik fought for control of his sanity. A moment before, his world made sense. He was number twelve in line, the most junior pilot in the carefully ordered hierarchy of a torpedo squadron. Suddenly, the familiar blue-gray corrugated wings of his airplane sprouted jagged, irregular holes. People he had never seen before seemed dedicated to shooting that hierarchy apart. And with it, Ensign Wayne Wik, USNR.

Wik caught a movement in his peripheral vision and turned his head. Off the starboard wing a sleekly elegant aircraft that he assumed was a Zero fighter climbed on a reciprocal heading at an incredible angle. It rocketed to a perch above and behind 3-T-13 and, with effortless grace, dropped a wing, nosed down and fell into a quartering gunnery run. Dowd fired again, his .30 Browning hammering out a long burst, but even Wik's frightened senses knew the fighter was out of range.

A separate compartment of Wik's mind opened in one corner of his consciousness and he saw himself, Dowd and Tare Thirteen from above and behind. The graceless Devastator grew in size with breathtaking speed, and then Wik snapped back to reality. He shivered under his goatskin flight jacket, but it was warm at 1,000 feet. And in that instant, he knew—knew absolutely. The image that had snapped in his mind was precisely what the Japanese pilot was seeing.

God in heaven, what do I do? All of Wik's training told him to maintain formation. How many times had the skipper pounded home the lesson? *Unless you're afire or a wing falls off, keep your position. Everybody else depends on your guns to defend your wingmen.* But Wik also knew that he was cold meat for the Zero. As last in line, nobody was covering him very well. *What do I do?*

In a position like this, you couldn't leave formation. You couldn't take evasive action, even if your airplane permitted it. You had to follow your leader as the exec, Lieutenant Hart, prepared to split the squadron in an anvil attack against the nearest carrier. What else could you do?

The A6M2 pilot—one of nearly forty airborne by then—answered the question. That was his ship down there, and the *Hiryu* Fighter Squadron fought savagely to protect her. His next burst was precisely on target. Three 20mm shells and seven 7.7mm bullets shattered the long plexiglass canopy behind the pilot's seat, penetrating to the bottom of the fuselage. The descending angle of one cannon shell and two bullets also penetrated the twenty-three-year-old body of Radioman Benjamin Dowd, who died without a sound.

Wik felt the 20mms explode, heard the high-pitched sounds, knew what they meant. Desperately, he jammed his right foot hard on the rudder pedal, slewing the big Douglas sideways. But it was not enough. Two hundred yards back, sensing an overshoot, the black-nosed killer elegantly barrel-rolled to maintain its aspect on the target. The pilot delicately jockeyed stick and rudder, placed his gunsight crosshairs slightly ahead of the TBD's nose and pressed both triggers again.

Foam kicked up well beyond Tare Thirteen, but Wik never knew it. The Zero pilot had in fact overdeflected, but he flew his sights back through the target. Two cannon shells tore into the Pratt and Whitney engine, knocking off a cylinder and puncturing the case. Four 7.7mms also hit, severing an oil line.

First came the smoke, dark brown and wispy from beneath the cowling. Moments later the smoke thickened, turned black and burned orange-red. Wik sensed more than saw the Zero pull up from its gunnery run, confident of a kill.

Wik glimpsed a plane crash into the water—an ephemeral impression of a cartwheeling aerodynamic shape swamped by white spray. "Was that a Jap?" he asked his dead gunner. The roasting heat of the engine fire swept over the top of his canopy and his thoughts of the outside world vanished. Panic rose in his throat and he screamed aloud.

Gotta get out. He rolled back the high-domed hatch and felt for his seatbelt latch. Gloved hands fumbled at the snap, found it and tugged hard. Impelled by the adrenaline surge of survival instinct, Wayne Wik gathered his legs beneath him, pushed hard and half-rolled, half-jumped onto the left wing. He felt the 100-knot wind, inhaled a mouthful of smoke and felt a scalding heat on his face. As he rolled off the wing he grasped his ripcord in his right hand, and his heart fluttered. *How high am I?* He hadn't checked the altimeter, hadn't even looked down at the water.

Falling through space, Wik had enough presence of mind for a quick three-count. Then he pulled, felt the ripcord disengage and heard a rippling, snapping sound. The water was awfully close. He shut his eyes for impact.

A violent, wrenching sensation. Wik was jerked upright as his canopy blossomed. Three seconds later he plunged feetfirst into the Pacific Ocean and the shock of water entry flashed a message to his dulled mind. *I'm alive!*

Wik grasped for the toggles of his CO_2 bottles and pulled both strings. He felt his Mae West inflate as he bobbed to the surface. With difficulty, he struggled out of his waterlogged parachute harness. A choking seizure overtook him and he felt he might vomit. Instead, he spat out seawater. Then he looked around. He could see very little besides smoke on the near horizon. Not even the noise of gunfire was evident.

Only then did Wayne Wik stop to wonder about Benjamin Dowd.

IJNS ARASHI, 1012

The junior watch officer turned inward to the bridge, breathless with excitement. "Captain! An aircraft just crashed in the water. Five thousand meters off the port bow."

Watanabe raised his glasses and studied the area. *There! Smoke and spray still visible. I hope it's an American plane.* He felt the division commander approach from behind. "An aircraft in the water, sir. I recommend we investigate."

Ariga nodded. "Conduct a rescue if it is one of ours. If it is American, search for prisoners and rejoin formation as quickly as possible."

Phil Rogers knew the meaning of frustration. Torpedo Three obviously was committed to an attack, following whatever other torpedo squadron had stirred up the Japanese. Lieutenant Commander Thach's half-dozen F4Fs were fighting for their lives, trying to keep some of the swarming Zeros off Massey's TBDs, but Bombing Three still hadn't jumped in. Rogers looked down again. A carrier—and a damn big one by the look of her—was turning into the wind. *She's about to launch!*

Max Leslie's calm voice penetrated the atmosphere and Rogers's ears. Through the static, the skipper called, "Wally from Max. If you read me, take the smaller carrier to the south. I'm attacking the bigger one." *Damn*, Rogers thought. *We don't even know if Short's been launched.* Still, Mr. Leslie—the astute old pro—was taking nothing for granted. Rogers again reflected on his admiration for the old man. *Things going to hell all around and he's still pushing for a coordinated attack.*

Descending through 15,000 feet, Rogers heard Leslie try to reach Torpedo Three one last time. "Lance or John, this is Max. I'm beginning my run from the southeast. If you hear me, start your runs now." Static crackled over the circuit, interrupted only occasionally by mostly unintelligible calls. Rogers's mouth was dry; he required no prescience to determine the likely fate of Torpedo Three. *God, please . . . not Wayne. Sally, say a prayer.*

Bombing Three, strung out in a line of vees by sections and divisions, began a northwesterly turn, still descending toward the pushover point.

Wayne Wik sorely missed the rubber raft that had gone down with Tare Thirteen—not only for enhanced chances of survival, but for just a little more elevation. The last he had seen of Torpedo Three, Mr. Massey had been driving head-on into the swarming Zeros and thickening flak. Apparently enough time had passed so that the torpedo attack should have produced results, assuming anyone got close enough to pickle a fish. If there were hits, Wik thought he might be able to see smoke from damaged ships.

He also figured that whatever happened to his squadronmates, at least he personally was out of immediate danger. He had glimpsed cruisers or destroyers nearby, but they were far too busy to notice one lone aviator bobbing in the water. *If the Japs come this way, I'll lie low in the water*, he figured. *Eventually a PBY or one of our ships will find me.*

He did not care to ponder the other two options.

OVERHEAD KIDO BUTAI, 1023

From his perch above the enemy carrier, Phil Rogers gawked at the scene. Wide open to attack, seemingly unaware or unconcerned of her peril, IJNS *Soryu* steamed upwind. He noted her starboard-side island, the stained yellow flight deck with the big red sun painted well forward, the densely packed aircraft arrayed for launch. *We've got her!* Rogers exulted. He shifted his gaze forward, toward Mr. Leslie's Dauntless. *Come on, Skipper, let's go, let's go . . .*

Then it hit him. Rogers jerked his head and shoulders around, left and right. The force of his motion was such that he unwittingly moved his stick hand, gently rocking the dive-bomber. *There's no fighters up here.* He keyed the intercom. "Barnes, you see any Zeros?"

The electronic crackle snapped in Rogers's earphones. "Ah, no, sir. Not a one. Strange, ain't it?"

A more experienced officer, a less optimistic aviator, would have marveled at the gift the gods of war had bestowed upon Bombing Three. Buck Rogers merely accepted the gift and was anxious to tear it open. He shifted in his seat, reached out to charge his two .50-calibers and looked down again.

Then Max Leslie waggled his wings, banking into a descending port turn. At 14,500 feet, completing 270 degrees of turn, the skipper abruptly nosed over into his dive. His two wingmen followed, as did the next three. Then the second division rolled in. Then the third.

Rogers, next-to-last in the long line of gray-blue Dauntlesses, counted to himself. When his section leader tipped over, Rogers mentally ticked off the proper interval. Then he shifted his left hand from throttle to stick, selected the diamond-shaped dive-flap handle with his right and activated the hydraulic pump. He felt the perforated flaps come open at the trailing edge of his wings, biting into the 180-knot slipstream. The yellow deck disappeared under his port wingroot.

Rogers came back on the throttle, coordinated stick and rudder and rolled into his dive.

Lieutenant Masatake Naito marveled at the events unfolding around him. Three squadrons of enemy torpedo planes had been destroyed in the past hour, to say nothing of the previous ineffective attacks by level- and glide-bombers. But this situation was different. *These torpedo planes are better coordinated with the dive-bombers*, he noted. If only *Kido Butai* could shake off this threat as well, all four carriers would immediately clear their laden decks of some eighty bombers and attack planes escorted by a dozen Zero fighters.

The captain clearly saw the fear in Naito's face. "Do not be so concerned, Air Officer. We have brushed aside every other attack this morning. This will be no different. You'll see."

Naito wondered whether he should hold his tongue. *No, there is too much at stake*. "Captain, it appears that all our fighters are occupied down here, dealing with the torpedo planes. If high-level bombers should appear—"

The lookouts all were shouting at once. "Helldivers overhead!"

It was a good dive, one of the finest he had ever made. Rogers felt the Dauntless steady and smooth in his hands, like a custom rifle fitted to a marksman's cheek and shoulder. For a moment he admired the way the skipper had set up the attack: diving out of the southeast, along the carrier's centerline from astern, sun at their backs. *Classic. This is the way it's done.*

But after all, this moment—these thirty-five seconds—were the payoff. This was the dividend based on the twenty-year investment the American people and government had made in a generation of naval officers like Maxwell F. Leslie. Not so much his individual skill—after all, he had no bomb—but his Annapolis education, all the fuel he had burned, all the practice bombs he had dropped, everything he had learned in four thousand hours of taxpayer-funded flying. The next few seconds would determine how well he had accomplished his primary purpose: preparing Bombing Squadron Three for this day and hour and minute.

Hanging by his seatbelt in a seventy-degree plunge, Rogers felt his dive was nearly straight down. He pressed his goggled right eye to the padded end of his optical sight and played with the controls. No major moves, just a little pressure on stick and rudder pedals to align the crosshairs. *Too soon*, he realized. *Can't see much of the target yet.*

Ahead of him was the third division leader, Lieutenant Shumway, whose Dauntless was followed by three more between himself and Rogers. The insignia-red interior of the splayed dive brakes on the preceding SBDs shone in the sun. Each plane had five flaps—an upper and lower at the trailing edge of each wing and a longer section beneath the fuselage. In all, they contained 318 perforations, allowing the 240-knot airstream to pass through them. The ingenious design reduced vibration on the speed brakes, affording the SBD the quality Rogers most loved about the airplane—exceptional stability in the dive.

The Dauntless plunged down its selected path and Rogers felt the familiar pressure build against his eardrums. He swallowed, then opened his mouth wide to flex his jaw and facial muscles. He saw the first tentative tracers curling up toward him and momentarily was distracted, then realized with a strange exultation, *Now I've been shot at!*

Still well below him, he saw the first three SBDs pull out of their dives—tiny toy airplanes crawling out of sight at the top of his crosshairs. A dark eruption down there. *Somebody got a hit!* Then sudden white rings on the water alongside the speeding, graceful ship.

As more planes dropped and pulled up, Rogers gained a better view of his target. *Wow, she's a big son of a bitch.* The mixed metaphor never occurred to him. But he could make out planes on deck, spotted aft for launch, and thought he glimpsed one blown overboard forward of the starboard-side island. Flak getting heavier now, with bursting stuff in addition to the tracers. None very close yet. *But one or two more hits. We're clobbering her!*

An unnatural movement caught his eye. Two blue-gray shapes peeled out of their dives, rolling into new headings as Baker Twelve and Sixteen diverted toward a bigger ship. *What, a battlewagon? No time to watch. But good headwork. Johnny and Obie see this carrier's done for.* Now Shumway's two wingmen, Baker Fourteen and Fifteen going for another nearby warship, maybe a cruiser. *Bob and Randy spreading the bombs around. Good deal.*

Must be down around five thousand feet and I still haven't fired a shot. Rogers's index finger clamped down on the trigger and he sensed as much as heard or felt the hammering of his two .50-calibers. His own tracers flashed outward toward the blazing dark-yellow flight deck, accompanied by the scent of burned gunpowder in the cockpit.

At length the exec dropped and hauled Baker Thirteen out of its nearly three-mile plunge. Rogers debated whether to make a high recovery and follow Shumway or continue strafing. In a prideful moment he made his choice. *I may never have this chance again.* He nudged the stick back a hair, raising the crosshairs to a point forward of the bridge, clear of the roiling, greasy black smoke. He saw orange-red tongues licking their way through the darkness and noticed Shumway's bomb striking home. Then, with three seconds to spare, he steadied up, nailed his crosshairs squarely on the doomed rectangle looming in his sight and thumbed the red button atop his stick. *Good release. I'd have got a hit!*

Feeling for the dive-brake handle, Rogers shoved it to the closed position, hit the accumulator and returned his right hand to the stick. A steady, two-handed pull brought four times the weight of earth's gravity down through the top of his head. His vision went from color to gray, from panoramic to funnellike, as Baker Eighteen bottomed out of its dive 1,100 feet over His Imperial Majesty's ship *Soryu.*

"Hey, Mr. Rogers, you see that?"

Phil had nearly allowed himself to forget Barnes in the back seat, vigilantly guarding their tail against interceptors during the half-minute dive. But as he picked up the mike and turned himself around, Rogers saw what his gunner meant. There, off to the south and west, were two more funeral pyres.

I J N S   T O N E,   1 0 3 0

"How is this possible?" asked the captain to no one in particular. Lieutenant Naito, standing at the rear of the bridge, had no reply. Nobody did. Naito risked a look at the captain's face as the twenty-six-year-veteran officer paced from port to starboard. Clearly visible were tears in the old man's eyes.

Naito did not trust his own voice. He barely trusted what his own eyes showed him. Nearby lay *Akagi,* flagship of the carrier striking force, blazing from a series of bomb hits. Farther off were *Soryu* and *Kaga,* both gushing smoke and flames. Destroyers steamed frantically near all three carriers, rushing to lend a hand with fire fighting or to rescue survivors. Another explosion rocked the flagship—Naito guessed an aircraft's fuel tanks had erupted in the searing heat—and he wondered how anyone could possibly survive.

"Is there any word on *Hiryu*?" asked the captain. His communications officer, slumped against a console, braced to attention. "No, Captain. But apparently the American attack only struck the southern part of the disposition." He waited for a response and, receiving none, added, "I can inquire if you wish."

The captain shook his head. "No, there is confusion enough just now. We will be informed." He turned back toward the gut-churning spectacle, unable to keep his eyes from the three blazing carriers.

Naito checked the chronometer. Azumano should be returning soon, and the cruiser's air officer needed to make preparations to recover the Number Four Scout. *He is in for an awful surprise*, Naito thought. *All his good work in discovering the American carriers may be wasted.*

Looking again toward *Akagi*, Naito marveled at the brilliant coordination of the American dive-bombing attack. To arrange for two formations to arrive simultaneously from different quadrants and hit three capital ships in a five- or six-minute period—incredible! The estimated strength of the American planes, at least two squadrons, told Naito that there had to be more than just the one carrier Azumano had reported.

We shall have to get our scouts refueled and launched again immediately, he reflected. Vice Admiral Nagumo—if he was still alive—would want updated intelligence immediately.

BAKER EIGHTEEN, 1031

Bill Barnes eyeballed the dark object, recognized it for what it was, and fumbled for his microphone. "We got a Nip out here, trailing us. Let's get him!" He forgot to say "sir," but neither he nor Phil Rogers paid any attention. Belatedly, Barnes added, "'Bout a mile back, eight o'clock."

Rogers turned his head and craned his neck. He was going to chastise Barnes for neglecting the enemy's altitude when the ungainly silhouette hove into view, slightly low. *Floatplane*, Rogers thought. *Must be from a battleship or cruiser.*

For the first time in his military career, Phil Rogers was faced with a command decision. Heading for the rendezvous, he was expected to join the other VB-3 aircraft circling southeast of the target. He could see two or three SBDs well ahead of him, en route to the rendezvous point. But this was an emergency. Besides, splashing a Jap would help make up for the lost bomb. *One pass*, he decided, *then I'll join up*. "Here we go, Barnes. Get ready!"

Rogers added power, coordinated stick and rudder and began a medium-banked port turn. As the SBD's nose came around he eased the stick forward slightly and drew a bead on the ancient-looking biplane. The range was still too great but he knew the Nakajima could not hope to outrun him.

He sees us, Rogers realized with a rush of adrenaline. The knowledge that he was about to engage an enemy aircraft prickled the nerves between his shoulder blades. With astonishing agility the awkward-looking floatplane stood on its port wingtips, stuffed its nose down and began a dive toward the water. Rogers was disappointed; a stern chase would take him back toward the Japanese fleet. He had seen no Zero fighters yet, but he could well imagine their pilots' attitude. Phil Rogers's white fangs receded as reason rose in his brain.

"Barnes, this isn't worth it. He can't keep up with us and we might miss the rendezvous. We're going back." With a look at the upper air where interceptors might lurk, he continued his turn and rolled out on the original southeasterly heading.

In the rear seat, Radioman Second Class William E. Barnes pounded the receiver of his starboard gun in frustrated rage. He did not realize it yet, but he had cut the heel of his hand through his calfskin glove.

IJNS ARASHI, 1040

From the bridge, Watanabe and Ariga watched the lifeboat return alongside. The khaki-clad aviator just fished from the crash site still wore his yellow life preserver, riding bareheaded in the stern. Once the boat was secured alongside, the American was prodded up the net. He received a helping hand over the chain rail and stood, dripping and scared, beneath the port wing of the bridge.

Watanabe turned to Fuji. "Navigator, you are the only one aboard who understands English. Interrogate the prisoner where we can hear you."

Fuji barked *"Hai!"* and descended the ladder leading to the main deck. On an impulse, he diverted down one deck to his quarters and retrieved his sword from its rack on the bulkhead. Back on deck, he gestured to the sailors attending the American. They had relieved him of his life preserver and shoved him along behind the navigator.

On the open deck before the bridge, Fuji stopped and turned to face the captive. An average-looking young man, half a head taller than himself. Brown hair and blue eyes. Nothing very remarkable, except . . . what?

One of the sailors handed Fuji the American's personal possessions: a wallet with photographs and money, a fountain pen and an official identification card. Fuji briefly admired the photo of an attractive white woman. Then he compared the expressionless face on the ID card with the one before him. Fuji suddenly recalled the petty officer who had stepped on his polished shoes a few days ago. This airman's eyes held the same look—fear and uncertainty. *Good, I can use that.*

Fuji slowly read the name on the card. Wayne W. Wik, Ensign, U.S. Naval Reserve.

EASTERN ISLAND, MIDWAY, 1048

Sunny Jim Carpenter jumped off the bed of the supply truck and waved his thanks to the driver. The sailor behind the wheel let out the clutch, added throttle and the Ford lurched away, leaving the marine in its dusty path at VMF-221's operations tent. Second Lieutenant Newton Callender ambled up to him. "Hey, Jim. Didn't 'spect to see you back from th' dispensary."

Carpenter looked closely at Callender, a survivor of the second division who had brought back the only undamaged airplane from the interception. Carpenter realized with a start that the twenty-three-year-old New Yorker was drunk. "I'm not hurt badly," Carpenter replied in a barely civil tone. He touched the bandage on his cheek, covering the cut made by his shattering canopy. He looked around. There were only a few enlisted marines, pushing useless airplanes out of the way. "Where is everybody else?"

"C'mon, I'll show ya." Callender took Carpenter's arm and led him toward a dugout near the mostly empty aircraft revetments. Stepping inside, Carpenter hesitated. He wanted to allow his eyes to adjust to the darkness, but there was something else. He sensed a depressing mixture of despondency and alcohol.

"Look, it's Jimbo," somebody said. "Siddown, Carpenter," slurred another voice. "Have a drink."

Carpenter squatted in the entrance, a hunched figure backlit by the bright sunlight outside. He made out a half-dozen pilots who passed a couple of bottles back and forth. A fifth of bourbon floated out of the gloom, apparently suspended in space before him. The gesture repelled him. He waved it aside. "No, thanks." *Christ, the squadron's fallen apart.* Carpenter wanted nothing so much as to leave this place. "Who's senior?" he asked to no one in particular.

"Who th' hell cares?" spat out the senior captain present. "I left the sergeant major in charge." Carpenter had seen enough. He stood up and took three fast paces outside. The sky was still cloud-flecked and blue, but Midway's fires continued to blaze. He smelled the reek of burning aviation fuel.

Not knowing what else to do, Carpenter walked to the operations tent. The duty NCO, an old-timer named Manning—whose face was a map of the corps' foreign duty posts—stood as the pilot entered. "As you were, Sergeant. I just came by to see if I can do anything."

The lined, leathery face tried to remain impassive. But obviously Sergeant Manning was surprised to see a sober officer. Carpenter took the vacant chair and slumped into a most unmilitary posture. "The lieutenant looks like he could use a drink, sir."

Carpenter threw a dagger glance at the NCO. "There's enough boozing in this squadron right now. As you well know."

Chagrined, Manning harrumphed. "Uh, yessir."

"All right, what's our status? Who's in charge?"

"Well, sir, we have two operational aircraft—Captain Carl's F4F and Lieutenant Callender's Brewster. The Grumman has eight holes in it, and one gun is still jammed. The Brewster . . . well, it's in fine shape. Good as when it took off." He looked significantly at Carpenter. "Captain Carl's sitting cockpit alert in his plane and Captain Humberd's in Callender's plane."

A lot of good two fighters will do, when twenty-five weren't half enough. "All right, I guess that's all we can do for now." He inhaled deeply, then asked the main question on his mind. "What about our missing pilots?"

"The navy picked up Captain Merrill. And they recovered Major Parks's body from the reef. He'd been strafed in his parachute. The bastards . . ." Manning's voice cracked. "We also lost four men here on the ground."

Carpenter absorbed that information. *Shouldn't be a surprise, I guess. The rape of Nanking, the Bataan death march.* He felt surprisingly little anger and realized he must be more tired than he had thought. "Any word on the scout-bombers?"

Manning picked up a paper and held it at arm's length. "Two-Forty-One put up twenty-eight SBDs and SB2Us. They took off right after you gentlemen. Apparently they attacked the Jap fleet, but results are pretty uncertain." His gaze returned to Carpenter. "They got fifteen back but half of 'em are junk. Pretty much the same with the torpedo-carriers: two of the army's four B-26s and just one of the six TBFs. I seen it come in—all shot to hell with a dead gunner."

Carpenter remembered the blond southerner, copilot of one of the Marauders. *I wonder if he made it?*

Manning was about to list the squadron's ground-personnel losses when both men heard the siren. Immediately a corporal poked his head inside the tent flap. "Hey, there's another alert! Carl and Humberd are starting engines."

Carpenter sprinted from the tent, running far enough down the line to watch the Wildcat and Buffalo taxi out. Shielding his eyes from the glare, he watched them turn onto the taxiway, setting a fast pace. Both stubby little fighters rocked on their spindly landing gear, paused briefly and accelerated down the runway. *God in heaven*, Carpenter thought. *Two against—what? Another hundred like this morning?* He wondered why anyone would do such a thing. Then he thought of his squadronmates in the dugout. He fervently wished for another plane of his own.

Manning was beside him, watching the mismatched pair climb under full power. "Hell, we'll never see them again."

The radio operator shouted from the tent. "Sergeant! The Japs are bombing again. PT boats report explosions in the lagoon. We better get under cover."

Carpenter started to follow Manning to the nearest shelter. *Wait a minute! Bombing the lagoon? That makes no sense.* "Sergeant, hold on . . ."

"Sir, excuse me." Carpenter turned to see the radioman close at hand. A sheepish expression confirmed Carpenter's suspicion. "Ah, sir. There's been a mistake. Midway Radio reports the bombs are from some *Hornet* SBDs. They're dropping ordnance before they land. There's been another snafu." He shrugged, a skinny kid in rolled-up sleeves stating the obvious. "They'll sound the all-clear pretty soon."

James Carpenter spun on his heel. So apparently the navy was having no better luck than the marines and army in this battle. Carpenter walked back to the parking area to await the return of the two unwounded VMF-221 pilots he still respected. He thought of his friends Buck Rogers and Wayne Wik. *I wonder if they're even still alive.*

Sitting on the deck, Wik took in his surroundings. He faced a semicircle of Japanese, most of whom stared at him with undisguised curiosity. The one with the sword—apparently a middle-grade officer—conducted a conversation with two other officers on the bridge above and behind Wik. He allowed his mind to wander.

Man, that was close. A hundred feet lower and my chute wouldn't have opened. He thought again of his gunner, who had gone in with the Devastator. Wik pushed the image from his mind.

The designated interrogator started to speak, stopped a moment to gather his thoughts, then carefully pronounced, "Name, rank-u." He shoved a paper and pen at Wik, who was pleasantly surprised. *This isn't so hard.* He took the pad and printed his full name, rank and serial number.

The lieutenant then pointed to Oahu on a map he held. "Ship? You ship!"

Wik looked up. The officer's brown eyes bored into his own. The American looked around, as if seeking an ally. *Shit! I can't tell them anything more!* He spread his hands, arched his shoulders. "I do not understand," he intoned, shaking his head.

The lieutenant picked up the pen and drew a crude sketch of an aircraft carrier. "Ship! Name ship!" He shouted this time. Again Wik played dumb. *If I can't understand them, I can't tell them anything.*

Twenty-eight inches of tempered steel, brilliantly polished, flashed in the sunlight. The sword made a ringing sound as it cleared the scabbard. With both hands on the pommel, the lieutenant placed the point four inches from Wik's face. *This can't be happening. What can I do? Why didn't the navy tell me what to do?* He swallowed hard and heard himself say, "USS *Yorktown.*"

The men of Bombing Three did not know that they and their *Enterprise* counterparts had just won World War II in the Pacific. In fact, they would not know it for days or years, according to their astuteness or optimism. But two and a half hours after *Yorktown* began launch, all seventeen VB-3 Dauntlesses were back over the task force. Phil Rogers felt the glow of accomplishment and the ease of relief. He ticked off his varied blessings: Obviously *Yorktown* was safe, steaming intact with her escorts deployed around her. The Japs had just lost three of their four carriers. Bombing Three so far had no losses. And, not least among these virtues, *I didn't screw up.*

For some, the good news was too much to contain. While waiting for Lieutenant Commander Thach's short-legged Wildcats to return, several of the radiomen-gunners unlimbered their hand-held blinkers and flashed Morse-code messages to the ships below. Bill Barnes rotated his seat to port, braced his elbows on the canopy rail and sighted on the bridge of the cruiser *Astoria*. He felt a kinship with his fellow communicator down there, who acknowledged Barnes's preliminary authenticator with the "ready to copy" signal. Barnes's practiced fingers blinked out the message: Victor Baker Three . . . Howe Item Tare . . . Jig Able Peter . . . Charlie Victor. Tare William Oscar . . . Mike Oboe Roger Easy . . . Charlie Victor . . . Baker Uncle Roger Nan Item Nan George. Endit.

VB-3 HIT JAP CV. TWO MORE CV BURNING.

IJNS TONE, 1140

Sakaida shoved up the power and urged the Type Zero floatplane through the waves. After landing on *Tone*'s wake, the rougher chop alongside took some extra-careful handling. At the last moment he cut his throttle and allowed the aircraft to decelerate to the ship's speed.

Standing in the middle seat, one hand braced on the canopy, Azumano reached for the hook that he would clip onto the aircraft hoist cable. With the latch closed and locked, he sat down again and Sakaida secured the engine. The three-bladed prop whirled into silence as the aircraft-recovery crane lifted the three-ton Aichi onto the port catapult. Once the plane was secure, Azumano scrambled down the boarding ladder to make his report. He had as many questions as answers for Lieutenant Naito. *Or maybe not*, he thought, looking around. Three burning carriers provided ghastly eloquent testimony as to what had transpired in Azumano's absence.

The aircraft commander brought his heels together on the deck and saluted crisply. The air officer returned the salute and came straight to the point. "Get your crew something to eat right away, Azumano. Battle rations are available in the hangar. We will be sending you and Number Three off again as soon as possible."

Battle rations, Azumano thought in disgust. *Rice balls and water. Tea if we're lucky.* He risked a question. "Air Officer . . ." He spread his hands in a helpless gesture. "What happened here?"

A refueling crew traipsed past both officers, nudging Naito's foot with a hose. He stepped aside and turned to Azumano. "Enemy dive-bombers. They attacked from the southeast and southwest almost simultaneously while our fighters were destroying their torpedo planes." He shook his head and bit down the bile he felt in his throat. "*Akagi*, *Kaga* and *Soryu* are all out of action."

Azumano pulled off his fur-lined flying helmet and ran his fingers through his hair. Realization lit a spark in his dark eyes. "Then there must be more than the one carrier we found . . ."

"Correct. That is why you are being launched again so soon." Naito placed a hand on Azumano's sleeve. "Find them for us again. You did well this morning, Azumano. If not for this damnable catapult"—he jerked his head toward the troublesome contrivance that may have doomed Operation MI—"you would have found the Americans a half-hour sooner. Our air groups might not have been caught fully fueled and armed on their decks."

Sakaida and Hara were now out of the plane, standing respectfully four paces behind Azumano. "Then, the battle continues," the observer said.

"Yes, of course!" Naito's voice carried an edge he did not intend. "*Hiryu* has launched a strike group based on your report. It should be nearing the enemy fleet now."

BAKER EIGHTEEN, 1152

"Get clear, we're being attacked!"

For a moment, Rogers was perplexed by the radio call. It made no sense. He was following Dave Shumway into the racetrack pattern, waiting a turn to land aboard, and now *Yorktown* was saying something about Japs inbound. The exec's Dauntless broke off to starboard, retracting its wheels as it went. Rogers had no choice but to follow. He heard part of another transmission to VB-3: "clear of own antiaircraft fire." *Well, that makes sense*, he thought. *Jittery AA gunners will shoot at anything that flies.*

The radio net now belonged to the fighter-direction officer, Lieutenant Commander Pederson. As Max Leslie, Syd Bottomley and Dave Shumway led their SBD divisions southeasterly—to the unengaged side of the task force—the airborne Wildcats began receiving orders. Rogers heard, "All Scarlet planes keep a sharp lookout . . . group of planes coming in at two-five-five, unidentified."

Various Wildcat flights checked in, either acknowledging orders or calling in status reports. Rogers realized that everyone's voice was progressively rising—a sure sign of tension. "Many bogeys, angels ten."

"Bandits above me, heading for the ship. Appears to be eighteen dive-bombers."

"Okay, break 'em up."

And finally, "Tallyho!"

13.

1201–1400, 4 JUNE

Repair Party Two stood by on the second deck, below *Yorktown*'s hangar deck. Cactus Jack Callaway glanced about, measuring his men's mood. All of the damage-control team had been through this at Coral Sea, one month before. *Is it only that long?* Callaway marveled. *Seems like years.*

As if reading his thoughts, a second-class petty officer said, "Just like old times, huh, Mr. Callaway?"

The damage-control assistant drawled, "We've fixed up Old Yorky before. We can do 'er again."

Another sailor thought aloud. "Maybe we won't have to . . ."

Even belowdecks, the sound and vibration of *Yorktown*'s antiaircraft guns was heard and felt. The loudspeaker blared, "Dive-bombers on the starboard quarter!"

Callaway shot a glance at the youngster. "Hold that thought, Nugent." Smiling, the DCA raised a hand with two fingers crossed. They all felt the ship begin to heel to starboard in a thirty-knot port turn.

Like ninety percent of the participants in naval battles, Repair Two saw nothing of the combat. They had no way of knowing that *Hiryu*'s dive-bomber squadron was chopped to pieces by Wildcats and AA guns; that only seven of the eighteen Aichis survived to dive on *Yorktown*, and that merely five of those escaped. But Repair Two crews knew what counted. They felt it and heard it.

A dull *ka-rump* sound came to Callaway's men. "That was well aft," he said. "A bomb hit." He surprised himself at his matter-of-fact tone of voice. The volume of AA fire increased, and even in their gray-painted steel world the sailors sensed the attack overhead was peaking. Moments later came another hit, apparently near amidships. The squawkbox directed Repair One and Seven to the second deck below the island, and Repair Three to the hangar deck aft.

The last hit was closest to Callaway. He felt the vibration through the soles of his shoes and knew it was bad—probably on this deck. The lights went out, but the emergency backup kicked in immediately. Moments later the sound-powered phone buzzed and Callaway picked it up. "Damage-control assistant, aye."

"Callaway, we've taken three direct hits and a near miss," began Commander Clarence Aldrich, the damage-control officer. "A bomb detonated on the flight deck aft of number-two elevator, but we can handle that all right. Our big problem is a delayed-action bomb that exploded on the second deck at frame ninety-five and blew the hell out of the intakes and uptakes to fire rooms two through six. Two boilers are disabled and we've got to try and relight the fires in five." *Damn*, Callaway thought, *one boiler on line. We're nearly dead in the water.* He chided himself to listen more closely. "The exec is down there now—the explosion gutted his office but he seems to have a handle on things." Callaway imagined Commander Dixie Kiefer, the ship's pixieish, popular executive officer, leading a fire-fighting crew.

Aldrich continued. "I need you to supervise the crews working forward. Another delayed-action went through the forward elevator and exploded on the third deck. Get up there around frame thirty-two. We got word of a bad fire spreading to adjoining compartments. Keep me informed."

"Aye, aye, sir!" Callaway hung up, and without explanation to his crew, he sprinted through the hatch, hollering "C'mon!" A few feet down the passageway he collided with another damage-controlman. Chief Riker's eyes were wide. "Mr. Callaway, there's a bomb hit in the number-one elevator pit. A bad fire around compartment A–Three-oh-five-A—lots of smoke."

"Yeah, I know, Chief. We'll handle it." Jack Callaway did not feel as confident as he sounded.

IJNS ARASHI, 1220

Wik began to grasp a terrible truth: there was no such thing as parting with a little information. Once he had given the name of his own carrier, it seemed he opened the floodgates to everything else he knew or ever had known about the U.S. Navy. The mere name *Yorktown* was the crack in the dam, the tiny fissure through which tons of pressure forced a treasure of intelligence. Now, still sitting on the destroyer's deck, Wik looked up once more at the face of his inquisitor.

Fuji saw the American's expression and knew it for what it was. With just a little experience, it was possible for a perceptive man to recognize vulnerability and weakness in another. And, with each halting answer, the enemy flier dug himself a deeper hole. It was all very logical, Fuji concluded. *If the barbarian answers Question One, he cannot logically deny knowledge of Question Two, and so forth.* The navigator had sheathed his sword; it had served its purpose. He felt his position growing stronger with each halting, poorly phrased query, his prisoner growing proportionately weaker with each answer. Fuji checked his watch and was surprised to find the interrogation had only been in progress about half an hour. Considering the language problem, things were progressing very well.

"Navigator!" Fuji looked up to the open bridge window where the captain and division commander watched the proceedings. "Ask the prisoner about task-force organization. The fleet commander will want to know which carriers are sailing together."

Fuji acknowledged Ariga's directive and turned his clipboard so the aviator could see the English-language notes. With a pencil the Japanese drew connecting lines between the names *Yorktown*, *Enterprise* and *Hornet*. "Ship with ship?" Fuji asked. He knew his language skills were poor, but he was not unduly concerned. By now the American knew the system.

With infinite weariness, Wik inhaled deeply, then let out his breath.

Let's get this over with, he told himself. He pointed to the last two names and held up two fingers. Then he poked at the first name, raising his index finger. Fuji nodded his comprehension and circled the block-letter names *Enterprise* and *Hornet.* He scratched a notation that they were teamed together, while *Yorktown* operated independently.

Wik leaned back against the steel bulkhead, staring into space. *What difference does it make?* he asked himself. *What the hell difference can it make?*

BAKER EIGHTEEN, 1237

"Mr. Rogers, did you hear that?"

The pilot pressed a gloved hand against his earphone, trying to sort out the stream of radio calls on the overloaded voice circuit. He picked up his mike and pressed the button. "I heard something about diverting to Red Base. That right?"

"Yes, sir. We're all supposed to land aboard the *Enterprise.* I guess we'll regroup for another mission." Rogers could tell that Barnes wished for nothing else. *Still wants his shot at a Jap,* the pilot mused.

One thing was certain—nobody was getting aboard *Yorktown* anytime soon. Even orbiting several miles away, it was obvious to Bombing Three crews that their ship had been hit hard. She was nearly obscured in a filthy cloud of smoke, streaming aft in the relative wind, that left only part of her bow visible.

The worms had returned to Rogers's stomach. He choked down the rising sense of impotence he felt—losing his bomb en route to the target, not being able to help defend *Yorktown* and now an uncertain future amid strangers. *Well, not exactly strangers,* he reflected. Bombing Three had, after all, spelled Scouting Six on *Enterprise* just two months previously for the Doolittle raid. *God, everything is happening so fast. Thirty minutes ago we had this battle wrapped up.* As he turned toward Task Force Sixteen, he hoped that he could keep up with events.

USS YORKTOWN, 1241

Compartment A-305A was on the third deck in the forward portion of the carrier. Each U.S. Navy warship was divided into four areas, lettered A-B-C-D, bow to stern. Thus, A-305A was on the second deck below the hangar deck, one of two storage areas directly beneath the forward elevator pit. Jack Callaway found the entire area choked with smoke from burning rags ignited in the high-order explosion from the armor-piercing bomb. That was bad enough. But the DCA also learned that A-405, one deck farther down, containing ship's stores, was affected.

All this information came to Callaway in a few moments, often related by confused, sometimes terrified men. One look, one breath, was enough to understand their concern. The adjoining bulkheads were already beginning to blister their paint from the intense heat.

"That ain't all, sir," Chief Riker continued. "Looks like we got a break in a fire main riser that's flooding A–Four-oh-five, Four-oh-six and probably Four-ten."

Callaway's Adam's apple performed a high dip at that news. "Four-oh-four's an ordnance storage area, isn't it?"

The chief nodded, briefly covering his mouth with one hand. "Yes, sir. Good thing it's flooding." He coughed in the foul air. "But that ain't all. Th' blast blew the control panels off the bulkhead in A–Three-oh-six-L. I was in there myself. Mr. Callaway, we got no way to activate the sprinklers in the forward magazine . . ."

"That's just aft of the fire," Callaway interjected. He thought for a moment. "All right, Chief. I want you to take most of Repair Two—they have CO-two if you need it—and show them where to hook a hose into a plug as far forward as you can. You may have to go back around frame seventy or eighty to find a plug with enough pressure." Riker nodded and turned to go. Callaway shot out a bony hand, patting the older man's round shoulders. "Good luck, Chief!" Riker never looked back.

Callaway felt better now, knowing what he was up against. A plan to kill the fire was forming in his mind. He turned to the officer in charge of Repair Seven, a serious-looking lieutenant (junior grade). "Fontaine, I want your crew to take an acetylene torch and start cutting through the deck in the elevator pit. It's the most direct way to the fire on the fourth deck. Soon as you get a big enough hole, feed some lines down there and douse the whole area. Flood it if you have to!"

The jaygee nodded eagerly, tapped his chief petty officer on the arm and plunged off into the gloom. Callaway coughed up some phlegm and pulled a handkerchief from his hip pocket. *Got to get some breathing apparatus down here,* he noted. He stepped into a nearby compartment and picked up the sound-powered phone to inform Aldrich of his plans. Despite the smoke and the godawful heat, Jack Callaway had a sense of optimism. *We can save this ship. By God, we can.*

"The prisoner was most cooperative, Lieutenant. You are to be congratulated." Captain Ariga's voice carried a trace of admiration that caught Fuji off guard. Nobody aboard—least of all Commander Watanabe—was accustomed to such compliments. Catching his commanding officer's expression, Fuji thought better of responding.

"Captain, as soon as the message is ready I shall relay it to the main body and the . . . strike group commander." Watanabe had almost said "flagship," but *Akagi* continued gushing smoke and flames. "Meanwhile, we will commence rescue operations."

Ariga nodded silently. Three of *Kido Butai*'s proud carriers—reduced to floating ovens in a matter of minutes. It was all too much. ComDesDivFour shook himself from his musing. "The prisoner held nothing back. This information must be passed along immediately, you understand?" Short, sharp barks indicated complete comprehension.

"Three enemy carriers, with *Yorktown* operating independently," Ariga summarized. "And the Americans knew we were coming. The fact that their carriers are out here is proof enough, but the prisoner also stated as much." He looked at Fuji again. "Is that correct, Lieutenant?"

Fuji drew himself to attention. "Yes, Captain! That is correct." The old Ariga was back. Still, Fuji ventured one question. "Sir, what plans for the prisoner?"

Ariga shrugged indifferently. "The commanding officer knows what action to take." The division commander looked meaningfully at *Arashi*'s skipper.

Watanabe called across the bridge. "Superior petty officer!" The man appeared as if materializing from midair and quivered to attention. "Dispose of the American and report back to me."

Fuji noticed the man flinch—a tension around the mouth. His name, the navigator thought, was Sato. But enlisted men's names were unimportant in the Imperial Navy. Fuji merely knew him as the senior superior petty officer aboard. After a heartbeat's hesitation, the sailor bowed deeply, uttered *"Hai!"* and disappeared.

Rogers and Burnett walked into the Bombing Six ready room with several other VB-3 pilots. The small compartment was crowded with the *Yorktown* overflow, but one glance at the empty chairs told the story. There were many empty chairs. Some of the *Enterprise* fliers were animatedly describing their recent experiences over *Kido Butai*; others sat glumly, staring at the vacant seats. Rogers sensed that nobody wanted to use the empty ones.

"Hey, Buck! Phil Rogers!"

Rogers turned at the sound of his name and searched the room. His attention was drawn to a waving hand at the end of an arm attached to a torso with a face he recognized. "Holy smokes, Bernie. That's Frank DiBella. We were roomies at Pensacola."

The former classmates edged through the press of bodies and spontaneously hugged, with much back-patting and hand-shaking. "Frankie, when did you get out here?"

DiBella rolled his eyes. He was of medium height with black hair under the cloth helmet that he had pushed halfway back on his head. "Only a couple months ago. I practically had to bribe my way out of Corpus Christi. Told my detailer that after two years of instructing, I'd go anywhere to fly anything—except P-boats."

Rogers nodded. "Then I just missed you back in April. We spelled Scouting Six during the Doolittle operation."

"Yup, that's right. I reported aboard at the end of April."

Rogers felt Burnett at his shoulder. "Oh, Frank, this is Bernie Burnett, the bull ensign of Bombing Three."

The two young men shook hands, sizing up one another. "Sure, I remember you," said DiBella. "You were a couple classes ahead of us."

"Roger. How you doing?"

DiBella took him literally. "Me, pretty good, I guess. At least I made it back. I even think I got a hit. But . . ." he gestured around the ready room. "This morning we launched thirty-three SBDs and fourteen TBDs. We got sixteen scout-bombers back, including two that diverted to the *Yorktown*, and four torpeckers. One of them had to be jettisoned." He bit his lip as if stifling emotion. "How did you fellows make out?"

"We clobbered one carrier and got everybody home," Rogers explained. "Except our skipper and his wingman haven't landed yet. But Torpedo Three . . ." He looked to Burnett for elaboration. Burnett merely shrugged. "Far as we know, none of them made it."

"Shit." DiBella said it like a prayer.

"Frank, you know Wayne's in Torpedo Three."

"Doggone, I'd almost forgotten that. The three of us drank a lot of beer at the San Carlos and chased a lot of girls together." He looked at his brown shoes, then glanced up again. "Got any dope on some of the other guys?"

"Just Sunny Jim. I heard from him a few weeks ago and he was still on Midway." Neither flier cared to speculate on the fate of their marine friend.

Burnett broke the awkward silence. "DiBella, you guys must have got both those other carriers. What happened?"

"Oh, hell, we searched half the goddamn Pacific. Our CAG's pretty sharp, though. When we got to the expected contact point we found zilch, so he started a square search. We came across a Jap ship hightailing it northeast so we followed his heading. That long search cost us plenty, though. A lot of fellows must have splashed out of fuel. I had fifteen gallons left. But we didn't have any idea you guys were around until we pulled out and saw the third carrier afire."

Rogers envisioned the geometry of the situation, the *Yorktown* squadrons turning to approach from the southeast while Bombing and Scouting Six attacked from the southwest. Three squadrons of SBDs attacking within the same five- or six-minute time span, leaving three-quarters of the enemy striking force blazing wrecks.

DiBella shifted his weight. "Say, what do you know about your ship? She gonna make it?"

The VB-3 pilots looked toward each other. Rogers shook his head. "Just don't know, Frankie. She was in plenty bad shape when we last saw her."

"Well, at least the odds are a lot better now. Between us and *Hornet* we should take on that fourth flattop no sweat," Burnett said.

DiBella shifted his feet again. Rogers thought he seemed slightly nervous at mention of his Task Force Sixteen partners. "The *Hornet* launched separately from us, so I don't know very much." He looked at the two Yorktowners. "Near as I can tell, it's just you fellows and us against that other Jap carrier."

Rogers allowed that thought to sink in. "Yeah. Now all we have to do is find the son of a bitch."

IJNS ARASHI, 1340

At least they haven't chopped my head off, Wik thought. Huddled in a corner of his tiny compartment in the destroyer's stern, he felt alternately numb and sick.

A couple of times he thought he would vomit. He wanted to sleep, to experience nothing, to awaken somewhere else. But his mind and stomach churned in a seesaw battle between guilt and resentment.

I told them everything, he thought. *Didn't even try to fool them.* He imagined a half-dozen ways he might have bluffed his way out of his horrible circumstance. But the image of that sword point playing inches from his eyes kept returning. The way it caught the light, the obvious willingness of the Jap lieutenant to use the blade on human flesh. Wik turned over into a fetal position, slowly funneling his outrage away from himself and focusing it onto the really guilty party—the United States Navy.

It's not my fault, he told himself. *They gave me a beat-up old dog of an airplane that'll hardly do a hundred and ten knots. Christ, a Zero must be three times that fast.* He ignored the fact that Tare Thirteen had been only four years old. But from there it was a logical progression. Send a torpron against an enemy fleet with only six F4Fs as escort—swarms of Zeros, flak of all types and calibers. And now this. *Nobody in the U.S. Fucking Navy ever told me how to handle this. Nobody ever told me I'd be a prisoner. Nobody ever said some screaming oriental would threaten to cut my head off. It's not my fault . . . not my fault.*

Still, obviously something had gone right. When rescued, Wik had seen one Japanese carrier burning furiously a few miles away. He was pretty certain that no torpedo attack had done that, so it must have been Bombing Three. *Good for you, Buck!* And there were two other burning ships—also carriers? Wik didn't know, and it was a cinch the Japanese weren't going to tell him. *They don't answer questions, they just ask them.* But apparently the *Enterprise* or *Hornet* air groups had gotten into the fight.

At that realization, Wik began feeling better. *If we clobbered three of their flattops, there's only one left. Jeez, we can win this battle.* He dared to hope that the information he gave the enemy would not hurt his friends after all.

IJNS TONE, 1359

The catapult fired and threw Number Four Scout into the air, accelerating from zero to sixty knots in two seconds. Sakaida kept the nose level, allowing the floatplane to build airspeed before easing back on the stick. Past 500 feet he reduced power slightly and turned easterly, climbing slowly. He wanted to conserve fuel as much as possible.

In the second seat Azumano slid his canopy shut and pulled his map from a leg pocket. Before examining the chart to confirm their outbound heading, he glanced backward and down. Lieutenant (junior grade) Hasegawa's Type 95, Number Three Scout, had just launched off the second catapult. According to Naito's briefing, Hasegawa would pick up the trail of the crippled enemy carrier struck in the first attack—apparently *Yorktown* since she was known to be operating alone—while Azumano searched for the second enemy force. Briefly Azumano wondered at the reliability of the report stating the Americans had three carriers north of Midway. *True, the information came from a prisoner interrogation*, he thought. But no flier worth his wings would part with such information. Azumano shrugged off the thought and consulted his track chart. *Americans are so different. What is the use in trying to understand them?*

14.

1401–1600, 4 JUNE

USS YORKTOWN, 1435

"We're doin' all right, Chief." CJ Callaway wiped his already-grimy handkerchief across his sweaty forehead and smiled at Riker for the first time in hours. The tall Texan's pride in his repair parties showed through the soot and sweat, and Chief Riker rubbed a hand at the corner of one eye. Callaway noticed it was the large reddened hand of a workingman—reddened from a first-degree burn.

"Yes, sir, Mr. Callaway." Riker managed to smile back. With all fires contained and the ship working up speed with more boilers on line, things looked better all the time. From merely five knots just forty-five minutes ago, *Yorktown* was steaming at nearly twenty—enough to operate aircraft if need be. "Maybe Admiral Fletcher will transfer his flag back here now."

The damage-control assistant shook his head. "I doubt it, Chief. We may not have full communications after all that bomb damage." Callaway knew that Fletcher and his staff had transferred to *Astoria* more than an hour ago, and the carrier was not out of danger yet.

Callaway turned toward the phone at his battle station and picked up the receiver, wanting to talk to Commander Aldrich again—when the loudspeaker intruded.

"Now hear this. Stand by to repel air attack! Estimated sixteen enemy aircraft twenty miles out."

Callaway turned to Riker, both men wide-eyed in disbelief. Callaway saw the chief petty officer's chafed lips mouthing the word for the emotion that stabbed his own mind. *NO!*

USS ENTERPRISE, 1445

"Listen up, men!" Dave Shumway stood at the head of the ready room, flight jacket unzipped, bareheaded with a message flimsy in one hand. "We've found the fourth Jap carrier. Lieutenants Adams and Dickson of Scouting Five made contact about fifteen minutes ago. Adams sent a precise voice message and followed it up with a coded report as well."

Rogers leaned forward in his seat and listened closely. *Lieutenant Adams*, he thought. *Sam Adams, the little red-headed guy from the Ford Island O-club.*

"The carrier is escorted by two battleships, three cruisers and four cans," Shumway continued, "bearing two-seven-nine degrees, a hundred ten miles from the scouts' launch." He fingered the map taped to the blackboard. "That's here, *Yorktown*'s 1150 position." Rogers copied down the information for double-checking after the briefing.

"Now the situation is this," the exec added. "The skipper and Swede ditched alongside the *Astoria*, apparently after covering a downed torpedo plane. Only two of our TBDs got back to the task force and both went in the water." *Wayne*, Rogers thought. He computed the odds. *One chance in six that he's all right. Not good.* "Mr. Leslie and his crews are safe, but obviously they're out of the battle," the exec continued.

Shumway checked his notes. "The strike leader on this mission will be Lieutenant Gallaher of Scouting Six. He's a good man—a year senior to me at the academy. But the two *Enterprise* squadrons can only put up ten SBDs between them. So Bombing Three will have to haul most of the mail. One of our remaining planes is a down, leaving us with fourteen operational, but that'll be enough."

Burnett raised a hand. "Sir, what about the *Hornet* Air Group? Aren't they going to launch?"

"I don't have full information on that. All I'm told is that we can't count on the *Hornet*." He shook his head. "Something is screwy over there." The exec's voice hinted at something—disappointment, even disapproval? Most of the pilots in the room knew men aboard *Hornet*: flight-school classmates, former shipmates, casual acquaintances. Rogers was close to a couple of ensigns in Scouting Eight and one in Bombing Eight. *I'll ask them about this when we get back to Pearl*, he thought.

Shumway paused for a moment, ensuring he had every pilot's full attention. "If we do this right, like we did this morning, we won't need any help. Then when we've put this last carrier on the bottom, we can all go home." He smiled slightly under his mustache. "Just remember to leave those goddamn electrical arming switches alone!"

A rush of laughter greeted the XO's last admonition. Rogers caught the eye of Roy Isaman, another pilot who had lost his bomb en route. The two ensigns grinned self-consciously at one another and Rogers laughed with everyone else—too loudly, he thought afterward.

USS YORKTOWN, 1445

By now the men of *Yorktown* knew the sounds, the rhythms and sequences—and what they meant. Belowdecks the sailors could hear the antiaircraft guns open fire, even feel the concussion through portions of the ship's steel frame. To CJ Callaway, standing with his crew in Repair Two, the sequence was all too familiar. *Three separate air attacks on this ship in less than thirty days*, he calculated.

"Torpedo planes to port," blared the 5MC loudspeaker system. Callaway felt the carrier lean into a hard left turn. *But not hard enough. At only nineteen knots she can't maneuver so good.* He grasped a stanchion with a bony hand and held on tight. The volume of gunfire increased: 5-inch, multiple 1.1-inch mounts, 20mm Oerlikons, finally jury-rigged .50-calibers.

Chief Riker braced himself in the corner near a cabinet. "Mr. Callaway, I got a feeling we're gonna take a fish this time."

"You may be—" *KA-WHANG!* Callaway never finished the sentence. The detonation of 450 pounds of TNT against the hull rocked 20,000 tons over to starboard. Callaway felt the carrier decelerate, quickly listing a few degrees to port. He swung himself around the upright he had been holding, reached for the phone and got a terse reply from Aldrich. Callaway hung up and turned to his crew. "It hit at frame eighty, below the waterline. There's flooding near the forward generator room." He looked around to assess his men's spirits. "Commander Aldrich thinks they can handle it."

Then another Type 91 Mod 2 aerial torpedo smashed into three-eighths–inch steel plating at forty knots and exploded sixty feet aft of the first. Callaway's compartment instantly was plunged into darkness. A few men shouted. Callaway felt and heard motion. He knew what it meant. "Stay put! That's an order, goddamn it!" He sensed that his blunt, harsh voice had blanketed the rising panic among some of the sailors. He also felt the ship coasting to a stop. He had to lean more to his right to remain erect. *We're taking on a hell of a lot of water.*

Long, long seconds dribbled past, each with its separate beginning, middle and end. The emergency lighting did not kick in. *That's a bad sign. Means widespread electrical problems—probably generators.* Callaway made an effort to control his voice before he spoke again. "Chief Riker, break out the battle lanterns and keep 'em handy. We'll turn on one for now."

The men heard scraping sounds as Riker lifted the nearest lantern from its rack. A wide, pale beam of light rent the total darkness of the compartment. Callaway thought that the highlighted features of the sailors' faces resembled the tortured gargoyles of Renaissance architecture. He could see the stark fear in those faces. And he could smell it. The sound-powered phone buzzed and he fumbled for the receiver.

"Repair Two, aye."

"Callaway, this is Aldrich. Sorry to take so long to get to you, but it's bad. We have two hits below the waterline. The first is flooding two fuel tanks, and the second destroyed the generator room forward of fire room two. We think everybody there is dead. Anyway, we don't have electrical power to pump fuel to starboard and correct the list. I just talked to the chief engineer, who says we're listing twenty-six degrees. The captain says to prepare to abandon ship, so get your people topside, now!"

CJ Callaway almost asked Aldrich to repeat the last sentence. *We can't leave my ship to sink! Not like this!* Then he heard himself say, "Aye, aye, sir." He hung up the receiver and turned to his men. "Cap'n says to prepare to abandon ship. But take it easy, men. We got plenty of time." He turned to Riker, who was already undogging the hatch. "Chief, you lead the way. Give me a lantern and I'll follow you all topside."

Azumano's binoculars seldom stopped moving. He knew that after more than an hour on course 070 the Type Zero floatplane should be back in the vicinity of the American task forces, and he was not about to miss the sighting. *If we do not find them, Hasegawa in the southerly sector certainly will.* Then the observer's practiced scan stopped. Beneath the spotty clouds were wakes—several of them.

Immediately Azumano checked his chart, then gave Hara a message for immediate transmission. *Enemy interceptors could attack us anytime.* "Number Four. Large American force bearing one-zero-two degrees, distance one hundred twenty miles from point of origin. Will amplify."

Sakaida already knew what his superior would want. Turning parallel to the ships' base course, he followed the heading for another five minutes. Hardly a word passed among the three crewmen, which pleased Azumano. He felt their coordination was excellent, and had grown sensitive to their moods. Turning in his seat, he noted Hara vigilantly searching the upper air, alert for fighters.

This time the pilot spotted the target. "Lieutenant," he said, his voice surprisingly calm over the intercom, "a large ship off the right nose."

Azumano slid back the canopy again and leaned into the slipstream. A cloud obscured his view forward, then was gone. Putting his glasses on the long, dark shape, he studied it closely. *Too far yet to be sure. But we had best report while we can.* "Number Four. There appears to be a carrier about twenty miles ahead of the first group reported." Suddenly, Toshiki Azumano realized that he had passed the point of caring whether he returned to his ship. *There is still a chance to win this battle,* he thought, *if we pinpoint the enemy for our carrier bombers.* It was surprisingly easy to give up one's life for such a purpose. He inhaled deeply, feeling better than he had all afternoon.

In the pilot's seat, Hiroyoshi Sakaida fought off delightful memories of the Nakadate twins stepping into the communal bath.

OVERHEAD TASK FORCE SIXTEEN, 1540

Twenty-four Dauntlesses climbed steadily upward, strung out in stairstep fashion. At the top of the stairs were the first planes to launch, already joined by sections and forming into six-plane divisions. These SBDs carried Mark XII 500-pound bombs—marginally effective against warships, but required for takeoff in the crowded flight-deck space.

Echeloned downward were the *Yorktown* bombers, straining under greater loads. All but three of these SBDs carried ship-killing 1,000-pounders, as longer deck runs enabled them to take off at near-gross weight.

No fighters tailed them upward. Rear Admiral Spruance, now conducting the battle in Fletcher's absence from *Yorktown*, had heeded his staff. Task-force defense remained paramount in the minds of the air-operations officers. They had already witnessed the competence and aggressiveness of Japanese squadrons in the face of alerted Wildcats. To reduce the fighter coverage seemed an unwarranted risk. The SBDs would tackle the last enemy carrier by themselves.

At the head of the mixed strike group—two dozen aircraft from three squadrons and two carriers—Lieutenant Earl Gallaher, class of '31, orbited for ten more minutes. Then, ensuring that his formation was intact, he set course into the westering sun.

NUMBER FOUR SCOUT, 1550

Lieutenant (junior grade) Azumano could not quite piece it together. He had heard Hasegawa's message only five minutes ago, reporting six heavy cruisers bearing 094, distance 117 miles from takeoff point. That was only about twenty miles from his own present position. *Is this a previously unreported surface unit or the escorts of the stricken enemy carrier?* He checked his chart again.

Azumano was beginning to understand that there was no such thing as complete information in a battle—especially a naval engagement. *All we can do is report what we find,* he told himself. He stuffed his chart away and returned to scanning the ocean.

The clouds parted and he was looking at two American flight decks.

He fumbled for his binoculars as he heard Sakaida and Hara shout over the intercom. "Lieutenant—"

"Two aircraft carriers—"

"Yes, I see them." His voice cut off the shouts like a samurai sword through bamboo. He focused on the nearer ship, concentrating on the distinctive island structure. *She is* Yorktown *class*, he told himself. Then, *Well, of course.* Enterprise *and* Hornet *are the other carriers out here, according to that prisoner. They are all of the same class.*

"Sakaida, back up in the clouds, quickly!" Azumano felt better as milky whiteness enveloped the floatplane. He ordered Hara to get on the radio immediately, confirming what was already suspected. The Americans had two untouched carriers operating together. Azumano felt a tingle between his shoulder blades. That meant at least thirty-six Grummans to hunt and kill him.

The Aichi broke out of the cloud cover and Sakaida immediately banked right toward another puffy white haven. "Gunner to commander. Enemy fighters above and behind us." Hara's voice was more controlled this time, his report more precise. *Experience teaches well*, Azumano thought. Azumano turned in his seat and again glimpsed the angular silhouettes before they disappeared behind a cloud.

"We have ample fuel," he announced. "We will try to stay in the clouds and report on the enemy's movements for a while longer." It was the correct decision, of course. But somehow, death in battle no longer seemed so easy to accept.

15.

1601–1800, 4 JUNE

NUMBER FOUR SCOUT, 1603

Azumano sat in his cockpit and listened to a friend die. Apparently while snooping the *Yorktown* task force, Hasegawa had been found by patrolling F4Fs, which boxed him in. The radio calls were necessarily brief and fragmented, and Azumano could not determine whether the fighters were in fact from *Yorktown*—which seemed unlikely—or from one of the two ships he himself had found barely ten minutes before.

First had come the relatively calm call, "Number Three. Grummans above me." Then, in successively higher tones, faster paced, "Enemy attacking me . . . they're firing!" Long moments of silence followed, in which Azumano imagined the talented floatplane pilot wriggling like an aerial weasel to escape the hungry Wildcats. He thought there was a short reference to counterattacking, then, "I am hit!"

Then nothing.

Sakaida was skimming a cloud deck, his floats cutting through the cottony swirls, when it occurred to Azumano that they would be silhouetted from above. "Commander to pilot . . ."

Hara let out a scream. "Fighter behind!" All his previous calm, hoarded during the mission, was expended in one lungful of air.

Sakaida knew better than to waste time gawking. He shoved forward on the stick, inducing negative G on the airframe, lifting Azumano and Hara from their seats. The blessed whiteness enfolded them again. "Report!" Azumano shouted.

"There was just one, sir. He came out of nowhere. I do not know . . ."

Sakaida was unsure how deep the cloud layer was at this point. He held his dive through the murk, fighting the onset of vertigo, and broke out underneath. Then he rolled into a starboard turn because the clouds seemed to extend farther in that direction.

There he is, Azumano said to himself. He was aware of Hara charging his Type 92 machine gun—rather belatedly. Not that it would do much good. One 7.7 against the Grumman's battery of 12.7s was no match. Azumano realized that only extraordinary flying could save them. That and an overdose of good fortune.

The F4F-4 pilot was the commanding officer of Fighting Six off *Enterprise.* He had tangled briefly with Hasegawa before two enlisted pilots had shot the Type 95 to pieces. Hungry for a kill of his own, he pressed in.

Sakaida flew with his head turned, gauging the fighter's approach. The instant the F4F's wings lit up with muzzle flashes, he broke hard down and into the attack, spoiling its tracking. Tracers flashed overhead. *That was close!*

As the Wildcat slid to the outside of the turn, Sakaida crammed on full throttle. The Kinsei 43 engine responded with 1,080 horsepower, and Sakaida climbed back into the cloud layer. He held his heading for several seconds, then banked forty-five degrees left. Moments later he broke into the clear. They were alone.

For ten seconds. The F4F's square wingtips appeared off the port beam in a medium-banked turn. Simultaneously, Azumano and Sakaida weighed the time-distance equation: should they duck back into the cloud or maneuver out here in the open? "Turn into him!" Azumano cried.

Sakaida would have done so regardless. The fighter had too much speed to allow it a straight approach to the floatplane. The Wildcat snapped out another burst that passed ahead of the Aichi as Sakaida ruddered through a level turn. Azumano took heart. *One Grumman cannot trap us*, he realized. *It must have help to box us in.* He shivered while something fluttered in his stomach. *Like they boxed in Hasegawa.*

On the next run the F4F made a high side pass, hammering out a long burst. Sakaida shoved everything forward—stick, throttle, prop and mixture—and dived back into the lowest cloud layer. Once in the misty haven, he abruptly honked back on the stick and pulled more Gs than Aichi Tokei Denki K.K. ever intended.

The next time Sakaida poked his nose out of the clouds, the floatplane really was alone.

BAKER EIGHTEEN, 1645

Phil Rogers took in the magnificent view from 13,000 feet. The sky above was wonderfully clear, turning cerulean in the afternoon sun. The ocean, appearing unrippled and calm, was only occasionally obscured by scattered low clouds. *Great hunting weather.* He had even seen three lingering plumes off to the southwest—satisfying evidence of the morning attack. He keyed the intercom. "Barnes, you all right?"

There was a slight delay. "Uh, yes, sir. Doin' fine. Kinda cold, though."

Rogers had only ridden in the gunner's seat twice—once on a familiarization flight and later catching a ride from Kaneohe to Ford Island with Lieutenant Bottomley. He had forgotten how noisy and drafty the rear cockpit of an SBD could be. Unless the canopy sections fit just right, they left a small gap that permitted high-speed air to enter the cockpit. It caused two minor but aggravating problems: a rippling effect on the top of your cloth helmet, and a persistent whistling sensation. Combined with the staccato beat of the Wright engine, it was surprising that most SBD gunners weren't grounded for hearing loss.

"It's kind of nice to fly in a different position for a change, isn't it, sir?" Rogers chuckled at the sentiment. Their usual place was in the last section, but since Mr. Shumway was acting CO, his division now led. Lieutenant (junior grade) Obie Wiseman now had the second section behind Shumway's three, with Rogers and Frankie DiBella of Bombing Six on Wiseman's wing. At first Wiseman had been concerned about inserting an *Enterprise* pilot into the VB-3 lineup, but it was necessary to round out the formation. Each squadron did things a little differently, which could lead to foul-ups. However, Rogers knew DiBella and trusted him. *Frankie always did fly a good formation.*

And he was alert. Rogers noticed the gunner in Six Baker Twelve gesturing, pointing forward. Rogers swiveled his head, peering into the increasing glare of the lowering sun. He pushed forward slightly on his stick, clearing the SBDs ahead of him. And there, thirty miles to the northwest on the beckoning sea, were the wakes of what remained of *Kido Butai.*

Callaway risked standing in the whaleboat as it neared *Hammann's* port quarter. He steadied himself with one hand on Chief Riker's broad shoulders and again counted heads. *I'm like a fussy old hen counting her chicks.* When the number tallied with those he had checked off before leaving the carrier, he turned to his lieutenant (junior grade). "Okay, Fontaine, they're all here. Soon's we get everybody aboard, report to me in the wardroom. We got a lot of work ahead of us tonight." The efficient young officer acknowledged and began urging the men to disembark.

Callaway sat down in the stern, keeping out of the coxswain's way, while his men and various others climbed the destroyer's ladder. He felt self-conscious, sitting there in his dry uniform, still wearing shoes like a civilized human being. True, his khakis were smudged and bore the odor of smoke, and he doubted the perspiration stains would be removed this side of Pearl. But he looked like a tourist compared to the sailors hauled out of the oil-blackened water. A surprising number had no flotation belts or lifejackets.

He could not help looking back toward *Yorktown*, riding uneasily with a severe port list. Tended by the cruiser *Astoria* and six destroyers, she resembled nothing so much as a wounded sea monster surrounded by her concerned, frightened young. *But there's still hope,* he told himself. *If she's still afloat in the morning, we can save her. I know we can.*

Toward that end, he had a battered cardboard box containing various engineering diagrams safely between his feet. They represented a hodgepodge of vital information: structural, electrical, fuel. Before departing the carrier, he had spoken again with Commander Delaney, the chief engineer, who insisted that such documents were important. Callaway and some other officers had gone back into the darkened, frightful spaces—some deep within an apparently sinking ship—to retrieve the papers. *Now if I just don't drop 'em.* Only moments before, he had watched a sailor lose a bag containing the flight-deck log, which promptly sank.

At length Callaway's long legs scaled the ladder. He badly wanted to lie down and close his eyes. *Or would I rather eat a real supper?* In pondering the dilemma, he missed a step and lurched forward, catching himself with one hand. *Guess I'd rather sleep than eat,* he decided.

OVERHEAD KIDO BUTAI, 1658

Rogers sucked in a breath, pressing his soft white mask against his face. Then he checked the high-pressure oxygen rebreathing system at his right knee. He knew they would not remain at altitude for long, but Lieutenant Gallaher's climbing, sweeping turn to the southwest had taken the two dozen dive-bombers toward 20,000 feet. Standard procedure called for aircrew to go on oxygen above 15,000.

Now the Scouting Six skipper was assigning targets. "This is Earl. Red Base aircraft, follow me down on the carrier. Scarlet, you take the nearest battleship." For a moment Rogers was disappointed. He badly wanted to hit a flattop, but then he reconsidered. *How often does an ensign get to sink a battlewagon?*

With the sun more or less at their backs, the Dauntlesses began letting down toward their pushover points from 19,000. Brief radio calls crackled through the upper atmosphere. "Fighters! Enemy fighters."

"Roger. Ahead of us and above."

Rogers strained to see the bandits. "Bill, I don't see 'em. Keep sharp."

"Aye, aye, sir!" *He sounds too damn eager,* Rogers thought.

Flak bursts blossomed below and ahead of the SBDs. Several more dark-brown eruptions magically appeared less than a hundred yards ahead. Rogers felt the mild concussion. *They're ready for us. It isn't like this morning.* Then he berated himself. *Nobody said it would be.*

He had an impression of the six *Enterprise* scouts peeling off, dropping into their dives. Glancing down, he saw a high-speed wake drawing a graceful arc on the water, turning to the south. More warning calls crackled—something about fighters. Tiny waterspouts appeared around the dark shape at the head of the wake. *No hits!* Rogers realized. *She's getting away!*

His earphones crackled again. "This is Dave. We are shifting targets. Repeat, we are attacking the carrier. Follow me."

Suits me fine, Rogers thought. *I'd rather sink a carrier anyway.* He busied himself with the drill: throttle to idle, prop to full low pitch, mixture rich, carburetor heat on, dive brakes open. *Watch the spacing on Obie, there . . . pushing over . . . now!*

"—ers on us!"

"Look out, Dave!"

Rogers heard Barnes's guns open fire; the abrupt noise caused Phil to flinch. Instinctively, he looked back and saw only the third section SBDs. Then a movement caught his attention. A darkish-gray aerodynamic shape flashed through his field of view, either overshooting Baker Eighteen or intent on one of the leading SBDs.

Can't think about fighters. Have to concentrate on bombing. Got to get a hit. With a conscious effort of willpower, Rogers forced himself to put his eye to the optical sight. Immediately he checked the ball and found it skewed slightly to port. He cranked in rudder trim with his left hand to compensate as speed increased. The ball obediently centered itself in its arced housing.

Barnes firing again. Flak bursting close aboard, jostling the Dauntless.

Rogers reached down to trim out the tail-heaviness he felt building. He looked at the target for the first time, played with the controls and aligned the crosshairs. This ship looked much like the first, except he noticed it had a portside island. And something else. *Something's not right. Her flight deck's jumbled. Don't think Dave's dropped yet. Scouts must've got a hit after all. But she's still going.*

A high, ringing sound startled Rogers, followed by one or two more. The twin .30s hammered out a long burst again. *We're hit! Goddamn Zeros are still with us. Don't look, don't look.* He now had the crosshairs well-centered on the ship's bow. An explosion briefly obscured his sight picture—Shumway's section definitely got a hit—then he focused again.

Rogers's left hand went down and forward, wrapping itself around the two-handled, black-knobbed manual bomb release. At an estimated 2,000 feet he tugged hard and felt the 1,000-pounder disengage from its rack. And unintentionally he put subtle back pressure on the stick.

"Oh, no. God, no."

From a seventy-degree dive 2,000 feet almost directly over the carrier's stern, the one-ton weapon took almost six seconds to fall. In that time a thirty-two-knot ship traveled almost 325 feet. Thus, an aimpoint squarely on the bow should yield a center hit on a 746-foot flight deck. But, despite a small error, Rogers had lofted his bomb in a ballistic parabola well ahead of the target. He did not take time to watch it—he knew to a certainty he had missed forward and a little to port. Belatedly, he realized he had also neglected to compensate for the changing wind vector over the turning target.

Flaps in, add throttle, carb heat off. Pull. Rogers wrapped both hands around the black plastic stick grip and tugged. Through his G-dulled senses he vaguely heard Barnes shooting yet again. *God, how many Zeros can there be in the world?* As the nose came up through the horizon, Rogers saw the enemy fighter overshoot to port and climb away. He also saw an airplane smash into the water.

Rogers turned southeasterly, heading for the rendezvous. He saw two SBDs nearby and felt better, then looked at the carrier—and felt much, much better.

She was a mess. Volumes of smoke and flames poured from the flight deck around the island. Another bomb rocked her—well forward, apparently like most of the others. Rogers did not know if the hit came from the last VB-3 section or Lieutenant Best's trio from Bombing Six. But this carrier definitely was out of business.

"Break right, break right!"

Rogers thought it was Barnes's voice but wasn't sure. Nevertheless, he stood on the right pedal and tugged the stick hard over. Leading with rudder, he slewed the Dauntless awkwardly, looked around—and gasped.

The disk of a Zero's propeller was clearly visible, perhaps 150 yards out, and growing with terrible speed. Tracers flashed from its nose and wing guns, passing just overhead. In the rear seat, Bill Barnes swiveled his twin mount, centered his ring-and-bead sights on the looming prop hub, and thumbed down both triggers.

For an eerie instant Rogers had the impression that both aircraft were linked in midair by fiery ropes of tracer ammunition 500 feet off the water. Bright motes of light played over the Mitsubishi's nose and propeller, then it was overhead, climbing almost straight up, pulling a brown smoke plume.

Rogers and Barnes gawked at the spectacle. Hanging nose-high a few hundred feet overhead, the graceful little fighter bobbled, began a tailslide and fell off on one wing. It went nose-down and dived headlong into the sea, exploding in a fountain of white spray, orange flames and dirty brown smoke.

Holy shit, Rogers said to himself.

"WAAA-HOOOO!" Barnes screamed his war cry into the intercom so loudly that it pained Rogers's ears. "IgothimIgothimIgothim! YouseethatMr.Rogers? Hotdamn!"

Rogers picked up his mike. "Barnes! Barnes, get ahold of yourself, damn it! Settle down!"

A chagrined silence followed. Then, "Ah, yessir. Sorry, sir. I just got carried away."

Rogers smiled to himself. "Good shooting, Barnes."

"Thank you, sir."

Rogers waggled his wings and joined formation on the other two Dauntlesses. Snaking low and fast over the waves, cloud-hopping when possible, they dodged through the outer flak belt and shaped course for the rendezvous.

Near the joinup, Rogers heard some strange radio calls. "Blue Base Leader to Blue chicks. The carrier is no longer the priority target. Attack screening vessels as follows . . ."

Blue Base, Rogers thought. *Hornet.* He looked upward, searching for the Bombing and Scouting Eight SBDs. But he saw only the darkening sky.

USS HAMMANN, 1712

The destroyer's wardroom had never held such a grimy assemblage of naval officers. Many were wringing wet, dripping where they stood while incongruously sipping coffee from blue-trimmed white cups and saucers, nibbling sweets and rolls off silver salvers. But more than eating, they listened.

Captain Elliott Buckmaster was taller than anyone else present, and wetter than most. But despite his appearance, any stranger entering the room immediately would have recognized him as the commanding officer. At the fringe of the group, CJ Callaway reflected that the thirty-year veteran inspired confidence. Sailors already were talking about the way the old man had rescued a drowning cook and pulled the frightened young Negro to the safety of a raft. A latecomer to aviation, Buckmaster had only won his wings in 1936, but he was *Yorktown*'s third captain and her sole wartime skipper. His sixteen months as CO were one month more than Callaway's tenure aboard the carrier.

"Our first job is to sort out survivors and identify key personnel," Buckmaster began in his Virginia drawl. "That will take some time because we have more than twenty-three hundred men spread among seven different ships." He looked around the room, seeking the reservist he wanted while wiping his pate with one hand. "Lieutenant Hilbert will visit each ship with a list of the salvage personnel we'll need over the next couple of days. We will assemble that crew on board the *Astoria* sometime tonight." Callaway was impressed. *We're not wasting any time.*

"Now, as for the actions of this force, I have word from Admiral Fletcher," Buckmaster continued. "We are withdrawing eastward to avoid enemy attack during the night." He waited for the murmur of dissent that he knew would run through the room. "Gentlemen, our escorts simply are in no condition to fight a surface engagement. Remember, they have hundreds of our people aboard."

He stood with hands on his hips, surveying the group, and saw he had made his point. "However, we have requested a tug which should arrive sometime tomorrow afternoon. It is my hope that towing the ship will at least keep her afloat until we get our salvage crew aboard. Then, with power from one or two destroyers alongside, we can get to work. But that easily can be another twenty-four hours. Any questions?" *Only a few dozen,* Callaway thought.

"Very well. I want to meet with the engineering and damage-control officers right away. Most of us will be transferring to the *Astoria* later tonight, so let's get organized, starting now."

NUMBER FOUR SCOUT, 1750

"Commander to crew. Keep a sharp lookout. There may be enemy aircraft in the area." Azumano replaced his microphone in its bracket and wriggled in his seat. He was mildly surprised to be alive this late in the day, but they weren't home yet. He had heard *Tone*'s frantic radio calls during the recent American attack. Apparently she was unharmed, but maneuvering to avoid dive-bombers could easily put her well out of position.

In the gathering dark, fires were plainly visible from the four stricken carriers—painful, lingering reminders of the power of the American navy. He would never say so aloud, but Toshiki Azumano felt let down by the rest of the striking force. *We have done our work exceedingly well*, he told himself. *Not only this crew, but all the scouts. Even* Soryu's *experimental Type 2 carrier reconnaissance plane confirmed the presence of three enemy carriers.* Now that speedy prototype aircraft had nowhere to land but in the sea. He thought again of his comrade, Lieutenant (junior grade) Hasegawa, and wondered if the pilot of Scout Number Three would receive a posthumous promotion to full lieutenant. That Hasegawa had an equally dead radioman never occurred to Azumano.

Returning to *Tone* could be a ticklish procedure, Azumano thought. He was certainly in the right vicinity—the burning carriers confirmed that much—but picking out their cruiser might prove difficult. He debated making a call to request a vector. But keeping radio silence was ingrained in aircrews, and Azumano wanted no blot on his record. He picked up the mike again. "Sakaida, are you sure enough of our position to land near our base? We should not use the radio unless absolutely necessary."

Hiroyoshi Sakaida felt more like his old self. After today, what could they do—send him to a combat unit? "Pilot to commander. The enemy already knows our location." He moved the stick to the right and showed Azumano *Kaga's* burning hulk, glowing dull red in the dusk just off the starboard wingtip.

"Scout Number Four to base," the radioman called. "Request homing for landing."

Moments later Sakaida reduced throttle and began his descent to the end of a very long day.

16.

1801–2000, 4 JUNE

Captain Kosaku Ariga found himself in a peculiar situation. A destroyer division commander, apparently he was the senior effective officer in *Kido Butai* since Vice Admiral Nagumo had been forced off *Akagi* and Rear Admiral Yamaguchi remained aboard the stricken *Hiryu*. And while his contemporaries knew him as an uncommonly ambitious individual, acting without direct authority for a vice admiral required some nerve. On the destroyer's bridge he turned to Lieutenant Takagawa, whose name he once knew but had forgotten.

"Signal Officer, have we communication with the flagship?"

Takagawa stiffened to attention. "Only by semaphore or signal flag, Captain. It is most unreliable in the smoke."

Ariga nodded and turned back. He brushed past Fuji as if the navigator weren't there. Then, turning about, he asked, "What is the bearing to *Kaga* and *Soryu*?"

Fuji was unprepared for the question. He knew the general direction—*Kaga* to the west, *Soryu* to the northeast—but the division commander had asked for specific bearings. Fuji spun toward the senior petty officer at the chart table and repeated the question. The man turned his compass, rose to begin a response and Fuji lost his temper. *This oaf is causing me to appear incompetent before the division commander.* He cuffed the man on one ear. "Answer me, idiot!"

Ariga pretended the incident had not occurred. "We have reports that *Hagikaze* has taken off *Kaga*'s crew and *Isokaze* is rescuing *Soryu* survivors. We may have to move rapidly to support them if enemy ships appear."

Beatings were common in the Imperial Navy, and Kosaku Ariga certainly never flinched from such disciplinary measures. But he had made his point. *Arashi*'s navigator would be prepared for the next question, whenever it came. And no member of this crew would hesitate to obey an order, no matter how distasteful.

USS ENTERPRISE, 1830

Rogers advanced his throttle to 1,500 rpm, then pulled the mixture to idle-cutoff. The Hamilton-Standard prop slowly wound down as he turned off the magneto switch, fuel selector and electrical systems. A plane captain was beside him on the wing, accepting his chartboard as he climbed out.

Barnes already had scrambled to the darkened flight deck and was excitedly showing four bullet holes to some deckhands. But when Rogers took the big step off the trailing edge of the wing, his gunner turned on him. "Boy oh boy, Mr. Rogers. We showed 'em, didn't we?" He democratically grasped Ensign Rogers by both arms.

A Cyclone engine growled overhead as some unfortunate pilot took a waveoff. Rogers barely glanced up. "Hell, *you* showed 'em, Barnes. I missed." He knew that Bill Barnes would become one of the hotshots of the aircrewmen's quarters after his incontestable success. *Well, he deserves it.*

The gunner chose to ignore his pilot's honesty. "But you set it up for me, sir. I seen this Jap coming at us from dead astern, see. And I figure, 'He can shoot at us but I can't shoot back.' So I call for a hard right turn, and you put him right in front of me. All I had to do was swing on him and shoot."

A growing crowd of fliers and handlers assembled to hear the post-mortem. Barnes was in his element. "I could see my tracers going in him. I mean, I was gunning him from the hip, it was so close. Must've killed the pilot 'cause the plane pulled straight up, stalled and went right in. Isn't that so, sir?"

"Yes, that's just what happened." Rogers thought that Barnes relished the phrase, "killed the pilot." Looking around, he waved to Burnett and walked over to him. "Who's missing, Bernie? I make us two short."

"Three Baker Ten and Twelve, sir. And Mr. Weber from Bombing Six." One of the LSO's writers was en route to the bridge. "We just landed Mr. Gallaher, sir. That's everybody."

Rogers and Burnett looked at one another. Neither knew what to say. *Obie Wiseman and Johnny Butler*, Rogers realized. He thought of the plane he saw crashing in the water just after recovering from his dive. "I saw somebody go in right after I pulled out," he said in a monotone. "That must have been Obie. We were under fighter attack right then."

Suddenly Barnes was notably quiet. Aviation Radiomen Second Class Grant U. Dawn and David D. Berg also were gone.

Burnett put an arm around his friend's shoulders as they trudged toward the island.

IJNS ARASHI, 1930

A petty officer and a rating appeared at the entrance to the berthing compartment and Wik sat up on the bunk. He was conscious of a damp, musty smell and wondered if it was the Japanese or himself in his still-damp flight suit. The sailor gestured toward the barbarian and uttered something unintelligible. *Guess the bastards want to quiz me again,* Wik thought. *This time I'll do better. I swear to God I'll do better.*

The enemy sailors led Wik topside where they emerged into the open, portside aft. He looked around, expecting to see the son of a bitch with the sword, but dark was falling and he saw only another petty officer. Wik felt himself pushed toward the railing, adjacent to a ladder from the first deck and the number-three turret. He noticed a fire-fighting station with equipment that resembled what he had seen on American warships—pumps, hoses, a wicked-looking ax.

Wik turned back seaward, savoring the open-air sights and sounds. He was aware of the thrumming of the ship's machinery turning twin screws beneath his feet. He looked aft, noting the wake glowing phosphorescent in the gathering dark. Only one burning carrier was visible; evidently the other two had sunk or been towed away. He wondered about Mr. Massey and the rest of the squadron. About Buck Rogers. Whether *Yorktown* was still afloat . . .

Searing pain at the back of the head. The ephemeral impression of a splintered skull. Wanting to scream but only a hollow moan escaping his lungs. Knees going very, very weak. Grasping the chain railing, trying somehow to stay on his feet. Seeing the dark water below, strength fading fast, feeling himself falling toward the ocean. Never hearing the splash but vaguely conscious of the ship's screws, fading as it rushed away. The inky blackness of the Pacific wrapping itself around him until there was only nothingness.

17.

2001–2200, 4 JUNE

Phil Rogers poured another cup of coffee for Dave Shumway, who nodded his thanks and turned back to the long, linen-draped table. Rogers poured another half cup for himself and settled beside Burnett and Isaman. "I don't know why I'm drinking coffee," Rogers offered. "It'll only keep me awake."

Burnett leaned one elbow on the table, his chin in his hand. "Not me. I'm all in." He looked left and right. "Anybody willing to carry the bull ensign of this squadron to his quarters?"

"I wonder where we'll bunk tonight," Isaman asked. "We don't have assigned billets yet, do we?"

"The ship's exec is working on it," Shumway offered. "He says we'll probably just move into most of the torpedo squadron's quarters." He picked up his cup. "There's plenty of room there."

Some of the ensigns traded knowing glances. Scuttlebutt held that after the morning strike there had been bad feelings between Torpedo Six and Fighting Six. Reportedly one of the four returning TBD pilots—an experienced noncommissioned pilot—had gone to VF-6's ready room with a .45 on his hip and blood in his eye. Losing three-quarters of his friends to Jap fighters was bad enough—getting shot at by his own fighters was definitely unsat.

Rogers exhaled, leaned back in his chair and stretched his arms over his head. "Mr. Shumway, is there any word on the flight schedule for tomorrow?"

"I checked with the air-ops staff a while ago. Dawn searches are scheduled, but there's another front moving this way. We may have to rely on Midway's PBYs."

"That's fine with me, sir." Rogers stifled a yawn. "Do we have enough operational airplanes?"

The acting CO took a folded paper from his pocket. "We're down to eleven. My airplane, Cooner's and Merrill's are all shot up." He put the paper back in his pocket. "This force will have to use the *Hornet* for the main air strikes from now on."

The fliers around the table fell silent. Burnett fidgeted in his seat and Rogers recognized the symptom. *He's about to ask an embarrassing question.*

"Sir, a lot of us are wondering about the *Hornet* Air Group." He spread his hands on the linen. "What gives?"

Shumway sat back, toying with his spoon. "Well. I have it on good authority that they've had heavy losses. Apparently their whole torpedo squadron and about one-third of their fighters." He did not mention that his authority was a first-class yeoman whom he had known on his first duty out of Annapolis, now on Spruance's staff.

Burnett was encouraged, and pressed on. "But, Lieutenant, we didn't see any of them over the Jap fleet this morning. And their SBDs arrived way late tonight."

Shumway eyed the ensign and was tempted to end the conversation. But he looked at a proud-tired young man who still might not survive this battle. One of *his* proud-tired young men. "Torpedo Eight apparently attacked alone and was destroyed. Their escort never made contact and presumably ditched on the way back. As for the scout-bombers . . ." He tapped his spoon on his saucer. "The ops office says they ran low on fuel searching for the Japs and some diverted to Midway. Took 'em most of the day to get reorganized.

"Then this afternoon—you didn't hear this from me, Mister—Captain Browning's staff neglected to tell the *Hornet* of our launch schedule against the fourth carrier. That's apparently why they were late." He dropped his spoon in his cup with a ringing clatter. Even junior ensigns had heard of Miles Browning, Vice Admiral Halsey's mercurial chief of staff now working for Spruance. Reportedly the man had two characteristics: an uncommon intellect and a totally abrasive personality.

"That fits the pattern, doesn't it?" Burnett muttered. He was greeted with a frosty silence. "Well, here we are running from the Japs after beating the bejesus out of them. Right?" Heads nodded up and down the table.

It was a sensitive point, and Rogers noted some scowls from *Enterprise* officers within earshot. Less than an hour ago Spruance had ordered the task force to turn eastward, opening the range between the Americans and Japanese.

Rogers sat motionless and wordless. He saw the tension in Shumway's neck muscles and wondered how the exec—actually the acting skipper—would react. At length Shumway said in a deadly, even voice, "I don't know about you, Ensign, but personally I don't relish tangling with a half-dozen Jap battleships in a night surface engagement."

Burnett's face turned crimson. "Uh, yessir. I see what you mean, sir."

Shumway rose and stretched. "I'm going to check on my wounded gunner in sick bay, then turn in. I suggest you gentlemen do likewise."

Rogers drained his coffee cup, then nudged Burnett. "C'mon, Bernie. Let's find a couple of bunks." They filed out of the wardroom, waving to some of Wally Short's scouting pilots. Phil diverted to their table.

"Hello, Rogers," Sam Adams greeted him. "We heard you fellows did a four-oh job on that last carrier."

"Thanks, Lieutenant." *I missed!* "Say, your contact report was real solid." In truth it had been thirty-five miles off, but that mattered little. Navigation had been easy under clear skies. "Ah, is there any word on the *Yorktown?*"

Adams shrugged. "Not much. She was torpedoed in the second

attack and has been abandoned. I suppose they'll try to put a repair crew aboard tomorrow."

"Yes, sir. That's pretty much what we heard." He looked around the table. *Nice to see some familiar faces,* Rogers thought. It occurred to him that after only a week with the makeshift air group, he was beginning to think of himself as a Yorktowner.

In the cruiser's smoky wardroom, a linen-covered table was spread with charts and diagrams, their curling ends secured by cups, saucers and ashtrays. "First things first," Captain Buckmaster said to the assembled officers. Most of them now wore borrowed khakis from *Hammann*'s or the cruiser's complement; all of them looked decidedly cleaner than they had aboard the destroyer a few hours ago. "Lieutenant Hilbert is already going to each ship of the screen, assembling men with the knowledge and abilities we need to begin repairs. I expect he'll be at it most of the night."

Standing with the damage-control officer, Callaway reflected that the U.S. Navy still did not possess personnel specifically trained for combat salvage operations. *Maybe this little episode will change that,* he thought.

Buckmaster continued. "I expect that we should have an adequate crew assembled in this ship by sunup. Then we'll see about getting them aboard *Yorktown* and setting to work.

"Now then. We need to clear the decks and reduce all possible weight, especially on the port side."

Commander Delaney, the engineering officer, responded. "Well, sir, there are two F4Fs tied down on the flight deck and a couple of bombers on the hangar deck. They'll be easy to jettison. There's also quite a lot of ordnance that we can dispose of. After that, it's hard work."

"What do you recommend, Aldrich?" the captain asked.

The damage-control officer leaned forward, palms down on the table. "Sir, the heaviest items we can jettison are the four five-inchers on the port side. We can cut them loose with acetylene torches and let them roll overboard." He thought for a moment. "That alone will rid us of six tons or more."

Buckmaster nodded. "Very well. Then we need to get at least one destroyer alongside to provide power as quickly as possible. I'm most concerned about that twenty-seven-degree list. The sooner we transfer oil from port to starboard, the sooner she'll come back to an even keel."

"Yes, sir," replied Delaney. "Then we should be able to light off some boilers and make headway on our own. Except . . ."

"Except the damn rudder is still jammed to port. Well, never mind. If need be, we'll rely on the tug. *Vireo* is underway to us from French Frigate Shoals. She should arrive in time to give us a tow if we can't steam on our own."

Callaway dragged on his cigarette, then crushed it out. He expelled a lungful of smoke and looked at the determined men around him. He was proud to stand with them. *Takes more than three bombs and two torpedoes to sink our ship*, he thought.

HONOLULU, HAWAII, 2000 LOCAL

Sallyann Downey was not hungry. The kitchen clock in her apartment off King Street said it was 8:00 P.M., and normally she would have finished dinner by this hour. Lately she had tried limiting herself to fruit and vegetables; Mary Tanaka's family were truck farmers who sold her good produce at bargain rates. *It's silly*, she told herself. Phil had made one casual remark about her "fuller figure these days" and she had almost worn out her bathroom scale ever since.

She put down the pen she had been holding and looked at the writing tablet. The top page boasted two lines: "June 4, 1942" and "Dearest Phil." She had almost written "Dearest Buck," but somehow that seemed inappropriate for her first love letter to him.

Sally reflected that there had been little opportunity for writing love letters to Phil Rogers. Somehow it was awkward because, after all, he was a navy man engaged in a war. She had expected to spend a great deal of time writing to him on sea duty. But the fortunes of war had kept her sailor "beached" (as he put it) for almost as long as she had known him. Only that three-week period in April, when his squadron went aboard the *Enterprise*, had prevented them from seeing one another almost weekly.

In the four months they had known each other, Sallyann Downey of Portland, Oregon, and the Library of Hawaii, and Philip Rogers of West Palm Beach, Florida, and Bombing Squadron Three, had fallen in love. They had both suspected it early on—he embracing it, she resisting it. *We've got it backwards*, she had thought. *The man is supposed to flee from entanglements*. But she realized that twenty-four-year-old men suddenly faced with combat and the prospect of violent death often needed an emotional anchor. She had become that anchor. But Sallyann was a sensible young woman, astute enough to know that love affairs born of crisis could prove fragile or painful. She had already seen it happen to two of her friends—otherwise-sensible young women much like herself who had become involved with servicemen. They had rushed to marry, and now one girl was the twenty-five-year-old widow of a dashing army pursuit pilot who had tied the world record for low-altitude flight. The other bride had a machinist-mate husband, on the submarine *Nautilus*, whom she hardly ever got to see.

But at least I told Phil I love him, she thought. Even if it had come at the last minute before he sailed off to the war, when all her emotions had caught up with her and blindsided her into Saying It. She wondered why she had been so fearful of voicing those words. *Well, that's the reason for the letter—to tell him what I couldn't before.* She knew what she wanted to say: that she was committed to him and him alone, but that she would not marry until after the war. She had told him all this in person, but somehow putting it in writing would make it "official."

Somebody was knocking on her door. She slid off the kitchen chair, pushed away from the table and pulled her knee-length silk dressing gown tight around her. She peeked through the curtain and saw the badges of office: the white civil-defense helmet and the air-raid warden's armband. She turned the knob and opened the door as much as she felt comfortable.

"Hello, Mr. Tarutani."

"Good evening, Miss Downey." Mr. Tarutani was well-known in the neighborhood; a cheerful, good-natured man of fiftyish appearance who befriended children, stray cats and young single ladies. But some residents called him the Hawaiian Vampire. It was said that when dusk fell, his personality changed and he turned into an officious boor.

"Ah, I hate to call on you like this—on official business, I mean—but I noticed your window shows quite a lot of light. It's a security violation." His pudgy right hand went to his pocket and the citation book contained there.

Sally glanced at her kitchen window and saw that one corner of the blackout curtain had caught on a potted palm. "Oh, dear," she said, placing a hand to her cheek. *Nice touch, Sally.* "I . . . I do believe that my cat, Muffin, has brushed against it again." She smiled charmingly. "You know what rascals cats can be."

Warden Tarutani's 260 pounds almost visibly deflated. He dropped his hand from his pocket, then touched his helmet in a nonregulation salute. "Well, seeing as how it's your cat . . . I'll let it go with a warning. This time," he added significantly.

"Oh, thank you so much. You're a dear." She blew him a kiss as she closed the door. As he walked away whistling, Sally shook her head briefly. *I have to get a cat.*

She giggled aloud. Rogers had told her of an acquaintance from the *Enterprise*—another SBD pilot—who had been home with his wife between deployments when an air-raid warden had come calling. "Say, don't you know a dive-bomber could spot that light from twenty thousand feet and drop one right in your lap?" the warden had scolded.

The Dauntless pilot had replied, "Well, sir, I've been flying dive-bombers for three years and that'd be a damn sight better bombing than I've ever seen." Telling the story to Rogers, the VB-6 flier also had added, "I guess I shouldn't have said that, because he started writing out the ticket right then."

Sally laughed again, savoring the story. She had to admit that she was very fond of most of Phil's friends. Especially that cute little Bernie Burnett, perhaps the least pretentious aviator she knew. Sally had come to understand three things about fliers: they were uniformly absorbed with their work; they were devoted to having fun; and nearly all of them were afraid of nothing so much as showing their fear. For some reason, Phil Rogers was more open about that sensitive fact than the others. *Maybe that's one reason I love him.*

Sally sat down at the table again. Now she had a good opening to her letter. Then she stopped in midmotion. For some reason the thought of fear caused her to think of one name. She realized she had forgotten to say a prayer for Phil's friend, Wayne Wik.

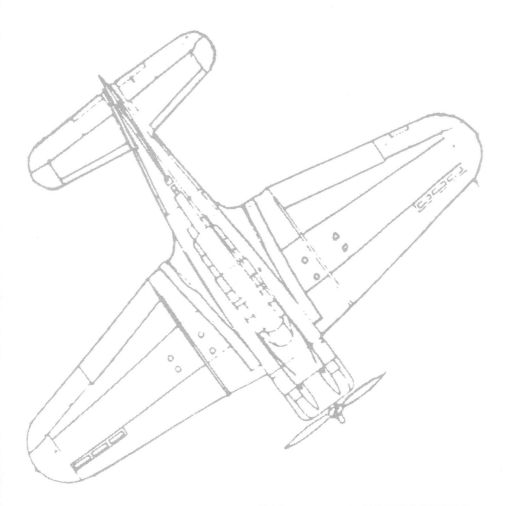

PART THREE

"Even against the greatest of odds, there is something in the human spirit—a magic blend of skill, faith and valor—that can lift men from certain defeat to incredible victory."

WALTER LORD
Incredible Victory

18.

FRIDAY, 5 JUNE

EASTERN ISLAND, MIDWAY, 0120

James Carpenter was undoing Candice Mulvaney's blouse again, being careful lest he pull one of the pearl-colored buttons off her expensive garment. Candice always had been particular about her appearance, but at that moment she was wonderfully disheveled from ninety minutes of escalating romance.

Her honey-blond hair was delightfully mussed; Carpenter had playfully untied the pink ribbon she wore, allowing her hair to fall onto her smooth, round shoulders. He had just unfastened the last button and peeled back the satin to reveal those shoulders and her blue bra straps. She was making little chirping sounds of pleasure or encouragement—it didn't matter which—as she slid from the living room sofa to the carpeted floor.

Then the front door burst open. The sound was like rolling thunder, yet somehow far away. Dr. Mulvaney's hand was roughly shaking Carpenter but the words didn't quite match. Something about the lagoon. *What lagoon?* Carpenter asked himself.

He forced his eyes open. Peering down at him from the darkened dugout was Corporal Pankratz. *You're not Doc Mulvaney*, Carpenter thought. Then he realized; he was glad he hadn't said the words aloud. Pankratz would never understand. *Or maybe he would* . . .

"Come on, Lieutenant, get up!" Pankratz spoke as if addressing a slow child. "A Jap sub's shelling us!"

Another dull boom, faintly heard, rolled through the early-morning air. "You said they're shelling the lagoon, Corporal?"

"Yes, sir. Don't know why. But it's definitely a submarine. The southern batteries on Sand are returning fire."

Carpenter forced himself to concentrate. "Well, then it's not an invasion." Pankratz stood motionless. "I mean, you don't start an amphibious invasion with a few rounds from one damn submarine. And you don't risk that submarine to lob a few shells into a lagoon. That just means they have no spotters."

"Uh, no, sir. I mean, yes, sir."

"Thank you, Corporal, you've done your duty. But I'm trying to go back to sleep. Let the goddamn Japs waste their goddamn ammo."

Pankratz raised a hand in the room. "Listen, sir. I think they've stopped."

Carpenter cocked an ear. The firing had in fact ceased. *The sub's pulled the plug and dived, so our gunners can't see it anymore.* He pointedly lay back down, turned his back to Jake Pankratz and pulled the covers of his cot up over his shoulders. It was an hour and a half until the predawn alert. He wondered if it was possible to resume a pleasant dream after being interrupted.

USS ENTERPRISE, 0400

Phil Rogers and Bernie Burnett awoke in two dead men's bunks and dressed in the dead men's clean clothes. Officially the Torpedo Six crews were missing in action, but few people held out much hope for them. The two VB-3 pilots knew little of the men besides their names—two ensigns from Georgia and Alabama. *Southern boys like me,* Rogers thought. Then, *No, not quite. At least I still have a future. However long that might be.*

Last night the displaced Yorktowners had self-consciously avoided handling the missing men's personal effects more than necessary, and neither had discussed them. When Burnett had gone to the head before turning in, Rogers had carefully placed the framed photos and the few other items in a drawer.

In response to dawn general quarters, Rogers and Burnett hastened to leave the berthing compartment for the ready room. They found the room filling with other aviators, looking and feeling much like themselves. There was little chatter as fliers settled themselves according to their preferences. A few were fully dressed in flight suits, leather jackets and Mae Wests, even wearing helmets. Most of the others wore only khaki shirts and trousers, hanging their gear on the bulkheads, draping items over their chairs or cramming them into the drawers under each seat.

As usual, Rogers sat down and began copying the weather and navigation data onto his plotting board. He found the simple task a welcome routine, a starting point for the rest of the day. Somebody nudged his elbow and his grease pencil traced an errant line on his board. Irritated, Rogers looked up to confront the careless jerk—and smiled. "Oh, hi, Frankie. How come you're up so early?"

Ensign DiBella stretched and stifled a yawn. "What, and miss all this excitement?" He smiled back. "Say, you can save the nav dope, pal. We're socked in and probably will be all morning. The PBYs are doing the searches today."

Rogers was impressed. "How does an ensign come by such lofty information?"

"Shee-it, Rogers. I play bridge with the exec and poker with the aerology officer." He tapped his classmate's arm with the back of one hand. "Stick with me, Mister. I have friends in high places."

Burnett overheard the exchange from across the aisle. "Uh, say, DiBella. Maybe you could use your influence to get us something to eat. Now, on the *Yorktown* I have an understanding"—he winked broadly—"with a steward's mate in the admiral's galley."

DiBella straightened up. "Well, we're scheduled to stand down from GQ after sunup. Breakfast in the wardroom on a rotational basis after that." He looked back at Rogers. "How 'bout it, Buck?"

Rogers leaned back in his chair. "Naw, I don't think so, Frankie. Somehow, I'm just not very hungry."

NUMBER FOUR SCOUT, 0650

Lieutenant (junior grade) Azumano was beginning to feel surprisingly comfortable: with his mission, with his aircrew, even with his unyielding seat in the Type Zero reconnaissance plane. *I am also learning to find the enemy more easily,* he told himself.

Since launch at 0440, Azumano's crew had searched the now-familiar quadrant north of Midway. It had taken some time to pick up the Americans' trail again, but for the past twenty-five minutes Sakaida's expert snooping technique had kept Number Four Scout in contact with the same battered carrier from yesterday.

The difference was plainly obvious: now the carrier was accompanied by a lone destroyer. Glassing the escort, Azumano assumed that it had detected his presence by radar. *Otherwise, why would it be maneuvering at high speed?* he asked himself. He swiveled his neck, searching the upper air for the fighters that could be directed onto him by that damnable device. But no other enemy carriers were known in the area, thereby precluding chances of interception.

Still, Azumano did not want to fall into complacency. He recalled only too vividly how the Grummans had barely missed finding him yesterday morning, and how *that one* had expended most of its ammunition at him in the afternoon. It had been a nasty scare.

Azumano looked forward, noting that Flight Petty Officer Sakaida remained vigilant as ever. Only Sakaida's expert maneuvering had prevented the F4F from shredding the Aichi floatplane with six .50 calibers. Now the pilot was just as careful, maintaining a respectful distance from the alerted U.S. destroyer.

The aircraft commander returned his attention to the crippled carrier. From this altitude the sun angle made perspective rather difficult—it was hard to tell which way the ship was listing. After further study, Azumano made an educated guess and determined the basis for his radio report. He passed it to Hara, who sent:

"Number Four. *Yorktown*-class carrier listing to starboard and drifting, escorted by one destroyer." The radioman then gave the position.

Sakaida, not given to intercom chatter, called with uncharacteristic formality. "Pilot to commander. We can remain here another two hours if our return position is unchanged. But if the fleet withdraws to the west . . ."

Azumano knew his pilot's intent. "Yes, Sakaida. You are right. We should head back." He hung up the microphone and felt the Type Zero bank away from the carrier. *No matter,* he thought bitterly. *Even if they send submarines to finish that American carrier, we have lost this battle.*

There was an English phrase—what was it? *Victory knows a thousand fathers, defeat is an orphan.* Listening to the constant purr of the fourteen-cylinder engine, Azumano imagined it repeated the word: *orphan, orphan, orphan . . .*

USS ENTERPRISE, 0815

"We've had some good luck," began the staff intelligence officer. He was a short, compact man named Freiburg—a commander nominally assigned to Vice Admiral Halsey but now working for Rear Admiral Spruance. The aviators sized him up as a businesslike individual, though a few cognoscenti said he had been a latecomer to aviation. In some circles, that was cause for skepticism—converts engendered less respect than homegrown true believers. Phil Rogers kept an open mind on the matter. Even Bull Halsey himself had only earned wings in 1934, unlike Captain "Pete" Mitscher of *Hornet*, who in 1916 became the U.S. Navy's thirty-third aviator.

"We are in contact with two widely separated groups of enemy ships," Freiburg said. "The main interest is this one, bearing three-two-four from Midway, distance about two hundred forty miles. It's composed of a burning carrier, reportedly accompanied by two battleships and two or three cruisers plus destroyers. Their course is generally westerly, last reported making twelve knots.

"Additionally, according to submarine and patrol-plane reports, two Japanese capital ships apparently collided late last night," Freiburg explained. "They are reported as battleships or heavy cruisers, but in any event their latest position bears two-six-four degrees from Midway, distance one twenty-five. Two PBYs are in contact, tracking them westward at about fifteen knots." He tapped a chart position west of Midway. "At least one of these ships is heavily damaged. It's trailing a wide oil slick, which happily for us simplifies the navigation problem." Freiburg's perfunctory smile brought the desired laughter from his audience.

"Now I know what you're thinking," the intelligence officer added.

"You'd love to put those babies on the bottom. Well, so would I." At this a few arched eyebrows and sardonic grins were traded. If Freiburg noticed the reaction, he ignored it and continued. "But Midway is dealing with them. We have to stand by to finish off that remaining carrier." He looked across the room, taking in the attentive, serious young faces. "We're convinced that three flattops have already sunk, but we're keeping an eye on the fourth. And remember," he emphasized, "we cannot assume that there isn't another one out there somewhere."

Dave Shumway raised a hand. "Commander, we're nearly out of torpedo planes and we're getting short on dive-bombers. My squadron is down to ten airplanes operational. I'd like to confirm the tactical organization with the other squadron COs and your ops officer right away."

"Of course," Freiburg said.

But in the back row two concerned ensigns put their heads together. Burnett whispered, "Jeesus, Phil, it sounds like Mr. Shumway's planning to shift the lineup."

Rogers nodded his assent. "Yeah, I know. But it *is* his decision." Burnett sat back, making no response, while Rogers glanced around, trying to gauge the other junior pilots' emotions. For reasons of pride, none wanted to be left behind, even for the militarily good reason of giving their aircraft to more experienced pilots. *And I haven't made a hit*, Rogers realized. He felt his heartstrings plucked in two directions: one toward the side of his psyche called Ego, the other toward Survival.

He closed his eyes. It was going to be another long day.

USS ASTORIA, 1035

"Hell, Chief, we shoulda stayed on that tin can for all the good it did us transferring over here last night." Standing in line with other salvage crewmen, Callaway pointed a long finger at *Hammann*, steaming alongside the cruiser.

Granville Riker's large, balding head nodded in agreement. His forty-four years were beginning to tell, though he was not about to admit it. *Just can't keep up with these kids like I used to*, he conceded to himself. "Well, sir, I guess the captain did what he needed to do. Mr. Delaney said there was no better way to get the salvage crew assembled." Riker leaned over the rail to spit into the gray-green sea. "How many are we transferring altogether?"

Callaway stretched expansively, inhaling the sea air. "Thirty officers, including the captain, and a hundred forty-one men. It'll take an hour or so to get everybody over to the *Hammann* by highline."

"You know, sir, in nearly twenty-five years in the navy I've only ridden a breeches buoy, oh, maybe two, three times." He smiled glumly at Callaway. "Thought it was a big kick when I was a lot younger. Now I can't say as I enjoy it much."

The Texan shifted his weight sideways, nearly rubbing shoulders with Riker. "I'll tell you a secret, Chief. I'd *never* done it until we transferred to this ship last night." He looked up and spread his hands as if expecting rain from the clear sky. "Now, shee-it. In daylight it oughta be fun."

Both men stopped to watch the next ship-to-ship transfer. Riker studied the intricacies of the endeavor more closely than Callaway because, though an engineering man, he was also proud to be a sailor. He noted that the crews on both ends of the suspension lines worked to keep tension on the ropes, minimizing the inevitable difference in seakeeping qualities between an 11,000-ton cruiser and a 1,700-ton destroyer.

Another sailor stepped into the canvas basket on *Astoria*'s deck, then allowed himself to be hoisted aloft. Suspended from a pulley, the basket was pulled across the gap between the two warships with surprising speed. The block-and-tackle arrangement worked smoothly, with only one dip toward the waves. Laughter broke out when spectators saw the potential victim pull himself higher in the basket, but his feet remained dry. As soon as he was hauled aboard *Hammann* he was helped from the contraption, which immediately was pulled back to *Astoria* for the next trip.

Riker turned back toward Callaway. "Excuse me, Lieutenant, but most of the boys are wondering. How soon will we head back to the *Yorktown*?"

"Not until this afternoon at the earliest." The disappointment in Callaway's voice was apparent. "We were told that Admiral Fletcher wants to refuel the destroyers from the *Portland* before she takes the rest of the crew back to Pearl."

Riker cursed under his breath. Callaway didn't catch the words but he recognized the sentiment. "I know, Chief. For what it's worth, I'd like to get going this morning, too."

Looking at the plain-faced, awkward officer, Riker took a chance. He glanced left and right, then spoke in a low, soft voice. "Mr. Callaway, I know it won't do no good, but . . ." He shook his head violently. "Damn it, sir, refueling that many cans will take eight hours or more. The *Yorktown* could sink in that time. Don't it make more sense to refuel a couple of us and let the rest catch up later?"

"Yup, it does, Chief." Now Callaway spoke in hushed tones as well. "But the admiral didn't ask my opinion. I doubt he even asked Captain Buckmaster. If we lose the ship because of Fletcher's decision, he's the one gets the blame." Callaway shrugged eloquently. "That's why admirals get paid more than lieutenants, I guess."

Riker was unconvinced. "If you'll excuse me, sir. Admiral Fletcher sure don't act like no Medal of Honor winner."

Callaway shifted his feet uncomfortably. He respected Riker too much to play the superior with the man, but that sort of talk made junior officers exceedingly nervous. Callaway had not even known that Frank Jack Fletcher wore the coveted decoration until the pale-blue ribbon appeared on the admiral's dress whites during an inspection. Afterward, Callaway had looked up the citation in the ship's library. What he read had surprised and disturbed him. In 1914 Woodrow Wilson's two-day expedition against Veracruz, Mexico, had resulted in fifty-five Medals of Honor to navy and marine personnel, including one to Ensign Fletcher. By comparison, fewer than thirty had been awarded to naval personnel during the nineteen months of American involvement in World War I.

Nor was that all. Criticism had been leveled at Fletcher for his handling of the aborted Wake Island reinforcement in late December. His *Saratoga* task force had turned back only 400 miles from Wake, leaving the defenders to the Japanese. On the other hand, Fletcher's defenders noted that then-CinCPac, Admiral Pye, had ordered Task Force Fourteen's return to Pearl. Callaway had to admit that Fletcher had handled Task Force Seventeen well enough since January, but the cruiser admiral had expert advice from *Yorktown*'s air staff. And the man was so . . . cautious.

At length Callaway was embarrassed into a response. He decided he could only speak from the heart. "Chief, I think I love Old Yorky as much as you do. If we get half a chance, we'll save her."

Both men advanced a few paces in line as another sailor took his turn in the breeches buoy.

IJNS ARASHI, 1105

Lieutenant Fuji carefully stepped over several prostrate forms slumped on the second deck. Though many of them rested on mattresses, most were content just to sit or lie on something firm. Fuji reflected that in other circumstances the passageway would be filled with seamen jumping to attention at an officer's presence. But not even a disciplinarian like Takeo Fuji could bring himself to berate *Akagi*'s pitiful survivors.

At least they look better than they did twenty-four hours ago, Fuji thought. Oil-soaked, begrimed men—some in tears, all visibly depressed—had settled on board the destroyer wherever room permitted. Several had been severely burned, and Fuji knew that some of those had already died. The sight of such wounds was bad enough; the smell was indescribable. Fuji wondered if he could bring himself to eat cooked meat ever again.

Fuji turned a corner and stepped into the enlisted men's mess to conduct a quick inspection. The ship's cooks had been working nonstop to feed the *Akagi* overflow, and there was genuine concern that supplies might not last for the return trip to Japan. Still, men had to eat, and Fuji edged himself through the crowded space.

He noticed a superior petty officer—the man's name did not register—animatedly relating the death of the American airman the night before. The sailor obviously relished the attention he received from his shipmates and a few *Akagi* men, even describing the arc of the fire ax as it split the prisoner's skull. The executioner then passed around the dead man's wallet, showing his friends some green American money and the photo of a white woman. An admiring seaman voiced a popular sentiment: "What a misfortune that we will not occupy Hawaii anytime soon."

Fuji was vaguely aware of international law concerning treatment of prisoners of war. The Geneva Convention of 1929 arrogantly reflected Western values, of course, which had almost nothing in common with Japanese military virtues. If the American had any honor, he never would have allowed himself to be captured, to say nothing of parting with such valuable information. But the thought seared itself on Fuji's brain: *If the Americans win this war, they will seek vengeance on us. And they will consider it justice.*

He made a mental note to learn the petty officer's name—just in case the information proved useful someday.

USS ENTERPRISE, 1128

"What's Dave all hot and bothered about?" Burnett asked.

Rogers leaned sideways in his aisle seat, looking toward the front of the ready room. Some pilots already were calling the composite unit

"Bombing Squadron 63," as Lieutenant Shumway was senior among the remaining VB-6 and VB-3 officers.

Shumway stood at the blackboard, forcefully speaking in low tones while conferring with Lieutenant Short of Scouting Five. *My gosh, they're arguing about something*, Rogers thought. Then he realized the two COs were merely confirming data of some kind, resorting to the familiar routine of a "chalk talk." Finally Shumway slammed down his chalk, breaking it on the holder. He said, "I'm going to see McClusky."

Heads turned as he stalked from the room. Rogers turned to his friend Frank DiBella. "What gives?"

DiBella looked over the high back of his chair. "I don't know for sure, but apparently there's a big problem with the staff's plan for this next launch." He looked left and right, confirming that nobody overheard the gossip. "My spies in the air department say that Captain Browning's ordered thousand-pound bomb loads for a 240-mile attack on that burning Jap carrier."

Rogers and Burnett exchanged goggle-eyed stares. "Holy smokes," Bernie said. He let out a long whistle. "We can't even . . ."

DiBella nodded. "Yeah. And that ain't all." He pointed to the plotting board laid across Rogers's lap. "Buck, you're the hot navigator. Run this for me. Take our projected 1400 position and plot it against the PBY's report on that burning carrier."

Rogers gave DiBella a gotcha smile. "Already have, Frankie."

"Okay. Now tell me how far we gotta go before we overtake the Japs, assuming they're still headed southwest at twelve knots."

Rogers laid off the time-distance problem on his circular grid and made a rough computation. He looked up and stared into DiBella's expressionless face. "Jesus, that's about 275 miles. I doubt we can make 240, let alone this!"

"And that last report is, what? Three hours old?" Burnett slammed back in his chair. "Damn!"

"You said it, friend." DiBella leaned closer. "I expect that Mr. Shumway is seeing our CAG, Wade McClusky, right now."

Rogers fervently replied, "I sure hope so. Somebody's got to talk some sense to those idiots on the staff."

I J N S   T O N E ,   1 2 0 0

Lieutenant Masatake Naito heard the knock and looked up from his desk. "Enter," he called. The visitor stepped into the compartment and came to attention.

"Oh, Azumano. I was going to ask for you shortly." Naito gestured toward a metal chair and Azumano accepted the invitation. He waited for his superior to speak again. "I am working on our battle report," the air officer explained. "I would like your comments."

Azumano was pleased to be asked, though more than a little surprised. Junior officers seldom were called upon for their opinions— only their professional knowledge. Still, this was a rare opportunity.

"Lieutenant, I am grateful for your willingness to record my thoughts. In all candor, I came here to offer my observations in hope that they might prevent a recurrence of our . . . misfortune." He had come perilously close to saying *our mistakes.*

"Yes. Please continue." Naito's tone was even, almost encouraging.

"Our doctrine must be changed, sir. We had too few scouts assigned to the important sectors. I realize that the naval general staff puts great emphasis upon striking capability over reconnaissance, but . . ."

"But without reliable information, our battleship guns and carrier aircraft are of little use." Naito finished the thought for his subordinate. "Yes, I agree. And my draft will state as much. Whether the captain chooses to keep that statement in his report . . . I cannot say."

"Sir, we cannot afford another battle like this one!"

Naito looked closely at Azumano. The man's face clearly showed fatigue and disappointment. Not even his own confirmation that USS *Yorktown* lay immobile and vulnerable to submarines had cheered him much. "Azumano, you sound as if this battle is already lost."

"Well, is it not, sir? Everyone knows that *Hiryu* was scuttled early this morning." Azumano instantly regretted his statement. For an Imperial Navy officer, Lieutenant Naito was uncommonly democratic toward his subordinates, but he was seldom indulgent.

Naito merely nodded. After a long silence he offered, "I am as much to blame as anyone. The catapult delayed your takeoff by thirty minutes . . ." He shook his head slowly. "If only we had those thirty minutes back again. If only Hasegawa did not have to search that other sector."

Of course! Azumano thought. Naito and Hasegawa had grown up in the same prefecture. *I had forgotten that.* He searched for some word of encouragement. "Lieutenant, we all take our chances in battle. The balky catapult . . . it merely happened that way."

Azumano had uttered the magic phrase, *Ko narimashita.* To a Japanese, the passive phrase "It happened that way" offered a grim but somehow acceptable explanation of great misfortune. Had he said, *Ko shimashita*—"someone *made* it happen that way"—Naito could have taken offense. And not merely because the damnable catapult was Naito's responsibility, but because such an attitude would have contradicted the Japanese sense of the logical order of things.

Naito straightened visibly in his chair. The expression on his face told Azumano that the subject was closed. "Do you have any other suggestions for my endorsement?"

"Yes, sir. Just one. I wish to recommend my pilot, Petty Officer Sakaida, for a commendation. His performance was exceptional."

Tone's air officer smiled an ironic smile. "Sakaida receiving a decoration! Now there really is something exceptional." Both men knew that awards to enlisted men were virtually unheard-of in the Imperial Navy. A nonconformist like Hiroyoshi Sakida—the clown of CruDivEight, the luster after Latin American women. Naito actually laughed. Then he raised a hand. "No, do not misunderstand me, Azumano. If a noncommissioned officer were to receive a decoration, Sakaida would be the one. But I doubt there will be any decorations from this operation."

"What do you mean, sir?" Then he remembered. *Defeat is an orphan.*

USS ENTERPRISE, 1300

Lieutenant DeWitt W. Shumway did not look like a naval officer who had just committed mutiny. In fact, he had committed no offense beyond preserving his own life and those of his pilots and aircrewmen, but it was not often that a senior lieutenant went over the head of a captain, chief of staff to a rear admiral.

Shumway cleared his throat, but not for attention. He was already the sole focus of every man in "VB-63's" ready room. "I've come from the flag bridge," he began. "Some of you know that originally we were ordered to launch on a 240-mile strike with half-ton bombs. Obviously, that wouldn't work very well." A few chuckles greeted his understatement. "It's a plan for a swimming meet," one Scouting Six pilot had said.

"I met with Captain Murray, Commander McClusky and Lieutenant Gallaher," Shumway continued. "We agreed that we should explain to the chief of staff that . . . his plan should be modified. After some, ah, discussion, we put the matter to Admiral Spruance." Rogers found himself leaning forward in his chair, like he had finished every *Flash Gordon* Saturday matinee back in Palm Beach. "The admiral said he would do what we pilots wanted." Scattered applause and whistles rippled through the room.

"Now, to get on with mission planning," Shumway added. "We will arm with five-hundred-pound bombs and launch thirty-two SBDs. The composition is . . ." He tugged a paper from his hip pocket. "Ten VB-3 and six VB-6 led by myself with Lieutenant Short leading seven of his planes plus nine from Scouting Six. The *Hornet* is supposed to put up a similar number."

Shumway turned to the wall chart, spreading his fingers wide to the west. "Wally's people will form a scouting line while the rest of us climb en route. We'll probably encounter an overcast with ceilings around twelve to fifteen thousand, but we'll stay as high as we can for best visibility. If we don't find the crippled carrier, we'll look for targets of opportunity." He looked around, seeking questions. There were none.

"All right, gentlemen. We launch in about two hours."

USS HAMMANN, 1400

Lieutenant CJ Callaway sat on a submersible pump, studying a sheaf of papers attached to a clipboard. Chief Granville Riker looked over his shoulder while Lieutenant (junior grade) Carlton Fontaine made entries on a pocket notepad. It was warm in the destroyer's machine shop, as much from the bodies crowded into the small space as from the ambient temperature.

"All right," Callaway began. "We know the heavy equipment we're going to need, but that's the easy part. Most anything necessary is still aboard the *Yorktown*."

"Yes, sir, that's right," Fontaine replied. "I think we might line up some spares, though. Oxygen bottles for acetylene torches, and maybe a portable welder or two."

"Good idea," Callaway replied. "Make a note of that."

As Fontaine scribbled in his notebook, Riker made harrumphing noises. "Yes, Chief?"

Riker tilted his dirty visored cap back on his head. "Lieutenant, it just occurred to me. Those cleanup crews from the destroyers that're already there. We don't know exactly what they're going to jettison, do we?"

Callaway was puzzled. "No, I don't think so. Commander Delaney just said they'd have the flight deck and some other spaces clear for us so we can get right to work once we're aboard."

"Well, sir, I just hope those boys don't toss somethin' we might need. Like Mr. Fontaine says, we might have to transfer some gear from this ship that's already on board."

Why didn't I think of that? Callaway wondered. But he knew why. *I'm so damn tired I can hardly stand up. Which is why I've parked my ass on this hard, uncomfortable pump.* "All right, Chief. You have a point. I'll take it up with Delaney."

As Fontaine and Riker ambled off to organize their respective crews and equipment, Callaway slumped back against the warm bulkhead. He tried to concentrate. *What else have I forgotten?*

OVERHEAD USS ENTERPRISE, 1540

Rogers could tell that the launch had not gone well. Both carriers were putting up SBDs, but most of *Hornet*'s scout-bombers remained on deck. *Another snafu down there*, he thought. *Well, nothing we can do about it.*

Now Lieutenant Shumway banked away from the task force, turning southwesterly. Rogers followed, rolling into a shallow bank, then centering the stick through the remainder of the turn. When Shumway in Baker Three rolled out on course, Rogers did likewise. He checked his instruments, found everything normal and waited until Barnes told him the task force escorts were well astern. Then he tugged the manual arming handle. He tensed for a heartbeat, then relaxed when nothing happened.

Flying wing on the new CO in the first section was another new experience for Rogers. He wondered again why Burnett had been displaced and he had not, but thought better of asking. *Dave's got his reasons*, he told himself. *Maybe just because I'm assigned to his division and Bernie isn't.*

Looking slightly down and forward, Rogers saw Wally Short's mixed squadron begin deploying into a scouting line—sixteen Dauntlesses fanning out line-abreast for greater coverage of the oceanic spaces they needed to search. It occurred to Rogers that while *Hornet*'s CAG and two SBD skippers were products of the Annapolis classes of 1923 and 1926, the combined *Enterprise-Yorktown* air group now was led by two lieutenants of 1931–32 vintage.

That knowledge troubled him. The squadron leadership ranks had been thinned terribly in two days: Max Leslie, out of the battle in *Astoria; Enterprise* CAG Wade McClusky sidelined with wounds; Bombing Six's skipper, Dick Best, grounded from a freak accident with his oxygen system; Scouting Six's Earl Gallaher almost immobile with a back injury. *They're all good men*, Rogers reflected. They, with Shumway and Short, had prevented a catastrophe by standing up to the chief of staff. Apparently Rear Admiral Spruance was astute enough to overrule Captain Browning, who reportedly had thrown a vicious tantrum and even now was sulking in his cabin.

But what if Dave or Wally don't get back from this hop? What if there's nobody senior enough to stand up for us against an egomaniac like Browning? With a start, Rogers realized that squadron command meant far more than training men for combat and leading them into flak and fighters. Sometimes it meant protecting your men from idiots with more stripes on their sleeves, or from the ambitious bastards the system inevitably produced.

Phil Rogers felt an involuntary shiver beneath his leather jacket. And it was not very cold at low altitude.

USS HAMMANN, 1740

CJ Callaway felt the destroyer begin a turn and knew its meaning. "High time we got going," he said to Commander Aldrich. "I like to thought we'd never finish refueling."

Yorktown's damage-control officer carefully placed his coffee cup on its saucer. There were relatively few diners in the wardroom, as many of the carrier's officers were catching much-needed sleep. "Jack, you might as well turn in. It's been a long day for everybody, and we'll start before dawn tomorrow."

Callaway leaned back in his chair. "Yes, sir. I'd like to check with my crew first, though. Chief Riker's about dead on his feet but won't admit it."

Aldrich knew what he meant. "Riker's a damn good man."

"What's the present situation? How does our schedule shape up?"

"You probably heard that the tug *Vireo* arrived from French Frigate Shoals this afternoon and reportedly is towing the *Yorktown*. But she's only making good about three knots. The *Hughes, Monaghan* and *Gwin* are standing by as escorts. I believe they've put a crew aboard to start clearing the flight deck and save us some time tomorrow. So with us, *Balch* and *Benham* there'll be plenty of help."

Callaway checked his watch. "If she can just stay afloat another eight hours or so . . ."

"Then we have a chance," Aldrich interjected.

BAKER EIGHTEEN, 1820

"Is that it, Mr. Rogers? All this way just for *that*?"

Rogers had to admit that Barnes had a point. In the twenty minutes since reaching the expected position of the damaged carrier, nothing had appeared on the surface of the darkening sea. By Rogers's reckoning the 240-mile search had stretched to 265, and *Hornet*'s first strike group apparently had gone beyond 300. Upon hearing Blue Leader call that he was attacking a cruiser, Shumway had recalled Short's scouts for a concentrated attack on that elusive ship.

Rogers looked down again. It was hard enough to tell much about ship types from 13,000 feet, and the haze only confounded identification. *She might be a light cruiser, more likely a destroyer leader. Whatever she is, she's making knots.*

Positioning his squadrons for the attack, Shumway judged the geometry of the situation. The warship was steaming west, making at least twenty-five knots into the lowering sun. His SBDs had been airborne some two and a half hours, and it was perhaps another ninety minutes back to the task force. No time to waste. "Scarlet and Red squadrons, this is Dave. I'm attacking now. Follow me in order."

As third to dive, Rogers had a relatively good view of the target. He was surprised at the puny antiaircraft fire at first, but the ship began a fast, arcing turn that required constant adjustment in tracking. He momentarily lost sight of the ship itself as he plunged through a wispy cloud layer, but had no trouble finding the wake.

A few flak puffs burst ahead of him, not close. *Good deflection but the range is off*, he thought. He moved the stick slightly and continued tracking the target, keeping his crosshairs well ahead of the bow. The ship appeared undamaged—apparently the *Hornet* pilots had all missed. He tried to judge the wind but the sea appeared calm, and no whitecaps showed through the thickening haze.

Moments later, Shumway released at 2,500 feet and began his pullout. Rogers saw the white bomb splash just off the port bow. The second bomb landed almost on top of the first. *Wind's more from starboard*, he thought. He finessed the controls, bringing his aimpoint to the inside of the ship's turn, almost on the starboard bow. *Looking good, ball's centered, hold it, hold it . . . Now!*

Rogers forced himself to hold the stick steady while he yanked on the manual bomb release. He felt the Mark XII separate as the five-hundred-pounder began its ballistic descent toward the ship's bow. Then he retracted his flaps, shoved on full power and began a steady pull. He realized he would not see the bomb strike, but he felt good.

As the nose came up through the horizon into level flight, Barnes was on the intercom. "Close, Mr. Rogers! That was a paint-scraper, just off the starboard beam." Disappointed, Rogers realized he had overcompensated for the wind. Then he heard Barnes open fire with the twin-mount .30s, trying to suppress some AA fire for the second-division pilots.

Running out to the east, Rogers occasionally veered left or right for a view of the attack. Barnes, facing aft over his guns, had a much better view and kept up a running commentary. "She's reversing her helm, going port now. A couple more near-misses. Gosh, she's putting up a lot of flak . . ."

There was not much radio chatter, which Rogers attributed to good training. He knew that a situation like this could breed laxity, where pilots only had to concentrate on putting their bombs on one target without fighter interception. He heard, "This is Wally, pushing over now." *Bombing Six and Scouting Six have already dived. I wonder if any of them got a hit.*

Long seconds of silence followed. Then a high-pitched babble of voices, fragments of calls. ". . . is hit!" "Pull out, Sam!" "Oh, God . . ."

Thirty-one SBDs slowly re-formed on course back to the east. Rogers knew that thirty-two had taken off.

APPROACHING TASK FORCE SIXTEEN, 1945

Enterprise and *Hornet* steamed into the night wind, trailing dimly visible wakes as two flocks of predatory seabirds winged homeward. In red-lit cockpits, nervous pilots tried to ignore fuel gauges that measured remaining flight time more in minutes than in hours. Below them was only the vast, empty darkness of the ocean.

Phil Rogers had eased slightly away from Lieutenant Shumway's
SBD, concerned about nocturnal formation flying. Rogers tried to
remember the date of his previous night carrier landing and could not.
He realized that his logbook still lay in its slot in VB-3's ready room on
Yorktown, and for a moment his thoughts about the documentation
of his professional life overcame his immediate interest in self-
preservation.

"Sir, do you see anything yet?" The concern was audible in Barnes's
voice.

Rogers picked up his microphone. "Nothing yet, but we're real
close. I'm backing up Mr. Shumway's navigation." He realized his tone
was more confident than the situation warranted. Finding the task
force was certainly possible at night—*Saratoga's* air group had conducted exercises for that very reason—but Sara had not been running
darkened through submarine waters.

Two beams of yellow-white light blazed up from the surface two
miles below. "Hey, there we are!" Rogers realized he hadn't depressed
the mike key. He tried again.

"I see it, Mr. Rogers!" Barnes beat him to it. "I never thought they'd
light up for us like that!"

Neither did I, Rogers thought. He replaced the mike, squirmed into
a more comfortable posture in his seat and closed up on Baker Three.
God bless Ray Spruance.

Shumway was dropping quickly now, obviously hastening to enter
the landing pattern and get aboard. *Don't want to keep the admiral
waiting.* Baker Three's wings waggled in the breakup signal and Rogers
reduced power, gaining interval as Bombing Three's first section flew
down the carrier's starboard beam at 800 feet. Rogers ran through his
checklist, got Baker Eighteen slowed with wheels, flaps and hook
down, and made the crosswind turn ahead of the ship.

Turning downwind, he glanced at the good ship *Enterprise* and
discerned her bow wave. As Baker Three broke left on base leg,
Rogers extended farther downwind, but kept the interval as close as he
dared. Seconds counted now—seconds given another pilot low on fuel,
or seconds denied a Japanese submarine captain.

Turning port, Rogers spotted the wake at right angles and continued the turn, rolling out over the twenty-six-knot wake. He instantly
sized up the view through his windscreen, past his optical sight, and
knew he was in the groove. He saw the landing-signal officer's
illuminated wands eerily suspended five feet off the deck and willed
them to remain level.

The lights bobbled up and down twice. *I'm a little high*, he told himself. He came back slightly on the throttle, keeping his attitude, and saw the flight deck looming out of the gloom to receive him. He resisted the impulse to chop the power and push the nose down for the deck. *Hold it, hold it . . .*

Lieutenant Robin Lindsey's gifted hands slashed downward and across his lanky frame, and the wands duplicated his gesture exactly. Rogers smartly retarded the throttle with his left hand and brought his right back against his seatbelt buckle.

Baker Three dropped to the Douglas fir deck, bounced once and the tailhook engaged the third arresting wire.

I made it. And I didn't screw up.

USS ENTERPRISE, 2038

Rogers made his way through the wardroom, threading himself amid the maze of chairs and press of bodies. En route to VB-3's table he cataloged a variety of conversations.

"That Jap skipper sure knew his business. I missed about a hundred feet astern."

"I told the intelligence officer it was probably a *Katori*-class cruiser."

"Nah. A *Katori*'s got one stack. This ship had two."

"I was just easing my way inside her door, even though she kept saying no. I mean, they all *say* no, but they don't all *mean* no."

"The Fighting Three exec, Billy Leonard? Yeah, he was up on the flight deck with his .45 when the first raid came in yesterday!"

"No, no. The last seven-game Series before 1940 was in '34 when St. Louis beat Detroit. It was in '31 they beat Philadelphia . . ."

"You're crazy. Roosevelt wouldn't dare run for another term."

Dave Shumway, Syd Bottomley and several other VB-3 pilots were seated at a table, talking to a lieutenant Rogers didn't recognize. Burnett eased alongside and the two ensigns stood together, apart from the group. "How'd it go?" Burnett asked.

"Not so good, Bernie. Thirty-two of us attacked a lone Jap ship—a cruiser or a big destroyer. No hits that we can tell. I near-missed to starboard, couldn't gauge the wind."

"Damn. That's a lot of gas and bombs to no good use."

Rogers thought of the rest of the price. "Worst thing is, the Japs shot down Sam Adams. You know, the red-headed lieutenant from Bombing Five? He's the one who found the fourth carrier."

Burnett nodded gravely. "Yeah, I heard. Short's people are mighty low about it. I guess he was real popular."

Rogers did not want to dwell on it. He almost felt he had been a friend of the charming little man who had been called "Goliath" at Annapolis. "Who's that talking to Mr. Shumway?"

"Oh, he's from Bombing Eight. He landed here because he didn't think he had enough gas to make the *Hornet*. His name's Green."

Rogers and Burnett took two chairs at the edge of the conversation. Both wanted to question Lieutenant Green, but thought better of intruding. Like most ensigns, they learned more by listening than by talking.

"Well, I can't say as I blame you fellows," Green was saying. "I guess if I was over here, knowing what you do, I'd wonder about our air group, too." He sipped his coffee, found it too hot and set the cup down. "I still don't know what happened tonight, but twenty-one of us were loaded with thousand-pounders instead of five-hundreds. We launched maybe fifteen minutes behind our CAG and his two divisions. By the time we reached the search area, we had to come back. We never found a thing."

Shumway and Bottomley exchanged glances. "More piss-poor staff work," another flier commented. Nobody responded.

Rogers could not resist. "Excuse me, sir. What can you tell us about your air group yesterday? We haven't heard very much." What he meant was, *Why didn't we see you over the Jap carriers?* Everyone present knew it.

Green looked Rogers full in the face for what seemed a long time. Three seconds later the VB-8 pilot began speaking slowly. "Well, you have to know our CAG. He conducted a long, very methodical search. Eventually the scouts and bombers split up. I took my division into Midway, where we refueled. The place is a mess, incidentally. The Japs really worked it over. Anyway, some of the fellows navigated back to the *Hornet* and got aboard on fumes. We got most of the SBDs back in time for the mission against that last carrier, but nobody on Admiral Spruance's staff gave us the launch time."

So that's why they were late, Rogers thought. *It wasn't their fault, after all.*

"We heard about your torpedo squadron," Burnett offered.

"Yeah." Green stared at his saucer. "Commander Waldron evidently went his own way and found the Japs while . . . we didn't." Rogers sensed that Green wanted to say something else—something not for the ears of strangers. "We lost all fifteen TBDs," Green continued, "and ten fighters. None of the escort made it back."

"This is turning more and more into an SBD operation," Burnett observed.

"Well, we got some of the *Yorktown* overflow. Our fighter skipper is missing from the escort mission and the exec went to sick bay. Lieutenant Commander Thach is running the show now. With elements of three squadrons, they call it VF-3/42/8."

"Like VB-63," Shumway added. There was a trace of a grin beneath his neatly trimmed mustache.

Rogers wanted to know just one more thing. "Mr. Green, I have a couple of friends from Pensacola in Scouting Eight. Do you know Ensigns Murtagh or Petersen?"

For the first time Green smiled broadly. "I'll say! So does our CAG. He grounded both of them at Ford Island shortly before we sailed. Accused them of 'disrespectful and insubordinate comments to a superior officer.'"

"Those are my boys." Rogers chuckled aloud. Then, fearing he was assuming too much, he asked, "Are they okay, sir?"

"Well, they were still alive six hours ago."

Rogers stood up to go. "Thank you, sir." *Alive six hours ago. That's par golf in this league.*

19.

SATURDAY, 6 JUNE

USS HAMMANN, 0415

"Hello, old girl." CJ Callaway realized he had spoken his thoughts, and was mildly embarrassed. But the dawn light barely illuminating the destroyer's deck showed that sailors on both sides of him shared the sentiment.

A few yards away, United States Ship *Yorktown* rode uneasily on the darkened sea. She canted dangerously to port, and Callaway determined by seaman's eye that, if anything, her list had only worsened in the thirty-six hours since she was abandoned. He imagined two of her huge fuel bunkers almost completely flooded—

each as large as a three-story house—and marveled that the bulkheads had withstood such tremendous water pressure for so long.

Less than five years ago, the American people had paid some twenty-five million dollars for the splendid new aircraft carrier. CJ Callaway knew as well as anyone how hard it was to come by that much money for a nation climbing out of what his generation always would know as the Depression.

Standing in the cool morning air, he thought for a moment of what that experience meant to an East Texas farm family. Failure of the local bank meant a perilously close brush with foreclosure on the mortgage. It meant ten- and twelve-hour days most of the year, working before daylight and after dusk, with school crammed in between. It meant one and sometimes two extra jobs for most of the kids—when work was available—and literally counting pennies. Callaway recalled thinking that things were tough for his family, but his mother always insisted the Callaways were more fortunate than so many of their neighbors, who had to sell out and move away.

But slowly—sometimes agonizingly slowly—things had improved. Rural electrification had been the most important; and about the same time, the farm got indoor plumbing. CJ, always mechanically adept, had recognized the growing opportunities for a smart youngster with an aptitude for studying engineering. His father, God bless him, had insisted that the boy attend college. *Son, there ain't nothing you can't do with an engineering diploma. Th' oil business, farm machin'ry, construction— you name it.* Jimmie Callaway had been proven correct, but not before dying in a tractor accident during CJ's junior year at A&M.

Daddy was sure-nuff right, CJ told himself. *Ain't nothing I can't do—including keeping Old Yorky afloat.* The thought occurred to him that maybe his generation had to experience the Depression to develop the character and the stamina and the enthusiasm to win this truly world war.

Callaway watched the lines being secured as *Hammann* lashed herself alongside the crippled carrier. As the sun rose higher and the distance diminished, he saw again the terrible damage his ship had sustained. But even in her critical condition, she was precious. Her twenty-five-million-dollar pricetag no longer had meaning, for her value was beyond computation. Other carriers, bigger and undoubtedly as well-built as CV-5, were under construction at Newport News this moment: CV-9–class ships with historic names like *Essex, Bon Homme Richard, Intrepid* and *Kearsarge*. But ten times *Yorktown's* cost would not replace her next month or anytime this year.

Callaway inhaled, let out his breath and turned to his salvage crew. "Come on, fellas," he said in a soft, low voice. "We got work to do."

"How many carriers can the Japs have out here?" Burnett asked. Rogers was mildly irritated by the whining tone in his friend's voice, but he understood Burnett's attitude. *Just when you think you've got a handle on things, something else pops up.*

A *Hornet* SBD, Eight Baker Two, had reported a Japanese carrier and five destroyers 128 miles southwest of Task Force Sixteen more than ninety minutes ago. Since then there had been no amplification, which put everyone on edge. Rogers was undecided about his reaction to the news. If true—and he knew it might be mistaken identity—it meant another ride through flak and fighters, spiraling downward, trying to ignore the tracers that curled up at you with deceptive laziness.

It also meant another chance to get a hit.

The ready-room teletype clattered again, with its same effect. Conversations ended in midsentence, reading concentration was shattered, and men fitfully dozing in their chairs were roused from thoughts pleasant or otherwise.

"Well, that's more like it," Burnett observed as the screen resolved a puzzle almost two hours old. HORNET SCOUT HAS LANDED. SAYS 0645 REPORT OF CV AND 5 DD WAS RECEPTION ERROR. PILOT REPORTS ONE BB, ONE CA, 3 DD. JAP FORCE HAS NO, REPEAT NO, CV.

Tension eased noticeably in the room as men resumed conversations or returned to reading or pretended sleeping. Rogers, increasingly aware of the laboratory in human stress in which he lived, glanced around. *Most are handling it okay. But some are irritated at the communications department for scaring them unnecessarily.* He recalled that *Yorktown*'s communications officer, Lieutenant Commander Ray, had gathered up all aviators' code books before the battle, insisting that contact reports be sent in plain language. Rogers wondered how an ensign could convince other ships to follow that sensible procedure.

"That still leaves the 0730 contact," Burnett noted. Obviously he wanted to talk. *Maybe he's nervous about being on the flight schedule*, Rogers speculated. *Well, so am I.* "I mean, the message drop from that other *Hornet* pilot reporting a cruiser and three cans," Burnett added.

"I wonder if it's a duplicate of the carrier report, without the flattop," Frank DiBella offered. He was sitting in his "usual" spot now, one row ahead of Rogers and Burnett.

Rogers sat up and shook his head. "Don't think so, Frankie. It's more than fifty miles southeast of that position. I just don't think there'd be that much difference in navigation error over that distance." Rogers looked again at his plotting board, with "Nearest Land" filled in: "Midway, 350 miles, bearing 145."

Burnett thought for a moment. "Hey, we're not all Magellans like you, Buck. Maybe DiBella's onto something. If you look at the ship types, they're not all that different. Five surface ships compared to four." He looked across the aisle. "Could be the same group seen from a different perspective, maybe through clouds."

Rogers stared back, seemingly looking through Burnett, out past the bulkhead to the western horizon. "Yeah, maybe so. I guess we'll find out soon enough, when we get our own scouts back."

"The *Hornet* launched SBDs with fighters about twenty minutes ago," DiBella added. "Maybe we'll hear something from them."

Rogers leaned back and closed his eyes. "I'd like to hear something from the *Yorktown*."

USS YORKTOWN, 0825

Damage control was the sole concern of Commander Clarence Ald-rich, who stood on the port side of the hangar deck, conferring with Lieutenant Commander Joseph Delaney, the chief engineer. Around them the rattle and clanging noise of work parties was unrelenting. Acetylene torches blazed fiery blades across the base of a heavy five-inch gun mount, four of which would go overboard to help reduce thc ship's list.

Delaney scribbled another note to himself, then looked up. "Bud, I don't want to take anything for granted. I almost croaked when I learned the *Hughes* found two more survivors aboard yesterday."

"Yeah. We're searching every accessible part of the ship right now." It had taken a while for word to circulate among a half-dozen ships, but most of the salvagers now knew that two wounded men, left for dead, had attracted the attention of the destroyer *Hughes* by firing a machine gun yesterday morning.

"Jack Callaway's checking progress on the second deck and lower," Aldrich added. "It's a time-consuming process, but without lights down there . . ."

Delaney nodded. "Yeah, I know. Slow going, and spooky." Nobody who had not searched the hell-black interior of a sinking ship could possibly imagine how spooky. The engineer referred to his checklist again. "Okay, we've got men from the gunnery department manning .50 calibers in case of air attack. The *Hammann* is standing off with the other DDs, monitoring the task force fighter-director net. If anything heads our way, she'll signal us."

"Good. We have communicators topside watching for flags or blinker messages." Aldrich shook his head slowly. "I'll feel a hell of a lot better when we get power. I think we may have to bring the *Hammann* back alongside. Otherwise we're stuck waiting for the other tug."

CJ Callaway appeared at the opposite side of the hangar bay and strode "downhill" to port in long, braking strides. He saluted perfunctorily, barely touching the brim of his hat. "I've got some good news," he began.

Aldrich managed a smile. "We sure can stand some."

"Fontaine's people have gone as far as the third deck and found nobody else alive. They're still at it and they'll report back when they're done."

"Very well," Delaney commented. "Did you find any more signs of structural damage?"

"No, sir. From what I could see of the transverse fuel-oil lines, we should be able to pump port to starboard and even up the list. Once we get power, that is."

"Yes, we're going to have the *Hammann* come alongside again and provide power," Delaney explained. "We can't wait indefinitely for another tug, and Captain Buckmaster agrees."

Callaway wiped his sweaty face on one sleeve. "Chief Riker's crew will need pressure to pump water onto that smoldering fire in A–Three-oh-five-A," Callaway began. "Oh, and I also saw Wiltsie's navigation crew. They're trying to bring the rudder amidships but it's slow going. She's still hard over to port."

Delaney heard a loud noise and looked over his shoulder in time to see the spectacular splash of a five-inch antiaircraft gun. He turned back to Callaway. "One step at a time, Lieutenant. One step at a time."

OVERHEAD TASK FORCE SIXTEEN, 1100

Lieutenant Wally Short led his thirty-one SBDs into one more orbit, allowing the tail-end sections to join up. The Scouting Five skipper also had a dozen Wildcats and three Devastators to keep track of—a senior lieutenant leading forty-six aircraft on a mission not too large for a full commander.

Twenty minutes had passed since *Enterprise* had begun launch, but the mission plan and the diverse aircraft involved had complicated things. The three surviving TBDs had only launched at the last minute, and Admiral Spruance had been specific—they were not to attack if there was any opposition. Ordinarily it would have been an absurd order. But this mission was not so much a combat as an execution.

The reported cruiser-destroyer force obviously was hurt, limping westward at ten to twelve knots. If the scout-bombers could set up the attack, allowing the torpedo planes to approach unhindered by AA fire, then Torpedo Six's survivors could exact a measure of revenge for the events of last Thursday morning. Otherwise, they would jettison their one-ton loads and return to base.

Short checked that his squadrons were formed up and set course into the eighteen-knot southwesterly breeze, climbing slowly to conserve fuel. He led his Dauntlesses in snaking S-turns en route to 15,000 feet, lest he outrun the TBDs. For once there was no hurry. This time there would be a chance for coordination, to do it according to prewar doctrine. Aircrews realized it would probably never happen again.

Riding his Dauntless just off Dave Shumway's starboard wing, Phil Rogers glanced back. Barnes was facing forward, guns stowed and canopy closed. *He won't have much to do today*, Rogers thought. *I hope.* Bombing Three now flew two five-plane divisions with five Bombing Six planes composing the third division. Attrition, and its attendant necessity, had forced the mirthful concept of "VB-63" into an operational reality. Rogers had not heard anyone talk about "Scouting 65," but Short's composite unit amounted to that, with sixteen aircraft from the two scout squadrons.

Barely clear of the destroyer screen, the strike leader got a call from *Enterprise*'s radio. "Scarlet Lead from Red Base. New orders; repeat, new orders. BB is your target. May be further along on course. Search for and destroy BB forty miles west of Blue Base target. Acknowledge."

The carrier wave crackled as Short replied. "Scarlet Lead. Roger. Will search forty miles beyond Blue Base's assigned target. This is Scarlet, out."

In the echeloned ranks of ordered Dauntlesses, pilots pulled their plotting boards from beneath their instrument panels. Almost unconsciously, Rogers slid away slightly from Baker Three in order to concentrate on his navigation. The expected contact point, penciled on his "ouija board," was 29–33 North, 175–36 East. *Make it 370 nautical, west-northwest of Midway.* He spun the circular grid and calculated the slight course change from the task force's present position. *About 180 miles total—okay for us but the torpeckers will have to stick with the original target.* He shoved the board back on its rails.

Rogers crayfished back toward his leader, using lots of rudder with opposite stick to offset the closure rate. It was not pretty, but it was effective. There wasn't much reason for tight formation, but he knew that Lieutenant Shumway liked for Bombing Three to look good. *Show the others how it's done.* He thought of the skipper, and wondered if Mr. Leslie knew how well the squadron had done so far.

From ingrained habit, Rogers rotated his head through the horizon, finishing with a quick glance overhead. He appreciated the weather again—CAVU above low, scattered clouds. He returned his scan to his instrument panel, registered everything in the green and continued his visual sweep. *Someday the historians are going to write about this,* he thought. He wanted to remember as many details as he could. The sunlight gleaming on polished plexiglass, dark bombs tucked up beneath light-gray bellies, gunners sitting with their seats facing forward or aft, according to their preferences. *Gosh, I wish I had a camera.*

Rogers inhaled and felt the thinning air fill his lungs. He felt good for no particular reason. A thought occurred to him and he pulled off one glove. Holding up his hand, he examined the fingernails for any sign of blue tint that indicated the onset of hypoxia. *Nope, they look okay. Better keep the oxygen mask handy, though.* He listened to the exhaust from the Cyclone's short stacks. The sewing-machine beat seemed to purr, *Gonna get a hit, gonna get a hit.*

USS YORKTOWN, 1120

The sound of pumps reminded CJ Callaway of the renewed beating of a stilled heart. He hastened up the ladder from the second deck, turned forward in the starboard catwalk and found Commander Aldrich. "We're still in business," Callaway reported.

The damage-control officer held up both hands with fingers crossed. "Here's hoping they can handle the load."

Callaway felt optimistic. "I don't know why not, sir. Commander Delaney's people and some of ours are checking lines and connections in each compartment. So far, so good."

He shifted his gaze to *Hammann's* mottled blue-gray shape, lashed alongside. Lieutenant Commander True, the destroyer's skipper, had informed Captain Buckmaster that it was not possible to hold station indefinitely with hoses linking pumps on both ships. Therefore, the DD had put out mattresses and woven-hemp fenders to protect her thin hull against *Yorktown's* exposed starboard bilge.

Aldrich asked, "How is Chief Riker coming with that fire in A–Three-oh-five?"

"That's the first place we got some hoses," Callaway explained. "The water pressure's holding up, and Riker thinks they'll have it whipped shortly. Anyway, it's no longer a danger."

"Okay. I'm having *Hammann* provide a couple of foamite hoses, too. We need to connect them to our own system here on the flight deck. You can use one of them if you need, but keep the other free for emergencies."

Callaway gave a curt nod. "Yes, sir. Now, what about counterflooding? Do we have enough power yet to handle it?"

"Vavacek's working on it now. Didn't I mention that?"

Callaway suddenly remembered. "Oh. Yes, sir. You did." *I'm still so damn tired. Can't remember everything.* Chief Emile Vavacek, the "oil king," knew everything there was to know about *Yorktown's* complex fuel-oil system—its layout, its requirements and especially its almost human idiosyncracies.

Aldrich pressed his concern on Callaway. "The chief's got a gang rigging an oil-suction hose to our port tanks. As that takes effect we'll naturally reduce the list. But we also need to put a hose into one of the starboard tanks. Then we can start pumping saltwater in there. You with me?"

Embarrassed, Callaway nodded decisively. "Yes, sir. Equalize the weight on both sides by adding to starboard and reducing to port." He felt like a grade-school student reciting multiplication tables.

"You got it." He slapped Callaway on the arm. "Stick with me, Jack. We'll get 'er done."

There was no longer any doubt. The mysterious battleship just did not exist. Rogers raised his microphone and called his gunner. "Barnes, I'm damned if I see anything down there. How about you?"

"No, sir," the reply shot back. "Just miles and miles of miles and miles." Under clear skies with only a few cloud shadows, the ocean was wide open to search. As a precaution Barnes had opened his canopy and deployed his guns, but the chances of enemy aircraft appearing clearly were zero. *No pun intended*, Rogers thought. Still, it had to be cold in that open cockpit at 22,500 feet.

Rogers looked forward again, past Shumway up to the scout formation. Wally Short had followed orders, swinging south around the cruiser-destroyer force, and hunted another thirty or so miles beyond those vessels recently pummeled by *Hornet* SBDs. Rogers mused that Burnett and DiBella had called it right. The Bombing Eight searches had almost certainly spotted the same enemy force, but one pilot reported it fifty-two miles from its actual position.

Radio static buzzed in his earphones. "Scarlet Lead from Red Base. Scarlet Lead from Red Base, over." Rogers perked up. He realized *Enterprise* may have some new information.

Lieutenant Short's clipped voice snapped back. "Red Base from Scarlet Lead. This is Wally. Go ahead."

"Scarlet Lead, you are advised to expedite your attack and return. Please acknowledge."

"Roger. Out."

That's telling 'em, Wally. Rogers felt that every pilot who heard the transmission probably held similar sentiments. *The staff sends us clear out here on a wild-goose chase, then tells us to hurry up and attack the original target.* DiBella had told some VB-3 pilots of a similar situation on Thursday. Evidently unable to stand the torturous waiting, Captain Browning had grabbed the microphone from a staff communicator and exhorted the air group to attack the Japanese carriers. *Enterprise*'s CAG, Lieutenant Commander McClusky, had flippantly replied, "Wilco. As soon as I find the bastards."

Short's division eased into a gentle starboard turn—the mark of a considerate leader. Too tight a turn would either throw the trailing sections to the outside of the turn or cause them to stall while pulling too hard to the inside. Shumway brought "VB-63" around in trail, heading back to the northeast as Short began letting down for a fast run-in to the attack.

Numerous radio calls competed for Rogers's attention. Few of the pilots identified themselves, further compounding the potential for confusion. He thought he recognized a fighter pilot who called, "There is a BB over there!"

Short cut through the chatter. "This is Wally. Target is one BB, ahead about forty miles." More calls ensued, including at least one from *Enterprise*. Apparently some pilots were uncertain of their targets. But Short would not be rushed when there was no need. Taking time to assign targets, he also ensured everyone was in place before attacking. "Smith from Wally. What the hell are you doing over here?" It was unlike the cheerful VS-5 skipper. *We're all tired*, Rogers thought. Four miles below, the victims became more identifiable—at least in size. Rogers eyed the largest. *It could be a battlewagon, then again . . .*

"This is Wally. Pushing over on rear ship now . . ." Something indecipherable as another pilot blocked Short's transmission. Then, "Our objective is the rear ship. Step on it!"

As Shumway nosed over on the rearmost ship, Rogers noticed that the standard, setpiece attack had turned to hash. Two- and three-plane sections, even five-plane divisions, had selected their own run-in headings. *Just as well*, he decided. *It'll split the AA defenses.* He glimpsed Fighting Six's F4Fs slanting down to strafe the two destroyers, suppressing their gunfire. A thought occurred to him. "Barnes, we won't worry about Zeros. Swing around and call the altitudes for me." The gunner acknowledged, stowed his twin-.30 mount and rotated his seat forward.

The target was a big one all right, but Rogers decided it was not a battleship. Somebody had said something about a *Mogami*-class cruiser, and the rakish silhouette seemed to fit the recognition card. Whatever her identity, she was making fifteen knots to the southwest. And she was in trouble. Aside from the severe oil leak trailing in her wake, her topsides were visibly battered from the *Hornet* strike.

Rogers watched for his interval on Shumway, then tipped over from 15,000 feet.

He began setting up the dive geometry. Running in downwind, bow to stern, was not the preferred method, but there wasn't much ack-ack to distract him. "Twelve thousand, sir." Barnes's attention alternated between his own altimeter and the big ship down below.

Let's see, I have to allow more lead than normal, for I'm diving downwind. That'll push my bomb farther along the fall line. But she's not moving very fast, so . . .

"Ten thousand, sir."

He adjusted his controls, placing the crosshairs between the first and second turrets.

"Eight thousand."

Some light flak coming up, but it's not bad. A few tracers crossed his field of view. He realized that one of the nearby destroyers was still in business. *Forget it. They can't hit you at wide deflection.*

"Six thousand."

Waterspouts geysered around the battlecruiser. He had the impression of cascades drenching the forecastle of the battered gray shape. Shumway was dropping and pulling out.

"Five thousand, sir."

The Dauntless was trimmed up, solid in that steady dive that designer Edward H. Heinemann had given to the aviators of the U.S. Navy. Rogers checked the ball in its arched housing below the crosshairs. *Nailed smack in the middle. This is good, this is very good.*

"Three thousand feet." More tracers, seemingly nearer.

It won't get any better. Is this how DiMaggio feels when he knows he's put one in the bleachers? Pull!

The Mark XIII, released at 2,800 feet and 240 knots, fell clear of the belly rack. The SBD's bomb-displacing fork lofted the half-ton weapon in a downward arc, clearing the propeller and sending the bomb toward its target. The fuse safety wires were stripped from the vanes, which began rotating in the relative wind around the aerodynamic shape.

Six point eight seconds later the solid-case weapon impacted on IJNS *Mikuma*'s C turret, two and a half feet port of the centerline. The Mark 21 nose fuse was crushed backward by the impact, and the Mark 23 tail-fuse plunger was impelled forward to initiate detonation.

One-hundredth of a second later 537 pounds of trinitrotoluene were ignited. The bomb's 460-pound casing was shattered into thousands of jagged steel splinters, hundreds of which slashed into the cruiser's bridge. Blast and fragments killed many of the personnel there, and Captain Sakiyama was instantly knocked unconscious with head injuries.

Still recovering from his dive, Phil Rogers felt Max Baer connect with a bare-knuckle roundhouse blow that knocked his right foot off the rudder pedal. Rogers's ephemeral confusion was instantly replaced by searing pain as Hideki Tojo inserted a red-hot poker into the pilot's calf. Rogers cried in surprise, pain and fear, and saw the Pacific Ocean filling the view in his windscreen.

"The captain says let's break for lunch in about ten minutes," Delaney said to Callaway. "Pass the word."

"Aye, aye, sir." Callaway turned to Riker and said, "Chief, I'd like you to round up Newland, Slagle, Moshafsky and Hilden. Soon as you can after chow, let's meet portside amidships to transfer the rest of the portable gear we'll need."

Granville Riker beamed his pleasure. He tugged on his chief petty officer's cap and set about organizing the crew he would need. Working topside in the sunshine offered a pleasant contrast to the semilighted confines of the fourth-deck generator room. But electrical power was being restored with *Hammann* alongside, and somehow that made a sailor feel better. The list was only slowly being corrected, but every degree represented a return to something approaching normalcy.

"Who's for sandwiches and coffee on the flight deck?" Callaway asked the work crew. In fifteen seconds he was the last man through the knee-knocker hatch into the passageway and the ladder leading topside.

BAKER EIGHTEEN, 1255

Rogers did not remember recovering from the dive. He was sure he had blacked out from the panic-induced hard pull on the control stick. Since his usual G tolerance was over four and one-half times the force of gravity, he assumed he had pulled five or more Gs. *Not that it matters*, he thought. *We're still flying.*

He checked the magnetic compass suspended from the canopy bow; the Dauntless was headed northeast. He scanned the gauges and found that he had to force himself to focus on them individually. His practiced scan was gone—destroyed by the pain in his right leg and the damage to his confidence. He remembered the dive, remembered the crossways tracers and his reaction. *They can't hit you at wide deflection.* Famous last words.

The R-1820 was running smoothly at cruise power. *Oh, yes. I did that after Bernie joined up.* He looked off his port wingtip and saw the other SBD less than a wingspan away. Burnett's face was plainly visible in the open cockpit, but somehow the features were slightly blurred. Rogers felt again the warm liquid running down his leg into his sock. *That's why.*

He tried to focus his thoughts, to concentrate on what was important. *Bernie will lead me back to the ship*, he thought. The irony struck him. The worst navigator in the squadron leading the best. Well, at least the best ensign. He estimated they were cruising at 6,000 feet—it was too hard to decipher the altimeter just now. *Got to clear my head.* He reached for his oxygen mask. Then, *No, not yet. Need to stop the bleeding.* But how? *Tourniquet. They don't give us medical kits but they should. Why didn't somebody in BuAer think of that?* He made a mental note to write an indignant letter to the Bureau of Aeronautics, Navy Department, Washington, D.C. *Gentlemen: I'm bleeding to death over the goddamn Pacific Ocean because none of you thought any of your aviators would get shot full of holes in the performance of their duties. Screw you very much. Philip Rogers, Ensign, USNR. Hee.*

He picked up the microphone and remembered to depress the key. "Barnes, I'm gonna try to put a tourniquet on my leg. Can you hold her steady for a while?"

"Yes, sir! Just one minute."

In the rear cockpit Radioman Bill Barnes leaned down to his left, unclipped the control stick from its bracket and carefully inserted it into the socket in the floor. He moved it side to side and saw the wings rock in response. "I got it, sir."

Rogers let go of the controls. He thanked God that Barnes had been so persistent in badgering him about getting some stick time. Many pilots refused to devote limited training time to showing their gunners how to control the plane. The navy had thoughtfully equipped the SBD-3 type airplane with stick, rudder pedals, throttle and flight instruments in the rear cockpit. There was no way to extend wheels, flaps or tailhook, but that was all right.

Unfastening his seatbelt, Rogers reached under his Mae West and fumbled with his jacket zipper. In frustration, he removed his gloves and stuffed them between his parachute and the seat. Once the jacket was unzipped, he unbuckled his cloth flight-suit belt and withdrew it from the loops around his waist. It was surprisingly hard work.

He noticed a slight change in engine pitch and saw the nose climbing above the horizon. But Barnes caught the error and leveled out. *Good boy.* Rogers had impressed upon him that flying perfectly straight and level was one of the most difficult of all aviation skills.

Rogers lifted his right leg, slipped the belt beneath it and fumbled with the buckle again. Once the belt was through the loop, he cinched it—hard—between knee and crotch. First-aid instructors said to release a tourniquet every five minutes—or was it fifteen minutes? Rogers decided to leave it tight.

He leaned back for a moment, his helmet against the headrest. He was tempted to close his eyes. *No, better not*. Instead, he reached for his oxygen mask and strapped it on. He turned the regulator to 100 percent and sucked in the vapors. *Slow and steady, don't hyperventilate*. In a few minutes his light-headedness began to abate a little.

He put his hands back on the controls and waggled the stick in the I've-got-it signal. "All yours, sir," Barnes said. Rogers moved the stick again. It was easier than talking.

USS YORKTOWN, 1336

Except for the slant of the deck, they might have been picnicking on a cruise ship. The early afternoon sunshine beamed down through low, broken clouds, providing a balmy atmosphere. Sitting on the deck edge in their respective groups, men were enjoying cold sandwiches and hot coffee, discussing the progress of *Yorktown*'s rejuvenation.

"Commander Delaney says the list's down to twenty-two degrees," Callaway told Chief Riker. "Funny, how only five or six degrees can make so much difference."

Callaway swung his legs into the starboard catwalk. He could look down on *Hammann*'s stern and count the depth charges on their racks. But he was more interested in the portable gear his gang would shortly move aboard the carrier: two submersible pumps and more hose lengths. He noticed lines rigged from the destroyer's bilges to the carrier's starboard tanks, further enhancing the counterflooding effort.

He looked back up the deck and called, "Chief Riker, I'm going over to the *Hammann* to make sure our gear's ready to move. Meet me there with your crew in a few minutes." Riker acknowledged with a wave and Callaway swung himself down to the destroyer's stern.

Automatic-weapon fire greeted his arrival. *What the hell's going on?* He sprinted to starboard and looked forward, toward the noise. He saw a 20mm mount unaccountably firing into the water. Then somebody yelled, "Torpedo attack!"

Now he understood. The gunners were trying to detonate a spread of torpedoes racing toward *Hammann*'s vulnerable starboard beam. Callaway saw white geysers several hundred yards out. Though he could not see the torpedo wakes, he knew that was where they were.

Hammann's port engine churned beneath his feet as the skipper ordered full astern in hopes of backing out of danger. Unnecessarily, general quarters sounded and sailors scrambled around Callaway en route to their stations.

But CJ Callaway had no GQ station on this ship. He looked back up at *Yorktown*, and thought he saw Riker staring down at him from the canted deck. The distance between them was measured in yards. It might as well have been millennia.

Callaway looked back to seaward. Now he saw at least two faint traces in the water, barreling toward him at forty knots. More 20mm bursts splashed across their path, to no effect. He gripped the rail, entranced by the scene as the scarlet thread of anxiety was double-woven into the tapestry of his consciousness. He heard one last chattering burst from the Oerlikons, then braced himself. *This is it*.

The first torpedo—one of four from the Japanese submarine *I-168*—smashed into *Hammann*'s number-two fire room. Callaway felt it as an impossibly vicious rending of ship and sea and even sky. The blast overpressure broke one eardrum as it broke the destroyer's back. He was never conscious of the 1,700-ton ship breaking apart beneath him as he was flung in an ungainly arc into the sea.

He had enough presence of mind to gulp in a lungful of air before dropping headfirst into the water. He crawled his way upward, out of darkness into the light, emerging from the roiling turbulence of the disturbed ocean. Breaking the surface, he had only a faint image of *Hammann*'s remnants sliding under—no longer secured to *Yorktown*'s side.

Then two more Type 95 torpedoes punched into the carrier's vulnerable belly, ripping her innards apart. She reeled terribly, settled back down and began to die.

Callaway and dozens of *Hammann*'s crew floundered in the water, some killed outright by the additional torpedo detonations. Some, like Callaway, were far enough from the impacts to survive with internal injuries from the blast pressure. But Callaway was dully aware of a sailor next to him, spitting water and crying and thrashing in futility to escape what was coming. "Good Christ! The depth charges aren't safetied!"

Moments later the destroyer's shattered stern reached the preset depth of the weapons intended to crush the hulls of enemy submarines like the one that had just killed *Hammann* and *Yorktown*. But CJ

Callaway, son of Jimmie and Clydia of Jacksonville, Texas; husband of Angela and father of Vernon, never registered that thought as the charges exploded and crushed the life out of him.

BAKER EIGHTEEN, 1349

Rogers heard Burnett make the call. "Red Base, this is Scarlet Flight. Three Baker Eighteen is returning with a wounded pilot. Request you take him aboard immediately."

There was no response, and Rogers thought Burnett would have to repeat the call. Then *Enterprise* came back. "Scarlet, please stand by." More silence.

"Mr. Rogers, what do you think's going on?"

"Don't know for sure, Barnes. I guess . . . I guess they're deciding whether to risk a fouled deck with so many planes in the air. They may tell us to ditch."

Barnes absorbed that information, then replied, "Want me to take it for a while, sir?"

Rest while you can. "Okay, thanks. Just keep it on this course. The task force is up ahead. I think Mr. Burnett has the ships in sight."

"Yes, sir." Barnes sounded remarkably calm for a young man who was about to trust his life to a wounded pilot in a deck landing attempt or a crash landing in the ocean.

Rogers bit off a moan, even though nobody could hear him. His thigh was almost numb from the tourniquet, but his lower leg now was in constant pain. He rubbed his thigh and, for the first time, pulled up the leg of his flight suit. He was astonished at the amount of dried blood on the khaki fabric. *Damn! I can't afford to lose any more.* He wasn't sure, but he thought the bleeding had abated if not stopped. It was a nasty gash, but only an entrance wound appeared on the right side. *Whatever hit me is still in my leg.* This time he did groan. *Damn it to hell—hurts like a son of a bitch.*

"Scarlet Flight from Red Base. We are recovering fighters first. Damaged aircraft will recover last. Over."

Rogers raised the microphone. "This is Baker One-Eight. I'm hit in one leg, bleeding like hell." *Well, I was bleeding like hell. And I damn sure can't get that blood back.* "Over."

Another "Stand by." Then, "Baker Eighteen from Red Base. Your choice—land in the water now or wait for the others to recover. The forward destroyer has been alerted. Estimate ten minutes to complete recovery. Over."

"I'll wait. Over." *Why did I say that?* He looked down at the surface. It was rippled by a strong breeze but there appeared little or no wave action. Good ditching weather. It occurred to him that he may have more gasoline than blood to spare. He took the controls again.

Burnett led 3-B-18 in a descending racetrack pattern astern of the carrier. He timed it well. As the last Wildcat snagged a wire, Burnett led Rogers into a straight-in approach, driving up the carrier's white wake. Rogers appreciated the setup. *I won't have to make any turns.* GUMP: gas—enough; undercarriage—*thump-thump*, down and locked; mixture—rich; prop—low pitch. Flaps and hook—down. Canopy—locked back. Rogers felt the Dauntless yaw awkwardly, and his pained leg protested against the movement of rudder correction.

Barnes's voice came over the intercom again. "Sir, our starboard flap's all shot up. Part of it's gone!"

That explains it. "Barnes, if we go in the drink, get out as soon as we stop moving. Don't wait for me."

"Aye, aye, sir," Rogers did not honestly think his gunner would leave the aircraft without him. Neither did Barnes.

"Baker Eighteen from Red Base. Be advised, you are approved for one pass at the deck. In event of a waveoff, you are to proceed straight ahead and ditch in front of the destroyer one mile off our port bow. Acknowledge."

"Baker Eighteen. Roger." *Now shut up and let me land.*

Approaching the ship, Rogers found his senses heightened. Still sucking oxygen, he thought the colors seemed brighter in the vivid sunlight. The sound of his engine was louder, clearer. Half a mile from the stern, he noticed the signal flags streaming from their halyards and the smoke from the large, rectangular stack. And there were the LSO's paddles.

Get me aboard, Lieutenant. Keep me coming. The colored paddles suddenly canted, right one up, left one down. *Level your wings.* Rogers corrected with a crisp movement of the stick. But the controls felt sloppy. *Looking better, lineup is fine, maybe a little low. Yes, there's the "low" signal. Two corrections on one pass—not so good. A tad of power. Careful, don't overcorrect! Level the nose. C'mon, where's the cut?* Rogers glimpsed a "high," then something that looked a lot like the cut. *Do it!*

He held slight back pressure on the stick, chopped the throttle and felt the Dauntless start to settle. Immediately he knew the LSO had given him a gift—a cut instead of a waveoff. Rogers felt the lurch as his hook snagged the wire before his wheels contacted the deck. *Damn—an in-flight engagement!*

The SBD's nose lifted as the arresting wire ran out to its limit. Then, with airspeed and forward motion depleted, the dive-bomber dropped eleven feet downward toward the unyielding wood planks. Rogers braced himself in his seat.

It came with more force, more concentrated violence, than anything he could remember. It was worse than any catapult shot. The landing-gear oleos compressed to their limits, hardly damping out the initial impact. Hitting port mainmount first, the SBD's weight blew the left tire, then the starboard wheel smashed down.

Rogers was pitched forward. His right hand shot out to brace himself, too late. His face went into the padded end of his sight, which imprinted itself below his right eye. He saw flashes of light and stars in daytime.

The Dauntless rocked tremulously, seemed to shudder, then quivered to a stop. When Rogers's vision cleared, he looked left and saw the bulge in the aluminum skin over the port wing. *Landing gear's busted*, he realized. *Almost came through the top of the wing. Good old Dauntless.*

Then the crash crew was there, unbuckling him and lifting him trembling from the cockpit, and one of them was saying, "We've got you, sir. We've got you."

USS VIREO, 1515

Captain Elliott Buckmaster stood bareheaded on the stern of the little fleet tug, borrowed prayer book in hand. Two dozen or more *Yorktown* salvagers arranged themselves in a semicircle around their skipper, heads bowed as he completed the service for burial of the dead at sea.

Standing in the second row, Chief Granville Riker found himself staring at the center flag-draped shroud. He wished he had not seen the remains of Lieutenant CJ Callaway, for until now that word had been merely part of the lexicon of the trade. But the crushing force of hundreds of pounds of overpressure had rendered several victims of *Hammann*'s depth charges unrecognizable. Riker had been the one who noticed the wedding ring on the officer's left hand. The gold band with the initials *CJC/ALC* was carefully wrapped in the lieutenant's handkerchief, secured in Riker's shirt pocket.

Callaway was not the only one, of course; some 80 of the destroyer's complement of 240 were dead or missing.

Buckmaster was reading, "Unto Almighty God we commend the souls of our brothers departed, and we commit their bodies to the deep, in sure and certain hope of the resurrection unto eternal life, through our Lord, Jesus Christ."

Riker glanced over at the doomed carrier. He marveled that she remained afloat, and to the casual observer she would have appeared almost normal. But those who crewed her, who served her—who loved her—recognized the awful truth. She was nearly on an even keel now, as the two submarine torpedoes had balanced her portside damage with comparable damage to starboard. But she rode sickeningly low in the water.

Riker suddenly heard Buckmaster intone, "Amen." The other sailors repeated the ancient word, Riker included. Then the burial party slipped the three sacks overboard; they hardly made a sound as they entered the waters of eternity.

USS ENTERPRISE, 1906

Rogers felt a touch on his arm. He twitched awake, turned his head on the pillow and focused. Two khaki shapes.

"Sorry to wake you," Burnett said. "We can only stay a couple minutes."

"How you doing, Buck?" DiBella asked.

Rogers shifted his weight, rolling onto his left elbow under the blanket. "Gosh, I'm glad you fellows came. I'm doing okay, I guess." He pointed at his right leg, bandaged and immobile. "The medicos say I have to stay down for a while. I'll get a full evaluation in Pearl."

"Well, it won't be long, then," Burnett offered. "We're headed back right now."

Rogers turned his head upward in puzzlement. "You mean it's over?"

DiBella folded his arms and nodded. "Affirmative. Admiral Spruance just ordered the task force back eastward." He grinned. "Looks like I'll get to meet this gal that Bernie's been telling me so much about."

Sally. I haven't even thought of her since . . . when? Rogers rubbed his eyes. He still felt the lingering drowsiness of the anesthetic. "What about the Japs?"

"Guess they're headed for the barn, too," DiBella replied. "We think the *Mogami* cruiser sank. Scouting Six flew a photo mission this afternoon. Dobson says she's in mighty poor shape—low in the water, guns drooping overboard."

Burnett touched Rogers's arm. "Hey, you got a solid hit, Buck. Smack on the third turret. I missed to starboard." He shrugged philosophically. "How's it feel to sink a cruiser?"

Rogers lay back on his pillow. "Hell, I didn't sink that ship." He looked up at his friends. "*We* sank her. Us and the *Hornet* squadrons." *It feels good, that's how it feels.* "Hey, how's my gunner? Barnes. I haven't seen him since—"

"He's okay," Burnett answered. "I checked on him for you. He got a sprained back in that arrival that you call a carrier landing, but he's okay. Said he'll come see you tomorrow."

DiBella glanced around the immaculately clean spaces of *Enterprise*'s sick bay. Only a few beds were occupied—far fewer than most people would have expected after the largest naval battle of the war. *That's because aircrew casualties usually don't come back*, he thought bitterly.

"Buck, we have to go," he said. "But now that we see how you're faring, propped up in the sack like the queen of Sheba, we won't lose any sleep worrying about you." Impulsively, he extended his hand. "See you later, shipmate." Rogers squeezed as hard as he could.

"I'll drop by tomorrow," Burnett said. "Get some sleep."

"Hey, Bernie."

Burnett turned back toward the bed. "Yeah?"

"Thanks for bringing me back."

Burnett's mouth turned up at one corner. "Oh, it was nothing, really. Anyone with a genius for navigation could have done it."

"Well, just the same, it would have been damn lonely up there without you." Burnett waved as he walked away.

As the footsteps receded, Rogers snuggled under the covers. He felt warm and pleasantly sleepy. Then his eyes blinked open. *I didn't ask them about the* Yorktown. *Well, I'll ask later.*

"Sally, look at this!"

Sallyann Downey turned from her station at the reception desk. Ordinarily, Mary Tanaka's call from across the room would have been considered a major breach of decorum in a library—even a library that had closed for the day.

Mary held aloft the evening edition of the *Star Bulletin*. From twenty feet away, Sally read the huge black headline:

MIDWAY BATTLE TOLL: JAPANESE SHIPS SUNK

Sally scurried around the end of her counter and ran to Mary's side. Together they read the announcement, released that afternoon from Admiral Nimitz's Pacific Fleet headquarters. Behind her rimless glasses, Sally's dark eyes scanned the subhead and the right-hand column, registering key phrases.

"Two or Three Carriers Down; Battleships, Cruisers Hard Hit."

". . . skill and devotion of our armed forces . . . momentous victory in the making . . . Pearl Harbor partially avenged . . ."

Then her heart turned over. "One of our carriers was hit and some planes were lost. Our personnel casualties were light."

Mary shook her head. "It doesn't really say very much," she sighed. Visually she scrolled the six columns, discounting items regarding camouflage in Hawaii, comments by the governor general, and the 250th career win by Yankees pitcher Red Ruffing, 3–0 over Cleveland. "Nothing about which ships were involved."

Sally looked at her friend. "No, but Phil's there, Mary. He can't be anywhere else. Can he?"

Mary lowered the paper, avoiding Sally's questioning eyes. "No, I suppose not."

Unconsciously, Sally tapped her fingertips together in a prayerful attitude. "Oh, Mary, I almost wish I didn't know about this battle. How long do you think we'll have to wait?"

Mary Tanaka's small hand rested on Sally's shoulder. "Obviously the battle is over. It should not be too long." She looked to the atlas resting on its table, opened to a two-page spread of the Pacific Ocean. "Midway is not very far. The ships should be back soon."

Sally stood staring at the newsprint, reading none of it. She wrapped her arms around herself and sought to straighten out her conflicting emotions. *I was right not to commit to marrying him*, she told herself. *It's bad enough just caring about someone in wartime. If you're married . . .*

But I do love him. I want him to know that. She decided she wanted to be the lover of Ensign Philip Rogers. *If only we can be together again.*

She looked again at the PacFleet announcement. She noticed that toward the end of the text Admiral Nimitz had added a little pun. "Perhaps we will be forgiven," he said, "if we claim we are about midway to our objective."

20.

SUNDAY, 7 JUNE

USS VIREO, 0455

"She's going fast now, sir." Chief Riker spoke without looking away from the spectacle that fixed his attention. Lieutenant (junior grade) Carlton Fontaine had just come on deck like everyone else not required below.

Fontaine glanced over his shoulder at the destroyers circling two miles from the sinking carrier. "I guess we should count ourselves lucky, Chief. We have a better view than the men who transferred to the cans."

"Yes, sir." Riker's voice carried no enthusiasm whatsoever. He felt as if he were back in his grandfather's cabin in the West Virginia hollow, waiting patiently for the old man to die. It was part of growing up, that was all. A boy took his turn sitting with the infirm and the aged, and in the presence of death he learned about life. He had respected Grandpappy Duncan more than he had loved the stern old mountaineer, and now, standing on *Vireo*'s unstable deck in the slanting early sunlight, Granville Riker realized that he loved his sinking ship more than he had loved most humans.

It wasn't an easy deathwatch, especially for a plank owner. The sea service accords special status to those who place a warship in commission, and Riker had been aboard since *Yorktown*'s commissioning pennant first fluttered in the Virginia breeze on 30 September 1937. Books and newspapers often wrote how great ships died "proudly," or even "like a lady." *Yorktown* was being denied that elegant death. Her severe port list became progressively worse until she exposed her entire starboard beam below the waterline.

"Oh, my God." Fontaine's expression was echoed up and down the rail of the little tug. Riker saw the two great holes blown in *Yorktown*'s side, the death wounds inflicted by that goddamned Japanese pigboat. With a professional precision he did not feel, Riker eyed the ugly shark-mouth gouges of the torpedo explosions and determined that they had struck around frames eighty-five and ninety-five.

From across the water came audible, grating sounds. Occasionally metallic *clangs* of heavy equipment tumbling inside the tortured hull could be heard, reminding Fontaine of a loose fitting inside the bass drum of his trap set back when he played in a college combo. Increasingly loud creaks and sharp groans came to unwilling ears, and the professional seamen knew their meaning. "Another bulkhead's collapsed," muttered a first-class boilerman next to Riker.

Moments later *Yorktown* rolled over on her port beam and her mud-red bottom turned skyward, her rudder and screws obscenely exposed to the early morning sky. Behind him, Riker heard a shuffle of feet and dimly was aware of an order from the lieutenant commanding the tug. Her flag was lowered to half-staff and, without command, men removed their caps.

Then came a low, rolling rumble from within the carrier, followed by a surging burble of water as air was displaced from the hull. With another loud protest—the sound of high-tensile steel being shorn by exceptional pressure—USS *Yorktown* (CV-5) dropped vertically from the sight of man, on her way 3,000 fathoms to the ocean floor.

Phil Rogers sat up in bed, reading a Zane Grey western loaned him by one of the medical orderlies. It was a 1934 volume titled *The Code of the West*, one of the many Grey novels Rogers had not read. But since the popular writer had died only three years before, Rogers determined there was ample time to catch up with the series.

For a moment Rogers wondered how the dentist-turned-novelist would have treated the recently concluded Battle of Midway. It seemed to feature all the essential elements: a conflict between Good and Evil, a desperate fight against odds, and a dramatic showdown ending in an unexpectedly lopsided victory for the forces of Good. *We're the posse in the white hats*, Rogers mused. Then he recalled that every fleet on earth boasted white hats, including the Imperial Japanese Navy and that of the Third Reich.

Well, so much for symbolism. Rogers harbored a secret theory—more a hope, actually—that long-lost letters of Herman Melville would be discovered, proving conclusively that *Moby Dick* was never intended as anything other than a rattling good sea story.

Rogers heard a medic say, "He's in that bed over there." Looking up, the pilot saw William E. Barnes, Aviation Radioman Second Class, approaching him.

"Good morning, sir." Barnes twisted his Dixie-cup hat in both hands. "I hope you're feeling all right."

"Lots better, thanks." Rogers motioned to a chair which Barnes pulled alongside the bed. "How are you, Bill?"

The gunner's face showed a trace of surprise. "Me? Why, I'm fine, Mr. Rogers."

"I heard you got a wrenched back in my so-called landing."

Barnes glanced at the bulkhead behind Rogers. "Well, ah, yes, sir. I mean, nothin' serious." He paused to gather his thoughts. "The flight surgeon says I'll be okay by the time we get back to Pearl."

"Well, I'm damn glad to know it. I really made a mess of that landing. I guess the plane's a washout, huh?"

"I don't think so, sir. The leading chief of Bombing Six seems to think it'll be salvageable at the depot level."

"Really?" Rogers wondered if he could check with the officer commanding Pearl Harbor Assembly and Repair. Somehow it was important just now that 3-B-18 should fly again.

"Uh, Mr. Rogers, I don't know if you've heard yet . . ."

His reverie broken, Rogers concentrated on Barnes again. "Heard what?"

Barnes crumpled his hat again. "Well, sir, it's all over the ship. The *Yorktown* sank early this morning."

Rogers fought to grasp the meaning of those words. "Ohh, no." He looked directly into Barnes's eyes. "What happened?"

"Don't know, sir. Just that she was torpedoed by a Jap sub yesterday and sank a few hours ago."

"Casualties?"

Barnes shook his head. "No word there, either. Apparently a destroyer was alongside, though. Both ships went down."

And I was thinking about a lopsided victory. "Well, maybe that's the end of it, Barnes. If we really are headed for Pearl."

"Ah, yes, sir. We're still headed southeast, anyway." Barnes leaned forward in his chair. "Mr. Rogers, how soon will they let you fly again?"

Rogers managed a smile. "I'd like to know myself. Guess they won't know until I get a full exam at Pearl Harbor."

"Well, sir, I was just wonderin' about that. You see, I'm afraid they'll transfer me out or at least put me with a new pilot, and . . ."

"Who said that?" Rogers's voice was clipped, pointed.

"Well, nobody, sir. Not yet." Barnes seemed taken aback. "But not knowing how long you'll be laid up, I just wondered."

Rogers got his voice and his emotions under control. "Hell, I'm surprised you haven't asked for another pilot. I nearly broke your back in that landing."

"Listen, Mr. Rogers. I don't want no other pilot!" At that, Barnes's eyes widened. Enlisted men did not take that tone of voice with officers of the United States Navy. He hastened to explain himself. "See, you and me, we've been through a lot together. I figure if I can't stay your radioman, well, I'd like to put in for flight training myself."

Rogers felt the lump rising in his throat. *Where does that kind of trust come from? That kind of loyalty?* "You mean it?"

Barnes's outthrust chin was answer enough. "Damn right I do. Sir."

Rogers thought that if he accomplished nothing else in this war, he wanted Bill Barnes to have the right to address him as Phil. *He's earned it, and then some.* "All right, I'll tell you what. If I can't stay with the squadron, I'll recommend that you go to Pensacola as soon as a slot's open. Otherwise, after our tour out here—whenever that is—I'll recommend it anyway."

Barnes's face looked as if the sun had just shone upon it. "Gosh, Mr. Rogers, that'd be swell. It . . . it's more than I ever expected."

"You deserve it, Bill. You're as good a radioman as we have in the squadron, and you've a Zero to your credit. I'm certain either Mr. Leslie or Mr. Shumway would endorse a recommendation."

Barnes rose from the chair and placed it back against the bulkhead. "I'd better get going, sir. Don't want to keep you from mending." He almost reached out to shake hands. "Well, I'll be seeing you, Mr. Rogers. Thanks very much."

"No, Barnes. Thank *you*."

IJNS ARASHI, 2358

The first watch, 2000 to 2400, was not a favored duty assignment in any navy, but Lieutenant Fuji consoled himself with the knowledge that he might have drawn the midnight to 0400 time slot. In another two minutes he would be relieved by the junior officer of the watch, who no doubt would read the captain's night orders and diligently perform as the emperor expected of a Japanese naval officer. *If he can stay awake with nothing to occupy him*, Fuji mused. After all, Takeo Fuji had once been an ensign himself.

The destroyer's navigator shifted his weight as *Arashi* dug her nose into a trough. It would be good to climb into his bunk and sleep away the rest of the night. Fuji allowed himself to contemplate the cool feeling of the sheets on his legs—

"Bridge, we have an emergency message!" The communications watch called up from the radio shack, accelerating Fuji's pulse. He leaned toward the speaker. "Watch officer of the bridge. State your message." He released the switch.

"Two destroyers collided a few minutes ago, sir. *Isonami* has lost more than three meters off the bow, speed reduced to eleven knots. *Uranami* reports capable of twenty-four knots."

Fuji's mind raced, cataloging the tasks that needed to be accomplished. "Casualties?"

"None mentioned, Lieutenant."

"Keep me informed."

Fuji smashed his right fist against the bulkhead. *Damn it to hades! Another collision, only two nights after* Mogami *and* Mikuma, *which led to the destruction of one and mauling of the other.* At least in this situation Fuji told himself the damaged warships were too far beyond enemy aircraft for the dreadful retribution the battlecruisers had suffered.

Fuji slumped into the captain's chair, pondering his options. Ordinarily he would wake Watanabe at a time like this; allow the skipper to decide what to do. Neither stricken ship had requested assistance, and others were closer than *Arashi*. Watanabe undoubtedly would be perturbed at having his sleep disturbed over an incident that did not directly affect his ship. Captain Ariga, though . . . he took a different view of such things. However, informing the division commander without going through channels to the ship's captain would be a breach of decorum as well as discipline. Fuji considered the options and decided to awaken both officers. *They will probably both berate me*, he gloomed. *I wonder what else can go wrong?*

21.

MONDAY, 8 JUNE

SAND ISLAND, MIDWAY

Dripping water from its landing gear and wingtip floats, 51-P-7 waddled up from the basin. As the PBY-5A strained awkwardly onto the seaplane ramp, First Lieutenant Jim Carpenter thought it resembled nothing so much as an ungainly pelican attempting a sea-to-shore transition. Like many marine aviators, he had opted for the leathernecks in part because the corps was "tactical," with few multiengine (and therefore noncombat) aircraft.

Now, however, as Peter Seven swung around under high throttle to its twin Pratt and Whitney radial engines, Carpenter had to admit that

PBYs were the most popular aircraft at Midway. Their long range and amphibian capability endeared them to downed fliers—and to those who waited patiently for their return from each search.

Carpenter noticed a VP-51 ensign whom he knew slightly, talking to a camera crew. The film unit seemed to be everywhere lately, reportedly led by "that Hollywood guy," a Commander Ford, USNR.

The ensign noticed Carpenter, walked over, saluted and addressed him almost casually. "Hi, Lieutenant. Still meeting each arrival, I see." Carpenter had spoken to the man occasionally over the past three days.

"Not every one. Just seems that way." He nodded toward the filmmakers. "What's with the movie crew? Something worth filming going on?"

The PatRon officer grinned. "Their CO is the director who did *Stagecoach, The Grapes of Wrath* and *How Green Was My Valley.* Apparently he has a special commission to show the folks back home what happens here." The ensign leaned close and spoke in a confidential tone. "Either he's as Irish as Paddy's pig or he works awful damn hard to give that impression. Anyhow, there are supposed to be some survivors on this plane and Ford's crew will shoot their arrival."

Carpenter's response was limited to a nod as the P-boat pilot ran up the engines to a deafening level, making speech impossible. Abruptly the R-1830s died in a roaring silence as fuel mixture was cut port and starboard.

Carpenter lowered his hands from his ears. "I wonder if there's any of our men aboard." He did not add that he was one of a handful of VMF-221 pilots ambulatory enough—and sober enough—to make the trip over from Eastern Island. Besides, nobody had said he couldn't catch a ride on the morning PT-boat run. But Carpenter did not want to explain that Sergeant Manning still was running the squadron on a de facto basis while Captains Humberd, Carl and one or two others rotated cockpit alerts. Nor did he feel like explaining his sense of obligation, diluted by decreasing hopes, that just one more 221 survivor might be found.

The groundcrew gathered around the PBY's port blister which an aircrewman raised. Carpenter kept his distance, aware that he appeared just another curious onlooker, but he anxiously scanned the figures moving inside the Catalina. There was no proof that this search had yielded anything. Sometimes the P-boats found nothing, or merely signs of flotsam. Yesterday Carpenter had heard a crewman casually mention they had machine-gunned a couple of empty black rafts. American rafts were yellow. *Well, no point letting some Japs find something to float on*. But still . . .

There! A khaki flight suit. Not the usual blue fatigues of a PBY crewman. The aviator moved slowly, almost painfully, accepting help descending from the blister. On the ground he was immediately wrapped in a blanket and shown toward a waiting ambulance. The man stopped and turned around, apparently to wait for a companion.

Carpenter took two paces forward, accidentally jostling a cameraman. *Something vaguely familiar about this one*, he thought. The second survivor alighted from the amphibian and accepted a blanket around his shoulders. When he turned to follow his escort, Carpenter's memory kicked in. "Excuse me," he called. "Johnny Stanley!"

Lieutenant (junior grade) John M. Stanley swiveled his sunburnt face toward the voice. After a moment's hesitation a light of recognition flickered in his eyes. "Why, Carpenter. Jim Carpenter." He extended his hand. "What the hell you doing here?"

The marine warmly shook hands. "Same as you. Surviving." He tried to smile. "It's a long way from Pensacola, isn't it?"

Carpenter's former classmate scratched his four-day beard and nodded seriously. "Yeah. Nobody told us about this end of the business." He noted the marine's face. "You get shot up?"

Carpenter touched the bandage on his cheek. "Morning of the fourth. Twenty-five of us intercepted a hundred or so Japs about forty miles out. Fifteen minutes later we had eleven pilots left."

"Jesus," Stanley said with feeling. "I thought *we* had it rough."

"Did you tangle with Zeros, too?"

Stanley's mouth turned from a frown to a sneer. "Hell, no. I haven't seen one damn Jap. Our skipper just ran us out of gas."

Carpenter leaned forward, hands on his hips. "Whaaat?"

"Oh, yeah. First-class snafu. You know I went to Fighting Eight in the *Hornet*?" Carpenter shook his head. "Well, like you say, the morning of the fourth everything went able-sugar. Our staff launched ten of us in F4Fs *before* the rest of the air group. We bored holes in the sky for almost an hour before the SBDs and torpeckers set course. Then our group commander led us all over the goddamn Pacific. Two of our ensigns finally convinced the CO to break off when we were down to half our fuel." Stanley's gaze dropped to the concrete ramp. "Far as I know, none of us made it back to the ship."

One of the PBY pilots appeared at Carpenter's shoulder. "Sorry to break this up, Lieutenant. But these men have to get to the dispensary."

Carpenter flinched slightly at the interruption. "Oh, sure." He turned to the ambulance crew. "I didn't mean to hold you up. It's just that Stanley and I . . ."

"No, it's okay," the survivor interjected. He looked closely and recognized his own pain and anger in his classmate's expression. "Good to see you again, Carpenter. Come look me up. We can swap war stories." The spite in his voice trailed him to the ambulance, spreading a pall in his wake.

As the vehicle drove off, Carpenter turned to the PBY pilot. "Where'd you find them, Lieutenant?"

The P-boat driver tipped his red ballcap back. "About a hundred thirty miles north-northeast." He shook his head. "Poor bastards had no idea where they really were—they thought they were somewhere northwest. Maybe after four days in a raft you lose track, but . . ." He shrugged. Obviously, fighter pilots weren't much at navigating.

"We told them about sinking four Jap carriers, but that didn't seem to make much impression," the Catalina pilot continued. "Your friend Stanley—you know what he said?"

Carpenter merely stared, expressionless.

"He said, 'If we just won such a big goddamn victory, why don't I feel like a winner?'"

Sunny Jim Carpenter absorbed that sentiment, then wrapped himself around it. "Well," he said slowly, "for guys like Stanley and me, maybe surviving is all the victory we can stand."

22.

SATURDAY, 13 JUNE

USS ENTERPRISE

"It doesn't seem like fifteen days, does it?" Burnett asked.

Rogers sat in silence for a long moment, secure in his wheelchair on the flight deck. "No," he replied slowly. "It feels more like . . . forever."

The two aviators watched the channel markers slip past as *Enterprise* returned to port. The crew lined the rail and the battle ensign flew from the mainmast in anticipation of a reception of heroic proportions. To the Big E went the honor of leading Task Force Sixteen's triumphal return to Pearl Harbor, but Rogers, Burnett and a handful of other fliers remained aboard—there were too few planes for everyone to fly off to Kaneohe. Most of their *Yorktown* shipmates already had returned aboard the submarine tender *Fulton*.

"Well, I'm looking forward to getting kissed a lot," Burnett chirped. "I've never been a conquering hero before. May not get the chance again."

Rogers looked up from his chair at the base of the island. "You know, Bernie, I still can't quite believe it was *me* out there. I mean, actually doing what we've trained for all this time. To put it to use, to see enemy ships burning . . ." He thought of his last view of *Yorktown*. "And ours, too. It just seems unreal."

Burnett knew exactly what his friend was feeling. But it did not seem a healthy frame of mind. Instead of responding, he nudged Rogers slightly. "Hey, we're coming abeam of Hickam Field. Looks like the air corps is out to welcome us." He rolled Rogers's chair forward a few feet and turned it to face outboard to starboard.

A long row of khaki uniforms lined the east side of the channel. From the slow-moving carrier, the initial impression was a waving, cheering crowd of well-wishers. Those sailors on deck heard the first faint words of welcome: "Navy!" *That's nice of them*, thought Rogers. He was surprised at the enthusiasm of the greeting from the navy's traditional rival.

As the ship passed nearer the embankment, more words became clearer. "Where was the navy?"

"Hey, did you decide to come out of hiding?"

"Okay, swabbies, the army will protect you!"

"Where was the navy?"

There were catcalls, obscenities and derisive gestures. Rogers and Burnett turned to stare at one another. Rogers saw a face growing red with boiling anger. Burnett looked back and perceived complete mystification.

"What the hell are they talking about?" Rogers asked.

"Fuck if I know," Burnett snapped out. The bull ensign joined a couple of whitehats in a single-digit salute to their comrades in arms.

PEARL HARBOR NAVAL HOSPITAL

Bernie Burnett and Bill Barnes held the doors open as Phil Rogers limped inside on crutches. His right calf, still heavily bandaged, protruded in a white bulk beneath a slit trouser leg. He stumped over to the reception desk as Barnes laid the brown file envelope on the counter for him.

"Ensign Rogers, reporting as per orders from the *Enterprise* flight surgeon."

The petty-officer yeoman at the desk stood to greet him. "Yes, sir. If you'll please be seated, I'll have you admitted in a few minutes." *Kind of cute*, Rogers thought. He turned toward the bench on the opposite wall and caught Burnett ogling the yeoman's wiggle as she walked toward a file cabinet.

"Nice gams," Burnett observed. He nudged Barnes. "Hey, she's a third class. You rank her." Burnett winked and made a *click-click* sound from the corner of his mouth. Barnes blushed and studied the shine on his shoes.

"Well, I'll be go to hell. The things ya see when ya ain't got yer gun."

Rogers perked up at the familiar voice. He looked toward the sound, saw a tall, blond marine aviator and shook his head in resignation. "Jeez, now I believe in miracles." He reached out to grasp the lieutenant's extended hand. "I thought sure old Sunny Jim would have stalled, crashed and burned by now."

Carpenter laughed and grasped Rogers with both hands. "Damn near did, Buck. I tangled with a flock of Zeros about forty miles out of Midway." He touched the small bandage on his left cheek, then looked at Rogers's leg. "I guess you were there, too."

Rogers made introductions all round, being careful to include Barnes. "He's my gunner who got me back alive and kicking," the pilot said. "Bagged himself a Zero, to boot."

Carpenter pumped Barnes's hand a few extra strokes. "Well, you did better than I did, then. I latched onto one—whew! If that Jap could shoot like he flew, I'd be on the bottom with fourteen other guys from my squadron."

Burnett's hand went to his forehead. "Holy Christ . . ."

Carpenter nodded gravely. "Yeah. Two-Twenty-One's all washed up. I'm being reassigned to a new squadron with F4F-4s."

"Well, we all took some hard knocks, I guess." Rogers thought for a moment of Wiseman and Butler. "Hey, guess who I saw on the *Enterprise*? Frankie DiBella! He's in Bombing Six, doing okay."

"What about Wayne Wik?"

Rogers sniffed, looked over Carpenter's shoulder and shook his head. "The TBDs never had a goddamn chance, Jim."

The marine seemed to shrug off the news with a physical motion. "Say, I hear that you guys sank four Jap carriers."

Burnett nodded enthusiastically. "And a cruiser besides."

Carpenter folded his arms and leaned back on the balls of his feet. "Well, all I can say is, enjoy it while you can. The army's already taken most of the credit."

Burnett and Rogers exchanged knowing looks. "We got a real heart-warming welcome when we passed Hickam," Rogers said. "What the hell's going on?"

Carpenter's mouth curled in a sneer. "Two days ago there was a big awards ceremony at Hickam. You can read all about it in the papers. How the B-17s and B-26s sank those Jap ships all by themselves. About all the credit they're allowing the navy is spotting the Japs."

"That's plain bullshit!" Burnett's voice turned heads behind the reception desk, but he hardly noticed. "Those carriers were launching deckload strikes when we found 'em."

"You know it, and even I know it," Carpenter replied. "But the flyboys got back here first and their story is the one that's being told. Even Lowell Thomas is interviewing them for his newsreel."

Rogers was about to say something uncharitable when he felt Barnes's hand on his arm. "Excuse me, sir. You're ready for admitting anytime." The radioman waved the processing papers.

"Oh, thanks." He looked up at his flight-school classmate. "Guess I'd better check in, Jim. But it's damn good to see you. Maybe we can get together in a couple days."

"I'll be at the Royal Hawaiian until I report to Ewa," he replied. "Good luck with the medics. Just nod your head, say 'Yes, sir' a lot and ignore them. Works every time."

Rogers tottered to his feet as Burnett gave him a hand. The trio headed down the hall and Barnes waved bye-bye to the yeoman, who smiled back. He saw the bemused looks on the ensigns' faces and broke into a self-conscious grin. "Her name's Agnes," he explained. "She gets off at 2000."

23.

SUNDAY, 14 JUNE

PEARL HARBOR NAVAL HOSPITAL

Rogers looked up as the door of his room opened. He laid down *For Whom the Bell Tolls* beside him on the bed, hopeful that somebody was coming to visit him. He had been skimming Hemingway's 1941 bestseller for the good stuff, but thus far Maria and Roberto had been too preoccupied with fighting the Spanish Nationalists to appease Rogers's literary libido.

Burnett's curly-haired head peeked inside. "Hi, guy!" Rogers was about to reply when Bernie interrupted. "'Bye, guy!" He disappeared behind the door, there was some quick whispering and then Sallyann Downey stepped into the room.

She stood motionless for a few heartbeats. Rogers raised himself on one elbow and whispered her name. She looked him up and down, from head to plastered leg, then stretched out her arms and ran the four steps to him. She collapsed into his arms and they lay there, awkwardly and wonderfully entangled.

They both spoke at once, then stopped, each insisting politely that the other proceed. Their noses touched, they laughed and kissed. She exhaled into his ear, then looked him in the face. "Are you really going to be all right?"

He patted her shoulder. "Oh, sure. Can't fly for a while, though."

She had known that would be his major concern. It would be fine with Sallyann Downey if Philip Rogers never climbed in another airplane until 1992. *Like Scarlett—I'll think about it later.* "Bernie told me what happened, Phil. Are you really okay? Do you know when you can get up and move around?"

He shifted his weight off of one elbow. "Honest, honey. I feel pretty good. The leg doesn't hurt too bad." Actually, it hardly hurt at all, but he didn't mind wringing some extra sympathy from the situation. She ran a hand along his hairline and he closed his eyes, savoring her touch.

At length Sally sat up and pulled a chair close. They held hands while they talked. It was awkward after the flush of greeting subsided. She could never fully share what he had been through, and he was prohibited from telling her very much. She knew of the squadron's losses, but was too embarrassed to mention the subject. Rogers, however, wanted to talk about the dead and missing.

"Do you know about Johnny and Obie?"

Her eyes lowered behind her glasses. "Bernie told me." She felt the wetness come. "Phil, I'm so sorry . . ."

He nodded, staring into space. "That's not all, Sally. Wayne . . . well, he never came back from the first mission." He squeezed her long, slim fingers. "Him and most of Torpedo Three."

She gasped audibly. "Oh my God . . ."

He lowered his voice conspiratorially. "Look, I don't know how secret this is supposed to be, so keep it under your hat. But scuttlebutt has it that all three torprons were wiped out." He decided not to mention *Yorktown*'s fate, but he suspected she knew.

"What will happen now?"

He shrugged, stroked her hand. "I don't know exactly. The

squadrons will start rebuilding, I guess. The skipper and Swede both landed in the water after the morning strike. They're okay, but they haven't rejoined us—don't know if they will. Dave's still running things. Doing a good job, too."

His mind is still out there, with his goddamned ships and airplanes. She made an effort to keep the anger from her voice. "I meant, what will happen to you? Will they keep you here?"

"For a while, at least." He smiled. "Maybe my ol' leg will get us some time together. Would you like that?"

Sallyann leaned forward, slipped her arms around his neck and delivered a soft, wet kiss on his ear. The only sound in the room for the next few minutes was that of heavy breathing.

KURE NAVAL BASE, JAPAN

Lieutenant (junior grade) Toshiki Azumano stood on the bridge, taking his turn as watch officer, and viewed the unloading process. It was a grim enough business, but to do it like this—almost in secrecy, in the dark. He shook his head in disgust.

Azumano recalled what the communications officer had told him of the directive. The four carriers' injured survivors—including those transferred to *Tone* and other cruisers to alleviate crowding in the destroyers—were to be closely "escorted" en route to isolation wards in designated hospitals. All other personnel, up to but not including fleet staff officers, were restricted to their ships or bases until further notice.

Looking portside and aft, Azumano discerned the white uniform of an aviation petty officer gyrating wildly. He did not need to confirm the owner's identity. Sakaida was back to his old form, swinging his hips in emulation of a Carmen Miranda rhumba routine. *Next, I suppose, he will have bananas and other fruit on his head,* Azumano told himself. But he felt an added appreciation for the clown of CruDiv-Eight. Aside from the fact that Sakaida's airmanship had saved his own life, the junior officer looked with warmth on Sakaida's antics to cheer the *Soryu* survivors standing or sitting in a semicircle around the petty officer. Many of them were swaying or clapping their hands to a Latin beat, smiling for the first time in ten days.

Still, not even Sakaida's antics could override the bitter, empty feeling of failure and loss. Azumano reflected that efforts to conceal the results of Operation MI from other elements of the navy spoke volumes. *We are pariahs,* he told himself, *untrusted and unwelcome even in our own land.*

He stepped onto the wing of the bridge and took in the dankness and the dark. He inhaled the odors of Kure and every other port in the Pacific: saltwater, sea air, rotting fish, fuel oil—and something else.

Defeat.

24.

WEDNESDAY, 17 JUNE

HONOLULU

The Diamond Head Dinner Club was down the beach from the Royal Hawaiian Hotel. Crowded with uniforms and laughter, the Diamond Head pulsed with activity and an undefined sense of anticipation. Heads turned when a Bombing Three contingent entered the foyer, showing much solicitation to the ensign hobbling on a cane with a dark-haired young woman on his opposite arm. The group stood at the entrance to the main dining room while Burnett informed the maître d' of their reservation.

"This is going to be great," Rogers said to no one in particular. "Everybody's going to be here."

"Sounds like a class reunion," Sally offered. She had hoped for a far more private dinner; obviously the table conversation this evening would be shoptalk.

"Well, it is, sort of," Rogers replied. "A couple pals of mine from the *Hornet*, and Frankie DiBella off the *Enterprise*, and Jim Carpenter."

As Burnett whistled and led the way toward their table, an older couple approached from the opposite direction. The naval officers and their dates stood aside to let them pass, but the plumpish, gray-haired woman stopped before Rogers. She had gray eyes that were moist as she touched Rogers's cane hand. "God bless you, son," she said. Her voice quivered. Then she was gone, hurried along by her husband.

Rogers turned toward Sally. He did not know what to say.

"Hey, Buck," Burnett interjected. "Can I borrow your cane tomorrow night?"

Sally shot a lethal glare at the bull ensign of Bombing Three. He pulled his head in, smartly turned about and made a forward-ho gesture.

Approaching their table, Rogers saw a familiar figure sitting with Jim Carpenter. "Shawn! How the hell are you, buddy?" Rogers switched his cane to his left hand and reached toward his Pensacola classmate.

Ensign Murtagh rose and warmly shook hands, then stepped back. "More's the question, how're you?" he asked.

Rogers slapped his leg, now requiring only a thin bandage. "Oh, I'm doing great. The flight surgeon says I can have an SBD again in a week or so." He remembered his social obligations and made the introductions, except for Sunny Jim's date: slender, blue-eyed, with a perfect complexion and cheekbones most models would envy. She was, in a word, gorgeous.

Sallyann took her in with one glance and instantly disliked her. *They belong together*, she thought of the marine and his companion. *Both tall, blond and beautiful.* Then she noticed the scar on Carpenter's left cheek and recalled what Rogers had told her. Some of the frost melted. She shook hands with the ice princess, whose name was Elaine.

Rogers eased himself into a chair between Sally and Murtagh. At that point Frank DiBella arrived with a short, curly-haired girl named Paulette, whom he introduced as his fiancée. Appropriate comments and congratulatory remarks made the rounds, then a waitress appeared to take orders for drinks. Burnett slapped a twenty on the table. "First round's on me," he claimed. "In honor of my impending status as the ex–bull ensign of Bombing Three." It was common knowledge that the Bureau of Naval Personnel had just released a list for promotion to lieutenant (junior grade).

"To ensigns everywhere," Murtagh said.

"Long may they wave," added DiBella.

Rogers turned to Murtagh. "Shawn, where's Bucky? I figured he'd be here for sure."

Murtagh laughed. "Oh, hell, he's still in hack."

Rogers remembered the wardroom conversation aboard *Enterprise*. "Oh, yeah. We had one of your pilots, a guy named Green, aboard for one night. He mentioned you two had got crossways to your CAG or something."

"Affirmative," Murtagh replied. "Just before we sailed. We didn't see him enter the wardroom so we didn't stand up. He braced us both and read us the riot act. Said we had no appreciation for naval regulations and customs."

Burnett leaned forward, intrigued. "He put you in hack just for that?"

"Well, not quite. I think we'd have been okay but Bucky said that, seeing as Commander Ring wore an academy ring all the time, it was sort of too bad he didn't have a college education to go with it."

"Ouch." Rogers flinched in sympathy.

"Yeah. He grounded us both on the spot. I only flew twice the whole time—just a couple of patrols on the way back. Bucky's still cooling his heels."

Carpenter leaned across the table. "Excuse me, Shawn. But what the hell gives with your air group? I met one of your fighter pilots getting out of a PBY. He says his CO ran ten planes out of fuel."

Murtagh's face blushed and he nervously tapped the tabletop. "Don't get me wrong, fellows. We have some really deluxe aviators in the *Hornet*. Gus Widhelm, Moe Vose, Johnny Magda, Hank Carey, a lot of others." He looked around and everyone there saw the pain in his eyes. "But our leadership is real erratic. On the first day, Ring led thirty-five SBDs around the god . . . goldarned Pacific . . . in parade formation, burning gas like there was no tomorrow. The fighter skipper wouldn't break off until too late, and apparently two of his guys drowned. Another senior VF-8 pilot refused a vector with bogies inbound and turned himself over to the flight surgeon for 'evaluation.'"

"You mean he turned yellow?" Carpenter's voice held no sympathy.

Murtagh shrugged eloquently. "Damn, I thought things were bad when the survivors of my squadron stayed drunk for three days."

The waitress returned with the first round of drinks, and Sally and Elaine exchanged knowing looks over their rum and Cokes. *We're in for a night of war stories and male commiseration.*

In the adjoining room the band was playing "Moonlight Serenade." Paulette slid her chair back and took DiBella's hand. "Frankie, I think it's time we had a dance." As some of the gentlemen gallantly rose to escort their ladies, Sally turned to Rogers, her chin cupped in one hand, her eyes dreamily half-closed. "Mmmm. That reminds me of Jantzen Beach and the dances on Saturday night." She rubbed against him. "You'll have to take me there when you visit Portland sometime."

He kissed her cheek. "It's a date. If you'll take a raincheck while I'm off the dance schedule."

"Well, my-oh-my. Lookit th' boys in their little white sailor suits." The voice obviously belonged to a drunk. Turning in his seat, Rogers saw it belonged to a very large drunk, wearing Army Air Force khaki. Two Hickam Field lieutenants smirked behind the vocal giant with the captain's bars.

Carpenter eased himself in front of Elaine. "You got a problem, mac?"

"Yeah, I got a problem," the army flier sneered. "I got a problem with navy heroes who leave the fightin' to the land-based bombers!"

Murtagh crowded next to Carpenter. "Hey, I bet you're one of those B-17 pilots we've read so much about in the papers," Murtagh said to the drunk. He turned confidentially to Carpenter. "You know what a multiengine pilot is, don't you, Jim? That's somebody who likes to fly but basically he's afraid of dying."

"What'd you know about dying, swabbie?" This from a first lieutenant who held a nearly empty glass in one hand.

Murtagh folded his arms across his dress whites. "Well, I know a couple of friends of mine died sinking a Jap cruiser. And I know my torpedo squadron died, except one pilot, trying to sink a carrier." His voice wavered and the veins stood out above his choker collar.

Sally looked around the room. All other conversations had ceased. The tension was thick enough to cut with a steak knife. *Why doesn't somebody break this up?* She saw the maître d' on the phone, presumably calling the MPs or shore patrol.

The captain poked a big finger in Murtagh's chest. "Well, we're the ones sank those goddamn carriers. We didn't see none of you swabbies anywhere around."

"Captain, we were all there, too," Burnett said evenly. He pointed at the newly awarded DFC on the khaki tunic. "If you really think you earned that medal, you're dead wrong. Those four carriers were virgins when we found them. They hadn't been hit by you or anybody." His voice was deceptively calm.

"Hah! What'd you jokers know 'bout virgins?" The giant looked back at his two companions, encouraged by their laughter.

Burnett took a grip on a chair, measuring the distance and angle to the giant's skull. Carpenter took one step closer. "You owe these ladies an apology, mac."

The army flier pressed against the dress-blue uniform. "Outa my way, shithead. Let a fightin' man pass!" He shoved Carpenter backward, into Elaine, who stumbled against a table.

Carpenter rebounded with a right cross that connected with an audible *crack* against the drunk's jaw. Instantly Sunny Jim grasped his right hand with his left, painfully aware of the abused knuckles. But the khaki giant, more surprised than hurt, shook off the blow and cocked a massive fist in retaliation. His jackhammer punch might have done genuine harm, but it was deflected by the arc of Burnett's chair.

At that point the fight became general.

DiBella grappled with one of the lesser khaki combatants, and they both went down in a tangle. Patrons scrambled to get out of the way, women shrieked, place settings crashed and pandemonium reigned.

Burnett impulsively jumped on the raging giant, who bellowed obscenities while trying to shake off the unwanted rider. Murtagh, meanwhile, was giving an impressive demonstration of South Boston street-fighting technique at the expense of the army second lieutenant.

Rogers belatedly gained his feet, uncertain of what he could do, when the khaki gorilla swirled in an attempt to shake off Burnett. Burnett's legs swung outward as if on a merry-go-round and clipped Sallyann on the neck. She staggered backward and sat down heavily.

Enraged, Phil Rogers felt his cane in his hand. He swung it in an overhand arc and landed a center hit on the giant's head. A loud *snap* rang over the grunts and shouts in the room—so loud that it commanded attention. People stopped shouting and aviators stopped fighting.

The army captain slowly turned back toward Rogers, with Burnett still clinging for dear life to the giant's shoulders. Rogers saw the uncertainty in the bomber pilot's eyes as the man tentatively felt the top of his skull. The whiskey-blurred eyes slowly focused on the cane, which had splintered in the middle. Rogers still held the useless implement as half its length dangled limply, held by a few wooden shards. Rogers felt like Errol Flynn's Captain Blood brandishing a melted cutlass.

Still rubbing his skull with one hand, the army pilot pointed at the broken cane with the other. "It's busted!" he shouted in triumph. "He broke his goddamn cane on my goddamn head!" The giant roared in laughter as Burnett took the opportunity to slide down the man's wide back.

The dining room rippled with laughter. The noise of relief and glee and emotion increased in volume and intensity as people caught the spirit. Some sat down, leaned back and allowed the cacophonous sound peculiar to human beings to wash over them and drain away their tension. Others leaned on one another or draped arms about friends, spouses, lovers and strangers.

Rogers sat down next to Sally, who hugged his neck. Over the laughter she said, "Sailor, you sure know how to show a girl a good time."

The Battle of Midway was over.

25.

SATURDAY, 20 JUNE

OVERLOOKING KAWAILOA BEACH

"I flew again yesterday," he said at last.

For a moment she stopped teasing his hair with her fingers as his head rested in her lap. Then she resumed the slow, steady brushing movement that he savored. After a while she leaned down and kissed him lightly on the forehead. "I love you," she whispered.

He decided not to tell her yet that his friend Randy Cooner, survivor of the greatest naval battle of World War II, had been killed on Tuesday taking off from Ford Island.

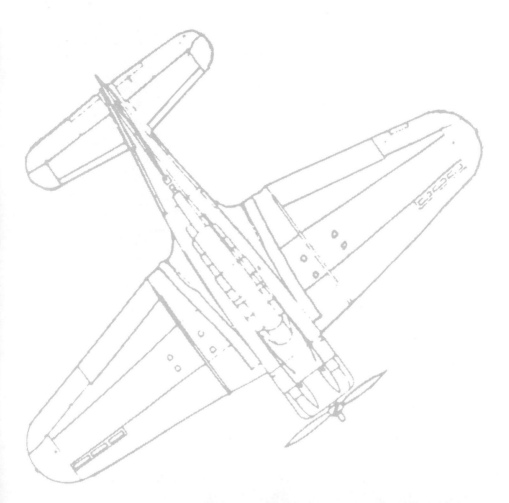

PART FOUR

"Guadalcanal is not a name but an emotion."

SAMUEL ELIOT MORISON

26.

SUNDAY, 28 JUNE

KAPIOLANI PARK

Rogers dropped the oversized picnic basket and joined it on the ground, inhaling deeply. Sally, all fresh and pretty, stood in contrast to his labored breathing and smiled down at the man she loved. "Poor baby," she cooed. She traced her fingertips along his hairline, then extended a blanket on the grass.

"Jeez, if I'd wanted to walk I'd have joined the marines," Rogers moaned. He rubbed his healed leg with both hands, giving just the trace of a grimace. Sally ignored the dramatics, sat beside him and opened the wicker basket. "Oh, Phil, it's only a quarter-mile or so from the road. Besides, the view up here is so nice."

Rogers rolled over, supporting himself on both elbows. "Easy for you to say," he replied. "I carry the food for a dozen people and you carry the damn blanket." He watched for a reaction to the mild profanity and realized she was becoming accustomed to aviators' language. *Four months ago she'd have corrected me*, he thought. It occurred to him that the Pacific Ocean had become a different place between February and June 1942. Certainly he was different from the way he was the day he had met Sallyann Downey.

As the other picnickers traipsed toward the foot of Diamond Head, Rogers took in the beauty of the park: well-kept grass, weaving palms and tropical orchids. *It's a damn paradise*, he thought. *Too bad half the squadron's back at sea.*

Burnett, Murtagh and the rest of the group arrived with their own hampers, blankets and other impedimenta. Rogers stretched out, hands clasped under his head, and looked up from behind his aviator sunglasses. "Hey, shipmates. Drop anchor."

"Roger," replied Burnett.

"Wilco," wheezed Murtagh. They slumped to the grass beside Sally, who shortly was joined by Mary Tanaka and Ginger Paisley, another girlfriend from the library, who began setting out plates, cups and utensils.

"Wonder what Sunny Jim's doing?" asked Murtagh.

Rogers shrugged. "Still busy with his new F4Fs, I guess. I thought we'd see more of him since we're all at Ewa now, but his CO keeps 'em busy as . . . anything." He thought he saw the ghost of a smile on Sally's lips.

"Well, I'm certainly glad you fellows moved," she offered. "It's more convenient than Kaneohe."

Burnett grunted. "Actually it's about the same distance straight-line," he explained. "The mountains make the difference."

Sally placed a friendly hand on Murtagh's shoulder. "Shawn, Phil tells me you're joining his squadron. That's wonderful."

"Thanks, Sal. I'm mighty glad to be . . . with Bombing Three." He had almost said he was frigging glad to be out from under his previous air group commander. The machinations behind the transfer had been fairly straightforward: VB-3 needed some replacements and the *Hornet* CAG was glad to part with some of his irreverent junior officers.

Mary took inventory of the baskets' content and raised her small hands. "All this food! Whatever will we do with it?"

Rogers laughed. "We'll have to eat it. I refuse to carry it back the way we came." Immediately he regretted his tone. With rationing in effect, it would not always be easy to pack such a varied lunch. He touched her fingers. "I'm sorry, Mary. I thought Frankie and Paulette would be here. He drew the duty this weekend when the watch officer got sick."

"Yes," Sally intoned. "I notice you boys don't have any problems getting away whenever you like."

"Strictly a matter of seniority," Burnett replied, flashing his new silver bar. "We senior officers try to look out for the interests of the hoi polloi."

Ginger, the other librarian, reached out and fingered Burnett's collar. He could smell her perfume, which he thought must have been applied with a ladle. "Ohhh, you're a first lieutenant!" she exclaimed.

Murtagh stifled a snort by faking a cough. Rogers merely looked down and shook his head. "Well, ah, that's right, in a way. You see, ah, Ginger. If I was in the marines I'd be a first lieutenant. But I'm a naval officer, so I'm actually a lieutenant junior grade."

"Golly, what's the difference?" Ginger asked.

Burnett looked around for help. Mary rescued him. "Well, Ginger, the army and the marines use the same ranks, such as second lieutenant and first lieutenant. The navy and coast guard have the same insignia, but call the ranks by different names, like ensign and lieutenant junior grade."

Ginger's big blue eyes widened in comprehension. "Oh, I get it. Same number of bars but different names."

Sally started pouring lemonade into glasses while Rogers closed his eyes and feigned sleep. But Mary interjected. "Well, it's like this, Ginger. My brother, Harold, is in the army. His battalion is on maneuvers in Louisiana, in fact." At this the three aviators perked up. *I didn't know she had a brother in the army*, Rogers thought. Then he remembered about the Nisei units formed from Hawaii and the West Coast.

"Harold is a second lieutenant," Mary continued. "He wears gold bars like Phil and Shawn, who are ensigns in the navy. When he's promoted he'll wear silver bars, because then he'll be a first lieutenant."

Ginger nodded. "Then when will he be a junior lieutenant like Bernie?"

Rogers symbolically pounded his forehead with a fist, but Sally swatted him down. Mary patted Ginger's hand. "Not for quite a while, dear."

Rogers exchanged glances with his two friends, who replied with knowing nods. Like most servicemen, they had assumed that civilians shared their basic knowledge of military lore in a nation at war. Sally was grateful when Murtagh changed the subject. "Hey, I hear Bombing Three's got a new CO."

Rogers picked up a sandwich and nibbled at the crust, his favorite part. "Affirmative. Dave Shumway just relieved Mr. Leslie." He was reminded of a story Barnes had related. "Hey, you want to know what a professional aviator's like? Listen to this."

Sally and Mary rolled their eyes at one another. Ginger leaned forward, elbows on her knees, all ears. "My gunner, Barnes, was talking to Mr. Leslie's gunner, you know? When the skipper ditched alongside the *Astoria*, his gunner jumped out on the wing to deploy their raft in case they needed it. But he noticed Mr. Leslie wasn't moving, just sort of slumped over in the cockpit. So his gunner walks up the wing to see if he needed help, and you know what? The skipper was just sitting there, calm as you please, turning off every switch in the cockpit!"

Murtagh and Burnett chuckled, sharing the sentiment. Rogers shook his head in admiration. "If that'd been me, I'd have got to the ship so fast my feet probably wouldn't have been wet. Man alive, that's a methodical pilot."

"So who's the next exec?" Murtagh asked.

Burnett answered. "Syd Bottomley. He has half the squadron on the *Saratoga* for a week or so, running up to Midway and back."

Rogers turned to the three women. "Ah, ladies, I hope you'll keep any military information to yourselves. It probably doesn't make a lot of difference in this case, but . . ."

"Oh, I know! Loose lips sink ships," Ginger automatically replied. Sally caught a trace of tension in Rogers's body and momentarily wondered at the reaction. Then she knew. *He's thinking of the* Yorktown *again.* She stroked his leg affectionately and felt him relax.

"Uh, yeah, that's right, Ginger," Burnett said. "Can't be too careful with Tojo's spies all around."

"Oh, I wouldn't tell anybody, Bernie. Honest!" She sat forward, earnestly looking at Burnett. "I mean, I don't even know anybody like that."

"Well, I don't imagine you get many spies at the library, honey."

Sally shot a frosty look at Burnett. "Oh, I don't know, Bernie. Where else would you go if you were looking for one source of information?" Rogers felt like burying his head in the ground. *Here we go,* he thought.

Burnett spoke slowly, as if controlling his anger. "I just meant that your work doesn't have anything to do with the military, that's all."

Rogers bit aggressively at his sandwich. Sally's dander was up and he knew the signs. Burnett was on his own, clearly outgunned.

"Tell me something," Sally said evenly. "How many friends did you lose on December seventh?"

Burnett was taken aback. "Well, none. Why do you ask?"

Sally spoke in a low, serious tone. "A Japanese bomb landed on the house of one of our custodians. It killed him and his baby. So I think the library has a share in this war, don't you?"

"Uh, yes, ma'am." He gulped some lemonade.

Later, walking hand in hand, Rogers and Sally stopped to hug behind a tree. He sensed the unspoken anger in her. "Okay, talk to Buck."

She leaned into him, the top of her head just under his nose. "Oh, damn. I feel the day's been spoiled, Phil. That tiff with Bernie."

He patted her back and stroked her hair. "He didn't mean anything by it, you know. Bernie's good people."

She looked up at him and lightly tapped a fist on his shoulder. "Maybe, but he had such a condescending attitude that I had to say something. Look, I know Ginger isn't exactly a genius, but she's a sweet girl. He was making fun of her and I resent it."

Rogers slid both hands onto her shoulders and faced her squarely. "Sally, he knows what you mean to me. You shouldn't take offense like that."

She shook her head and her short, black hair swirled around her ears. "Maybe it's not just Bernie. Maybe it's every man in uniform who treats girls that way. I even see it at work. People don't take me seriously because I'm 'just a librarian.' As if it isn't a real job, or as if it doesn't matter." She shrugged. "That's why I challenged him on the library and the war."

Rogers chuckled aloud and she relished the sound of him. "It's a cinch he won't do it again. I think you cured him." He paused, realizing that this was the moment he had waited for. "Sally, I want you to know something. When I was wounded, when the blood was running down my leg and the pain was driving me crazy, Bernie took over. He slid up on my wing and led me back to the ship." He let those words take effect.

Her eyes misted behind her lenses. "Oh, Phil." She reached up and kissed him briefly on the mouth. "I guess we'd better go back."

When they returned to the picnic area, they found two esoteric discussions underway. Murtagh and Mary were comparing Catholicism and Buddhism while Burnett valiantly tried to explain to Ginger the difference between army captains and navy captains. "Now look, honey," he was saying. "A navy captain is three ranks higher than an army or marine captain . . ."

Sally hugged Rogers's arm and giggled to him. "Maybe the day hasn't been so bad after all."

27.

FRIDAY, 3 JULY

MARINE CORPS AIR STATION EWA, HAWAII

"Six guns instead of four, and folding wings to boot." Standing on the flight line, the base engineering officer patted the cowling of the first F4F-4 that the marine pilots had ever seen. He even kicked the port tire, reminding Jim Carpenter of nothing so much as an earnest used-car salesman.

"Yeah. Extra weight, less ammo than the dash three, and folding wings that do us no good ashore." Captain John L. Smith, the blunt Oklahoman who had established Marine Fighting Squadron 223 barely two months before, stood with his arms folded among his pilots.

The engineering officer, a major, bristled slightly. Smith had pointedly omitted the obligatory "sir" from his comment, but his observation—like his aerial gunnery—was smack on target. The major sought a line of defense. "Smith, this is the latest model. It's the only one being produced now. Besides, I'd think you'd be delighted to get rid of your F2As."

Smith remained unconvinced. "Major, the handbook shows me that this airplane weighs nine hundred pounds more than the F4F-3 at all-up weight, without any increase in power. It's at least ten knots slower, its service ceiling is a good two thousand feet less, and it climbs about five hundred feet per minute slower." Some of the pilots of VMF-223 smirked at one another. They'd learned quickly that John Lucien Smith knew his business. "As for the Brewsters," Smith added, "at least we didn't have to crank up our wheels by hand."

Recognizing a no-win position, the major walked toward his jeep. "I'll give you people all the support I can. If you need anything—anything at all—just let me know. You and Two-twenty-four will receive your full allotment of new airplanes over the next few days. Meanwhile, good luck." He climbed in, started up, gnashed the gears twice and drove off.

Smith turned toward his pilots. His rawboned frame seemed larger than it really was, only increasing his command presence. "I want pilot checkouts in this plane at the earliest possible moment. Those of you with previous F4F time will oversee the transition. I am especially relying on you pilots with combat experience to help with gunnery and tactics training." He looked at Marion Carl, Roy Corry, Jim Carpenter, a handful of others. "All right, let's get busy. We have a hell of a lot of work to do."

28.

SATURDAY, 4 JULY

HONOLULU

Sally heard the three rapid raps on her door and her pulse accelerated. In her haste she nearly tripped over the large cat idling on her small living-room rug and, in a pique of anger, kicked at the tabby. "Out of my way, Muffin!" She wondered whether acquiring a pet in order to lend credence to her blackout cover story was worthwhile. Mr. Tarutani had not been around much lately.

Rogers saw the doorknob turn, then looked into those big hazel eyes. "Hi, honey." He leaned down to kiss her, secretly pleased with the warmth of her response yet fearful of her reaction to the news he bore.

"I'll be just a minute, Phil," she said as she turned to pick up her purse. "We still have enough time to get to the park."

Rogers pointedly sat on the sofa and patted the cushion next to him. "Sally, I'm awful sorry. But I don't have as much time as I'd thought."

Looking over her shoulder, Sally paused a moment. Then she knew. She slumped into a chair at the kitchen table. "You're leaving again, aren't you?"

The aviator nodded. He felt every inch of the fifteen feet between them. "I can't say when, of course. You know how it is."

Yes, I know damn well how it is, she thought bitterly.

"I have to get back tonight," he added. "Do you still want to go to the park?"

Wartime Honolulu on July fourth offered a variety of activities, each guaranteeing a warm welcome for servicemen. Suddenly none of that mattered as Sally felt the anger building inside her. *I can't let myself take it out on him. After all, it's not his fault.* She covered her mouth with one hand and fought down a sob.

After an awkward moment Sally rose from the chair and curled up beside him on the sofa. They sat entwined for several minutes before she said, "Let's just stay here, okay? I'll fix us something for dinner."

"Okay." He kissed the top of her head.

They sat shoulder to shoulder at the kitchen table, she shredding lettuce and he slicing fruit and vegetables. His sleeves were rolled up and his collar was open, his black tie on the living-room floor where Muffin lazily batted at it. Her blouse was partially unbuttoned, no longer tucked into her skirt. They both needed several minutes with a comb.

Rogers was mildly surprised to find he did not mind spending the evening in the kitchen rather than in bed. "It's the wrong time of month," was all she had said, and it had been enough. She was grateful for his understanding, and relieved at the tacit message. *If we make love tonight, he'll think it's because I'm afraid I'll never see him again.* She leaned over and kissed his neck.

"Ummm. Thank you," he muttered. He dumped the mixture of fruit and vegetables into her bowl, and she began tossing the salad.

At length she said, "You know, I think I'm getting used to being a sailor's girl. You're gone three weeks at a time, I eat my heart out pining away for you, and you come back for a while." She laughed aloud and hoped it sounded genuine.

He leaned forward, one arm braced on the table. "Sally, you need to understand something. This cruise may not be like the other two. There's no guarantee we'll only be gone three weeks. I mean, *Yorktown* was at sea for three months before . . . Midway." He shrugged. "I just don't know where we're going or how long we'll be there."

Sally absorbed that information and began dissecting it. She realized she may have assumed too much, for her knowledge of wartime deployments was limited to her familiarity with Bombing Three. First the Doolittle raid, then Midway—both relatively quick operations. She searched for some source of comfort. "Well, at least you'll be back on the *Saratoga*, won't you?"

His eyes locked onto hers. He allowed a few seconds to pass before he responded. "Yes, we will," he said evenly. "But that's—"

"Confidential information. I know." She smiled. "But doesn't that make you feel better, being on your own ship?"

Rogers stared at the cupboard, giving a noncommittal grunt. He wondered how much to tell Sally now that *Saratoga* was back in commission. But he also wondered how he could make anyone understand the feeling a carrier aviator had for his ship. He still hadn't told Sally the full story behind VB-3's unusually long stay in Hawaii.

He thought back to that terrifying eleventh of January, when the submarine torpedo had connected as Sara steamed southwest of Oahu. He could still remember his discussion with Bernie and Randy when the jarring blast interrupted all talk. How the lights had blinked out and a wardroom full of officers sat in eerie silence, nerves drawn bowstring tight, waiting for the next torpedo or—far worse—for the unknown.

And he certainly could not tell her about the junior officer in the next compartment, abruptly faced with a horrible decision. How two Filipino steward's mates had panicked and began undogging a hatch to escape from the steel confines. How the young jaygee had drawn his pistol, chambered the first round from the magazine and, in a faltering, choked voice, ordered the men to secure the hatch and sit down. How they had ignored him, never dreaming that an equally frightened young man would follow procedure.

"Phil?" Sally's voice cut through the haze of his memory.

"Oh, sorry." He grinned in embarrassment. "I was just thinking that you and I owe something to a Jap submarine skipper."

"Whatever do you mean?"

"Well, if the Sara hadn't been torpedoed, you and I probably wouldn't have met."

Her hands grasped his, their lips met and they finished the evening back on the sofa. When at last he had to leave, neither minded missing dinner.

29

TUESDAY, 7 JULY

USS SARATOGA

". . . Three-thirty-three, three-thirty-four, three-thirty-five!" Phil Rogers abruptly stopped at the edge of the flight deck, almost lurching forward into the carrier's twenty-knot breeze. He turned around and beamed at Burnett and Murtagh. "Still three hundred thirty-five paces stern to bow!" He stomped his right foot on the wooden planking. "Good old Sara."

Lieutenant (junior grade) Burnett turned to Murtagh and spoke in a detached, almost scholarly, tone of voice. "You will note, Ensign, the peculiar behavior of certain lower orders of human beings when exposed to saltwater. The effect becomes more pronounced with greater exposure to sea air, until at last the subject begins squirting semen from his ears."

Murtagh chuckled in appreciation; he was beginning to feel accepted in his new squadron. "Yeah, I understand at that point they promote the subject to lieutenant jaygee!"

Rogers pretended not to hear the exchange. He felt surprisingly good, considering he had recently left his girlfriend behind for the uncertain future of another combat deployment. "Come on, Bernie. You have to admit that it's nice being back on the *Saratoga* again. Just like old times."

Burnett looked over his shoulder, taking in the distinctive island forward of the huge funnel. "Well, almost like old times. It's good to be aboard with Scouting Three again, but I was hoping we'd have the whole air group together."

"Yeah, I know what you mean. It's kind of ironic, isn't it? I mean, last time we went out on the *Yorktown* with our torpedo squadron and now we're back aboard our ship with the *Yorktown*'s old fighter squadron." He remembered to include Murtagh in the conversation. "And Shawn's torpeckers."

"Hey, I'm not complaining," Murtagh interjected. "I'd have volunteered for goddamn patrol planes to get out of the *Hornet* Air Group. I just wish Bucky could have joined us."

Rogers expelled a breath. "That'd be swell. But like you say, he's probably not bitching either, now that he's in the fleet replacement pool."

"What's Torpedo Eight like?" asked Burnett.

"Oh, I don't know any of those fellows very well," Murtagh offered. "Lieutenant Larsen had the TBF contingent at Pearl when Commander Waldron took most of the squadron to Midway. Those were the guys I got to know." The freckle-faced Bostonian stared at the horizon, remembering his dead friends in their antiquated TBDs.

Rogers felt an awkwardness that made him fidget. He thought of Wayne Wik and Torpedo Three and decided to change the subject. "Anybody know anything about Fighting Five?"

"Sure. I have a classmate with them, Benny Nichols," Burnett replied. "The skipper's Roy Simpler; exec's named Harmer. Both academy types, both good guys from what I hear. The squadron was transitioning from F3Fs to F4Fs on seven December, so VF-42 moved over from the *Ranger*."

"And here we are with squadrons from three air groups," Rogers said. "Well, I guess there's no point worrying. After all, we did okay with a mixed lineup at Midway."

Murtagh's voice carried a trace of bitterness. "A damn sight better than the *Hornet*, with all four squadrons intact."

Rogers tapped his classmate's arm with one hand. "C'mon, Shawn. That's all behind you now."

The Irish street fighter looked at his brown shoes and shook his head. "Yeah, I know. I guess . . . I just miss the prewar organization, you know? When you knew what squadrons went with which carrier. Things made sense."

"Friend, those days are over." Burnett hoped his voice did not give the impression of lecturing. "But the *Lexington* Air Group's gone now, and *Yorktown*'s is scrambled. So is ours. Not even the *Enterprise* and *Hornet* outfits are all together anymore. I guess the only air group still intact is the *Wasp*'s, and they haven't seen any action yet."

"Hey, speaking of the *Enterprise*, did you hear about Mr. Leslie? He's the new air group commander." Rogers was almost as pleased with Max Leslie's promotion as the former VB-3 skipper must have been.

"Yeah, and scuttlebutt has it we're joining up with the *Enterprise* and *Wasp* task forces," Burnett offered. "Must be something big about to happen."

"Well, whatever happens, Shawn here is right." Burnett and Murtagh looked toward Rogers in anticipation. "This war sure screwed up a damn good flying club."

30.

FRIDAY, 10 JULY

MARINE CORPS AIR STATION EWA

Jim Carpenter rolled out on his downwind leg, slid back the canopy and checked his instruments. *Eight hundred feet, eighty-five knots. Good enough.* Approaching midpoint of the northeast-southwest runway, he moved his left hand from the throttle to the stick and, with his right, loosened the friction lock on the landing-gear control. He began turning the crank, fighting against tension as gravity wanted to whip the control from his hand. He had heard about the F4F's landing-gear handle—how the device positively *lurked* in wait for the unwary. If it slipped from a pilot's grasp, the control unwound with devilish speed and the only way to stop it was to jam your right knee in the path of the whirling handle. A VF-42 pilot had remarked that you only did that once.

On the twenty-eighth rotation the handle stopped, and Carpenter remembered to force it over the hump to lock the chain-driven landing gear full down. He noticed he'd lost almost 100 feet altitude and chastised himself for the lapse. *Never thought I'd miss my old Brewster,* he thought. A quick scan of his gauges told him that temperature and pressures were in the green. He adjusted the cowl flaps, then lowered the vacuum-powered wing flaps. The little Grumman nosed down slightly and Carpenter easily corrected.

Abruptly he realized he was too high at the upcoming left turn onto base leg. Fighting the natural urge to stuff the nose down—which would only increase his airspeed—he came back on the throttle, keeping the nose almost level. The words of the navy check pilot came to him again. *The trick to a good carrier approach in this airplane is speed control on downwind. Everything proceeds from there.*

Carpenter felt the Wildcat settling. He estimated he reached about 250 feet by the time he rolled into his final approach and added a touch of power. He shot a glance at his airspeed indicator—seventy knots.

Up ahead, standing on the left side of the runway, Carpenter saw the landing-signal officer's paddles outstretched. He mused that probably no other squadron commander in the Marine Corps was a qualified LSO, yet Major Bob Galer of VMF-224 was the right man at the right place. Carpenter had only met Galer twice before—most recently at the briefing for this carrier-qualification session. Rumor had it that Galer and some of his pilots had pirated the jeep assigned to the officer of the day and had liberated some hard-to-find solid-rubber tailwheels for carrier planes—a rarity on Marine Corps air stations.

Almost immediately Carpenter saw Galer's paddles raise in a "high" sign. The pilot reduced power and pulled his nose up slightly. When the paddles returned to shoulder height, Carpenter pushed the throttle up once more and was pleased as the F4F maintained a steady descent to the end of the runway. Then Galer slashed his paddles down and across his body, and Carpenter's left hand brought the throttle all the way back as he eased the stick into his lap with his right.

With the R-1830 snapping at him from its short exhaust stacks, Carpenter felt the impact of touchdown, tailwheel first. The little fighter lurched to port, but Carpenter caught it with a mild application of right brake and rudder. He had learned on his first flight that the

Wildcat's high center of gravity and narrow landing gear often gave false alarms of impending ground loops. *Not too bad*, he told himself. *Not bad at all*.

He kicked right rudder, advanced the throttle to the stop and heard the Pratt and Whitney wind up again. Moments later he was flying once more, cranking up his wheels for his next simulated deck landing. Momentarily he allowed himself to think that all this was leading somewhere. Everyone knew that marine squadrons seldom were assigned carrier duty.

31.

SATURDAY, 11 JULY

IJNS TONE

Hiroyoshi Sakaida knocked at the entrance to the air officer's cabin. A voice beckoned him to enter and Sakaida stepped into the compartment, cap in hand. He was surprised to see Lieutenant (junior grade) Azumano as well as Lieutenant Masatake Naito, but he bowed and said, "Flight Petty Officer Sakaida reporting as the air officer ordered."

Naito looked up from his seat behind the steel desk, then leaned back. "Stand at ease, Sakaida. I believe I have welcome news for you."

Sakaida looked at Azumano, who stared back impassively. *I know that look*, Sakaida thought. *He's hiding something.*

Naito came to the point. "Sakaida, your performance during Operation MI was most commendable. In fact, Lieutenant Azumano has recommended you for a commendation but . . ." his voice trailed off. "But none have been approved for this ship."

Sakaida bowed toward both officers. "I am humbly grateful that my efforts were considered worthy." *If I were an officer I would have a promotion for my work*, he thought.

"Instead, I have decided to grant your wish," Naito continued. "I understand that you desire combat duty with a fighter squadron. While I cannot guarantee that exact assignment, I am recommending your transfer to a float-fighter unit. If the request is approved, you should report to the fighter conversion unit in about two weeks."

Azumano's lips curled in the beginning of a smile as Sakaida's eyes widened in disbelief.

32.

MONDAY, 13 JULY

MCAS EWA

"The CO says we're going to concentrate on gunnery," Carpenter told the three new pilots assigned to his division. They sat in one corner of VMF-223's hangar where Carpenter had placed a blackboard for briefing purposes. "That means two hops a day, including weekends, for as long as we can arrange towplanes and a slot on the gunnery range." He noticed dissatisfied scowls on the faces of two of the youngsters. His attitude may have seemed officious to the second lieutenants fresh out of Pensacola, but Jim Carpenter told himself that he no longer cared. *No, that's not right. I'm going to ride these kids because I do care.*

"I know what you're thinking," he continued. "Smitty is going to fly our asses off while other squadrons are working a five-day week and chasing skirts. Well, I don't know any more than you fellows, but it's obvious that we're going someplace while those other squadrons stay here."

"Lieutenant, when do you think we'll know?" Second Lieutenant Mike Stankovich, a husky ex-linebacker out of Northwestern, seemed the most eager of Carpenter's pilots.

"I haven't any idea," Carpenter replied, picking up a piece of chalk. "What I do know is that we're going to shoot a hell of a lot of fifty-caliber over the next few days." He was about to launch into his review of the standard gunnery patterns when another thought occurred to him. He laid down the chalk. "I want to tell you guys something.

"You know I was at Midway. So were a few others. We were given a lousy forty-eight hours at the Royal Hawaiian and then reported here, to an understrength squadron still flying F2As. Some of us began feeling pretty damn sorry for ourselves." He controlled his voice, trying to keep it modulated and sincere.

"Well, I'm here to tell you that we have it better right now than we ever did in Two-Twenty-One. We're flying better airplanes and we're getting more support and training time than we ever dreamed of on Midway." He held up a finger. "And I learned something else. When I tangled with the Zero that gave me this"—he touched the healed scar on his left cheek—"I realized that I wasn't ready for combat." He saw the effect of his words as Engel, Gentry and Stankovich exchanged puzzled glances. He pressed the point.

"Remember, I had over six hundred hours in fighters and thought I was a pretty hot gunner. But that Jap crawled all over me. I tried to fight him like I'd done in dogfights with other Brewsters, and it was damn near suicide. When he dived in to finish me off, he made his only mistake. He pulled up almost straight ahead of me—practically a no-deflection shot. My mom could have blown him out of the air." Carpenter paused for emphasis. "I got one burst at him, got a few hits and he climbed away."

The second lieutenants squirmed in their chairs. They saw where Carpenter was leading. "You guys have, what? Maybe three hundred hours' total time? Less than fifty in fighters." He shook his head. "You ain't ready for combat. But you will be by the time we ship out."

Barely an hour later, Carpenter led his three Wildcats into the gunnery area, checking in with the range officer by radio. He entered a holding pattern at 12,000 feet and looked back over his shoulder. Bobby Engel, his wingman, was tucked in reasonably close. Stankovich, leading the second section, was properly positioned, but his wingman lagged badly.

Carpenter picked up his microphone. "Number Four from Bulldog Lead. Close it up, Gentry." There was no reply, but the fourth Wildcat skidded awkwardly into position. Carpenter shook his head. *Have to keep an eye on him.*

Static crackled in Carpenter's earphones. "Bulldog Lead, this is Ewa Range Control. Your target plane is entering the area at ten thousand feet, west to east. Over."

Looking down to his left, Carpenter saw the SBD towplane streaming its canvas-sleeve target on a 1,000-foot cable. He called for his division to fall into trail and began a descent parallel to the target tug's heading. "This is not a firing pass," he called. "Follow me through the high-side run and regroup on the port side." With that he waggled his wings, accelerated ahead and, about 3,000 feet off the target's right nose, began his descending reversal toward the target.

Carpenter had chosen the high-side approach first because it was one of the easiest gunnery patterns to fly. However, he knew it was possible to turn too late, allowing the target to gain excessive horizontal separation. In that situation, the fighter inevitably got "sucked" far behind the target and completed the run out of range. Equally troubling, it gave a bomber's tail gunner a clear view of the fighter.

Completing forty-five degrees of turn, Carpenter saw the sleeve drawing level with him. He smoothly coordinated stick and rudder, flying his illuminated sight from the rear to the front of the target at ninety degrees deflection. Then, continuing what the Army Air Corps called a curve of pursuit, he angled into a right bank, closing the range before passing 100 yards astern of the sleeve. At two points in the run—at ninety and at forty-five degrees to the target—he had fired imaginary bursts. From previous experience he knew he would have made hits at both firing points.

Carpenter pulled up and watched the other F4Fs complete their dry runs. As expected, Stankovich was the smoothest. After re-forming on the left side of the towplane, Carpenter waggled his square wingtips again. "Okay, gang. Here we go again, this time from port." He looked at his instrument-panel clock and thought, *If only we have enough time to teach these kids. Got to have more time.*

33.

MONDAY, 27 JULY

USS SARATOGA

The new gold oak leaves on Dave Shumway's collar reflected the overhead light in the dining room that served as the SBD ready room. Sitting in his chair, Rogers reflected that the skipper of Bombing Three deserved the recent promotion to lieutenant commander, but not merely because the Bureau of Naval Personnel had authorized it. And though he would never admit it, Rogers also took pleasure from Burnett's elevated status as a jaygee.

But after Midway, Rogers secretly felt that he also had earned a promotion. *Well, Bernie's two classes senior to me*, Rogers told himself. *Shawn and I should get ours soon.*

"Fellows, your attention, please." Shumway now faced the roomful of pilots, most of whom were Midway veterans. "You all know that we had a bargeload of brass aboard yesterday, including General Vandegrift of the First Marine Division. Vice Admiral Fletcher will be the senior carrier commander in this upcoming operation, so that makes *Saratoga* the flagship of the support group."

Shumway half turned toward a chart of the Southwest Pacific on the bulkhead behind him. "Eleven days from now, we're going to put Vandegrift's marines ashore in the Solomon Islands." Bombing Three reacted with whistles, shouts and scattered applause. The CO waited for the commotion to abate, then continued. "That's right. It'll be the first American offensive in this war.

"The landings will be twofold," he continued. Pointing to the southern end of the island chain, he said, "Marines will occupy Tulagi, where the Japs have a seaplane base, and this airfield on the north coast of Guadalcanal."

Rogers stirred in his seat. *Guadalcanal—what an odd name. Wonder what it means?*

"In support of the landings I'm told that seventy-five ships are gathering here, south of the Fijis," Shumway added. That information also brought a reaction. Nobody in the room had ever seen that many ships at sea. "As I said, Admiral Fletcher will command the carrier force, which includes the *Enterprise* and the *Wasp*. Admiral Turner's in charge of the amphibious group that will put the troops ashore."

Shumway already knew the questions stirring in his pilots' minds and hastened to address them. "We expect to take the Japs by surprise, because even though the Tulagi seaplane base is operational, the airfield on Guadalcanal isn't. That's why we want it. With land-based air in there, we can support further amphibious landings all the way up the Solomons."

The skipper's finger went toward the top of the map. "The reaction will come from here, the Japs' big naval-air base at Rabaul on New Britain. It's about five hundred miles from Rabaul to Guadalcanal, but intelligence says the Japanese navy has land-based bombers there, plus heavy surface units." He looked around the room. "Everybody follow me so far?"

Burnett raised a hand. "Skipper, any idea how long we'll be in the Guad-a-canal area?" The name was still new, unfamiliar.

"I'm coming to that, Bernie. Admiral Fletcher has committed us to three days in support of the landings. That's supposed to be enough time for the transports to unload the marines and their equipment. I don't know for sure, but I suspect Fletcher doesn't want three carriers tied to a beachhead much longer than that." He indicated the blue area near the bottom of the map. "We'll be limited to an area south of Guadalcanal, flying patrols and air support for the infantry during that time. After nine August, I don't know. My guess is we'll head southeast, beyond land-based bomber range, to be in position if the Jap navy comes out in force.

"One thing seems sure," Shumway added. "They won't let this landing go unopposed."

35.

SUNDAY, 2 AUGUST

USS LONG ISLAND, PEARL HARBOR

Carpenter ducked under the wing of an SBD parked far aft and wound his way forward through a forest of propellers and hedges of stabilizers. "There's hardly room to swing a cat aboard this spitkit," he marveled.

Big Mike Stankovich, slightly shorter than Sunny Jim but definitely beefier, agreed. "I dunno how those swabbies packed this many airplanes on this deck." He looked around, taking in the nineteen Wildcats and twelve Dauntlesses that had been craned aboard the day where he peered outside. It was difficult to gauge the altitude, but he saw the night was clear with low, scattered clouds.

The H8K1 flying boat was a prestigious aircraft, in size and performance as well as in quantity. Sakaida had heard that to date fewer than a dozen had been produced, including prototypes. Consequently, he knew that the aircraft commander was a commissioned officer—in this case a full lieutenant—and the rest of the nine-man crew were senior petty officers and ratings. But Sakaida also knew that airmen loved to talk shop and to show off their equipment. He decided to make friends.

Moving to the flight engineer's compartment aft of the cockpit, Sakaida nodded to the third-class petty officer monitoring the engine gauges. "It's no good trying to sleep on a night like this," Sakaida began. He introduced himself to the man at the console, who replied, "Hajime Uesugi, Yokohama Air Group."

"I never saw so many gauges," Sakaida began. *I'll play the farm boy visiting the big city.* He flashed his most ingratiating smile. "I am just a floatplane pilot—I never saw anything so advanced as all this!"

Uesugi gave a sideways glance, as if trying to determine the passenger's motive. The red-lit cabin was a contrast of light and shadow, accenting the engineer's high cheekbones. Apparently glad of the diversion, he replied, "You would sell your virgin sister for an assignment like this, Sakaida. This is the most powerful flying boat in the world—more than the English Sunderland or the American Coronado."

Sakaida leaned closer to the panel. "What are your engine specifications?"

The engineer swept a hand across the gauges. "Four Kasei 12s, rated at 1,530 takeoff horsepower. We are cruising at 160 knots at 4,000 meters and will continue that speed most of the way to Guam."

A low whistle escaped Sakaida's lips. "What is your top speed at altitude?"

"Oh, almost 250 knots at 5,000 meters." Uesugi kept his exaggeration within ten percent—well under the worldwide norm for aviators.

Sakaida caught a movement in his peripheral vision. A form emerged through the hatchway leading to the flight deck, and he recognized the aircraft commander. Awkwardly, Sakaida braced in the low overhead.

"Who are you?" the lieutenant asked sharply.

"Flight Petty Officer Sakaida, sir!"

"Oh, yes. I saw your name on the cargo manifest." The officer's tone implied that Hiroyoshi Sakaida was another piece of His Imperial Majesty's property, along with the high-priority aircraft engine parts the H8K was delivering to Rabaul. Which, in a real sense, was the case.

"What is your aircraft type?"

"Sir, I am a floatplane pilot. Previous assignment, cruiser *Tone*. Now joining the rear echelon of the Yokohama Air Group in the Solomon—"

"Floatplanes, is it?" The aircraft commander thought for a moment. "Well, make yourself useful while I take a two-hour rest. Join Hatano on the flight deck. If you cannot help fly this type of aircraft, at least you can keep him from falling asleep." The officer brushed past Sakaida as if he were no longer there.

34.

FRIDAY, 31 JULY

OVER THE PACIFIC

Sakaida could not sleep. It was not so much the constant drone of the Kawanishi's four engines as the uncomfortable fold-down bunk. The priority passengers—two officers from the Twenty-fifth Air Flotilla—had the best accommodations, of course. Lesser mortals rotated on a "hot bunk" system, and Sakaida thought he could smell fish on the pillow from the bunk's previous occupant.

Swinging down from the cot, Sakaida pulled on his shoes and climbed the ladder to the upper deck. He ducked under the dorsal 20mm gun turret and passed the waist blister aft of the starboard wing, before. Glancing up the escort carrier's 490-foot length, he shook his head. "And *we* gotta be first off!"

"Well, sure," Carpenter replied. "An F4F's a lot lighter than an SBD with a five-hundred-pound bomb."

Nearby, some mechanics from VMSB-231 were loading additional gear into the rear cockpit of a Dauntless. "Say, I bet with the tools and spare parts they're cramming into those SBDs, they'll be over gross weight for launch," Stankovich observed.

The two enlisted marines struggled with a tool kit, awkwardly lifting it toward the dive-bomber's rear canopy rail. Without a word, Stankovich walked over, took the big step up to the wing and one-handed the bulky box into the gunner's seat.

"Gosh, thanks, Lieutenant!" The PFC's pimply face expressed gratitude and admiration.

"Think nothin' of it, lad." Stankovich dropped off the trailing edge of the wing and walked back to Carpenter, dramatically brushing his hands together.

"Showoff." Carpenter grinned.

The ex-fullback polished his nails on his shirt, then blew on his fingertips. "Ah, it was nothin'."

"Now hear this. Single up all lines fore and aft." The flight-deck bullhorn blared the old litany. "Set all special seakeeping details and stand by to get under way."

The fighter pilots looked at one another, their faces reflecting the orange light of the low sun. "Jeesus, here we go," intoned Stankovich. "Wonder where we're headed?"

"One thing I've learned," Carpenter replied evenly. "If you wait long enough, you always get the Word."

36.

MONDAY, 3 AUGUST

Sakaida was not at all certain that Lieutenant Azumano had done him a favor. Stepping to the door of the Type 97 flying boat, Sakaida felt the tropical heat and humidity envelop him like an oppressive towel. Fatalist that he was, he tossed his duffel bag down to the whaleboat idling alongside the H6K2.

It had been a long, uncomfortable trip, even in the spacious H8K: first a 2,100-mile overwater stretch to Guam, then a mere 600 to Truk in the Caroline Islands and another 700 to Rabaul, New Britain, for a day's layover. The final 250-mile leg to Buin in the H6K had been a tea party by comparison. In all, 3,500 nautical miles in four days had shown Hiroyoshi Sakaida most of the empire's Pacific region. He had not seen a great deal other than the inside of the H8K, including part of one night spent in the pilot's seat, but stops for offloading cargo and awaiting VIP passengers had been worthwhile. He made notes to write his family about his odyssey—something remarkable for his mother, who had never been more than a week's travel from her mountain village.

During the boat ride to shore, Sakaida tried to evaluate his new surroundings. At first glance he regretted accepting Azumano's well-intentioned offer of a transfer to a front-line unit with high-performance combat aircraft. Buin, on the south coast of the largest of the Solomon Islands, must have been a desolate place before the war, because it certainly looked godforsaken now. Rude buildings were spread along the shoreline, apparently temporary structures pending completion of permanent facilities. Sakaida ventured a word with the coxswain while the boat's lieutenant chatted with the VIPs.

"How long have you been here?" Sakaida asked.

The coxswain checked forward to ensure his officer did not mind him talking with another lowly rating. "Two months," the man replied. He said his name was Niitake, and that he came from the Kurile Islands.

Sakaida smiled in sympathy. "You must wish you were back there right now."

Niitake shook his head in an unmistakable sign of woe. "This cursed place is hell. The heat, the insects." He leered at the lieutenant's back. "The officers. Be glad you're going south toward the combat zone."

Sakaida was intrigued. "How do you know where I'm going? I don't even know that yet." His orders merely required him to report to the rear-area component of the Yokohama Air Group.

"This place is a mess," Niitake explained. "The airfield is supposed to be operational before the end of the month, but the schedule has been changed once already. I am told that the footing for the runways is very poor. So our land-based air attacks on the Americans are flown from Rabaul." He turned the tiller to maintain course toward the coconut-log pier. "The only operations flown from here are seaplanes. Are you a seaplane pilot?"

Sakaida nodded. "Yes, I was transferred from cruiser *Tone*. I wanted to fly fighters." He thought better of mentioning his role in Operation

MI. Azumano had been forceful in his warnings about discussing Midway with anyone, including junior officers.

"Well, the only ones between here and Guadalcanal are Type Zero and Type 2 sea fighters. You will probably go to our new operating base." Niitake looked earnestly at Sakaida, envying the aviation rating on the pilot's left sleeve. "It's a place called Rekata Bay."

37.

THURSDAY, 6 AUGUST

Sakaida had seen them upon arrival—A6M2-N floatplane fighters resting on their beaching dollies or riding at moorage offshore. His pulse had quickened at the prospect of combat in the Type 2 Nakajima modification of Mitsubishi's fabled Zero-Sen carrier fighter.

Now, sitting in the cockpit of one of the precious aircraft—destined for the advance base on Santa Isabel, he learned from mechanics' gossip—he felt in his element. He relished the presence of the reflector gunsight atop the instrument panel and the twin receivers of 7.7mm machine guns. *This is a real combat aircraft!*

The local checkout was a simple but effective reprise of what he had learned at the Oppama transition unit: pass a blindfold cockpit check, learn how to start the engine, then fly the airplane.

Sakaida had seldom flown a single-seat aircraft. At first he felt vaguely uneasy without the familiar presence of an observer and gunner behind him. But with the fourteen-cylinder Sakae engine ticking over, he left his doubts in his wake as he advanced the throttle, steering with blasts of power and taps on the rudder pedals. Aligned with the wind, he shoved throttle, mixture and prop controls full ahead and felt the little fighter bounce over the waves, throwing spray over the empennage. At an indicated seventy-eight knots the Type 2 was up on "the step" of the main float, and moments later he was flying.

His first impression was the rudder's unusual responsiveness. The floatplane needed about forty percent more rudder area than the standard Zero fighter, more for water taxiing than in flight, but the aerodynamic dividend was obvious.

Sakaida reduced power and propeller controls to climb setting and relished the Nakajima's performance. He estimated he was climbing at least fifty percent faster than he ever had in his Type Zero reconnaissance plane from *Tone*. Feeling safe at 6,000 feet, he leveled off and took stock. The little fighter seemed surprisingly stable as he took it through a series of ever-tighter turns. Then he tried power-on and power-off stalls, eagerly assessing his weapon's capabilities.

Satisfied after twenty minutes of experimenting, Sakaida decided, *Enough of that. Now for some fun.* He added power, nosed down steeply and watched the knots build on the airspeed indicator. With the engine pitch rising, windstream screaming past the canopy, he began a steady pull on the stick. The horizon disappeared under the nose, the airspeed bled off and Sakaida felt the controls beginning to slacken. He realized he should have pulled a tighter radius, as the Type 2 barely reached the apex of the loop. Then he was over the top, arcing down the back side. He retarded throttle and eased out of the loop into level flight.

Accelerating downhill once more, Sakaida felt confident this time. He kept the circumference of the maneuver nice and tight, smiling with pleasure when he felt the mild bump as he recovered at the bottom. *Flew through my own turbulence—a perfect loop!*

He noted the clock and realized his time was up. Other pilots were waiting their turns to fly. But as he banked toward Shortland, Hiroyoshi Sakaida was a happy man.

"You know, Bernie, I was just thinking." Rogers lazed in the upper bunk, a book open on his chest.

"Don't you know that's dangerous for an ensign?" The drowsy voice from the lower rack was muffled by the pillow over Burnett's head to blot out the light.

Rogers leaned over the edge of his bunk. "No, I mean our situation. Just think what we were doing sixty days ago, tonight."

There was silence while Burnett backtracked the events of 6 June. He remembered the attack on *Mogami* and *Mikuma*, and visiting Phil in *Enterprise*'s sick bay. "I was tryin' to get some sleep. Nothin' ev'r changes." He exaggerated the drowsiness he felt.

Rogers ignored the humor. "That's just my poir ," he insisted. "Look how things *have* changed. This time two mor ihs ago we were outnumbered, trying to defend an important island from the Japs. Now we're the ones on the offensive. We're ready to take the most important base in the Solomons, three thousand miles from Midway."

"Umm-hmm."

Rogers refused to be put off. He raised himself on one elbow. "We're going to win this war, Bernie."

Burnett pulled his pillow tight around his eyes and ears. "You and me. Burnett and Rogers, like Lewis and Clark." He contemplated for a moment. "Or Burns and Allen." *I'm Burns, you're Allen*, he thought. "Say good-night, Gracie."

Rogers slumped back, irritated at being shunned when he wanted to talk. He picked up the book and tried to find his place. Then Burnett's curly hair surfaced alongside the bunk, followed by his pillow-creased face. "Okay, Buck. What's on your mind?"

Surprised, Rogers felt the onset of guilt at rousing his friend on the eve of battle. "Well, it's just that . . . I'm starting to believe I can see an end to this."

Burnett shook his weary head. "Are you nuts? This war is gonna last years, Rogers." He yawned broadly.

"Yeah, I know. But we *are* going to win, and—"

"Well, hell's bells. *Of course* we're going to win. I don't think I know anybody who thinks different." He peered closely at Rogers. "What's with you?"

Rogers exhaled a deep breath as an explanation formed in his mind. It was long and complex—or was it? He heard himself say, "I'm going to ask Sally to marry me."

Burnett slumped, softly banging his forehead against the edge of the bunk. "I should've known. Girl troubles." He looked up at Rogers again. "What's that got to do with the end of the war?"

"Bernie, Sally always said she wouldn't consider marrying anybody because the war was going to drag on. But now, like I said, we're on the offensive. Don't you see? Midway completely changed things in the Pacific."

"Yeah. We're on the *Saratoga* instead of the *Yorktown*, standing off the Solomons instead of Midway. Tomorrow morning we'll get shot at by a whole new bunch of Japs and we'll drop bombs on a whole new bunch of targets."

Rogers shook his head. "Doesn't matter. Whenever we get back to Pearl, I'm going to pop the question."

Burnett was careful to remove the previous cynicism from his voice. "What if she says no, Phil?"

He shrugged. "Like Scarlett O'Hara said. I'll think about that tomorrow." Burnett thought, *You better think about your flying tomorrow, buddy.*

Rogers reached up and turned off his reading light. "Good-night, Bernie."

"Good-night, Gracie."

38.

FRIDAY, 7 AUGUST

OVER BEACH RED, GUADALCANAL

Smoke rising from across the sound was proof that *Wasp*'s aircraft were working over the Tulagi seaplane base. Barnes's voice came through the intercom, excitedly familiar. "How come those guys get the juicy targets, Mr. Rogers?"

Picking up his microphone, Rogers suppressed the mirth he felt at his gunner's eagerness. "New kids on the block, I guess. But stay on the ball, Barnes. Maybe some of those Jap floatplanes got up before we arrived." Actually, Rogers doubted any hostile aircraft escaped the early morning attack. But he knew the possibility of a shot at another Japanese plane would keep Barnes alert.

So far Ensign Philip Rogers's fifth combat mission had been anticlimactic—no antiaircraft fire, not even any identifiable targets to bomb. He was almost disappointed.

Rogers noticed the lead SBD swinging into another port turn in the holding pattern and banked to follow Bernie. Shawn Murtagh, flying number three in the section, smoothly kept station to starboard.

From his perch 8,000 feet over the beach, Rogers again looked down at the traffic jam of shipping. He had never seen an amphibious operation before, and the organized confusion captivated him. Landing craft trailed faint wakes like water bugs from Transport Area Yoke into Beach Blue on Tulagi while cruisers and destroyers in Area X-Ray maintained a bombardment of Beach Red on Guadalcanal's northern plain.

The size of the island impressed Rogers. Somehow it was larger than he had envisioned, even after plotting its ninety-mile length and average thirty-mile width. From over the landing beach he noted a row of coconut palms offsetting the light-colored sand and rippling waves of surf. Farther inland, beyond the grassy plain containing the uncompleted Japanese airfield, loomed green-jungled 6,000-foot mountains. But the staff aerologist had insisted that, ten degrees below the equator, Guadalcanal's wild beauty hid disease and rot, its humid air a suffocating blanket.

Rogers noticed his temperature gauge showed a few degrees into the yellow. He opened his cowl flaps for better cooling and thanked God that he was not expected to operate from the dark, brooding island.

USS LONG ISLAND

Sunny Jim Carpenter knelt to kiss the grease-smeared belly of the fattest chief petty officer aboard the little carrier. Wearing an oversized set of "diapers," the "Royal Baby" put on a childish pout and wailed something unintelligible to his "parents," King Neptune and the Queen of the Deep. The bearded *Neptunis Rex*—who bore a remarkable likeness to the ship's engineering officer—idly waved a regal finger at a pair of his fishnet-clad acolytes.

As he rose to a crouch in order to back away from the serene presence of the royal infant, Carpenter smelled a foul concoction. He turned just in time to see two gleeful sailors pour a ladle of galley scraps over his head. The rancid odor of warm bacon fat, lovingly stored and reheated for the solemn occasion, stained Carpenter's skivvy shirt.

A "one-eyed" pirate, leering ominously and brandishing a genuine cutlass, directed the marine to the end of a conga line of other "pollywogs" who had never entered the Golden Realm of Neptune. En route, Carpenter passed Mike Stankovich, who was obliged to maintain watch over the fantail with a pair of Coke bottles for binoculars. At the first sign of mermaids, Big Mike's standing orders required that he dive overboard and join the lovely creatures in "the rapture of the deep." To ensure acceptable grooming for the mermaids, the ship's barber had clipped Stankovich's hair right down to the scalp.

At length the miserable pollywogs were herded again into the royal presence and made to kneel in homage. Then, regal as always, Neptune waved his trident and declared the assemblage to be "trusty shellbacks" worthy to share his company in future line-crossing ceremonies. (And, incidentally, qualified to inflict similar indignities on other fresh-caught pollywogs.) High-pressure hoses then were turned on the motley crew to cleanse the offenders of their foul odors.

Thus did USS *Long Island* mark her transit south of the equator, en route to points unknown.

39.

SUNDAY, 9 AUGUST

USS SARATOGA

Holy Christ, four cruisers! Rogers's back felt a prickly sensation between the shoulder blades, and not from the tropical heat. The scout-bomber pilots in the main dining room encased a stunned silence.

"That's the word from flag country," Shumway was saying, relaying the catastrophic news from Admiral Fletcher's staff. "Details are sketchy, but it's confirmed that the *Astoria, Quincy* and *Vincennes* all went down during the night. The Aussies scuttled HMS *Canberra* this morning." He paused in the litany of disaster, then pressed on. "But there's more. The *Chicago* is damaged, out of action, and a destroyer is missing as well."

"Skipper, what the hell happened? Were our ships caught napping?" Burnett didn't mind vocalizing the question that hung like a curtain in the ready room's confines.

"Well, obviously they were surprised. A Jap cruiser-destroyer force came around Savo Island and . . . apparently the whole thing was over in about thirty minutes." The CO's voice carried a gravelly sadness; the reservists began to realize that the Annapolis graduates undoubtedly had friends and former shipmates in the slain cruisers. *It must be hell, not knowing*, Rogers thought.

Somebody in the front row asked, "Any word on what we did to the Japs?"

Shumway shrugged eloquently. "Not for sure. But it's a hell of a lot less than they did to us." He brushed a finger over his mustache and continued. "The big question is why the Japs didn't press their advantage. They could have cleaned up the transports with a mop, but they steamed around Savo and headed back north to Rabaul.

"Anyway, we're hightailing it southeast. Apparently Admiral Fletcher wants to prevent any chance of another night surface engagement, especially since the transports have lost most of their protection."

A hard-edged murmur spread through the room, striking sparks wherever it alighted. For the first time, Rogers was aware of Murtagh's clenched fists on the armrests of his chair. "We're running! Can you frigging believe it?" Rogers looked at his classmate and saw the purple tint rising beneath the skin. Rogers was certain that Shawn Murtagh had never run from a fight in his twenty-three years on earth.

A dreadful thought forced its way through the fogged confusion and injured pride in Rogers's mind. Raising his voice over the chatter, he asked, "Skipper! What about the troop transports? If we pull out, won't they be left . . ."

Shumway raised a cautionary hand. "I know what you're thinking, Rogers, and you're right. The transports are hoisting anchor with most of the marines' heavy equipment still aboard. I don't imagine that Admiral Turner's very happy with Admiral Fletcher this morning."

Rogers leaned back in his chair, berating himself for his previous optimism. *About thirty-six hours ago I was trying to convince Bernie that we almost had this thing whipped.*

I'll never make that mistake again . . . never.

A celebration definitely was in order, and the party was progressing nicely. But observing the destruction of nine enemy warships took a lot of celebrating. Sakaida extended his cup toward Special Duty Ensign Kono, who was democratically pouring for the petty officers at the moment. Someone—Sakaida no longer remembered or cared just who—had suggested a round of sake for each American ship sunk. Besides, some of the new arrivals had been alerted for assignment to the Shortland Seaplane Base in a few days. The sake supply there was reputed to be distressingly erratic. *Best to drink up now,* Sakaida thought.

"This is to ship number seven, is it not?" Kono slurred his words in most-unofficerlike fashion, but then Sakaida remembered that his new friend Yusuke had been an enlisted man for thirteen years. "Or is it number eight?"

"Yes!" Sakaida blurted. He clinked his cup against those of the ratings squatting on the mat to either side of him. The man on his left burped loudly, and pounded his chest with his free hand. This display of comic genius inspired an outburst of laughter in the rude barracks.

"We have drunk to five enemy cruisers," Kono explained to his inebriated companions. "But the radio report also said four destroyers. Now . . ." He paused in midsentence to catch his breath. ". . . are we on destroyer number two or number three?" It was a matter of serious import.

"Yes!" Sakaida responded again, raising his teacup in triumph. He looked around, disappointed that his humor was apparently wearing thin. Rising on unsteady feet, he announced, "I know . . . what we need." He trod carefully outside and returned from the twilight evening with a bunch of bananas in one hand.

"You like Latin American girls?" Sakaida asked rhetorically. "Well, I have one . . . right here!" With one hand he raised the bananas to the top of his head. Then, fumbling with his free hand in a pitiful attempt to snap his fingers, he began prancing around the circumference of the convivial circle. A series of imitation-Latin cadences, punctuated with "Ayeees" and "Aye-aye-ayes," accompanied his routine. A second-class airframe mechanic beat a syncopated tattoo on the wood floor, and Hiroyoshi Sakaida won a new circle of friends while celebrating the deaths of 1,077 American and Australian sailors.

40

THURSDAY, 13 AUGUST

USS LONG ISLAND

Captain John L. Smith faced a roomful of VMF-223 pilots and delivered a cold-water dousing. "We're putting into Suva this afternoon," he began. "And I expect some of you will leave the squadron for additional training."

Most of the men present were second lieutenants who realized the CO's words were directed at them. He waved down the rising protest building in the compartment and swept the assembly with a patented Quantico stare. "It's no reflection on your potential ability," Smith added by way of explanation. "But after consulting with Commander

Barner and Major Mangrum of Two-Thirty-Two, we're recommending that many of the pilots in both squadrons receive another six weeks of training before going to combat."

From the front row, Jim Carpenter looked down the aisle at Mike Stankovich, Bobby Engel and Sam Gentry. As a division leader, Carpenter had given Smith an assessment of the men's abilities, apparently at the request of *Long Island*'s skipper, James D. Barner. Carpenter winked at Stankovich, who was solid. But Engel was regarded as marginal, and Gentry, whom Carpenter considered "nervous in the service," had to go.

"If the transfers are approved, we'll pick up replacements from VMF-212 in the New Hebrides," Smith continued. "That means that we'll be getting some new pilots with more experience than some of you who are staying. Section and division leads may need to be changed accordingly, but I won't know about that until I see who we get from Lieutenant Colonel Bauer." The merest trace of a smile cracked the granite edifice of Smith's jaw. Carpenter and a few others knew that Smith had been a very junior squadronmate of Bauer's long, long ago—in 1940. Now Smitty, shortly in line for major, was raiding "Indian Joe's" talent pool.

"One more thing," Smith added. "We all know about the situation where we're headed, on Guadalcanal." It was an understatement, as discussion on the tiny carrier had centered on nothing else for the past few days, since word of the disaster at Savo Island. "The navy hauled ass out of there with the transports as well as the carriers. General Vandegrift's troops haven't seen an American aircraft since the ninth, but the Japanese are bombing the place every day." He swept the room again, left to right, reinforcing his message. "If any of you are feeling sorry for yourselves about being left behind for now, that's too bad. But it doesn't count for a thing compared to the help the marines need on that island."

41.

TUESDAY, 18 AUGUST

Another damn sector search, Rogers told himself. He knew perfectly well he was unlikely to find anything in the expanse of the Solomon Sea south of Guadalcanal. But as he turned onto his outbound 200-mile search leg, he also welcomed the chance to get off the ship after a couple of days of inactivity.

Rogers slid his canopy forward to reduce the wind swirling into the cockpit. He glanced back at Murtagh, joining him in a rendezvous turn, and waggled his wings. Ordinarily two ensigns would not fly together, but Bombing Three now boasted a high degree of corporate experience. Though Rogers secretly relished leading his old classmate on this mission, he knew that the senior position easily could be reversed next time.

"All set back here, sir." Barnes had deployed his guns, as usual, and had his daily code pad ready for use in event of a contact.

Rogers finished trimming the scout-bomber for a slow climb before responding. "Okay, Bill. Try to keep me from falling asleep, will you?"

"Sure thing, Mr. Rogers. I'll just cut loose with a long burst." Barnes laughed over the intercom.

That would do it, all right, Rogers mused. The pilot was increasingly comfortable with an easy relationship toward the gunner, to the extent of addressing Barnes by his given name in private. Occasionally, on long searches like this, Rogers was tempted to gossip over the intercom. He knew that Barnes had dated that female yeoman from the Pearl Harbor hospital, but not much beyond that.

Rogers scanned his gauges again, swept the horizon and squirmed in his seat. *Best let it go*, he decided. *If we get in the habit of gabbing, we might miss something important.* His mind withdrew to the afternoon of 4 June, when Barnes had spotted that vengeful Zero just in time. Turning his head, Rogers checked port and starboard, focusing beyond the tail of his Dauntless. *Got to keep sharp*, he told himself. *If I want to see Sally again.*

LIBRARY OF HAWAII

Mary Tanaka pointed to Sally's homemade lunch. "So you're brown-bagging it, too."

Somehow, the slang was slightly humorous. Ordinarily Mary was correct and precise in her choice of words—what most people would expect of a librarian, Sally thought.

Sitting on a cement bench in the courtyard, Sally kicked off her shoes and stretched her feet into the grass. She nibbled at her tuna-salad sandwich and pointed a toe at one of the nearby bomb shelters. "I wonder if they're going to leave these here."

Mary chomped an apple and shrugged. After a moment she swallowed and said, "I think so. You know Mr. Kuhio, the custodial supervisor? Last week he said there was a problem keeping the shelters drained properly, and they would have to make some improvements."

Sally looked at the mounded earth over the shelter and remembered the air-raid drills. At length she said, "Phil doesn't think there'll be another attack on Hawaii."

Mary nodded vaguely, then looked at her friend. "I suppose he's right. The newspapers all say the war has entered a new phase, now that we are on the offensive." She thought for a moment. "I suppose Phil and Bernie and their friends are somewhere in the Solomon Islands."

Sally put away part of her sandwich and folded the paper sack. "I haven't heard anything yet. Phil warned me that the mail could be awful slow." She studied her toes and said, "I keep thinking about that picnic we had in the park. Mary, do you think I was too rough on Bernie? I mean, his crack to Ginger about Tojo and the library?"

Mary stared into space. "Well, no. Actually, I thought you handled it pretty well." She smiled. "Besides, as I remember, Bernie and Ginger were getting along pretty well by the end of the afternoon."

Sally leaned close, her shoulder rubbing Mary's. "Actually, I think Ginger gets along pretty well with *any* man in uniform." Mary broke into a giggle, one hand covering her mouth.

"I didn't get to ask you," Sally added. "What did you think of Phil's friend, Shawn?"

"Oh, I liked him. But I think he was surprised when he met me. He didn't seem to expect that I would be Nisei."

Sally nodded. "Yes, but I really don't think it mattered."

"No, it didn't. He was easy to talk to. But you know, Sally, I can't get involved with a Caucasian. Or anyone else. My parents—"

Embarrassed, Sally hastened to interject. "Oh, gosh, Mary! Of course I know how your family feels. I hope they don't think I was trying to set you up with somebody. It was just a picnic, after all."

Mary patted her friend's arm. "Yes, I know. It's just that my parents are quite traditional. Even Harold had trouble when he joined the army. My mother thought there were other ways he could show his loyalty to America. And with the way things are on the mainland . . ."

Sally inhaled and thought before speaking. She had waited for this opportunity. "Mary, I don't think I know anybody who doubts Nisei loyalty. The relocation camps on the West Coast . . ." She shrugged in frustration. It was a sign of wartime hysteria, she knew, but that did nothing to alleviate the pain. Because of her friendship with Mary, she had read as much about the situation as she could find: how President Roosevelt and California Attorney General Earl Warren had dispossessed families of Japanese ancestry. Apparently one of the few to protest was FBI Director J. Edgar Hoover, who contended that American citizens were being deprived of due process.

"It's just different here in Hawaii, with the Japanese descendants being forty percent of the population," Sally continued. "But I know there are people who can't see past . . . the racial part." She looked at her friend. "Do you ever feel it?"

Mary nodded slowly. "Oh, yes. It's not very obvious, but it's there. Sometimes when a soldier or sailor comes in, he will divert away from the circulation desk when he sees me. Or he waits to talk to someone else."

Sally did not know what to say. So she listened.

"There's something I haven't told you," Mary added. "When I was very young, maybe three or four, we went back to Japan for a visit. My father's family is from a village in the mountains near Tokyo. It's the only time I ever met any of my grandparents, and I don't remember them at all. Harold remembers a little of that trip.

"I have several cousins in the Japanese military, Sally. I've never met them and I don't even know all their names. But one of them, named Fuotoka, is an officer in the army. My mother thinks he's in China. Another is a naval aviator. His name is Sakaida."

42.

WEDNESDAY, 19 AUGUST

OVER TONOLEI, SHORTLAND ISLANDS

Sakaida saw the lead A6M2-N bank away to the left as Ensign Kono rolled into a gunnery run on the target 2,000 feet below. Waiting for the proper interval, Sakaida then followed his leader down on the floating target, fairly squirming with anticipation. Aircraft checkouts were fine, and certainly necessary, but after 1,100 hours flight time, Sakaida felt that one floatplane handled pretty much like another.

Gunnery was a different matter entirely.

Trailing Kono by ten seconds, Sakaida studied the leader's approach heading and dive angle. The attack run was shallower than expected, but Sakaida realized that the combat-experienced officer must know what he was about. Abrupt smoke puffs spurted back from Kono's nose as he opened fire with his 7.7mm machine guns. Sakaida had been disappointed to learn that no 20mm ammunition was available for practice missions. The Shortland aviation-matériel officer said his supplies were insufficient for such luxuries just now.

That information had bothered Sakaida. *How can we fight a war without ammunition?* He considered it an ill omen. Then he pushed the thought from his mind, concentrating on the immediate problem.

In admiration, Sakaida registered white geysers smothering the oil drums lashed together in the bay. Kono fired a second burst which spumed the water just beyond the target, then he was nose-level and climbing away in a port turn, clearing the area for his new wingman.

With delicate movements, Sakaida arranged the target in his Type 98 reflector gunsight. Kono had instructed him to fire his first rounds just short of the target, walking his bullets through the center. As engine pitch steadily increased, Sakaida was fascinated with the sight picture presented him. He pushed slightly forward on the stick, placing the center aiming dot below the barrels, and fired.

The sound and vibration of two machine guns erupting in the cockpit comprised a bedlam of violence. Sakaida had been unprepared for the sensory overload—nobody had warned him about it. The tang of burnt gunpowder was tangible, though he had reflexively stopped firing after a short burst. Sakaida glanced down at the twin receivers projecting through the instrument panel, not knowing what to expect.

When he looked up, he saw whitecaps filling his windscreen. He realized that Kono was screaming at him over the scratchy radio circuit. Sakaida placed both hands on the stick grip and pulled, hard.

In six years of flying, Sakaida had never experienced blackout. He could not remember the last time he had even grayed out, as floatplane operations seldom involved such stress. But when his vision cleared, Sakaida found himself nose-high with the Type 2 sea fighter shuddering on the edge of a stall. Instinctively, he shoved the nose down and added power. Then he looked around.

Kono was just off his port wingtip, canopy slid back, shaking his head in admonition. *He warned me*, Sakaida realized. *He said I might become entranced by the target.* Sakaida raised his hands in a mea-culpa gesture, then indicated with a circular motion that he wanted to try once more. He was not certain, but he thought he could see a knowing smirk on his leader's face.

The carrier wave itched in Sakaida's earphones as Kono said,

"Follow me again, and do what I do!" Sakaida rocked his wings in awkward acknowledgment. He gave little thought to the unshielded ignitions in most Japanese aircraft engines, which often interfered with radio transmissions. Visual signals would usually suffice.

Kono broke down and away so abruptly that Sakaida was momentarily taken by surprise. *He's showing me that fighter flying is different. I have to forget my reconnaissance days*, Sakaida realized.

As before, Kono put his first rounds on target. Sakaida remembered to throttle back slightly, understanding that the shallow strafing pass was for his own protection. With more time to concentrate on his sight picture, he fired three bursts. The first hit short, but the next two swamped the barrels, which appeared to be sinking.

After two more passes, the target barrels and ammunition were expended. "All right, boy. Now let's see you, fly!" Kono swerved behind Sakaida and fixed the student squarely in his sight. Two seconds later Sakaida was sliding around a hard port turn, throttle against the stop in a descending spiral, feeling more alive than at any time in all his twenty-six years.

For the next ten minutes, two sea-fighter pilots had the South Pacific sky to themselves in an arena bounded by towering cumulus clouds and white-capped azure waters.

43.

THURSDAY, 20 AUGUST

Carpenter responded to the plane director's "come on" gesture by nudging more power to the R-1830. In response, the fully loaded Wildcat waddled onto the escort carrier's single catapult, where handlers shoved its square tail into line.

Looking forward past the F4F's round nose, Carpenter lost sight of the catapult crewmen who scurried about their arcane business beneath the wings. He knew they were attaching the bridle to his aircraft, and felt a slight motion as the hydraulic catapult took up the tension on the cables. The sailors scrambled back into the open, signaling all-clear to the catapult officer.

In response to the man's circular motion, Carpenter advanced throttle and prop controls full forward and released the toe brakes. He checked his instruments, ensured that his flaps were lowered and the tailwheel was locked. Then he nodded to the officer and braced his head against the padded cushion on his armor plate.

The wait seemed interminable, and Carpenter wondered if there was some snag. *I shouldn't run a lashed-down engine this long at full power*, he thought. His left arm, fully extended to keep throttle, prop and mixture controls firewalled, began to twitch faintly.

As the carrier's nose came up in the swell, the catapult fired ten seconds after Carpenter ran up the engine. He felt as if a Missouri mule had kicked him in the small of his back. The canopy slammed forward, jolted loose from the violence of the catapult's momentum, and for an instant Carpenter's heart rose in his throat. *I'll be trapped and drown if I go in the drink.*

Then he realized he was flying. He eased into a clearing turn, raised his flaps and began cranking up his wheels.

With his wits about him, Carpenter joined the loose pack of Wildcats climbing for altitude over the little task force, including a light cruiser and two destroyers. He saw Stankovich's fighter flung off the deck and noted that the launch was proceeding as planned. *Damn little bucket's only got one catapult*, he thought. *This'll take all day.* He saw the other planes waiting their turn, parked well aft on the tiny flight deck. With insufficient room for a deck-run takeoff, launch depended on the catapult, so the procedure was bound to be slow.

Eventually all nineteen Wildcats and dozen Dauntlesses were formed up. Carpenter took encouragement from the faultless launch process. *Our twelve new guys did fine*, he told himself. *But of course, they're more experienced than those we left in Efate.* The squadron's hasty tactical reorganization had "demoted" Stankovich from section leader to Carpenter's wingman—a change Carpenter welcomed.

According to the ship's navigator, launch had commenced 190 miles south of Guadalcanal, off the southern tip of San Cristobal Island. But the southeasterly trade wind had required *Long Island* to steam away from the objective, thus lengthening the flight. Carpenter mentally computed the navigation geometry and checked his compass against the late-afternoon sun. *Something's screwy*, he concluded.

At the head of the formation, flying VMF-223's spare F4F, was Lieutenant Colonel Pike, executive officer of Marine Air Group 23.

Carpenter knew little about him, other than scuttlebutt that he had more rank than flight time. Carpenter noticed the skipper's Wildcat leave the first division and pull alongside Pike's. *What's Smitty up to?* Then the realization dawned. *He's showing Pike the way home!*

Thirty-one blue-gray aircraft turned onto their course for Guadalcanal, flying northwesterly through a reddening, cloud-flecked sky.

HENDERSON FIELD, GUADALCANAL, 1630

Carpenter looked around at the object of Operation Watchtower and was not impressed. Swirling dust and the dimming light obscured his vision as other planes landed on the 3,500-foot dirt-and-gravel runway. *Oh, well. At least we all made it.* He unfastened his seat belt, slid out of his parachute harness and dismounted.

Immediately the aviator was surrounded by "mud marines." Their jubilation overrode military courtesy as a bulldozer driver democratically pounded Carpenter on the back. "Boy, oh, boy. Are we glad to see you!" Another enlisted man, with an '03 Springfield slung over his shoulder, shook the pilot's hand and started to speak. But no words came from the dried, cracked lips in the grimy face. The rifleman merely nodded and turned away.

What the hell is going on here? Carpenter wondered. He slowly made his way through the well-wishers to join the rest of VMF-223, but he was intercepted by a second lieutenant who saluted, then extended his hand. Carpenter shook again, feeling like a politician campaigning for office. "Welcome to Henderson Field," the staffer said. "You're a sight for sore eyes. I'm Glenn Burkett, First Division staff."

Carpenter pulled off his helmet and mussed his blond hair. "Henderson Field?"

"Yes, sir. It's been named for a marine flier killed at Midway."

"Oh, my gosh . . . yes. Joe Henderson." Carpenter had hardly known Major Lofton Henderson of VMSB-241, shot down while attacking Japanese carriers.

Looking around, Carpenter asked, "Burke, what's the story here?"

"Uh, Burkett. We've been bombed almost every day since the landings on the seventh. We have a perimeter around the field, and there's a lot of patrol activity." He shrugged. "The rest of the island is pretty much owned by the jungle and the Japs."

"Well, I didn't see any sign of bomb damage from the air. How bad has it been?"

Burkett tipped his helmet back on his head. "Actually, not terribly bad as far as damage goes. But you have to understand, these men haven't seen an American airplane in about two weeks. General Vandegrift himself met the first of your planes to land. The effect on morale is—"

"HIP-HIP, HOORAY! HIP-HIP, HOORAY!" A vocal group of infantrymen cheered the arrival of another SBD.

Carpenter turned to Burkett. "I see what you mean."

44.

FRIDAY, 21 AUGUST

Only nineteen hours after arrival on Guadalcanal, Carpenter wanted to lay down and sleep. Gunfire had awakened the airmen around 0200 when a Japanese probe of the perimeter had been checked barely a mile from the field.

Stankovich came sprinting slightly downhill from 200 yards north of the runway. "Smitty's tangled with some Japs over the sound," Big Mike gasped. "He's comin' in right now."

Carpenter looked back from where Stankovich had come—the ramshackle Japanese structure everyone called the Pagoda. It served as headquarters for air operations on Guadalcanal, or "Cactus" in the code-name slang that had become a second language.

"Any word on the action?" Carpenter asked.

Stankovich breathlessly shook his head. "Radio contact ain't too good." The lieutenant leaned forward, bracing his hands on his knees. Carpenter did not press the issue. He knew that operational details such as radio frequencies and flight schedules were still being worked out.

A faint hum throbbed the tropical air, capturing the attention of everyone within earshot. Carpenter looked up toward the noonday sun, shading his eyes while searching for the source of the sound. "Radial engines," Stankovich said. It was a useless comment—both Japanese and American naval aircraft used air-cooled engines.

"There!" First Lieutenant Ben Morgan, formerly of VMF-212 and Carpenter's section leader, pointed a finger to the north-northwest.

Carpenter saw it. "He's landing dead-stick. Damn."

Now plainly visible, the first returning Wildcat turned from base leg to final approach, its three-bladed propeller motionless. Streaming a thin trace of oil, the F4F continued its approach, wheels still tucked neatly into the fuselage. The pilot astutely landed long to clear the runway for those coming behind him.

As the battered Wildcat touched down, bumped, then crunched onto the gravel again, Carpenter read the aircraft number. "It's Johnny," he said. A crowd of spectators sprinted toward the spot where their friend would slide to a halt.

Moments later three other F4Fs swung into the pattern, touching down in controlled landings and taxiing to the parking area. Carpenter stood watching the new combat veterans. He folded his arms and looked down at his dusty shoes. "Goddamn . . ."

Stankovich gave his leader a querulous look. "What's the matter, Jim? They're all back."

Carpenter finally looked up. "Hell's bells. Every one of them has holes in it." He pointed to the third fighter, just shutting down. "That one's worse than my F2A at Midway." Stankovich looked closer and made no reply. It was obvious from the profusion of 7.7 and 20mm holes that the Wildcat would never fly again.

Pilots and mechanics crowded around John L. Smith as he dropped off the wing. The CO idly poked a finger in a machine-gun hole aft of his cockpit. He was swamped with questions.

"What happened, Skipper?"

"Did ya get one, Smitty?"

"Johnny's okay. His plane's a write-off, though."

Smith removed his helmet and goggles and began shedding his Mae West. "We were at fourteen thousand south of Savo Island when I saw about six Zero fighters maybe a half mile to one side and five hundred feet above us," he began. "We turned into them and naturally they turned into us." He shrugged his big shoulders and looked at his riveted audience. "After that, it's hard to say just what happened. I shot at one with his belly to me as he went by, but then two more got on my tail."

The CO handed his gear to his plane captain and, in a flat, unemotional voice, continued the tale. "I turned toward the field and they left me alone. But when we counted noses, Johnny was missing, so we went back to look for him. Then the Zeros jumped us again and shot some more holes in us. But like before, when we headed back they turned away."

An operations officer made his way through the crowd, a smile on his face. "Captain Smith? Oh, good news, sir. We just had a report of a Japanese plane in the water off Savo Island."

Cheers and applause broke out, and a few daring souls even patted Smith's back. He stared down the celebrants. "Don't let this go to your head. Remember, we might have got one of them, but we've lost the use of two planes." His hazel eyes scanned the crowd. "All this means is that the Japs are as scared of us as we are of them."

IJNS TONE, OFF RABAUL

Lieutenant Masatake Naito paced briskly to the Type Zero floatplane undergoing maintenance in the hangar bay. He looked up to the wing, where his senior aircrew officer was leaning into the middle cockpit. "Azumano! A word with you, please."

Startled at hearing his name, Toshiki Azumano glanced down. He muttered a quick word to the petty officer in the observer's seat and turned toward Naito. "At once, Air Officer." Azumano scrambled down the ladder and saluted with precision.

Naito returned the salute and turned with a follow-me gesture. He felt the cruiser beginning to roll to port and automatically shifted his balance. Safely away from the enlisted men, he dropped the formality and spoke in a confidential tone. "Azumano, you are my most experienced aircraft commander. I want you to know more of our role in the upcoming operation."

Azumano knew that the air officer had just come from a staff meeting with Rear Admiral Hara and Captain Anibe. It had not taken long: the entire task force was composed of the elderly light carrier *Ryujo*, escorted by *Tone* and two destroyers.

"We will continue our southerly heading, in advance of Carrier Division One," Naito explained. "*Ryujo*'s mission is to launch an attack against the Americans on Guadalcanal before rejoining *Shokaku* and *Zuikaku* to the northeast."

Azumano caught his breath. "But, Lieutenant, *Ryujo* only has nine attack planes. Does this mean that we . . . are to be sacrificed?"

Naito's dark eyes remained fixed on his subordinate's. "Officially we are designated the Detached Strike Force. But . . ." He sought the precise words. "We may draw the enemy upon ourselves if necessary, in order that CarDivOne may strike a decisive blow against the enemy."

"Very well." Azumano did not know what else to say. In the Imperial Navy, one served His Majesty's cause without complaint. He shook his head almost imperceptibly.

"Something is on your mind," Naito said evenly.

"I was just thinking, sir. In a situation like this, I wish I had Sakaida flying with me again." Azumano's new pilot, Flight Petty Officer Tachibana, was competent enough. But like so many replacement aircrew, he lacked seasoning.

Naito tugged at his visored cap. "I imagine that Sakaida is completing his transition course at Oppama. The new float-fighter units are being organized at Kanoya Kokutai one at a time."

Azumano stood to attention and saluted, his face an expressionless mask. *Sakaida*, he thought, *in granting you your wish, I may have doomed myself.* Toshiki Azumano turned away with an empty feeling beneath his belt buckle.

45.

SUNDAY, 23 AUGUST

USS SARATOGA, 1445

Spotted near the front of the pack, Rogers waited his turn to launch. The noise of thirty-seven radial engines was a sign of latent power that pulsed with kinetic energy. He could feel as much as hear the change in rpm and pitch as pilots went through their checklists, running up full power, testing magnetos and cycling propellers.

The sixteen-year-old giant carrier swung into the wind, heeling slightly in the turn. Rogers sensed the canted angle of the flight deck and told himself it was perfectly normal, but he never fully adjusted to the sensation. When he had first joined Bombing Three, he had imagined himself going over the side, strapped into his aircraft and sinking like an anchor. It still had not happened, nor had he even seen it happen. But the thought was always there, twitching in his brain.

The air group commander's SBD began its run down the deck and Rogers saw the Dauntless settle off the bow. Seconds later it reappeared in a slow climbing turn. "There goes Queen Bee," Rogers called over the intercom. Barnes made no comment, but none was necessary.

Rogers felt confident serving under Commander Harry Don Felt, who seemed to be the flyingest CAG in the U.S. Navy. Hailing from Kansas and the Annapolis class of '23, he had been skipper of Bombing Two when *Lexington* received the fleet's first SBD-2s during 1940. Since then he had probably logged as much Dauntless time as anyone, and his pet was the SBD-3 with the numeral zero painted on the cowl. It was a joke in *Saratoga*'s ready rooms that Queen Bee would fly for no one but Commander Felt and Radioman Snyder.

As his own turn came, Rogers told himself to concentrate on the fundamentals. Taking off with a 1,000-pound bomb and a full fuel load required careful handling, even in as simple and reliable an aircraft as an SBD. When he felt Baker Five leave the deck, he left full power on while he made his clearing turn, cleaned up gear and flaps, and then adjusted throttle and prop control for a 130-knot climb.

Beneath a gray overcast, *Saratoga*'s air group took shape as Rogers formed on Burnett and in turn was joined by Murtagh. In a climbing spiral he alternately kept formation and watched the launch proceed below: thirty other SBDs behind Felt and six of the reformed Torpedo Eight's new TBF-1s. Rogers studied one of the big Avengers as it rose into the relative wind with deceptive ease. *It's that huge wing*, he thought. *You could lift a house with that much wing area.*

He saw Wayne Wik's face, murky yet identifiable against the gray sea and sky. *Wayne never got to fly the TBF.* Rogers shook his head, clearing away the apparition like a cobweb from his memory. *He's been gone—what is it? Ten weeks now?*

After another circuit over the task force, CAG Felt led the strike force out on course. Rogers pulled his chartboard toward him and checked the time-distance equation. *Let's see . . . 275 miles to the reported position of the Jap transports.* The briefing had made clear that it was well beyond the radius of an F4F escort, so the scout-bombers and torpedo planes would go alone.

Rogers felt the chances of success were marginal. The PBY contact report of enemy transports and destroyers was hours old by the time it reached Vice Admiral Fletcher; the weather was increasingly dirty and daylight was running out. But, according to the staff intelligence officer, the threat of Japanese reinforcements ashore was too great to ignore. The long-range strike continued, seeking an elusive target in the stretch of open water known as the Slot.

BAKER FIVE, 1530

"Bill, strap yourself in tight. We may be in for a bumpy ride."

"Ah, yes, sir. All buttoned up back here."

Rogers could tell that Barnes had closed both canopy sections over the gunner's cockpit—the familiar windy whine was gone. In worsening weather like this, he saw no point in deploying the twin .30-calibers against the infinitesimal chance of interception. *The Japs aren't dumb enough to fly in this crud*, he ruefully told himself.

It was obvious now that Commander Felt meant to push his orders to the limit. A series of dark-gray line squalls stretched seemingly into infinity under ragged, scalloped clouds. Raindrops spattered with increasing frequency on the plexiglass canopy, streaking backward in the 160-knot slipstream.

A quarter-mile ahead, Queen Bee drove into the obscuring cloak of a rain cloud. Rogers inhaled deeply, slowly exhaled and set himself for instrument-flight penetration of the front.

He wanted to be on the gauges before he actually entered the clouds, so he concentrated on his needle and ball for attitude and the airspeed indicator for vertical reference. "Needle-beedle-speedle," it was called—the most basic form of instrument flight. With the turn-and-bank needle centered, as well as the ball indicating yaw, he knew he was tracking straight. Occasional reference to his compass reinforced that information. With his vision focused on his instrument panel, he hardly noticed when Baker Five entered the moist confines of the dank, gray cloud until rain beat a warning tattoo on his canopy.

But Rogers was groping his way blindly through three dimensions, not merely two. Therefore, his instrument scan constantly alternated from turn-and-bank to airspeed indicator. If the needle showed an increase beyond 160 knots indicated, he knew he was diving. If the airspeed dropped off, he was climbing.

Rogers was thankful of Barnes in the rear seat. It was a luxury to have another set of eyes in the airplane, alert to an imminent collision. That was always a possibility when flying formation on instruments.

But he sensed the darkness enveloping the world outside his cockpit and realized that any warning probably would come too late.

How long can this last? Rogers asked himself. The eight-day clock was stuck on noon—he had paid no attention to it before launch. He wanted to peel back his left glove to check his watch, but dared not break his concentration. The rain whipped harder against the SBD's airframe and canopy, the propeller throwing occasional torrents onto the windscreen. *Needle-ball-airspeed*, he told himself.

"Sir, it's getting light up ahead." Barnes knew that his pilot would not try to pick up the mike, but saw him nod vigorously.

Rogers sensed the gloom growing less oppressive. *Don't look, don't look. It may clamp down again.* Then the rain shower abated and subdued sunlight glowed around him. He raised his eyes from the instruments with their luminous numbers and needles, and saw sky and airplanes again. The lead section was closing up behind Queen Bee, and Rogers eased back into position off Bernie's port wing. There was Shawn in good formation to starboard.

Rogers heaved a sigh of relief. Then he withdrew his plotting board once more and ticked off the estimated position. He looked forward and down, but saw nothing other than gray waves and cloud shadows on the darkening waters of the Slot. *We're at the briefed contact point*, he calculated. *But no Jap transports.* He slid the board under the instrument panel again and caught Commander Felt's gentle left turn.

"Bill, I think we're going to search to the west. But my guess is we'll land on Guadalcanal." Of the three air groups in the area, only *Wasp*'s was fully trained in night carrier operations. Far better to spend the night ashore than try to get thirty-seven planes back to *Saratoga* in darkness and uncertain weather.

Barnes replied over the intercom. "Gosh, I hope the marines know we're coming. I hear they shoot at anything that flies after sunset."

Rogers fidgeted on his seat-pack parachute. "Yeah. I hear the same thing."

HENDERSON FIELD, 1835

Carpenter slid off the wing of the Wildcat and gratefully felt his feet on solid ground. "I don't *ever* want to do that again," he croaked.

"That bad, sir?" The plane captain, Corporal Ames, noticed his pilot's voice carried the telltale high pitch of breathing pure oxygen.

"Most miserable damn weather I've ever flown in. Low ceilings, squall lines, lousy visibility." He checked his wristwatch and rubbed the oxygen-mask crease on his face. "We turned back less than an hour after takeoff. Didn't find a thing."

Stankovich waddled up in the gathering gloom. "I guess the Japs must have turned back, Jim. The poop is they knew they'd been spotted."

Carpenter shrugged eloquently and rolled his shoulders to ease some of the tension. "Probably. But we could've missed them in that crud out there."

Both pilots stood quietly while Ames busied himself securing the F4F for the night. At length Carpenter turned away for the long hike to the Pagoda. "We're just damn lucky we got everybody back. General Vandegrift must consider things pretty grim to commit nearly his entire air force on a late-afternoon search through miserable weather." The mission's nine SBDs and dozen F4Fs represented three-quarters of the island's remaining air strength.

Stankovich glanced left and right. Seeing no one in earshot, he offered an opinion. "I overheard one of the staff guys right after this afternoon's briefing. He said if the Japs land those fresh troops, we may not be able to hold the field."

Automatic-weapons fire blazed up from the west end of the field, evenly spaced tracers slanting into the dark. Somebody shouted, "Take cover!" as two or three more machine-gunners chipped in.

Carpenter stopped in midstride and stood with his hands petulantly on his hips. "Damn those idiots. No fire discipline at all. They can't see anything."

Stankovich, with an athlete's reflexes, already was stretched prone on the ground. He tugged on the leg of his friend's flight suit. "You gonna stand there and direct traffic or what?"

High-pitched voices shouted, "Cease fire, cease fire!" There was a rush of aviators, mechanics and support personnel in both directions along the flight line.

Two operations officers sped by in a jeep, its headlights partly blacked out to reduce glare. Carpenter waved them down and scrambled aboard, giving Stankovich a hand over the rear. "What's doing?"

The passenger, a captain, held onto his helmet with one hand as the jeep lurched across the rough field. "The *Saratoga*'s air group is landing here. They've been out looking for the same transports you were after."

Carpenter perked up. "Yeah? Hey, that's swell. I have some friends on the Sara." He thought for a moment. "But how the hell are they going to land in the dark?"

"We're parking jeeps along the runway," the captain replied. He pointed to the left and directed the driver to stop with the headlights shining on the rude gravel strip.

Stankovich leaned toward the ops officer. "Uh, excuse me, sir. But if we leave the lights on, won't the Japs . . ."

"Gentlemen, as soon as this vehicle stops, I suggest you follow my example."

"What's that, sir?"

"Run like hell."

HENDERSON FIELD, 1935

It took a while for Carpenter to find his friends.

Rogers and Murtagh stood with their gunners on the south side of the runway, watching while marines and Seabees manhandled Burnett's SBD in the dark. "I never heard of this procedure," Murtagh observed. "Think it'll work?"

"Damn if I know. But these guys seem to know what they're doing." Rogers looked on as some beefy ordnancemen raised the tail of Baker Four, which already had been relieved of its half-ton bomb. They swung the SBD almost 180 degrees, then set down the tail. When parked in this manner, the twin-mount .30 calibers from Burnett's plane overlapped the field of fire from Murtagh's.

"I don't know, Buck. If we have to rely on our own gunners to protect the airstrip, we're in deep—"

"What's the matter, you little Irish squirt?" Murtagh heard the familiar voice in his ear and felt the hands on his neck. "You never heard of advanced air-base defense?"

Murtagh and Rogers turned to see their Pensacola classmate smiling in the dark. Handshakes, punches and friendly insults were traded as Carpenter gushed, "Welcome to Guadalcanal. We call it the cactus patch."

"Some welcome. Do you always shoot at visitors?" Rogers had been spooked by the eerie, deceptive slowness of the tracers that curled toward him.

"There's a lot of itchy trigger fingers on this island. It's famous for things like that."

Unsatisfied, Rogers persisted. "Like what else?"

"Ha! Stick around long enough and you'll see for yourself. Like somebody said the other day—Guadal's the only place in the world where you can stand up to your ass in mud and still have dust blow in your eye."

Murtagh punched Carpenter's arm again. "How you doing, Jim? We don't hear much about air ops here."

Carpenter shifted his weight and folded his arms. "Well, we're holding our own against the Zeros. Smitty, our CO, splashed one day before yesterday. We've had a couple of fights since then, but so far nothing like Midway, We're down to about ten SBDs and sixteen F4Fs, but the army just arrived with a squadron of P-400s."

"P-400s?" Rogers was puzzled. "Never heard of 'em."

"They're P-39s built for export to England," Carpenter explained. "I see why the RAF turned them down—no altitude performance and they don't turn worth a damn. Word is they're going to be used for ground support. You guys get settled in?"

"Not yet," replied Rogers. "We've been helping Bernie and some of the others arrange their airplanes to repel boarders. I guess we'll have to refuel by hand pump."

"This is a low-budget operation," the marine observed. "Whenever you're squared away, I'll show you where to bunk. I hope you enjoy camping out."

Murtagh gave an exaggerated shudder. "Sleeping in the open with jungle creepy-crawlies. Ugh."

"Yeah." Carpenter smiled. "This place actually makes me homesick for my dugout on Midway. At least there, the only thing I worried about was the rising water table. Here, the sky falls in almost every night."

46.

MONDAY, 24 AUGUST

HENDERSON FIELD, 0200

Rogers, Burnett, Murtagh and their shipmates had dozed fitfully since turning in. Wrapped in captured Japanese blankets after dining on captured Japanese rice and their own emergency rations, they twitched and turned through the early morning hours. Once, when gunshots stabbed the darkness, Burnett had sat up wide-eyed and nudged Rogers.

"Phil, you hear that?"

Rogers was fully alert but feigned drowsiness. "Whaat?" *Now it's my turn.*

Burnett ignored the ruse. "That was gunfire!"

Rogers rolled over. "Well, of course it was gunfire. This is a war zone."

"I wonder if the Japs are coming. They must've seen us land."

Rogers could tell now—Burnett was genuinely frightened. "Bernie, Jim said there are patrols out all the time. Remember?"

"Well, what if some commandos sneak through our lines?"

"C'mon, Bernie. Who's going to get past two squadrons of SBDs with their free guns trained on the perimeter?" A malicious thought occurred to Rogers. "Besides, you're armed, aren't you?"

Burnett groped under the shelter half intended to keep the drizzle off them. He came up with his hunting knife—the only survival gear he carried. "You mean this?"

"Sure. But I prefer this." Rogers hefted the .38 revolver he wore in a handmade shoulder holster. Burnett had kidded him mercilessly about the arts-and-crafts class held aboard ship.

Burnett replied in hushed tones. "Can you really use that thing?"

"Well, yeah. My dad was our Scoutmaster back home. He helped us form a National Rifle Association club for junior shooters."

"I mean, could you really shoot somebody?"

"A lot easier than you could kill 'em with that Bowie knife you're so proud of."

Burnett was considering a response when he heard a whistling rumble in the air. "Listen . . ." The rumble ended in an explosion northwest of the field. Seconds later came a second.

Someone shouted, "Take cover! Condition red!"

The two pilots scampered from under their shelter, pulling on shoes and picking up equipment. "Are we gonna take off?" asked Rogers.

A third explosion flickered in the Lever Brothers plantation to the north. Burnett and Rogers jumped into a sandbagged trench that was ankle-deep in mud. "Don't think so," Burnett responded at length. "They don't seem to be after the field."

Other men crowded into the trench, elbowing the previous occupants for room. A familiar voice said, "Hey, Navy. Welcome to the Marine Corps." Sunny Jim Carpenter's brilliant smile cut through the murky drizzle.

"Screw you," Rogers replied. Another shell burst a mile away.

"It's a Jap destroyer out in the sound," Carpenter explained. "I told you the overhead caves in here."

"Why the hell doesn't the . . ." Burnett caught himself.

"Yeah," added Big Mike Stankovich. "Why the hell don't the navy chase that Jap tin can away?" Other marines in the trench chuckled in delight. But none mentioned that destroyer *Blue* had been scuttled that evening from torpedo damage inflicted by another Japanese destroyer.

Carpenter decided to change the subject. "Hey, Buck. You still seeing your librarian?"

A fourth shell whined into the plantation but Rogers ignored it. *They must not have any spotters,* he concluded. "Not lately. The navy's real peculiar that way." He nudged Burnett, who smiled back. "How about you? Any word from that tall blonde?"

"Naw. We haven't been here long enough for any mail to catch up with us." He paused, as if musing whether to pursue the thought. "I called Elaine a couple days before we sailed."

"What'd you tell her?"

"I said I'd look her up when the marines have won the war."

"That's odd," quipped Rogers. "That's just about what Sally told me . . ."

HENDERSON FIELD, 0855

Standing beside Baker Five, Rogers and Murtagh shook hands with Carpenter. "Thanks for a lovely evening," the Bostonian said. "We really must do it again sometime."

"Better yet," Rogers interjected, "you come see us next time. Emily Post says that reciprocity is entirely proper."

The big marine tipped back his blue ballcap and laughed. "Buck, what the hell do you know about etiquette?"

"Me? Nothing. But Sally knows all that stuff."

Carpenter turned his head as a nearby TBF started its big Wright engine. "Too bad our morning search didn't find those Jap transports. PBYs found 'em headed back north." He shook his head. "It would've been nice to hit 'em while we had all you fellows here."

"Maybe you need some U.S. Navy scout-bombers to conduct your searches," Murtagh jibed.

"Say, don't sell our guys short. Dick Mangrum is one fine squadron leader, and he has some good people in Two-Thirty-Two."

Rogers pointedly checked his watch. "Jim, we have to man up for the 0930 takeoff. We're due back at 1100, and the Sara can't wait." The two friends warmly shook hands once more.

Murtagh, sensitive to his previous comment, made an extra effort.

He squeezed Carpenter's hand with both of his. "Keep your tail clear, Jim. And I hope your SBDs get to use the presents we left you." He turned and walked toward Baker Six, sloshing past a long row of 1,000-pounders lying in the mud.

IJNS TONE, 1 2 2 3

Azumano heard cheering behind him and turned aft. Looking down toward the midships secondary battery, he saw sailors waving their caps over their heads, accompanied by loud shouts of *"Banzai."*

"They are new. Give them time," Naito said. He turned his attention to the launch in progress from carrier *Ryujo.*

"Air Officer, I merely hope they do not have to learn as we did . . . in June." Azumano found it difficult to say, "Operation MI," let alone "Midway." Strict security remained in force, and there were tales of secret police scooping up some talkative sailor and hauling him away.

Naito merely nodded, focusing his binoculars on the 11,000-ton carrier. *She is not an* Akagi *or* Kaga, *but she is our responsibility*, he told himself.

"Sir, what is the attack force?" Azumano asked.

Another Zero lifted off *Ryujo's* flight deck and turned to join the growing number of circling aircraft. "Fifteen fighters and six carrier attack planes. Lieutenant Notomi is leading them against the enemy airfield on Guadalcanal."

USS SARATOGA, 1 2 5 5

Rogers bit into a thick roast-beef sandwich and chewed slowly, his eyes closed to savor the taste. "Mmm-mmm, that's good. Those jarheads can have their cookouts and camping. I'll take clean sheets and hot food every time."

Burnett slid into the chair beside him in the wardroom, fresh-scrubbed and wearing a clean set of khakis. "You missed water hours, Buck." He sniffed pointedly in Rogers's direction. "In fact, I think I'm going to move upwind. I can still smell that frigging island on you."

"The skipper wanted me to update the navigation dope," Rogers replied in self-defense. "We're spotting the deck for another full strike: thirty SBDs and eight torpeckers."

"Yes, I heard. Transports again?"

Rogers swallowed another mouthful and sipped his coffee. "Don't think so, Bernie. Evidently Admiral Fletcher thinks that PBY reports can't be trusted after the transport force disappeared yesterday. Now there's word that it was found way the hell up the Slot after turning around. But the P-boats also found a Jap carrier to the northwest."

Burnett leaned closer, despite the faint odor. "No kidding?" His eyes widened in concern, and Rogers was reminded of the same expression under the canvas tarp last night, with gunfire nearby. *Is he getting edgy?*

"How far?" asked Burnett.

"About two hundred and forty, two hundred and fifty miles from us, as of 1130. The *Enterprise* has scouts out looking to reestablish the contact." Rogers thought of his classmate Frank DiBella and wondered if he was one of the searchers scouring the waters 200 miles north of Guadalcanal.

"I didn't think we'd tangle with carriers again so soon," Burnett admitted. "I mean, after Midway."

Rogers resisted the temptation to lick some mustard off his fingers. Officers and gentlemen did not engage in such hamburger-stand behavior. "Well, it makes sense. I hear they still have more carriers than we do," he replied evenly. He looked around. "Hey, where's Shawn?"

Burnett laughed aloud, and Rogers felt better about his section leader. "He got caught in the showers when they turned off the water. You know the drill—all soaped up and no way to rinse. He's madder than hell."

Rogers shared the humor. Murtagh, the former choirboy, could employ most impious language when aroused. But everyone who had ever sailed in a naval vessel knew the risk of lingering too long in the shower when water was constantly rationed. "Well, if I can't clean up, I'm going to catch a catnap. How 'bout you, Bernie?"

Burnett reached for a sandwich. "I'm going to eat something besides Spam and Jap rice." He looked up at his friend. "Then I'm going to see the ordnance department about a pistol." He winked.

THREE BAKER FIVE, 1410

The electronic babble and the screechy-scratchy noise in his earphones were driving Rogers crazy. *Marconi can take his invention and—*

"Sir, did you hear that?" Barnes interrupted the pilot's opinion of wireless communication. "Something about Jap carriers to the north."

"I didn't even get that much," Rogers barked into the mike. "The goddamn atmospherics are terrible. What did you make of it, Bill?"

"It was from an *Enterprise* scout, sir. He reported at least one carrier about two hundred miles from his launch position."

Rogers waited for the rest of the information. When it did not come, he asked, "Well, what bearing?"

"Ahhh . . . either he didn't give it or I couldn't read it."

Rogers was confident that Barnes's interpretation was correct. The radioman had not yet failed to copy a full contact report. "Okay, Bill. Keep your ears peeled."

Rogers replaced the microphone in its bracket and nervously tapped his feet on the cockpit floor. From force of habit he scanned his instruments. *Fuel pressure, good. Oil pressure, good. Cylinder-head temp, okay.* He turned to look at Murtagh, who waved casually from his position on the other side of the three-plane vee formation.

He checked his watch and saw that only twenty-five minutes had passed since Commander Felt had led thirty SBDs and eight TBFs off *Saratoga*'s deck. Rogers supposed that the CAG was keeping his strike group low in order to stay under the fifty-percent cloud cover that might hamper the hunt. It made sense, but as the radio circuit snapped and popped again, Rogers wondered if reception would be better at altitude.

OVER GUADALCANAL, 1425

There they are, Carpenter thought. It was only the second time he had seen Japanese aircraft. *At least the odds are a lot better this time.* Two and a half months previously, VMF-221 had been outnumbered more than four to one. This time the odds were nearly even: sixteen VMF-223 Wildcats and a pair of Airacobras from the army's 67th Pursuit Squadron against twenty-one Japanese carrier planes.

Carpenter glanced around, checking that his two sections were intact. Stankovich had slid out to an abeam position, slightly stepped up. The second section—Lieutenants Buzz Hilyard and Rick Pine—was farther upsun. *Time's a-wastin',* Carpenter thought. *Let's go!*

From well above the Japanese formation, Carpenter saw the lead division roll inverted and pull through into overhead gunnery passes.

The first Wildcat fired an economical burst, gray-white smoke puffs trailing from its wings. One of the carrier bombers gushed flames, nosed down—and exploded. Carpenter was filled with admiration. *Marion makes the most damn* beautiful *overheads I ever saw!*

Carpenter shoved everything forward with his left hand, sizing up the fight. He quickly estimated that some of the bombers could make Henderson Field from their present position south of Malaita, and turned to cut them off.

In a few moments he reeled in the remaining Type 97 carrier attack planes, noting their air discipline. *Five left, still keeping formation.* He began tracking the farthest right-hand aircraft, gauging the range by its wingspan in his illuminated gunsight. It all came back to him: the morning of 4 June. A long line of carrier bombers identical to these, escorted by arrogantly aggressive Zeros. He shot a quick look over his shoulder. *I'm clear—Mike's still there.*

Turning back to his gunnery, Carpenter saw the Nakajima's wingtips fill the 100-mil circle in his reflector sight. *Boresight range, dead astern. Easy shot.* He depressed the trigger and his six guns fired.

The dark-green upper surfaces of the bomber sparkled with white motes that played over the wings and canopy. Armor-piercing, ball and incendiary rounds punched through the airframe, penetrated fuel tanks. In the rear seat, facing aft, the seaman first class tried to line up his 7.7mm machine gun at the blunt-nosed Grumman 300 yards behind. But his bomber's own tail was in the way. The twenty-two-year-old Japanese heard high-pitched *whangs*, saw aluminum pieces chopped out of the plane's skin. Then he shrieked in surprise, anger and pain. Two half-inch-diameter bullets went through his torso, punching cloth and webbing into lung tissue. The world went red, gray, black.

Carpenter now had a visible overtake on the doomed bomber. He wondered if he should throttle back. *No, it'll give the others more time to shoot at me.* He pressed his run into 100 yards, fired again, saw more hits and broke away in a diving right turn.

He was surprised to find himself pulling out at 7,000 feet. Then he realized the Japanese had only been flying at 9,000. He looked back, cleared his tail and saw his Nakajima coming apart. Another bomber fell toward the cloud-flecked waters north of Lunga Point. *Where's Mike?* He stomped left rudder, skidding to check his blind spot. *Not there.* Carpenter felt the onset of dread. *Oh, God. Like Griff all over again . . .*

An angular silhouette hauled into Carpenter's peripheral vision.

There's an F4F! Carpenter squinted hard, saw the number ten on the fuselage and waggled his wings. He banked into a climbing turn, setting up a level side pass at the remaining bombers.

He wanted to call down more Wildcats to finish off the Nakajimas before they bombed Henderson Field. But the single radio circuit was a cacophony of calls, warnings and human-electronic noises. It did not matter. The others were keeping the Zeros off him.

Carpenter coordinated stick and rudder, put a Type 97 in his sight from starboard and mentally computed the deflection. *He's making maybe 200 knots; 130 mils at full deflection but I'm on a quartering run so use three-fourths of that.* He placed the sight reticle one and a half diameters ahead of the bomber's nose, and fired. His tracers passed just behind the target's tail and Carpenter knew he was still too far out. He waited a few more seconds. When he touched the trigger, he heard the six M2 Brownings and immediately saw the flash. *My God!* He pulled up, clearing the fireball.

Carpenter shook his head in amazement, then realized he must have detonated the Nakajima's bomb load.

His attention was caught by explosions on the ground, producing billowing dust and smoke. He was mildly surprised to realize the fight had taken him southward over the shore of Lunga Point. *They're bombing the field*, he realized. He shoved up the power, hoping to intervene.

Then the Zeros arrived.

Carpenter saw them as small, fast darts arrowing toward him from slightly above and well to port. He was surprised at how acute his vision seemed, even allowing for the clear afternoon sunlight. He turned toward the threat, thought, *Oh, Jesus—nose to nose*, and tried to draw a bead on the leader. There was no way to practice a head-on shot.

The little fighter's nose lit up with yellow sparkles and Carpenter almost ducked reflexively. His own aspect was too shallow to cut the corner in time but he hosed off a burst just to reply. Then the first Zero was past him, lost to sight somewhere behind. He had a better shot at the wingman and laid off 150 mils lead before firing. *Close*, he thought, *but low.*

Carpenter's instinct was to wrap the Wildcat around in a flipper turn—ninety degrees of bank and pull. But he thought, *I tried that at Midway and it didn't work worth a damn.* He left everything firewalled and stuffed his nose down, accelerating back the way the bombers had come. Two Wildcats passed 800 feet over him, apparently chasing the Zeros, and he felt better.

Then he was alone. Judging from the radio calls, the fight was over.

THREE BAKER FIVE, 1518

Rogers caught the turn just as Burnett's starboard wing dipped slightly. *Here we go again*, Rogers thought. *Another damn contact report that may or may not mean anything.*

This time he had discerned even less of the radio message than before. But obviously Commander Felt thought the latest report merited investigation, otherwise he would not lead his remaining twenty-nine Dauntlesses and seven Avengers off their base course. The long, slow climb to medium altitude had resulted in two aborts—an SBD and a TBF—but Rogers regarded that as merely an annoyance. What bothered him was the consistently poor communications and the jumbled picture of Japanese forces.

He studied his plotting board again. It was speckled with lead-pencil measles representing enemy ships reported by *Enterprise* search teams. Between them, Rogers and Barnes had monitored a variety of contacts: at least two separate carrier groups and two or three surface units. He ticked off each one, spread roughly in a line west to east in the northwestern quadrant from Task Force Sixty-One.

Yet Rogers was skeptical. He knew that one or more of the reports might be a duplicate contact from another search team, with the built-in certainty of navigation error amounting to dozens of miles. *The* Hornet *scouts had a fifty-two-mile difference on those cruisers at Midway*, he told himself. He put his pencil away and shoved the plotting board back under the instrument panel.

After several more minutes of uneventful searching, Rogers saw the lead aircraft bank lazily to the left. He picked up his mike again. "Looks like we're turning back to the west, Bill. Maybe CAG knows something we don't."

Barnes's voice seemed atypically indifferent. "Well, there's nothin' to see out here, sir."

Rogers looked to his right, back northward as the formation resumed its previous heading. *It's kind of pretty, actually.* Almost three miles below, the blue-gray sea lay rippled by a sixteen-knot tradewind, dappled with purple-blue cloud shadows.

Everybody was talking at once. The harried intelligence officer, sitting at a makeshift desk in the Pagoda, tried to inflict order upon the proceedings but hardly anyone paid him much attention. At length he stood on his chair, put two fingers in his mouth and emitted a shrill whistle.

I never could do that, thought Carpenter.

"Right now it looks like we got sixteen planes," the IO began. "Maybe we'll get additional confirmation from one of the coastwatchers, but I'm showing claims for nine carrier bombers, three twin-engine bombers and four fighters." He looked around. "Everybody happy with that?"

Stankovich looked at Carpenter. "Twin-engine? I didn't see any twin-engine stuff. Did you?"

Carpenter smirked at his wingman. "No. But what the hell? At least we stirred 'em up. Believe me, Mike. This is one hell of a lot better than we did at Midway."

Stankovich seemed unconvinced. "Well, I just can't help thinking about Rick Pine. He was a good guy. And the other two . . ."

Carpenter rolled his shoulders again in the gesture Stankovich knew so well. "It happens. But like I said, this was a whole lot better than Midway. Carl, Corry, myself . . . we've all been through worse than this." He nudged Big Mike with one elbow. "Besides, you got one confirmed your first time up. That's more'n I could say."

"Lieutenant Naito reporting, Captain!" The announcement was delivered in a gasp as Naito quivered to attention. He had sprinted from the big cruiser's hangar bay as soon as he had heard the summons to the bridge.

"Air Officer, there is a report of unidentified aircraft to the southeast. You will remain on the bridge and assist with identification." The captain hardly looked at Naito, preferring to scan the cloud-flecked sky with his binoculars.

Naito bowed in acknowledgment and stepped out onto the wing of the bridge. He would have preferred to have one of his aircrew officers like Azumano, who was preparing to launch on a search flight in the Number Four Scout.

The task group radio net squelched in ship-to-ship conversation. Then, "Fighting Dragon to all ships! Probable enemy aircraft bearing one-four-zero!"

The broadcast from *Ryujo* told Naito what he needed to know. He swung his glasses in that direction and forced himself to search methodically. Then he glimpsed them—ordered high-altitude specks behind the clouds. *Too far yet for identification*, he thought. But instinctively, he knew. He had seen identical formations at Midway.

Midway. He shuddered. *There we could not defend four carriers with sixteen ships. Now we have this cruiser and two destroyers against—what?*

He felt the cruiser beginning to accelerate to battle speed.

OVERHEAD IJNS RYUJO, 1550

"Here we go again, Bill." Rogers felt suddenly edgy, as if he knew a surprise was about to be sprung on the *Saratoga* Air Group. A thought occurred to him and he pressed the mike button again. "The Japs have had almost fifteen minutes to get ready for us. Keep a sharp lookout for fighters."

"Aye, aye, sir!" Crisp, eager, attentive. Rogers knew that Barnes was anxious to paint another "meatball" flag below his cockpit, and this looked like a prime opportunity. *But it can go the other way.* He thought of Obie's plane splashing near *Hiryu* the evening of 4 June.

Something else bothered Rogers—communications were still troublesome. Apparently Don Felt's radio receiver was out, which meant the only information the CAG could gather was what he could see. Not good for the officer responsible for coordinating a three-phase attack on an enemy task force.

Rogers watched briefly as Dave Shumway's six planes broke off toward the northeast, coordinating with Lou Kirn's fifteen scouts from the northwest. Then he heard Lieutenant Bottomley on the radio. "Second division, this is Syd. We're going after the cruiser." Rogers lost track of Shumway and Kirn as he banked away, following his exec toward the warship with the distinctive four turrets mounted forward.

He looked down through the thin undercast and sized up the situation. Four high-speed wakes were visible, heading generally west at about twenty knots. A thought occurred to him. "Barnes, do you see the TBFs?"

The radioman-gunner shook his head. *Now I'm "Barnes" again. Must be force of habit.* From his rear-facing position he looked port and starboard, seeking the big torpedo planes. "No, sir. I think they split off when Commander Felt assigned targets."

"Okay . . . Bill." Rogers remembered that nobody was listening on their intercom. "Watch for 'em when we pull out. They should be making their runs about then."

Barnes acknowledged and felt better. *He's thinking ahead. That's real good.*

Rogers saw the familiar drill being played out. As Bottomley's three planes shifted into echelon, the entire second division nosed over toward the roll-in point. He saw the dive brakes' red interiors gleaming at him in the afternoon sunlight and began his own combat checklist. It was almost automatic now, but he concentrated on each item. *Don't let me screw up.* The items came in sequence: carburetor heat, high blower, prop pitch, cowl flaps, dive brakes selected, hit the hydraulic power pack. *There goes Bernie. Pushing over . . . now!* For the fifth time in eleven weeks Rogers pointed his nose downward at a warship of the Imperial Japanese Navy.

IJNS TONE

Naito saw the attack coming and knew what to expect. He shot a concerned glance across the disposition to *Ryujo*, pounding along at twenty-plus knots and flinging Zeros off her short deck. Two white geysers spewed upward from the ocean as the first American bombs rained down.

For a moment the air officer forgot his own immediate concern—the other helldivers slanting into their long, straight dives on *Tone*. A lookout also had reported enemy torpedo planes on the periphery of the screen, but Naito paid no attention. An observer would have thought him properly dispassionate for an imperial officer; his expression never changed. But Naito had seen this before, knew that invincibility was terribly changeable.

The bombs kept falling—some close, but most beyond harmful distance of the carrier's 10,000-ton hull. Naito saw the long bow come starboard and immediately was filled with admiration. *Captain Kato is turning crosswind. It will complicate the Americans' bombing.*

The next 1,000-pounders smacked the ocean along *Ryujo*'s previous path, before her wake carved the first arc in the dark-blue water. Naito realized that those weapons had been released while the carrier held to her original course.

"Enemy planes retiring!" a lookout shouted. Naito glanced upward and saw no more dive-bombers over the carrier. He had counted each splash, waiting tense and prayerful for the "Fighting Dragon." And now he realized his prayer had been answered. *Twelve bombs*, he thought. *At least twelve—and they all missed!*

Then he remembered the bombers coming after *Tone*.

The first thing Rogers noticed was the flak. The cruiser was belching brownish clouds of medium-caliber stuff, and tracers scarred the air in long strings of glowing light. Then the radio caught his attention, unaccountably clear for a change.

"This is Queen Bee. Syd, shift targets. I say again, shift from the cruiser to the carrier."

It's Midway all over again. Rogers marveled at the similarity to the evening strike of 4 June. He pulled in his flaps, added throttle and eased out of his dive just as he had when Lieutenant Gallaher had called Dave Shumway off the battleship in order to finish the fourth carrier. *Maybe it'll always be like this—Bombing Three batting cleanup.*

The high-altitude pullout required additional time to regroup, but Rogers noted that Syd Bottomley had the second division well in hand. The exec brought his seven SBDs around to the heading of the little carrier—she was nowhere the size of those sunk at Midway—and resumed the attack.

Nearing the pushover point, Rogers saw the target describing a complete circle on the water. She appeared unharmed, and he knew that her Zeros had to be up and waiting, just as *Hiryu*'s had been. Briefly he wondered if the U.S. Navy would ever stock enough fighters aboard its carriers both for strike escort and task-force defense. Then he nosed over from 15,000 feet.

As he settled into his dive, Rogers began tracking the carrier. *Hello there*, he thought. Then he glimpsed something on the deck—the briefest flicker amidships. It was not a good view because of Burnett ahead of him. But there was only one explanation. *Commander Felt must have got a hit! He's the only one flying alone.*

Rogers's mind began sorting priorities. He knew there was still time to refine his dive heading, thankful for the SBD's wonderfully balanced ailerons that made last-second corrections possible. He envisioned the problem in spatial geometry—the constantly changing aspect between Bottomley's lead section and Burnett's, and both of those in relation to the turning target down there on the surface of the water.

Rogers thought himself through the problem in the first ten seconds of the dive. He saw that Lieutenant Bottomley was taking his section down from a different angle. *Good*, Rogers thought. *It'll force the Japs to split their AA fire. Bernie's got us lined up from astern.*

Halfway down, Rogers selected his aimpoint. *Wind's from the southeast*, he remembered. *Target's turning in that direction, so adjust upwind.* He jockeyed stick and rudder to place his crosshairs slightly forward of the carrier's bow.

Round white rings bloomed around IJNS *Ryujo*, then a darkish cloud appeared on her dark-yellow deck. Rogers realized that Bottomley's section had just scored, but he forced himself to concentrate on his own bombing.

Nearing the drop point, the flak increased. Brown-black puffs magically appeared in space, silently violent. Rogers recalled the dictum that if you couldn't hear flak, it wasn't dangerous. Ever since the *Mikuma* attack he had told himself his bad luck with antiaircraft fire was over. He felt two or three near-misses jostle his aircraft, but the Dauntless immediately returned to its trimmed-out, steady dive. He shot a glance from the crosshairs to the ball indicating yaw error. *It's pegged in the middle. Looking good. This is good, this is very good. Steady . . .*

He thumbed the red button on his stick, felt the bomb leave the aircraft and kept a neutral touch on the controls. Then, satisfied that the half-ton weapon was on its way, he moved the diamond-shaped flap-selector handle and activated the power pack. He felt the SBD accelerate slowly as the perforated flaps retracted, then he began his pullout.

At 1,600 feet Rogers had a thought. With his nose coming level with the horizon, he rolled into a steep left bank. He searched for the ship, found it just aft of the wingroot—and saw the explosion as his bomb smashed into the flight deck forward of amidships.

"Yeah!" He screamed to himself, to the Western world, and to nobody at all. He thought of Barnes's war whoop after splashing that Zero at Midway; recalled little of his own emotion after hitting *Mikuma*, because of his leg wound. But this was different. This hit was right there for him to see, to savor. He knew it would be a bragging point back in the ready room.

He looked around, seeking Burnett or Murtagh, then realized his folly. By rolling into that bleacher-seat vertical bank he had put himself outside the radius of the ship's turn. Therefore, he had deprived himself of the support of his squadronmates.

Rogers reversed his turn, pulling hard while trying to cut the corner to the rendezvous. Then he heard Barnes firing and knew what it meant.

IJNS TONE, 1558

It all came rushing back to Naito. The blue-gray dive-bombers, the white geysers around the carrier, the roiling black smoke of fuel-fed fires on the flight deck. *It's Midway all over again.* The air officer felt a sickly turmoil in his stomach—the depressingly familiar sensation that comes of watching a friendly aircraft carrier burning.

"Enemy planes retreating!" shouted an enlisted lookout. "We shot down six or eight of them!"

Naito's impulse was to thrash the idiot. But he asked himself, *What is the point?* Eventually the young sailor would learn that even if the shootdown claims were accurate—and Naito knew they seldom were—it was a poor exchange. He turned to the cruiser's captain. "Sir, shall we launch the duty scout to search for the enemy?"

Captain Anibe shook his head. "We will stand by to assist *Ryujo*." He paused briefly and exhaled a breath of sadness and pride. "She will not float much longer."

BAKER FIVE, 1559

Rogers heard Barnes's twin .30 calibers chatter again and judged that the threat came from port. He firewalled throttle, mixture and prop controls, popped the stick forward and dived for the water. It looked a long way off from his position at 1,600 feet, ahead of the burning carrier.

Looking back, trying to find the fighter intent on killing him, Rogers realized that Barnes had had no time to call a warning. *That was a stupid move,* he told himself. *Just to admire my handiwork. If I get out of this, I swear I'll never—*

"Turn right, sir!" Barnes's voice was high-pitched and rapid over the intercom. Rogers stepped on the rudder pedal and snapped the stick hard over, pointing his starboard wingtip at the water now only 200 feet below. He saw a gray shape pull into an abrupt dive-recovery overhead and realized the Zero had been forced to abort its gunnery run. *Pull out or hit the water—good.* He nosed down even more, leaving himself minimal room to maneuver.

Then Barnes fired again and Rogers began to understand. *Christ! There's two of them!*

White spume flecked the water around the SBD and Rogers began jinking as much as he dared. It was a fine distinction: too much evasive action and he would spoil his gunner's aim. Too little, and the fighters would have an even easier target.

Rogers craned his neck all the way back, trying to keep an image of where the first Zero went. He glimpsed it almost directly overhead, perhaps 800 feet high—a graceful shape silhouetted against the sky. For a moment Rogers was confused about the fighter's aspect. *Is he coming toward me or going away?* Then the geometry became clear. *My God, he's looping back down on me for an overhead pass!*

High-pitched, metallic *whangs* announced that the Japanese wingman was scoring hits. Rogers abruptly kicked left rudder and skidded to port, spoiling the fighter's tracking. He was vaguely aware of more bullets and cannon shells impacting the water around him. "They're coming around again," Barnes announced.

Rogers forced himself to think. *I can't outrun them, so I have to keep turning. But don't get predictable. Mix up your plays like the football quarterbacks do.* He feinted left, then cross-controlled and lurched the Dauntless back to the right. Three hundred yards out, diving in once more, the first Zero seemed to bobble in uncertainty. It pulled up without shooting.

Seconds later the wingman was positioned again, and firing. Rogers glanced back, saw the winking lights of muzzle flashes from nose and wings, and turned toward the threat. Miniature lightning bolts of tracers flashed around him, and more bullets impacted the Dauntless. Rogers tried to line up for a shot, but the Zero was too fast. He lost sight of it somewhere overhead.

Rogers turned back to his southeasterly heading, weaving thirty degrees either side of base course. He ran frightened eyes over the visible portions of his SBD and noted two jagged 7.7mm holes in one wingtip plus a smooth hole in the fabric over one aileron. He was aware of the sandpaper dryness in his throat, the acidic bile in his stomach. The adrenaline rush was barely subsiding when Barnes called him. "Sir, I think they're gone."

Rogers made a methodical search of the airspace around him. He found nothing and marveled at that fact. "I guess you're right. They must be low on ammunition. Can you see anything else?"

"Ah, no, sir. Just that Jap carrier burnin' like hell behind us."

"Okay. Stay sharp back there." He thought for a moment. "How's your ammo?"

"I figure I got enough for another set-to." Barnes sounded apologetic. "I didn't get one this time, sir. They stayed out of effective range."

Rogers allowed himself to chuckle. "I'm not complaining, Bill. I'm not complaining."

From ingrained habit, Rogers scanned his instruments. *Holy smokes—tach's redlined and cylinder-head temp's into the yellow.* He had been running the engine at high rpm and manifold pressure for—how long? He looked at his clock but the time was meaningless. He throttled back, opened his cowl flaps for maximum cooling and started an easy climb to cruise altitude.

APPROACHING TASK FORCE SIXTY-ONE, 1705

The radio circuit was one prolonged babble of man-made and electronic noise. Commander Felt's returning dive-bomber and torpedo-plane crews heard a succession of calls between airborne fighters and shipboard radar controllers.

"Red Two, arrow three-one-zero. Acknowledge."

"Hey, what's that down there, Chick?"

"Enemy aircraft departing Red Base from the . . ."

"Wow! I got him!"

Rogers pressed his earphones close and squinted in concentration. *The Japs are attacking the task force. But from where?* Then he remembered. *The* Enterprise *reports of more carriers to the north.* He shook his head in frustration and reached for his mike. "Bill, what do you make of this mess?"

"It's our communications net, sir. Us radiomen have said all along we need more frequencies, and somethin' better than AM radios that won't stay tuned."

Rogers thought that Barnes's voice carried an I-told-you-so tone.

Well, he's right, the pilot thought. Under the daily rigors of carrier operations, the crystals in current aircraft radios often bounced off the desired frequencies.

Rogers decided to ignore the chatter while heading for a holding pattern on the disengaged side of the task force. He knew Barnes would be on point for another shot at a Japanese aircraft, but that seemed an unlikely prospect with an estimated fifty Wildcats airborne. *Those Japs will be like I was an hour ago—eager as hell to get out of the target area.*

A vaguely familiar voice broke through the string of radio calls. Something about "Lou," and "Jap planes heading our way." Rogers tried to sort it out. He knew that "Lou" could be Lieutenant Commander Bauer, the skipper of *Enterprise*'s Fighting Six, or Lieutenant Commander Kirn, leading *Saratoga*'s scouts. He grasped the mike again. "Bill, there might be Japs coming this way. If so, they'll probably tangle with Scouting Three up ahead of us."

"Ah, yes, sir!"

Rogers double-checked his forward-firing .50 calibers and satisfied himself that both had rounds chambered. Moments later the low clouds parted, and he saw two formations on a collision course perhaps three miles ahead. Tracer fire spit upward from the VS-3 group, converging overhead at a small gaggle of alien-looking aircraft. Rogers thought he saw at least one plane fall in the distance, arcing downward at the head of a greasy finger of smoke. "Bill, get set! Here we go!"

Rogers forgot his previous concern with his engine temperature. He shoved everything forward and turned slightly port, descending on an interception course for a fixed-gear aircraft approaching from his ten o'clock position.

Closing the range, he saw that the carrier bomber—he thought it was an Aichi Type 99—had already been hit. Its engine dragged a long, thin plume of brown smoke that seemed to be worsening. *You're my meat,* Rogers thought. He called Barnes once more. "Bill, we'll pass him on this side. You rake 'im as we fly by, then I'll swing around and come up beneath."

"All set, sir." Barnes sounded calm and steady.

Apparently at that moment the Japanese pilot saw his peril. He banked away to starboard, turning north, to open the distance. The increased radius of the turn necessary to join on him put Rogers in trail, back at the Aichi's seven o'clock position. *Screwed that up,* he told himself.

Rogers was going to advise Barnes of the situation when the gunner came up on the intercom. "It's okay, sir. Get abeam and I'll shoot him."

No need, Rogers thought. He banked slightly to starboard, put his crosshairs on the black-nosed bomber and pressed the trigger. His M2 Brownings pounded at his senses and he saw his tracers going into the airframe ahead of the cockpit. Then he realized he was going to collide.

Rogers popped the stick forward, passing below and beneath the Aichi and emerging 100 yards off its starboard wing. The Japanese pilot rolled into a left turn, the big elliptical wing tipping almost vertically. Rogers noted the fixed landing gear, and briefly wondered why the enemy gunner wasn't shooting back.

As the Japanese nosed downward, trying to accelerate away, Rogers got his answer. Whoever had worked over the Aichi previously had been thorough. The long greenhouse canopy was shattered, and the fuselage from the rear seat aft was nearly split open by bullet strikes. *This guy's done for. Let him go.* Then he thought of Wayne and Johnny and Obie. And the two Zeros that had him trapped near the burning carrier an hour and one eternity ago.

Rogers kept formation a respectful 100 yards away, edged forward slightly and pressed his mike button. Then Barnes opened fire. *He doesn't need any orders for this*, Rogers realized.

Bill Barnes did a methodical job of execution. With his twin mount trained to port, the gunner worked his way aft from the Aichi's propeller, putting short, well-aimed bursts into the engine, wingroot and cockpit. Rogers knew he would always remember the way the .30-caliber bullets struck sparks as they impacted the airframe, the way more canopy glass glittered as it shattered. The way the Type 99 dive-bomber rolled to the left and dropped headlong into the ocean in a geyser of white water and dirty-brown smoke.

That's another meatball on Bill's platter, Rogers told himself. He banked to the right, heading back for the rendezvous.

USS SARATOGA, 1755

The ready room was jammed with excited pilots exchanging a delighted babble of impressions, observations and misinformation. Rogers edged his way to a chair, where he unburdened himself of his plotting board, parachute harness and Mae West. He felt a hand on his shoulder and turned to see Burnett.

"My gunner says you got a hit, Phil!"

"Yeah. I saw it, too. Damn near got me killed." He shoved his cloth helmet back over his matted hair. "I'll *never* do that again. Ever."

Burnett shook his head querulously. "What do you mean?"

Rogers leaned close to his friend and section leader. "Bernie, I pulled out and rolled into a vertical bank to watch my bomb." He held up one hand, palm outward. "I saw my hit, all right, but that stunt cost me plenty. I got separated from you and Shawn." He rolled his eyes expressively. "Goddamn Zeros almost ate me alive."

Burnett realized that Rogers was still slightly shaken. *Well, he's entitled*, Burnett thought. *A hit on a carrier and two scrapes with enemy aircraft.*

"How'd the other fellows do?" Rogers asked.

"We're still taking statements. But it looks like three or more bomb hits on the carrier and at least one or two torpedoes. The TBFs also think they hit the cruiser."

Rogers decided there was no point being polite. "Good deal. But what about losses?"

Burnett uncased a smile. "Everybody's back, Phil. Hardly a scratch."

"Wheeew!" Rogers let out a low whistle. "I wouldn't have guessed it. Barnes and I counted fourteen hits in our plane alone. And with all that flak and the fighters . . ."

"Well, we don't know the score from the *Enterprise*," Burnett interjected. "She took a bomb and her flight deck's damaged. Most of her F4Fs are landing here."

"Then our fighter defenses are . . ."

"Thinned out. And there's another couple strikes still airborne, without escort. Elder and Gordon launched less than an hour ago, along with five torpeckers. And the *Enterprise* has about twenty SBDs and TBFs looking to finish off the carrier we hit. Dave says Commander Leslie's leading."

Rogers felt a little electric shock at the name of his former skipper. He looked at his watch. "Gosh, they'll have to land after dark . . ."

"Waaahoooo!"

"Hey, CAG!"

Rogers and Burnett turned toward the shouts and merriment. They saw Commander Felt enter the room to a chorus of cheers and congratulatory greetings.

"Great hit, sir," Murtagh exclaimed. "Square amidships."

Felt accepted the accolades like a benevolent warlord acknowledging the cheers of his men-at-arms. But Rogers was reluctant to assume too much. He turned back to Burnett. "I wonder if we really sank that ship, Bernie."

IJNS TONE, 1950

Standing amidships of the cruiser, Naito watched the number-two motor whaleboat bobbing its way through the chop. In the evening sunlight the sea had an eerie reddish tint, accented by orange flames from the doomed *Ryujo*.

"This should be the last trip, Lieutenant," remarked Ensign Yanagiya, the officer of the deck.

Naito, with little to do, stood idly by. "Are there many casualties?" he asked.

"Yes, sir." The young officer looked at his clipboard. "The executive officer estimates two hundred or more missing."

Naito stared at the crimson sea. "It was like this at Midway," he muttered.

Yanagiya, not so young that he had missed Operation MI, sought consolation. "We were fortunate that the enemy torpedo planes missed us this afternoon."

"Yes," Naito replied softly. "We were fortunate."

47.

WEDNESDAY, 26 AUGUST

"We're short of everything except insects," Carpenter told Stankovich. "If we don't get replacement aircraft and new oxygen bottles by tomorrow, we're out of business."

Big Mike casually swatted a mosquito, as if confirming Carpenter's assessment. Not even the Pagoda was immune to Guadalcanal's teeming parasites, but those were the least of his concerns.

Representatives of VMF-223 and VMSB-232 sat around a crude table, taking stock of their situation. A radio operator sat in one corner, monitoring the island's air-defense network. The status board showed twelve Wildcats and nine Dauntlesses still operational from the thirty-one planes that had landed six days previously.

"Well, isn't Smitty sending some of the Two-Twelve guys back to fetch more F4Fs?" Stankovich was visibly concerned about being off the schedule this morning, but there weren't enough Wildcats to go around.

Carpenter nodded. "Affirmative. We put four of 'em on a B-17 for Espíritu Santo this morning. But they can't be back here before a few more days." He looked at the marine SBD pilots in attendance. "At least you fellows got reinforcements."

Captain Bryce Stosser, whom Carpenter had known slightly on Midway, laughed aloud. "Yeah, but I don't think the navy is going to double our complement again anytime soon." He nudged Lieutenant (junior grade) Harold Bellinger of Scouting Five. "How do you like joining the marines, Hal?"

Bellinger pointedly tugged at his sweat-stained khakis and wrinkled his nose in distaste. "Just 'cause the skipper brought us here don't mean we gotta like the company. Besides, haven't you heard? The marines are part of the navy."

"*Yes—the best part!*" The chorus of voices overwhelmed Bellinger, one of eleven SBD pilots from *Enterprise*'s Flight 300 that had landed after a dusk search on the twenty-fourth.

"Well, I guess we're gonna be here awhile," the carrier aviator admitted. "That's why I'm at this meeting—to learn your setup. I guess it's like Carpenter says. We're short of everything."

"Except bugs and Japs," Stankovich said. He looked at his watch. "We should be hearing from the coastwatcher anytime now."

Bellinger cocked his head in curiosity. "Coastwatcher?"

Carpenter suppressed the mild surprise he felt. *Don't expect too much*, he told himself. *These guys have only been ashore for thirty-six hours.* "Our air-raid warning system depends on the coastwatchers," he began. "Most of them are Australians—prewar planters, missionaries, district officers. A few Royal Navy types. They work with loyal natives on all the islands from here on up the chain. When they see Jap planes headed our way, they radio ahead."

Bellinger was intrigued. "How much warning do they give you?"

Carpenter shrugged eloquently. "We need about forty-five minutes to get the F4Fs to thirty thousand feet. Since the Japs have to bomb in daylight to do any good, their transit time from Rabaul puts them overhead around noon." He pointed at Stankovich. "That's what Mike meant."

"Well, we can handle the Jap reinforcement ships—what you fellows call the Cactus Express. Assuming we have gas and bombs. But I sure don't like the prospect of tangling with Zeros. We tried that at Coral Sea." He paused and looked around. "I don't guess you have any fighters to spare for escort, do you?"

The marines eyed one another. A few of them had former classmates—SBD pilots who had encountered Japanese fighters on 8 May, trying to prevent speedy Nakajima torpedo planes from attacking *Lexington* or *Yorktown*. Others, like Stosser, had survived Midway.

Carpenter felt he should make some reply. "Well, the fact is, we just don't have enough fighters for air-base defense and bomber escort. At least not now." He avoided Bellinger's eyes. "Like Smitty says, it's up to us to make things work as well as we can with what we've got."

Privately, Carpenter felt the Cactus Air Force was going to stand or fall on the strength of its junior officers. He had seen almost nothing of the group exec, Lieutenant Colonel Pike, since landing on the twentieth. The very capable Dick Mangrum of VMSB-232 was the next senior aviator, but the other squadron COs were captains: Smith; Dale Brannon of the 67th Pursuit Squadron; and the leader of Flight 300, Turner Caldwell, a navy lieutenant.

"Sir, there's sixteen twin-engine bombers passing New Georgia. Heading our way!" The radio operator turned back to his console, concentrating on coastwatcher Donald Kennedy's report.

Carpenter checked his watch. In twelve minutes every flyable aircraft on Henderson Field was airborne.

HENDERSON FIELD, 1345

"Smitty's really pissed," Stankovich whispered. Sitting in VMF-223's ready tent near the flight line, Carpenter had to agree. It was obvious that the CO intended to unburden himself of whatever was bothering him.

"Gentlemen." Smith's posture, to say nothing of the veins prominent in his athletic frame, belied the soft tone of his voice. "Look around you. Go ahead." Several of the pilots turned to take in the carnage behind them. A raging fuel fire had nearly burned out, consuming 2,000 gallons of aviation fuel that Cactus could not afford to lose. Furthermore, the field radio station was damaged, and two of the 1,000-pound bombs left by the *Saratoga* Air Group had been detonated.

"Twelve of us intercepted sixteen bombers," Smith continued. The assembled pilots turned back toward him, now intent on his tone as much as his words. "We attacked with good position from higher altitude. And we knocked down three stinking bombers!" The debrief had shown that Smith had destroyed two; his exec, Rivers Morrell, got one.

He paused to let his words take effect. "The other thirteen, as you will notice, bombed with good effect. I am told they dropped some fifty bombs, including a mixture of fragmentation and incendiaries." Holding up a cautionary hand, he continued. "I know what you're thinking. You think that we got four Zeros as well, and we lost just one. Well, that isn't good enough."

Smith leaned forward, his square jaw aggressively thrust outward. "Most of you people forgot everything you ever learned about gunnery! You were flock-shooting the whole goddamned formation instead of picking out one airplane and concentrating on it, like you were taught!" His voice rose an octave. "That's why, out of twelve pilots, only five did any good." Carl, Frazier and Trowbridge had bagged Zeros, but Corry—a Midway veteran—was gone.

"Gentlemen, if a fighter pilot can't shoot, he's no damn good to himself, to his squadron or to the Marine Corps. We're getting more pilots shortly, and I hope to hell they're better than some of you who were up there today." He stalked from the tent before anybody could react.

Carpenter sensed what Smith was about. Gunnery was a fetish with the corps; it defined a marine's purpose in life. Perhaps an appeal to that fetish would turn the trick. Carpenter approved. It struck a chord deep in the American psyche—a frontier pride in marksmanship. He shook his head. *We've got to do better.*

48.

SATURDAY, 29 AUGUST

OVER GUADALCANAL, 1155

Carpenter swiveled his head from side to side, then turned his gaze upward. Other than Smith's ten Wildcats, and fourteen army Airacobras somewhere behind and below, the sky seemed empty. *Damn, where the hell can they be?*

The coastwatcher report, as usual, had been timely. Cactus had scrambled twenty-four fighters in anticipation of the noon attack—far better than the system had done early this morning. Carpenter briefly recalled the shock and surprise of three Mitsubishi bombers streaking in low and fast out of the dawn, their bombing unhindered but ineffective. *A lousy way to start the day,* he thought. *We need night fighters.* But Cactus needed everything.

Carpenter adjusted his oxygen mask, easing the pressure on the bridge of his nose. He was thankful for the resupply of oxygen bottles, essential to high-altitude interceptions. He reflected that the P-400s were unable to reach the level of the Japanese bombers, so the F4Fs would have to deal with the primary threat—wherever it might be.

Smith swung the formation—two four-plane divisions and a separate flight of two—around to the north. Carpenter checked Stankovich's spacing and rolled into a medium-banked turn, figuring the CO had anticipated an alternate approach route.

"This is Cactus Radio! The field is being bombed! Repeat, the field is being bombed!"

For a heartbeat, Carpenter sought to make sense of the broadcast. *How can that be?* He looked backward, past his tail. True, there were heavy clouds, but the bombers should not have been able to attack undetected. Then he shoved the thought into a far corner of his mind as he stood his Wildcat on its port wingtip.

In a high-speed descent, Carpenter led Stankovich down through the scattered lower cloud layer. Dust and smoke blossomed from the kunai-grass plain east of the river, and Carpenter cursed to himself. Then he saw the ordered ranks of eighteen Type One land-attack bombers, pulling away to the west. Carpenter shot a worried glance overhead, seeking the Zeros that had to be present. He thought he heard Carl's division engaging fighters. Reaching up, he pulled his goggles over his eyes for additional protection, then rolled into a high-side pass.

Carpenter began tracking the nearest bomber, the right-hand wingman in the second three-plane section. He remembered Smith's blistering lecture from the day before. *Most of you people were flock-shooting the whole goddamned formation instead of picking out one, like you were taught.* Carpenter thought, *Not me, Smitty.* He estimated a 200-knot target speed and waited until the squat silhouette filled his 50-mil ring. Then he laid off a full ring-and-a-half deflection and depressed the trigger.

Brief impressions stamped themselves on Carpenter's mind. He saw his first tracers streak ahead of the target, then twinkle their way back along the right wing and upper fuselage. He was aware of a muzzle flash from the bomber's dorsal gun; pieces of aluminum peeling back from the wing; a white steam of fuel vapor gushing out.

Then he was diving under the formation. Glancing up, he saw the pale-blue bellies. Stankovich was hollering on the radio. "He's burning, Jim! We got the son of a bitch!" *Mike must have shot at my target, too.*

Carpenter left everything firewalled and hauled back on the stick. A gray mist wrapped itself around the periphery of his vision. He turned port, climbing back for another pass at the harried bombers, when something small and fast caught his eye. *Zeros!* His adrenaline surged as he rolled left, turning to meet the Japanese fighters head-on in a climbing turn.

Carpenter and Stankovich traded snapshots with the three Zeros, which pushed into steeper dives and disappeared behind the Wildcats. Carpenter knew it was a no-win setup. *They're faster and they outclimb us.* He twisted his neck but could not see them. "Mike, where'd they go?"

Stankovich seemed to take his own sweet time replying. One second dragged past, followed by the snail's-pace duration of another. "Ah, I think they're climbing right."

Without responding, Carpenter stood on his right rudder pedal and laid the stick hard over to starboard. The Wildcat slewed inelegantly in the air, swinging around to confront the Zeros head-on once more. Anxious eyes behind tinted lenses sought out the Mitsubishis, but they were gone. The fight, now audibly trickling out, had bypassed James Carpenter and Michael Stankovich.

Carpenter made a clearing turn and retarded the throttle. He estimated the combat had lasted less than two minutes. Down to 8,000 feet, he shed his oxygen mask, lifted his goggles and wiped a grimy glove across his clammy face. He reached up, released the canopy lock and shoved the hatch back. He inhaled deeply, savoring the cool air. He was sweaty and thirsty and alive.

49

SUNDAY, 30 AUGUST

OVER TULAGI, 1230

"Everybody pick out one," Smith called, "and don't shift targets."

Carpenter could hardly believe the setup. *It's goddamn beautiful!* he exulted. He had never expected to find so many Zeros at so serious a disadvantage, especially today. Heavy clouds had hampered the search for the inbound raiders, but the army pilots had found them first.

Or the Japs found them, Carpenter thought. He saw a swarm of Zeros mauling Captain Brannon's P-400s, caught at low level over the beached transport *William Ward Burrows* just off Tulagi. Carpenter checked left and right, seeking the bombers that surely were there. But he saw only Zeros and a fiery gout falling toward the water 15,000 feet below. *The army's taking a beating.*

Hauling into firing range, Carpenter put a Zero in his illuminated gunsight. The overtake was visible now and he came back on the throttle, seeking valuable seconds to track the clip-winged fighter. *This Jap doesn't know I'm here—too busy chasing that 400.* Carpenter slid to the inside of the Zero's turn, placed his gunsight pipper ahead of the nose and pressed the trigger.

Orange flames erupted from the wingroot as the Mitsubishi exploded. Carpenter realized that his six .50 calibers had ignited a fuel tank. He added throttle, pulled up and saw another Zero crossing his path. He hastily lined up a full deflection shot, fired and missed.

Carpenter looked around for Stankovich. *No good being alone up here.* "Behind you, Jim!"

Tracers flashed past his canopy as Carpenter heard rounds impacting his airplane. Without looking, he kicked right rudder and pulled the stick hard back and left. The Wildcat swerved awkwardly in midair and the hammering stopped.

The Zero magically appeared in front of Carpenter's port wingroot, climbing from his belly side. *Can't believe it—the same stunt from Midway!* Carpenter crammed on full throttle, brought his sight to bear and allowed more lead than he needed. He clamped down on the trigger again and allowed a long, hosing burst to fill the air in front of the Zero's zoom climb.

It was not efficient, but it worked. At no deflection, inside boresight range, the pattern of six machine guns ripped the lightweight Mitsubishi apart. The wreckage dropped away, trailing smoke and debris.

Carpenter joined on Stankovich and took stock. *No bombers. The Japs must have sent a fighter sweep against us,* he thought. *They're trying to wear us down.* The water was littered with the carcasses of dead airplanes, widening splash rings and burning debris. After forty minutes of hunting through the towering clouds, fuel was low. Carpenter estimated he had expended more than half his ammunition, and did not know the extent of damage to his own plane. He rocked his wings, leading Stankovich in a descending turn toward Henderson Field and home.

HENDERSON FIELD, 2115

Jim Carpenter stirred the dying fire with a long stick and watched the embers rise into the night air. He felt better than he could remember since Midway. Sitting in front of the squadron's ready tent, sipping precious scotch with his squadronmates, was wonderful. John L. Smith had been holding court all evening. It reminded Carpenter of a medieval king recounting a day's hunting with his barons.

Sitting beside him, Stankovich yawned broadly. Big Mike wore fatigue pants and a light-blue pajama top. If he was disappointed at not getting a kill, he concealed it well. "I still can't believe that second Jap, pulling up in front of you like that."

"I couldn't believe it myself," Carpenter said evenly. "It was just like that Zero who clobbered me at Midway. Only I missed that one."

"It's a sign of overconfidence," Smith rasped from across the circle. "He thought he couldn't miss and figured it was safe to dive below and pull up ahead of you." The CO's chiseled-granite face turned to take in the other pilots. "Remember that and you'll live long enough to kill more of 'em." Smith's own four victories had run his string to nine, while Carl's tally stood at eleven.

"We probably knocked down eight of them in our first pass," Smitty continued. "You guys did what you were told this time—picked your targets and didn't get distracted. Keep it up."

The pilots knew that "Keep it up" was about as high an accolade as their skipper would grant. Though three F4Fs had sustained battle damage, there had been no losses. But Carpenter had stopped by the 67th Pursuit Squadron compound and knew that four Airacobras were missing. Somebody had seen two parachutes, so there was still some hope.

"Things seem to be going our way, Smitty," Stankovich volunteered. "With Colonel Wallace's two squadrons, are we going to start going after the Japs now?"

Smith gave a tight-lipped smile in the firelight. "I don't think so. We still need more than two F4F squadrons if we're going to provide escort for the SBDs."

The advance element of Marine Air Group 23 had arrived over the past two days, including Major Bob Galer's VMF-224. Carpenter had chuckled when Galer climbed out of the Wildcat with the LSO flags he had used for field carrier-landing practice in Hawaii. But VMF-224 and VMSB-231 still were settling in. The Cactus Air Force yet had some growing to do.

50.

MONDAY, 31 AUGUST

USS SARATOGA, 0745

Phil Rogers chalked the ship's expected morning and evening positions on the blackboard and returned to his chair, shaking his head.

"What's wrong?" Burnett asked.

Rogers slid into his chair. "We're using the same point option as yesterday and the day before. I don't think that's such a good idea."

Burnett looked at the lat-long position and nodded slowly. "Yeah. Why would Admiral Fletcher want to do that?" Most aviators felt that recovering search aircraft at the same position several times in a row could draw unwelcome attention.

"I just work here," Rogers sighed. He flipped a page in his *Time* magazine and tried to ignore Shawn Murtagh's snoring in the chair beside him. The dining room was filled with dozing, gossiping and otherwise idle aviators following stand-down from dawn flight quarters—normally a quiet time of day.

Burnett hoisted his coffee cup and heard Rogers chuckle. "What's that, Phil?"

"Oh, I'm reading some magazines that I got from home. This one's only about six weeks old." Rogers's voice carried no trace of irony. Receipt of a periodical in less than two months from publication was unusual. "There's a guy in Oklahoma who wrote a poem to his ration board:

> *'And when I die, please bury me*
> *'Neath a ton of sugar, by a rubber tree.*
> *Lay me to rest in an auto machine*
> *And water my grave with gasoline.'"*

Burnett shook his head in disgust. "I suppose those people think they really have it rough."

"Some more than others, I guess," Rogers replied. He pointed an accusing finger at a photo of James Caesar Petrillo, don of the American Federation of Musicians. "This bastard, for instance. He makes $46,000 a year, and he's got nothing better to do than make things tough on school kids. It says here the day before the National High School Orchestra was scheduled to start its thirteenth concert season, Petrillo ordered NBC Radio to stop the broadcast. One hundred and sixty students couldn't play because they aren't professional musicians."

"Unions are the same all over," Burnett said. The spite in his voice reminded Rogers that Burnett—son of a Detroit automobile executive—had no love for organized labor. "One of the marine officers aboard said that the Guadalcanal landings were almost delayed on account of New Zealand dockworkers. They wouldn't help reload the transports if it rained, and had to have their goddamn tea breaks." He snorted in derision. "The marines ended up doing all the work themselves."

Rogers cast a sideways glance at Murtagh, still sleeping soundly. The Massachusetts native, fiercely proud of his shanty Irish origins, was Democratic body and soul. Burnett and Murtagh had learned not to discuss politics in general or Franklin D. Roosevelt in particular.

Rogers flipped the page again—and inhaled. "There's an article about the *Lexington* being sunk at Coral Sea."

Burnett leaned over to look. "Anything about the *Yorktown* or Midway?"

"No . . ." Rogers quickly scanned the article. "Just says the Lex had 'an unnamed sister carrier' is all . . ."

Saratoga heeled over in the start of a radical starboard turn. But her 33,000-ton bulk could not respond as quickly as smaller, more agile ships; the roll to port was not as pronounced as *Yorktown*'s had been. Rogers and Burnett exchanged concerned glances. "What the . . ."

Those men standing quickly slipped into their chairs. Rogers saw the duty officer pick up the phone, seeking an answer to the squadron's tacit question, when the loudspeaker erupted. "General quarters, general quarters. All hands man your battle stations. This is not a drill."

The duty officer slammed down the phone. "Submarine contact! *McDonough*'s dropped depth charges but reports torpedoes in the water." He braced himself. "Captain Ramsey's turning toward the wake."

Murtagh, roused by all the commotion, reached for his plotting board. "What's goin' on?"

Burnett could not resist. "Oh, nothing, Shawn. Buck and I were discussing labor unions, and the captain went to GQ."

Rogers tried to stifle a laugh. It came out as a snort. In response to Murtagh's puzzled expression, Rogers explained. "A destroyer's attacked a submarine but there's torpedoes headed this way."

Murtagh's Irish-blue eyes widened. "Holy Mother . . ." He crossed himself almost without realizing it.

Rogers could tell that Burnett was about to launch another wisecrack, and interjected, "It's okay, Shawn. Even if we get hit, Sara's been through this before."

Bombing Three's other veterans overheard the remark, and most of them reacted similarly. They pulled up the January memory from the recesses of their consciousness, recalling how the torpedo explosion sounded, how it felt. What it was like, sitting in blackness as a list developed. It was a lot like this—sitting and waiting and being unable to do a blessed thing about it.

Then the torpedo speared *Saratoga*'s starboard side, amidships.

USS SARATOGA, 1525

Rogers and Murtagh watched the last Scouting Three Dauntless lift off the deck and turn to join its companions. "I hate to see them go,"

Rogers said. "The air group's SBDs have hardly been together since the war began."

Murtagh leaned forward on the rail from "Vulture's Row," where sailors lined the island to observe flight operations. "I guess they're really needed at Guadalcanal." He looked in the direction of the twenty-one scout-bombers and nine torpedo planes the damaged carrier had launched. "How far did you say it is to Espíritu Santo?"

"Almost three hundred and fifty miles. The skipper says they'll regroup there before they fly up to Cactus in a few days." Rogers shook his head in recollection of the night he had spent at Henderson Field. "Poor bastards."

"Well, better them than us." Murtagh laughed. He nudged Rogers's elbow. "Good luck for you, Phil. You'll get to see Sallyann again before long."

Rogers feigned indifference. "Depends. It's still about thirteen hundred miles to the anchorage at Tonga. But we were lucky, Shawn. Word is the torpedo didn't do much structural damage, but Dave checked with Engineering and said they're concerned about getting our speed up to thirteen or fourteen knots. This ship has turboelectric drive, and apparently the explosion screwed up some of the circuits."

"That explains the tow," Murtagh said. He pointed forward, where the cruiser *Minneapolis* strained at her cable, tugging the big carrier into the southeast trade wind to aid launching aircraft. "Man, now I've seen everything."

Rogers shot his friend a knowing grin. "No you haven't. You ain't seen the bare-breasted maidens of Tongatabu."

Murtagh's freckled face took on the expression of a child who has been invited to the candy store. Then he turned skeptical. "Go on, Rogers. You haven't been there, either."

"Well, no . . ." Rogers allowed the confession to be dragged from him. "But the *Yorktown* was, right after Coral Sea. That's all the guys aboard her would talk about. They'd been at sea for three months solid when they put in to reprovision. And there were all these native girls, walking around without any tops on."

Murtagh inhaled deeply and set his chin. Holding up a scarred fist, he vowed, "Rogers, if you're pulling my chain . . ."

Rogers leveled his most sincere gaze. "Would I lie about anything that important?"

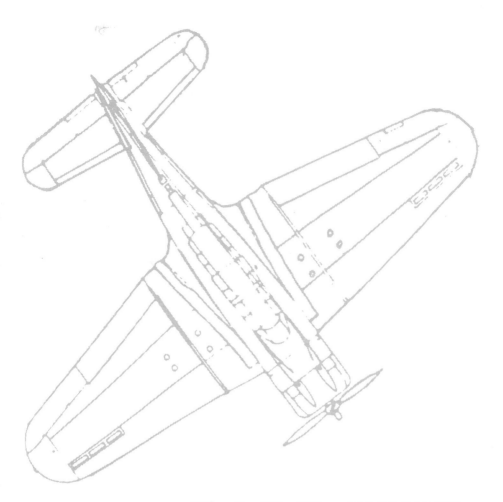

PART FIVE

• —— • —— • —— • —— •

"There were many famous battles . . . But
after the war we talked only about two,
Midway and Guadalcanal."

CAPTAIN Y. "TOMMY"
TOMAGAWA, JAPANESE NAVY
Guadalcanal, by Richard B. Frank

51.

WEDNESDAY, 2 SEPTEMBER

GUADALCANAL

Carpenter ignored the liquid rumbling in his bowels and continued tramping through the grass 600 yards from the Pagoda. He had all he needed for emergencies—a hip pocket full of precious toilet paper and a round chambered in his .45 with the flap holster unfastened.

The fighter pilot had forded the narrow branch of mostly stagnant water immediately west of Henderson Field and continued to the bank of the Lunga River. There he found other men with similar intentions: to rinse off some of the island's mud and dust, to wash filthy clothes, or simply to float in the cool water.

Carpenter stripped and waded knee-deep into the stream, remaining within reach of his pistol on the bank. He began wringing his khaki trousers, alternately scrubbing them with a quarter bar of soap he had scrounged. It occurred to him that in America's front line of a global war, he owned two of the most valued commodities of all—toilet paper and soap.

Eventually satisfied with the pants, Carpenter laid them on a rock to dry in the sun. He began on his shirt, but before he was finished he had to retreat into the bush, carefully picking his way barefooted. *I must look ridiculous*, he thought. *Bare-ass naked with a cocked pistol in one hand and toilet paper in the other.*

Emerging onto the riverbank again, he caught the eye of another bather, equally naked. The man looked at Carpenter with undisguised curiosity, then smiled. "You don't have to explain, buddy. We've all had the trots." He eyed the .45. "But is that for snakes or Japs?"

Carpenter shrugged. "Whatever. There's supposed to be plenty of both in the boondocks." He tried to determine the man's rank or branch of service, but everybody wore khaki or nothing.

"Have you had to use that thing?"

Carpenter laid the pistol down and re-entered the water. "Naw. Hope I never do. I'm a fighter pilot."

The man stood upright from his own laundry. "Yeah? Me, too." He extended his hand. "Glen Benson, Sixty-seventh Pursuit."

"Jim Carpenter, VMF-223." Somehow, ranks weren't important.

Benson showed genuine interest. "Were you involved in the fight this morning?"

Carpenter shook his head slowly. "I should have been. We were headed for the Zeros when I got a bad case of diarrhea. Barely made it on the ground before it was too late." He felt awkward, explaining the embarrassment to a stranger, let alone a fellow aviator. "I'd have been useless in a fight. But our guys and VMF-224 got about seven or eight, I think."

Benson nodded absentmindedly. Finally he looked at the marine. "I was in that combat over Tulagi last Sunday. It's our only big air-to-air action so far. You know, we lost four planes and two pilots."

Carpenter knew. "Yeah, I heard." He fumbled awkwardly with his shirt. "How'd you do, Benson?"

The army pilot shrugged. "Got a piece of one but he climbed right away from me . . ."

"Well, the same thing happened to me at Midway." Carpenter

explained that long-ago episode in the universal sign language of fighter pilots.

Benson seemed unconsoled. He slumped into the water and leaned forward on his knees. "If we had anything like your planes. P-40s, even. But the Brits wouldn't even take our P-400s." His voice choked. "You know what a P-400 is, don't you? A P-39 with a 'zero' after it." Benson's facial skin stretched taut as he tried to smile.

He's about done in, Carpenter realized. *My God, do I look like that?* He tried to think of something to say that would not sound condescending. "The mud marines say you fellows are doing a fine job of ground support."

Benson leaned back, bracing himself with his hands. "Yeah, that's what we hear. But we never know for sure. All we can do most of the time is strafe the jungle or drop some light bombs."

Carpenter decided to change the subject. "Hey, the Sixth Seabees are starting on the new fighter strip. It's supposed to be ready in about a week. And our own radar's operational. Things are looking up."

"I guess so." Benson sounded unconvinced. "Well, I'm going to try the deep water. Good meeting you, Carpenter."

"Good luck, Benson." The marine watched the Airacobra pilot swim into midstream, where his white bottom upended before submerging. "You're going to need it," Carpenter muttered sadly.

52

SUNDAY, 6 SEPTEMBER

REKATA BAY, SANTA ISABEL ISLAND

Sitting with a few other newly arrived aircrew, Sakaida looked around at his environment. He had known that advance-base conditions would be primitive, but the newly opened floatplane base at Rekata Bay made Buin look positively gracious. He had stowed his personal gear in a wooden hut with woven-reed "windows" that opened when the weather gods withheld wind, rain or both. Even at that, he counted himself fortunate after seeing the tents and lean-tos where non-aviators lived.

The place buzzed with insects, and the equatorial heat sucked moisture and energy from the body day or night. However, Sakaida felt reasonably comfortable. He had already made acquaintances among his new companions, though most of them were so young and inexperienced that he doubted many would appreciate his Carmen Miranda routine.

"Attention!" someone shouted. Two dozen airmen scrambled to their feet as a senior-grade lieutenant in tropical whites strode to the front of the room. He was of medium height for a Japanese—about five feet four—with wideset eyes in a moon face. Sakaida knew better than to judge the officer impulsively, but his finely honed instincts said, *Self-important. No Azumano, anyway.*

"As you were," the lieutenant snapped. When the fliers were seated, with an ensign and a lieutenant (junior grade) in the front row, the man began. "I am Lieutenant Mitaka, commanding the *Kamikawa Maru* squadron. I wish to acquaint you with the situation here." He turned to the regional map on the wall behind him.

"We are part of the R Area Air Force, which is composed of all floatplanes in this region. From this base," he said, tapping Rekata Bay on the north coast of Santa Isabel, "we can conduct reconnaissance and attack missions against the American forces on Guadalcanal." He pointed to Henderson Field, 140 nautical miles southeast.

"On seven August the enemy landed on Tulagi and Guadalcanal," Mitaka explained. "We had a detachment there from the Yokohama Air Group, with Type 97 flying boats and Type 2 float fighters. All the aircraft were lost to enemy action on the first day, but the surviving officers and men fought valiantly in land combat."

Mitaka straightened visibly, and Sakaida feared the onset of a patriotic speech exhorting fighting spirit and selfless devotion to duty.

"We will strive to uphold the example set by those men. Previously we have had minimal support," Mitaka explained. "But seaplane tender *Kamikawa Maru* has arrived from Yokosuka, bringing eleven fighters and two floatplanes."

The detachment commander then referred to a paper in his hand. "Therefore, I now have a full roster of our flight crews. Besides myself we have Lieutenant (junior grade) Sawa and Special Duty Ensign Kono, who has earned a meritorious commission for his long service in China and the early phase of this war." Sakaida noticed that most of the others looked at Kono with undisguised curiosity. Meritorious promotions from the ranks were about as common as Christians in the Imperial Navy.

"Among our noncommissioned pilots, the most experienced apparently is Petty Officer First Class Sakaida, detached from the Yoko-hama Air Group." Mitaka looked over the assemblage. "Which one is that?"

"Here, sir!" Sakaida leapt to attention.

"Ah, yes. You are well recommended by your former commanding officer from cruiser *Tone*. I expect good things from you, Sakaida." Mitaka almost seemed to smile.

Sakaida stood riveted in place for a moment before he realized he had actually received a compliment. He remembered to bow to Mitaka and sat down, unable to think of a reply. It occurred to him that Mitaka had described him as the most experienced petty officer—not the most senior. In the rank-conscious Japanese military, that was a startling comment. Sakaida could tell that the two junior ensigns did not like the direction this discussion was taking.

"All of you are qualified floatplane pilots, but many of you are fresh from training," Mitaka explained. "This means that we must make maximum use of those with the most experience. Lieutenant (junior grade) Sawa will lead the reconnaissance contingent because that is our primary mission here. His deputy will be Flight Petty Officer Nishida. Ensign Kono, who has combat experience, is designated the senior fighter pilot. Sakaida will be next in line."

There was subdued murmuring in the room. Sakaida noted that Mitaka had not taken a flying role for himself, but the man's leadership style might emphasize administration and maintenance over operations. In any case, he reflected that in matters of personnel assignment, Lieutenant Mishizo Mitaka was a most astute officer.

53.

WEDNESDAY, 9 SEPTEMBER

GUADALCANAL

Carpenter checked that his landing gear and flaps were down, scanned his engine gauges and lined up on the new fighter strip. He felt the queasy postcombat jitters wriggling in his stomach. Combined with the debilitating effects of his recent dysentery, he sensed his competitive edge slipping away. *Only two damaged this time . . . second fight in a row without a kill*, he chided himself.

He forced himself to concentrate on his landing. The fighter strip, only three-quarters as long as Henderson Field, lay about a mile southeast of the first airstrip. He realized he was almost past the first third of the runway and milked the stick back, compensating with just a touch of throttle. The increased sink rate dropped the little Grumman onto the hard-packed strip tailwheel first. *Good. I'm down in plenty of time.*

Carpenter's gaze swept left to the parking area. The field was still new to him, and he wanted to be sure he made the correct turnoff. When he looked back forward, the runway appeared twenty degrees askew. His pulse leapt. *Damn it to hell!* He shoved on the throttle, heard the Pratt and Whitney wind up, booted right rudder and hoped the extra airflow over the small tail would straighten him out.

Not enough. He carefully depressed his right toe brake and gingerly coordinated throttle and rudder. The errant Wildcat came back into line on the left side of the runway, rocking gently on its narrow landing gear.

Carpenter caught sight of the "follow-me" jeep and turned onto the taxiway on the north side of the strip. There he shut down and switched off. He pulled his sweat-darkened cloth helmet off his head and closed his eyes against the overhead tropical sun.

"Lieutenant, you all right?"

Carpenter forced his eyes open. The plane captain was beside him on the wing, concern obvious under the red ballcap. "Yes. I'm okay." *I feel like a twisted dishrag.* He unstrapped and slowly climbed down.

"I'll get to work on the bullet holes right away, sir." The corporal fingered two 7.7mm holes in the F4F's rudder. Carpenter stared at them in disbelief. "I guess . . ." He stopped. *I didn't even know about them! When did that happen?*

Stankovich came bounding up from the next fighter, all grins and enthusiasm. "We cleaned 'em out that time! Did you see my bomber?"

Carpenter nodded. "Affirmative. That was good shooting, Mike." The blazing Mitsubishi was one of the few clear memories he had of the mission.

"Hey, if you're not careful, your wingman's going to catch up with you." Stankovich nudged Carpenter's shoulder playfully.

"Hope you do." Carpenter managed a smile, then turned and trudged toward the squadron tent. He supposed Stankovich was talking about their respective scores. *I used to be like him. Before Midway.* First Lieutenant James Carpenter, USMC, knew that he had been credited with four confirmed aerial victories of his own and one shared with his wingman. Stankovich's tally was two and a half or three and a half—it didn't matter. What mattered was enough food and enough sleep, and not feeling so damned *tired* all the time. There were a few, like Smith and Carl, who seemed to thrive on combat.

Carpenter wondered if his friends Phil Rogers and Shawn Murtagh were as tired as he was.

TONGATABU, TONGA

Sitting on the beach, nursing their warm beers, the three aviators luxuriated in the island setting. Rogers had shed his shoes and socks and wriggled his toes into the sand. He raised his gaze from the waterline to the familiar silhouette riding at anchor in Nukualofa Roads.

"Now you have to admit, that's one beautiful sight," he said admiringly.

Burnett swallowed a mouthful of the New Zealand brew. "Yeah. Every Jap sub skipper in the goddamn Pacific would agree with you." He picked at a particle of sand in his teeth. "Torpedoed twice in eight months. That must be some kind of record."

"Well, she's still a beautiful lady," Rogers insisted.

Murtagh stirred beside him. "Hey, speaking of beautiful ladies, what about all the bare-breasted maidens you were bragging about?"

Rogers feigned ignorance. "Me, bragging? I haven't seen any unattached females. How 'bout you, Bernie?"

"Nary a one," Burnett responded from beneath his hat. "If there was any here, I'd have sniffed 'em out."

"Well, hello, Yanks." The accented voice came from behind the trio. "Enjoying our scenery, no doubt."

Rogers turned and smiled. "Oh, hi, there . . . Bob?"

"Right." The New Zealander extended his hand and the two shook. "Bob McKenzie. Still at your service."

Burnett hoisted his bottle. "We're still enjoying the beer, Lieutenant. Mighty good of you to scrounge for us."

McKenzie waved a deprecating hand as he squatted in the sand. "Not at all. We did the same for your *Yorktown* chaps when they were here in May."

Murtagh sat up, his interest piqued. "Say, Lieutenant, I hear that the *Yorktown* crew got acquainted with the, ah, native girls." He looked pointedly at Rogers, who glanced away to conceal a smile. "Uh, where do they . . ."

McKenzie laughed aloud, his big shoulders rolling. "You mean the famous island girls who dash about half-naked?" He laughed again. "As near as I can tell, most of them are still hiding in the hills on order of Queen Salote. And those I've seen are fully dressed." He shook his head in amusement. "I've no idea how these rumors get started, but every American sailor seems to believe them . . ."

The Kiwi was nearly bowled over as Ensign Rogers burst out of the starting blocks, barefooted, three strides ahead of Ensign Murtagh.

54.

SUNDAY, 13 SEPTEMBER

HENDERSON FIELD

Lieutenant (junior grade) Bennett Nichols of Fighting Squadron Five was just senior enough to draw an unwelcome bit of responsibility. He was also senior enough to know where to find help; that was why he had tracked down First Lieutenant Jim Carpenter of VMF-223.

Looking out from the Pagoda, Nichols surveyed the area and asked where the *Saratoga* squadron should establish its compound. "We only arrived day before yesterday," he explained to his marine companion, "and we're still learning the ropes."

"Yeah, Smitty said he'd briefed you fellows when you landed

Friday afternoon. He probably mentioned that our squadron and Bob Galer's Two-Twenty-Four are in the Cow Pasture." Carpenter pointed southeasterly toward the Fighter Strip.

"I'd recommend you set up in the coconut grove," Carpenter continued. "It's accessible to the field but far enough removed that you'll be away from the worst of the bombing and shelling. And it's cooler there." He grinned. "But the damn parrots sit in the taller trees and squawk at all hours."

Nichols shook his head slowly. "You know, I was almost looking forward to this. Exotic island settings, palm trees." He slapped a mosquito on his neck. "Man, I'll take the Sara anytime."

"Say, do you happen to know a couple of Pensacola classmates of mine? Phil Rogers and Shawn Murtagh, Bombing Three."

"Yeah, I've met them. They're flying with Bernie Burnett, who was in my class. But the carrier air groups are all mixed up now. Our squadron's originally from the *Yorktown*, and Torpedo Eight's off the *Hornet*. It's hard to keep track of all the old gang."

"Japs in the traffic pattern!"

Carpenter heard the shouted warning at the same moment he heard two radial engines growling in a high-speed pass. He sprinted from the Pagoda and took in the scene. He muttered a fervent prayer. "Oh, my God. Please, no."

Sakaida knew that he and Noichi would get away clean. He had timed the fifty-eight-minute reconnaissance flight from Rekata Bay to perfection, arriving east of the airfield near Lunga Point to begin his fast run-in. And the war gods had rewarded him with a golden opportunity.

The American aircraft was caught at the worst possible moment. Flaps and wheels down, slowed for landing, it had no chance of escape.

Sakaida shot a quick glance at his airspeed indicator, which registered 220 knots. He calculated that he had a moment in time to maximize his opportunity, and slightly retarded the throttle to reduce his overtake. As the American's wingspan loomed in his range finder, Sakaida flipped the safety covers off his cannon and machine-gun triggers.

When the wingtips filled the diameter of his ring sight, he opened fire with all guns.

.   .   .

Carpenter stood transfixed at the spectacle. The lead Zero floatplane was firing 7.7 and 20mms into the SBD, which only now seemed aware of its peril. Tiny details stamped themselves in Carpenter's consciousness. He estimated the float Zero had opened fire at 200 yards, the muzzle flashes from its nose and wings clearly visible. He even noted the slower rate of fire from the cannons, not quite as audible as the high chatter of the 7.7s.

He clearly saw bullet impacts on the scout-bomber, almost from prop to rudder. Shattered canopy glass twinkled briefly in the afternoon sun, then the Dauntless plunged headlong from 500 feet into the pioneer battalion's area across the river. The SBD exploded on impact, leaving a brilliant fireball where its 500-pounder cooked off.

Sakaida streaked through the smoke of the explosion, shoved on full power and leveled off in his high-speed pass. He glimpsed Noichi strafing the length of the airstrip. He knew better than to pull up too soon, where every antiaircraft gun on the field could track him. Glancing back over his shoulder, Sakaida confirmed the fire on the ground where the American had crashed. *A Grumman fighter!* he exulted. Once over the river and climbing northward for home, a cry of triumph filled the cockpit, briefly drowning out the roar of 900 horsepower.

Nichols's gray eyes met Carpenter's, and the marine saw mirrored there what once would have been his own reaction: shock, disbelief, terror. But now, after a tropical eternity of more than three weeks on the island, Carpenter merely said, "Welcome to Guadalcanal."

55.

TUESDAY, 15 SEPTEMBER

GUADALCANAL

Carpenter appreciated the irony. Cactus had scrambled his division fifteen minutes previously, and now he was likely going to get wet to no good purpose. It was not confirmed yet, but apparently the takeoff was generated by a false alarm. He looked again at his cylinder-head temperature gauge, whose needle had quickly crossed the yellow arc into the red. Dark flecks on his windscreen told him the likely problem, but Stankovich confirmed it.

"Jim, you're losing a whole lot of oil. The bottom of your fuselage is covered with it." Stankovich emerged from beneath Carpenter's F4F and reappeared off the port wing. The wingman called again. "You better head back while you can."

Carpenter mentally computed his chances. From 12,000 feet and twenty-five miles out, he might make Henderson Field if everything worked exactly right. He glanced down at Savo Island's brooding shape in the area now called Ironbottom Sound. Then he raised his gaze toward Lunga Point's flat plain, and the haven of Henderson. He reduced power to idle and nursed the faltering Wildcat in the most efficient glide he could manage. *I need to arrive overhead with a few thousand feet for a dead-stick landing,* he told himself. *This thing will glide like a greased safe.*

Then Stankovich's voice was back in the earphones, high-pitched and concerned. "Jim, there's smoke now from under the cowling." Carpenter shot another glance at his instruments. The temperature gauge was nearly pegged and his oil pressure was bouncing off zero. He smelled a faint trace of burnt oil. *Damn, damn, damn. It's a wonder any of these crates still fly. Best mechs in the world can't work without enough spares.*

He keyed his microphone button. "Mike, stay with me in case I have to jump."

"Roger. I'll follow you down."

At 10,800 feet, Carpenter was forced into a decision. If he held a straight course for Henderson, he would have to make an over-water bailout if the airplane began to burn. That meant he might drown. If he turned south, toward the shoreline, he could parachute to dry land and pray that friendly natives found him before the Japanese.

He was mulling over the options when a gout of flame licked at his feet. Simultaneously Stankovich was screaming. "Fire! You're on fire, Jim! Get out!"

At Pensacola, Cadet Carpenter had been advised that the only reasons for abandoning an aircraft in flight were structural failure and fire. He pulled his radio lead, unfastened his seat belt and shoved back the canopy. Then, with thickening smoke sucked past his face into the slipstream, he laid the stick over and watched the world rotate. As he sensed himself becoming light in the seat, he kicked the stick forward and immediately was floating in space.

Carpenter estimated that he had left the aircraft at a little over 10,000 feet. Falling toward earth, he knew intellectually that he had plenty of time to open his parachute. But the primal fear building inside shrieked for him to pull the D-ring before it was too late. He marveled briefly at how the doomed Wildcat had disappeared, then clutched at his harness, found the metal handle and gave a tremendous tug.

A ruffling, fluttering sound came to his ears. Then the world was viciously reoriented in an upward surge that left him gasping. He looked up, saw the beautiful white canopy fully deployed and uttered a heartfelt "Thank you."

He looked down and spotted his aircraft by its smoke trail. The Wildcat was spinning slowly toward the water, and Carpenter calculated it would splash three or four miles off Doma Cove. He heard an engine growing louder and looked left and right, then spotted Stankovich approaching from the northwest. The Wildcat dropped a wingtip in greeting and Carpenter waved energetically, indicating he was safe.

Carpenter checked his drift and determined that an onshore breeze was taking him nearer to land. Almost nine minutes later he descended into the water and began disentangling himself from his heavy parachute harness. The canopy settled partially, then caught the wind and Carpenter felt himself slowly being dragged along. It was almost pleasant, but the motion impeded his ability to release his leg straps. Then he felt his feet drag bottom.

Moments later Carpenter shucked his harness and gathered up the canopy. He paused briefly to wave as Stankovich made a low pass parallel to the beach, rocking his wings. Then Carpenter dashed into the treeline, crammed his parachute under a fern and drew his pistol from his holster. He chambered a round, thumbed on the safety and, in a low crouch, eased away from his tracks in the sand. He had a canteen of water, a hunting knife and twenty-one rounds of .45 ACP ammunition to get him twenty miles to home.

LIBRARY OF HAWAII

Mary Tanaka brushed Sallyann Downey's arm. "Battle stations," Mary whispered, and nodded significantly over her shoulder.

Looking up from the circulation desk, Sally immediately perceived the threat. Two sailors—both second-class petty officers, she saw—were looking at her and whispering to one another at the newspaper table. *Oh, lord. Here we go again.* She had come to realize that eventually lonely servicemen discovered that libraries had librarians, who by law of God and Nature must perforce be unmarried and therefore available.

Sally noticed that the two navy men shook hands, as if sealing a bet, and one of them stood up. He hitched up his white bell-bottom trousers with the thirteen buttons on the flap—Sally knew the conventional wisdom that it gave a sailor thirteen seconds to change his mind—and advanced confidently toward the desk.

He isn't bad looking, she admitted. *Curly hair, well built, probably popular with most girls.* He looked about her age—maybe a year or two older at twenty-four or twenty-five. Sally was prepared to let him down easy.

"Hi, there, honey." He had a nice smile, but the approach was all wrong. She had expected "Excuse me, ma'am," which was not only more usual, but more polite.

"May I help you?" She kept any tone of warmth from her voice and hoped her eyes appeared calm and disinterested behind her glasses.

The second-class leaned casually on the counter. "Well, I hope so, sugar. See, my friend and me are scouting for a get-together next weekend. We're at the navy yard and some of the fellows—"

"I'm terribly sorry, but we only discuss library business here. If you have a question about books or periodicals, I'll be glad to help you, sir."

The sailor's forehead creased in an exaggerated gesture of disbelief. "Ah, c'mon, honey. Don't 'sir' me. My name's LaMunyon, but you can call me Rick."

Sally could not stop the grin she felt curving around the corners of her mouth. "You can call me Miss Downey."

LaMunyon straightened up, hands on his hips. "Well . . ." Sally knew he had just bitten off a profane remark. "Okay, sure, I understand. You gotta be proper when you're on the job." He looked at her in a decidedly unromantic manner. "But what about after work? Maybe—"

"No, *sir*, not after work, either. You see, I'm engaged." *Well, I am, sort of.*

He looked at her hands and Sally folded her arms. "Sister, you ain't very much engaged if you ain't got a ring."

She fought to keep her voice down. "Not that it's any of your business, sailor, but my fiancé is with the marine commandos. He just got back from Guadalcanal. He was wounded in action, but he's still able to kill people quickly and quietly." She drew a finger across her throat and smiled sweetly.

Petty Officer LaMunyon plainly did not know whether to believe

Miss Downey or not. He retreated as gracefully as possible—which meant hardly at all—and collected his partner.

Mary rejoined Sally as the sailors left. "A marine commando? Wait until Phil hears about this!" The two young women laughed so loud that nearby patrons were disturbed in their reading.

Across Punchbowl Street, Rick LaMunyon entered a drug store and borrowed the phone book. He traced a shaking finger down the column until he came to Downey, S. Despite his anger and humiliation, he knew enough to recognize that single women seldom were listed by their full names. He made a note of the address on King Street.

USS SARATOGA

"Did you hear the *Wasp* was torpedoed today?" Burnett's voice was hushed, but the latest carrier loss was the main topic at dinner.

Rogers leaned across the table, fork in hand. "Then it's true? I figured it might be scuttlebutt, or an exaggeration." He looked around *Saratoga*'s capacious wardroom and recalled that she had now survived two submarine attacks.

Burnett nodded solemnly. "Yeah, I got it from one of the communications staff. A sub—or maybe two, I don't know—shot a whole spread of torpedoes. Three or more hit the *Wasp* and she's in plenty bad shape. The *North Carolina* and a destroyer also were hit."

"Goddamn." Rogers quickly calculated the remaining balance of power in the Southwest Pacific. He laid down his fork and slumped in his chair. "Damn, Bernie. Here we are, two days out of Tonga, bound to be laid up for—what? Last time it was six months. With the damage to the *Enterprise*, that means only the *Hornet*'s fully effective."

Shawn Murtagh, seated beside Rogers, made a deprecating noise. "All I can say is, I hope the Big E gets back in commission in a hurry."

Burnett ignored the sentiment, though he knew Murtagh's feelings were deep-seated. "What I don't understand is why the Japs are so much more effective with their subs than we seem to be. Look," he said, ticking off each item on his fingers. "We got nailed in January, out of business until last month. Then, after three lousy weeks in combat, we're tagged again and Admiral Fletcher's wounded.

"Then there's Midway. *Yorktown*, sunk by another submarine when she'd have made it home otherwise. And now the *Wasp*." He grimaced as if his dinner were an undigested lump in his stomach. "The way I count it up, Jap subs have done us three or four times as much damage as their carriers."

Rogers thought back to a long-ago conversation with a dead friend. "You know, Wayne Wik said before Midway that our torpedoes weren't very reliable. There probably isn't much difference between aircraft torpedoes and the submarine kind." He looked around the table at his friends. "The longer this war lasts, the more it seems a long way from being over."

G U A D A L C A N A L

Carpenter knew better than to try to move through the jungle at night. Not only was navigation a problem, but he might stumble into a ravine or—far worse—run across a Japanese patrol or observation post. He could have made progress along the beach, but if he was seen in the open he would surely be caught.

Darkness had settled with tropical speed that seemed accelerated by loneliness and isolation. He had cut some palm fronds with his heavy-bladed knife and fashioned a marginally comfortable bed, then laid other fronds across some branches for cover. But he knew the roof of his crude lean-to would blow away in the first good wind. And, of course, the cloudy sky promised rain. He settled down to contemplate his situation.

He knew that Stankovich had a good fix on his location. That was the most important break, besides landing unharmed. He had been surprised to notice his right shoe and trouser cuff were singed, but his heavy socks had protected the skin. It could have been much worse.

And there were heartening examples of returned aviators. In his own squadron, Marion Carl had just returned from five days in the boondocks, fetched back by sympathetic natives. Lieutenant Amerine of VMF-224 had survived a week in the bush, including a couple of run-ins with Japanese. He had sustained himself by eating nonpoisonous insects and plants. *If they can do it, there's no reason I can't*, he told himself. But he wondered how hungry a man had to get in order to eat insects.

Between the rain and the bugs, he got precious little sleep. For lack of anything else to do, he decided to practice reloading his .45 in the dark. He had no idea how many magazine changes he executed that night: thumbing the release button, allowing the seven-round maga-zine to drop out while he felt for one of his two spares and slammed it home.

By sunrise, James Carpenter figured he had the fastest reload in the South Pacific.

56.

WEDNESDAY, 16 SEPTEMBER

"Enemy bombers reported headed for Buin. Available aircraft take off immediately for interception!"

We will never intercept them in time, Sakaida thought as he raced from the rude hut. It was 165 nautical miles from the Rekata Bay floatplane base to the southern tip of Bougainville. He called to his wingman for the day, Flight Petty Officer Second Class Masao Mizuno. "Follow me to the west. We will try to attack them on their way back from Buin." Mizuno waved in acknowledgment, then dashed toward the second A6M2-N on its beaching dolly.

An agonizing fifteen minutes passed before Sakaida turned into the wind, advanced throttle, mixture and prop controls and began jolting across the bay. He lifted off, water streaming from his centerline and wingtip floats, and almost immediately made a climbing turn to the west. He glanced back, saw Mizuno following and settled down.

Sakaida realized that he needed more information. He did not know how many bombers were involved, nor the type. But at the last minute he had been told by Lieutenant Mitaka that observers reported multiengine aircraft.

Assume they are Boeings, Sakaida told himself. He knew only the barest specifications of the impressive airplane the Americans called B-17, and that data came via the Japanese Army Air Force. The Boeing was reportedly large, well-armed and fast—420 kilometers per hour with a 6,030-kilometer range. To the Imperial Navy, which thought in nautical miles, that meant 225 knots top speed and a ferry range of 3,200 miles. Mission radius with a useful bomb load would be far less, of course, but Sakaida had been told that the U.S. Army Air Force based two or more squadrons of Boeings in the New Hebrides and staged them north through Guadalcanal.

Sakaida turned the crank on his radio to the designated frequency and tried to contact Buin. He was rewarded with a carrier wave and some unintelligible noise. The unshielded ignitions of most Japanese aircraft interfered with radio communication so he was, as usual, on his own.

He looked down off his right wing and saw he was abeam of Vaghena Island, at the southern tip of Choiseul. He continued his climb, leading Mizuno toward 8,000 meters.

GUADALCANAL

Carpenter had been awake before dawn. He decided to start moving as soon as any light broke through the jungle canopy, making the most of his travel time. But he reminded himself to move slowly, cautiously, stopping often to listen to the jungle.

He had been under way about half an hour when he came to a faint trail crossing his path. He crouched beside the trail, behind a tree. He felt a temptation to follow the path, knowing he could make better time than picking his way through the bush. But he also knew that the Japanese undoubtedly would use such trails. They had launched a large-scale assault on the ridge south of Henderson Field in the past two days, and they owned the western half of the island.

Something made a rustling noise in the foliage ahead and to his right. His heart accelerated and he drew his .45. He rolled his shoulders to alleviate some of the cramped sensation from lying on palm fronds all night. Hearing nothing more, he decided to parallel the trail as long as it headed generally east. If it turned more southerly he would resume his trek through the boondocks.

A gunshot cracked past Carpenter's right ear and he instantly dropped flat. When he looked around, eyes following the muzzle of his .45, he saw a tall white man emerge from the brush. Two natives accompanied the stranger; one of them looked about twelve years old.

"Beautiful offhand shot if I say so myself," exclaimed the man in a British accent. "Glad to have witnesses."

Carpenter noticed the .303 Enfield that the stranger carried at port arms. The man walked calmly forward, sending one of the natives ahead into the brush. "You will be Carpenter," he declared. Then he extended his right hand. "David Llewellyn. Presently of the coast-watcher organization, late of the Church of England."

The marine holstered his pistol and stretched himself off the ground. He grasped the man's hand. "Yeah, I'm Carpenter." He looked back across the trail. "What the hell did you shoot at?"

Llewellyn smiled triumphantly. "Not shot *at*, old man. What I *shot*. We can always use some pork." He pointed, and Carpenter saw the youngster dragging a sixty-pound boar from the brush. It had been hit just below and behind the shoulder—a heart shot.

Carpenter scratched his head in bemusement. "Are you nuts? The Japs will be swarming here in a couple minutes."

Llewellyn shook his head and tugged at his goatee. His red beard was laced with gray, and his face showed prolonged exposure to the tropical sun. "Don't think so, laddie. They're well ahead of us, beyond Tassafaronga."

Carpenter was unconvinced. "How do you know that? And how did you find me?"

The hunter smiled again. "Why, it's my job to know, old son." He patted Carpenter on the back. "Come on, then. How do you like your roast?"

Mizuno saw them first. He waggled his wings to attract Sakaida's attention, and the lead fighter turned toward the north.

Sakaida noted four large aircraft, flying in pairs, heading straight down the channel between Vella Lavella and Choiseul. He realized that he would probably have time for one pass—certainly no more than two. In the thin air at 25,000 feet, the ungainly floatplanes were at a serious disadvantage against the turbo-supercharged, multiengine bombers.

Sakaida double-checked his armament, ensuring that all four guns were charged. He turned up the rheostat on his reflector sight, glanced over at Mizuno and saw that all was ready. He inhaled, flexed his fingers to alleviate some of the tension and let out the breath. Then he lowered his goggles and pointed his nose at the lead Boeing. Even from several hundred meters, the size of the aircraft was apparent. Sakaida allowed himself a moment to contemplate glory. *After the victory over the enemy airfield, if I bring down one of these giants, I will truly be noticed.*

The shape grew alarmingly in his gunsight. As the wings filled his inner ring rangefinder, muzzle flashes blinked at him from the bomber's nose and top turret. He centered the target as well as he could—the controls were a bit sloppy at that altitude—and began firing.

He was aware on the second burst that his tracers were falling short. Then he remembered. *The Boeing's wingspan is thirty-two meters—three times that of a fighter or attack plane. It is still out of effective range.* He made himself endure the sustained fire from the Americans a moment longer. Their gunfire also was falling short or going wide, but the sensation was exceedingly uncomfortable.

Now the giant's wings filled the outer ring of the rangefinder. Sakaida thought with a start that the relative closure must be more than 400 knots. He depressed both triggers, sending a continuous stream of 7.7 and 20mm ammunition toward the B-17. He heard two or three bullet strikes on his own aircraft, but could not tell where they hit.

Passing close under the bomber's belly, he had a glimpse of color on the nose. Then he was diving into a port turn, hoping for a shot at the next pair of Boeings.

On the flight deck of the Eleventh Bomb Group B-17E called "Battlin' Betty," the pilot called his second section, warning them of the danger. Then he polled his crew for damage. There was none to report, but upon landing the bombardier would notice a 7.7mm hole in the paint where the curvaceous Betty's navel used to be. A crew chief would find two more in the right wing.

By the time he completed his reversal, Sakaida realized his original assessment had been correct. He could not overtake the lead bombers, but the trailing pair still were within range. He hoped to coordinate with Mizuno in order to split the defensive gunfire, but his wingman had broken in the opposite direction.

Sakaida rolled into a gunnery pass from the right rear of the fourth B-17, slightly low. He found he could stay in position long enough to shoot, but the tail gunner, right waist and belly turret all tracked him, firing steadily. He heard a few more impacts on his airframe. *This is no way to fight*, he told himself. *Five or more heavy machine guns against two cannon and two light guns.* He fired most of his remaining ammunition in a long, desperate burst and thought he saw hits on the wing. Then he stuffed his nose down and dived out of the searching, angry tracers.

GUADALCANAL

David Llewellyn's camp had much to commend it. Several well-constructed thatch huts were clustered around a well, which Carpenter inferred was a source of some pride to the missionary. "Saves us from hauling water back from the Bonegi," had been the explanation.

Llewellyn showed his guest into the most comfortable hut and sent a small boy scampering off on an errand. Moments later the islander returned with a variety of tropical fruit. "I expect you'll want something to tide you over until dinner," the host remarked. Carpenter dug into the wood bowl and began peeling a banana.

"We'll inform Cactus that you're safely with us," Llewellyn explained. "But you must be patient. It may be a week or so before we get you home."

Carpenter tried to appear nonchalant, but he devoured the first banana and started on a second. Between swallows he asked, "How did you find me, sir?"

The ironic smile returned. "Well, laddie, first you must accommodate an old man. Please do not call me 'sir.' True, I'm older than you—twenty-five years or so, I'd guess—but the connotations are distressing to me.

"Now, I don't wish to offend. Perish forbid. But once we heard from Cactus that you were down near Doma Cove, it wasn't very difficult. Some of my boys picked up your trail early this morning. The chopped ferns were a dead giveaway." Llewellyn lowered his head slightly and gave a professorial glance from under bushy eyebrows. "But we expected you to do what Americans and civilized people usually do, by following the paths. Once we realized you were cleverly making your way through the jungle, we estimated where you'd turn up. And there you were." He snapped his fingers.

"So you put a rifle bullet right past my head."

Llewellyn smiled through his reddish-gray beard. "Not to worry, lad. I seldom miss from sixty yards. We saw you the same time as the pig. Seemed a pity to risk losing a good meal."

Carpenter wiped his hands on his pants and pulled his canteen from its case. *A sharpshooting missionary. Well, why not?* He took a swig and screwed the cap back on. "Uh, I don't want to be too nosy, Padre. But how do you keep the Japs from . . ."

Llewellyn held up a hand. "Another thing, old son. I'm not exactly a padre anymore. It's a long story. But you ask a legitimate question. We keep our radio well away from this place and we move it frequently. I think it best we let it go at that."

He stood up, grabbed his rifle and motioned Carpenter to remain. "I'll go make that radio call at our scheduled time. You tuck up in here, have a nice lie-down and I'll be back in an hour or two."

Carpenter took off his clothes and stretched out on a woven hammock. In ten minutes his snoring had a crowd of children laughing to one another outside the door.

REKATA BAY

Sakaida fingered a half-inch hole in one of his wingtip floats. The mechanics already were cutting metal patches to cover the battle damage to his aircraft, which would be operational again tomorrow. He turned away, joining Mizuno on the wooden walkway from the beaching area.

Both enlisted pilots abruptly stopped and came to attention. They saluted in unison as Lieutenant Mitaka approached, followed by Ensign Kono. Mitaka came directly to the point. "You intercepted the bombers?"

"Yes, Lieutenant," Sakaida acknowledged. He was senior and would make the report. "We found them at eight thousand meters west of Choiseul."

Mitaka swatted a mosquito and looked up at the heat-filled sky. "There is no sense in standing around here. Let us compile the mission report in the operations office."

Sakaida pulled off his fur-lined helmet and undid his life preserver. Walking toward the patched-together "office," he continued his narrative. "They were Boeings, four of them flying in two sections."

Mitaka looked back as he walked. "Yes, Buin told us that five or six bombers attacked shipping."

Petty Officer Mizuno ventured to speak. "Excuse me, sir. Does that mean that two were shot down over Buin?" He was concerned that the Buin defenses were more effective than he and Sakaida had been. If so, the loss of prestige would be unbearable to him.

"No!" Mitaka rasped. "It means that ground observers are less reliable than those in the air." He looked significantly at Kono, who obviously shared that opinion.

Entering the office, Sakaida and Mizuno deposited their equipment on a table. Mitaka sat down and began making notes for his report. "Continue, Sakaida."

"Sir, we were . . . unable to bring down any of the enemy aircraft." He wanted to explain that two floatplanes against four multiengine bombers at high altitude was a poor match, but he thought better of making excuses.

"Yes, I know that, Sakaida." The officer's tone was even and matter-of-fact. He continued scribbling notes.

Kono interjected while Mitaka wrote. "At what range did you open fire?" From the tone, Sakaida knew that the perceptive veteran suspected one of the problems.

"Sir, I fired too early on my first approach. The aircraft's size, it is deceptive." Kono grunted an acknowledgment and furrowed his eyebrows. In combination with his bald head, the appearance would have been frightening to anyone unacquainted with the man.

"I would say you did well to find the Boeings, considering you had no directions," Mitaka said. He looked up. "What do you conclude from this experience?"

Sakaida relaxed as much as he dared. "Sir, we need a method of attacking them in greater force. Their firepower is . . ." he paused, searching for the phrase. ". . . overwhelming. I hit one on my second attack. My bullets went into its wing, but I was exposed to several guns at the same time." He shrugged in a helpless gesture. "The bomber merely kept flying. It showed no damage."

Mitaka scratched some more notes on the paper, then looked up. "Yes. The Boeing is known for its strength and armament. The Americans call it Flying Fortress. In my report I am comparing it to our H8K flying boat in speed, construction and size. But there is an important difference."

"Sir?"

Mitaka looked back and forth between the two pilots. "We have built such aircraft in their dozens. The Americans are building them in the thousands."

USS SARATOGA

Dave Shumway stood at the head of the room, hands on his hips. The chatter in the room abated. He looked left and right, then began in a low, even tone. "As I'm sure you all know, the *Wasp* was torpedoed off the Solomons yesterday morning. Some of you also may have heard that they couldn't save her. Well, it's true. She was scuttled last night."

The buzzing chatter resumed as aviators fidgeted in their chairs, exchanged initial impressions or merely looked around to observe their friends' reactions. The squadron CO pressed ahead. "You all are wondering what this means to us, and I wish I could tell you more. But since we flew off the scouts and torpeckers, and then the fighters, we need to keep something aboard for emergencies. That's us."

Shumway had a tentative operations schedule in his pocket, but he did not need to refer to it. "We'll be conducting limited flight ops until we reach Pearl, but at the ship's reduced speed you need to stay sharp and pay attention. Launch will be especially tricky, even with light loads.

"Now, it's fairly obvious that we'll be on the beach for a while. That's okay, we have plenty of practice at it." Heartfelt laughter swirled through the confined space and the skipper allowed himself a wry smile. "We expect to make Pearl on the twenty-first. Leave will be granted in rotation, starting a few days after we drop anchor. Incidentally, you can see Mr. Burnett to make your contribution to the anchor pool. But be warned—I saw him passing some cash to the navigator this morning."

More laughter erupted as Rogers nudged his friend, who flushed in embarrassment. Somebody launched a dollar bill folded into a paper airplane in his direction. Murtagh grabbed it out of the air and quickly pocketed it.

"One more thing. The latest AlNav has been published. I think you'll find that some ensigns currently in this room will have to spring for a wetting-down party when they sew on that extra half-stripe."

Rogers and Murtagh warmly shook hands. It had been a long stretch from ensign to lieutenant (junior grade), but the all-navy distribution list was official. Rogers basked in the glow of the moment. Things were looking up: a promotion and an unexpected chance to be with Sally again.

Yet he felt vaguely uneasy. He sat back in his comfortable chair and began dissecting his emotions. While the sinking of *Wasp* was a shock, he knew nobody in her air group. He had never been aboard her, and had only seen her a couple of times from the air. USS *Wasp* (CV-7) was just another wartime entity. She had existed on the periphery of his consciousness just as *Saratoga* and *Yorktown* had surely existed for other men.

Loss of *Wasp* and however many men died with her had no direct effect upon Lieutenant (junior grade) Philip Rogers. And that was what bothered him.

GUADALCANAL

David Llewellyn picked his teeth with a long thorn and suppressed a contented belch. The pleasant aroma of medium-done pork still filled the air around the pit where the boar had roasted slowly through most of the day. "Ahh, there's nothing like a good cookout under the stars. Puts a chap in a philosophical mood." He cradled the Enfield that never was beyond arm's reach.

Carpenter looked up and tried to identify a constellation. The inky tropical sky was partially obscured by cloud, but through occasional breaks in the layer he saw astonishingly bright stars winking at him across thousands of light-years. "There's lots worse ways to spend an evening on this island," he replied. He thought of the sleepless, horror-filled nights at Henderson Field, alternately shelled and bombed.

A seminaked girl approached the fire, holding out an orchid to Llewellyn. The missionary accepted the gift from the child, whom Carpenter estimated at four or five years old. Llewellyn spoke a few words of an unintelligible dialect and the little girl squealed in delight. She toddled off to find her mother.

Carpenter turned back to his host. "What did you say to her?"

Llewellyn scratched his beard self-consciously. "I told her I'd pass on her lovely gift." He held out the white flower to the marine. "It's for you."

Carpenter accepted the orchid and pointedly stuck it in his shirt pocket. "You seem to have won over these people."

"Ah, you've got it backwards, lad." He looked around at the villagers, who politely allowed the white men their privacy. "These islands are populated by Melanesians. Now, most encyclopedias will tell you they've still one foot in the Stone Age. Cannibals and headhunters. But it isn't entirely true. As you've just seen."

"The difference between book knowledge and personal experience," Carpenter observed.

"Ah, now I detect you're a philosopher." Llewellyn threw back his red-maned head and laughed at the stars. "This can be a very long evening, James."

"I'm not going anywhere." He ventured a question. "Llewellyn, how the . . . how did you get here?"

The missionary leaned forward, his elbows on his knees. He seemed deep in thought, as if deciding how to answer the question. At length he looked directly at Carpenter and said, "Old son, this is one of my stops on the road to hell." He stared into the embers of the fire pit, and Carpenter knew better than to interrupt.

"I was in the Great War," Llewellyn began. "A chaplain, I was, in a territorial regiment. Quite young, oh-so-earnest. Well, to keep the story within bounds, one evening in 1917 I was seeing the lads along a trench line when Jerry came to visit. His calling card was a shower of grenades and trench-mortar bombs. Even in the dark it wasn't hard to see what they were about. They'd isolated our section of trench long enough to overrun us and get away with prisoners for questioning. Both sides did it all the time.

"I happened to be near a Vickers gun. Understand that most chaplains are averse to bearing arms. In fact, they're prohibited by law. But those were my lads, some of whom I'd known in civilian life. I saw them being blown apart, bayoneted, clubbed, whatever, and I went a little mad. I pulled the dead gunner off his Vickers and began firing. Fine weapon, the Vickers. Reliable. I went through a two-hundred-and-fifty-round belt, then picked up a rifle and took after any

German within reach. Some of the others recovered their senses and we pushed old Jerry back through our wire."

Carpenter sat spellbound by the missionary's tale. Without knowing how, he sensed that Llewellyn's incredible story was fact.

"Those few minutes ruined my life," the man continued. "I discovered a fundamental flaw in my character. After over a year in the army, most of it in the front lines, I realized where my calling lay. I did far more good for my flock in five or ten minutes than I had in months and months of ministering to them. I tell you, Carpenter, I don't think I saved one blessed soul in that war. But I saved quite a few lives." He caught himself approaching a peak of heartfelt anger. Smiling in the dark, he returned to his jovial banter.

"My battalion commander was an understanding sort. After all, he was a Welshman, too. He poured me a dram and said, 'Davie, if you was a line officer I'd get you a Distinguished Service Order for certain, and with a bit of luck, a Victoria Cross.' But I was a chaplain and, quite apart from the sin of slaying my fellow man, I had undeniably violated king's regulations. There was nothing for it but to resign my commission."

"What did you do then?" Carpenter tried to imagine this demonstrably good and caring man resolving a moral dichotomy.

Llewellyn grunted in the dark. "I turned from a fisher of men into a hunter of men. Reenlisted as a ranker and, because I could shoot, I found myself posted to the First Army sniper school at Linghem. I finished the war as an enthusiastic assassin and fornicator. Got a Military Medal for the former and a common social disease for the latter."

Carpenter sat in awed silence. *Why is he telling me this?* But he recalled that people sometimes unburden themselves to strangers about things they would never discuss with relatives. In as polite a tone as possible, he asked, "David, after all that, how did you come here?"

The Welshman unwrapped himself from around his legs. "Well, that's an even longer story, James. If ye don't mind, I'll save it for another time." He pointed to the hut behind him. "You're welcome to the 'guesthouse' for the duration of your stay. We'll leave for Henderson Field after breakfast. I'll send Ezekiel to fetch you."

As Carpenter spread the mosquito netting over the hammock in the darkened hut, he found himself saying a prayer for the peace of mind of David Llewellyn, a Welshman a long, long way from anything like home.

57.

SATURDAY, 19 SEPTEMBER

GUADALCANAL

Llewellyn called a halt and the little party moved into the shade of a line of bushes. Carpenter slumped beside the missionary and noticed the four islanders sat facing outward to the points of the compass. "Your troops are well trained," he offered.

"Ah, 'tis nothing any good soldier wouldn't do. But I try not to regard them as troops, Jamie. They're more like . . . parishioners. We look out for each other."

"Say, I haven't figured out yet—what religion do you practice here? You said you were formerly Anglican."

Llewellyn smiled archly. "That's a question I've not quite answered meself, laddie. I'm like our organist back home in Maeshafn Mold—I play it by ear."

"Well, do you preach a general Protestant faith or what?"

Llewellyn bit into a banana and thought while he chewed. "Generic Christianity, I suppose. I try to combine the best elements of several faiths. Of course, I still adhere to Anglican doctrine with watered-down ritual. But I throw in some good Catholic guilt—there's both good and bad guilt, you know—and mix in some evangelism for spice."

Carpenter grinned in response. "Sorry I won't get to hear you deliver a sermon. I think I'd enjoy that."

"Well, now, maybe we can arrange that before you leave this blessed island. Tell me, James, what's your faith?"

Carpenter had wondered when Llewellyn would get around to that. "I was baptized in the Unitarian Church. But to tell you the truth, I have no idea how it differs from any other Protestant religion. Since then I've become a devout United States Marine."

"Well, you make a valid point, old son. A fighting man needs a faith of that sort. The best warrior's religion, of course, is Muhammadism. But you marines have a splendid hymn. Too bad it isn't played on bagpipes." He thought for a moment. "You know, after the war, whenever I heard the pipes, I got this powerful urge to go out and kill somebody who needed killing."

Carpenter chuckled at the sentiment. "What do you do for music?"

Llewellyn glanced down in disappointment. "We have to sing *a cappella*, I'm afraid. I had an accordion when I came to the Solomons nine years ago, but it didn't last long in this climate. Somewhere I picked up some Baptist songbooks. 'Jesus Loves Me,' 'The Old Rugged Cross,' that sort. You want a Baptist hymn every time. Forgot to mention that in my ecclesiastical mixture."

Finally Carpenter summoned the nerve to ask the question that had preyed on his mind. "David, whatever drove you to come here? There are so many other places you could have gone."

Llewellyn leaned back against a tree, his Enfield across his knees. "Well, thereby hangs a tale, ye might say." He spoke carefully, choosing his words. "After the war, I was at a loss. I'd no future in the Anglican Church after my shameful conduct, though my mother, God bless her, never knew just how badly I'd behaved. But you know, James, some Welsh women have what we call the Sight. And my mother was one of them. One evening in 1919 she took my face in her hands and she said, 'Davie, you're cursed with a long life of suffering. And I see it's of your own making.'"

The missionary sniffed and rubbed his nose in a way that made Carpenter want to look away. But Llewellyn continued. "I decided that organized religion had no hold on me, but I felt the need to make amends for my behavior in the war. So I signed on with a nondenominational group devoted to good works among the heathen. I served as an administrator in Kenya and China before I fetched up in New Guinea." He leaned forward, with fevered eyes locked onto Carpenter.

"James, I've seen hell," he said softly. He patted the ground with one hand. "It exists here, on earth." He leaned back again and continued his tale. "I'd made a good record on my first two postings— exemplary, you might say. For that reason the London office sent me to the worst place of all. That was New Guinea in 1931.

"Now, a bit o' background. New Guinea has about seven hundred languages and dialects, so nobody can possibly communicate with all the tribes and clans and whatnot. But I went to the southeast interior, where there was a Papuan tribe of Anga speakers." He shook his head at the recollection. "Most of those people are animists who worship nature, but some are in the grip of evil headmen. They have shamans—witch doctors if you like—who possess the power to summon up the furies of hell."

Carpenter felt a little chill run through him.

"I mean that, James. Late one night my interpreter and I heard jungle drums outside the village we were in. We got curious and crept through the brush, and there was an unholy rite in progress. The tribal shaman was an ancient black man—really black, with dried, wrinkled skin and red-lined eyes. What he did that night was far more than mumbo jumbo. He conjured up from the earth something—a creature, for lack of a better word. Through the smoke and the darkness we couldn't see it very well, but it was so unspeakably foul that I cannot describe it. There was a smell of sulfur about it, and it seemed to do his bidding. The shaman threw a straw icon at this . . . thing . . . and my interpreter passed out. That's God's holy truth.

"Now, the next morning the interpreter came to me, absolutely terrified. He said one of the shaman's acolytes told him the old man had cursed him because he had dared turn his back on the old ways. He was going to die before the sun set.

"Well, I was ready to believe anything. We packed up and left, making our way to the river where we embarked in our canoe. About an hour before dusk the boy gave a cry, grabbed his throat and died."

Carpenter stared at the missionary, disbelieving but intent on his words. He waited for Llewellyn to continue.

"I know what you're thinking," the Welshman said. "The power of suggestion. You say the boy died because he'd been told that he would. But when I lowered his body over the side, there was a red welt around his neck.

"James, I know when I'm beaten. I had no faith in my ability to deal with that situation. Not even my own faith in God Almighty, and that's why I'm cursed. I was tested and I failed, so I went home for a year. Then I came here, where I could do some good."

The American simply stared at his companion, unable to think of anything to say.

"There, I've told you," Llewellyn said. "You can think me a liar or a fool or a madman—or all three. But you asked me a question, and I told you the truth as I know it."

Llewellyn used his rifle as a prop and pulled himself upright. "We can still make three miles before dark."

HONOLULU

Sallyann paid little attention to the people in the park. She turned the corner with her bag of groceries for the coming week and was thinking of her next letter to Rogers as she climbed the steps to the apartment-house door. Saturday evening was a good time for shopping, as few people pushed the curfew to visit the stores that were open. Preoccupied with her thoughts and her key ring, she had not noticed the two sailors who had spotted her from their park bench.

She had just turned the key in the lock when she felt a hand on her shoulder. A slurred voice, the scent of liquor and a sense of dread came to her. "Lemme help you, Miz Downey."

She turned to see the slack-jawed face of Petty Officer Rick LaMunyon. His companion from the library stood close beside him, holding a paper bag with an open bottle. "Oh, no, thank you," she said. She turned back toward the door.

"Not so fast, honey." Her left arm was firmly gripped and the voice insisted, "Ain't you gonna invite us in?"

"Yeah, jus' a coupla lonely sailors," the other intoned.

Sally's mind raced, seeking options, but she was spinning her mental wheels. No alternatives occurred to her. "I really must go . . ."

She felt herself pulled backward down the steps, absurdly still clutching her groceries. She realized that her only weapon—the keys—remained in the door. *Stay calm, don't get them excited.* Belatedly, she told herself that she should have asked them in, then run next door to Mrs. Thomas or the apartment manager down the hall.

The second sailor took the bag from her arms as LaMunyon pressed her against the wall, around the corner where they were hidden from the street. She felt her skirt lifted and a pair of strong hands clutching at her. She began to scream, but another hand covered her mouth and forced her head back against the wall. *This can't be happening.*

"Relax, sugar," LaMunyon said evenly. "We're gonna enjoy this, so you should, too." He reached his fingers under her panties and began pulling them. "Your big, tough marine isn't around, is he? An' if you wanna say anything, we'll jus' say you invited us." Through tear-blurred eyes she saw him grin and breathe more whiskey fumes into her face.

She felt one hand leave her and realized that LaMunyon was fumbling with his trousers. *Thirteen seconds to change his mind.* She waited as long as she dared, then opened her mouth and bit hard.

"Ow! God damn you . . ." The other sailor withdrew his hand and looked at the teeth marks on his palm. As Sally shrieked a high-pitched, visceral scream, he backhanded her right cheek. The force of the blow knocked her glasses askew and whipped her head aside. She saw varicolored spots floating before her, competing with the evening sky. She screamed again before the hand was back over her face, pressing a white sailor's hat to her nose and mouth and obscuring her vision.

Both hands were back under her skirt. She sobbed and tried to move her arms, but they were pinned.

Abruptly the hat was gone, and with it, the hand. She had the impression of the second man reeling backward and there was a third voice, distant yet familiar. LaMunyon's head turned in that direction as Sally's vision cleared.

A white doughboy-style helmet sat atop a large head belonging to a huge man who was pounding the sailor's skull against the stucco wall. Mr. Tarutani dropped the inert body like a sack of wheat and reached toward LaMunyon with ham-hock hands bearing thick, stubby fingers.

LaMunyon turned toward the big Hawaiian, freeing Sally's arms. She brought her right hand up toward the face and, with as much power as she could manage, drove her thumb into the left eye. She felt her long, manicured nail penetrate something soft and liquid.

Then LaMunyon was rising vertically off the ground, gripped by the throat in those massive hands. Sally heard the sailor scream, heard Mr. Tarutani shout something unintelligible and saw LaMunyon beating ineffectually at his assailant. She quickly calculated that the Hawaiian air-raid warden had 80 to 100 pounds on the sailor, and apparently could hold him aloft indefinitely.

Moments later, Mr. Tarutani released the white-clad form, which flopped to the ground with a purple face and a trickle of blood from the left ocular socket.

58.

SUNDAY, 20 SEPTEMBER

GUADALCANAL

Carpenter knelt in the shade of a grove and wiped a sleeve across his sweat-streaked forehead, then looked over Llewellyn's shoulder. The marine knew the little group was now deep in Japanese territory, but the exact position was a mystery to him. "Where exactly are we?" he asked.

The missionary oriented the rough map and searched briefly with a dirty forefinger. "About here," said Llewellyn. He tapped a point upon the Kokumbona River, east-southeast of Point Cruz. "We should cross the Matanikau tomorrow, then it's straight on to the Lunga."

"Aren't we likely to be ambushed trying to get through the lines?"

"It's only a bother if we're caught at close quarters, Jamie." Llewellyn's blue eyes continued scanning the hummock, reading the ground. "And if we keep our wits about us, we won't go anywhere that might happen."

Carpenter instinctively wanted to trust the Welshman, whom he recognized as more of a soldier than a missionary. But an alarm bell rang somewhere in the marine's mind. "David, I don't understand. If we . . ."

"It's historical, laddie." Llewellyn finally turned his face toward the American. "Think upon it. Your Jap-o-nese, he's got no tradition of marksmanship. A military tradition, aye. There's no braver soldier on earth than your Japanese. But when it comes to long-distance shooting, he's a loss. He isn't trained as a genuine rifleman, and his weapon has open, imprecise sights.

"Now you and me, we're products of cultures with long traditions of marksmanship. When Conan Doyle wrote of 'the yew wood, the true wood, the wood of the English bow,' he meant Welsh longbows. The blasted English overwhelmed and absorbed us, as the Frenchies learned to their sorrow at Crécy and Agincourt. Then at Mons in '14, our Old Contemptibles shot the Prussian guardsmen to pieces with precision, long-range riflery." He prodded Carpenter in a friendly way. "Like your ancestors did to the poor redcoats in the insurrection."

Carpenter's expression showed a sincerely dubious outlook. "Relax, laddie." Llewellyn tapped the marine's arm in a confident gesture, and smiled. "If there's any ambushing to be done, I expect we'll do it ourselves."

That was not what Carpenter had hoped to hear.

59.

MONDAY, 21 SEPTEMBER

GUADALCANAL

"We should be getting close," Llewellyn said. He sat beside the worn track in the tall grass and glanced around, ensuring his scouts were dispersed in the evening light. Carpenter, with a marine's professional eye, appreciated the way the islanders deployed without an order, without speaking, rifles ready.

Llewellyn studied his chart again and looked to the northeast. "The problem is, old son, that I don't know your chaps' disposition." He waved some insects away from his face. "The perimeter seems to change rather frequently." He noted a squiggle on the map, running from Guadalcanal's north coast well inland. "I think we're almost to Alligator Creek. Most likely your defensive positions will be on any high ground overlooking this plain, so that's where we'll head."

The two men stood to resume their trek when one of the scouts trotted soundlessly up to Llewellyn. "Jap-man, he come," said the Melanesian called Ezekiel, pointing down the trail. "Musket he fire up quick."

Carpenter looked quizzically at the missionary. Pidgin English seemed to require as much interpretation as French. "How many Jap-man?" Llewellyn asked in kind.

Ezekiel, a stout, cheerful man of indeterminate age, thought for a moment. He held up six fingers, then knelt and drew an esoteric diagram in the dirt. Llewellyn and the scout exchanged a few words Carpenter could not follow.

"Right." Llewellyn stood up, hefting his rifle. "A Japanese patrol has established a night ambush position astride this trail," he told Carpenter. "We can either go to ground here and wait until dawn, or try to slip past them and hope we're not spotted."

"Sounds risky," the marine replied.

Llewellyn nodded. "It is. Either way, we'd be on the defensive if we're discovered." He looked directly at Carpenter. "Or . . . we can determine the point of contact."

"David, are you suggesting—"

"Remember what I said before? I am suggesting, Jamie, that *we* do the ambushing." He turned and sent two of his men toward the Japanese position, one from each side of the trail. Without further explanation, he showed Carpenter to a secluded spot well clear of the trail. "You wait here. If one of us doesn't come for you, stay put. Understand? If need be, wait all night, then head due east." He smiled at the flier. "Like Peter Pan said, straight on till morning." Then he was gone.

Carpenter sought the position that gave him the most flexibility. He decided to sit facing the trail with his arms braced on his knees, holding his .45 in both hands. The minutes dragged by, accompanied by the incessant buzzing of insects and the itch of dried grass.

A gunshot split the evening, somewhere up the trail. Then another, and another. Then silence.

Carpenter risked a look. He glimpsed Llewellyn kneeling on the same side of the trail, fifteen or twenty paces away, looking down a straight stretch of the path. Another shot shattered the heavy air. This one seemed closer. Carpenter released his right hand, wiped a sweaty palm on his pants, then gripped the heavy pistol again.

Llewellyn instantly shouldered his Enfield, and Carpenter saw the Welshman stand waist-high in grass. Carpenter realized, *He's going to shoot somebody.*

Llewellyn saw what he wanted—three panicked Japanese soldiers fleeing toward him, single-file on the trail. He got a quick sight picture and pressed the trigger. The .303 copper-jacketed bullet took the nearest Japanese high on the sternum and the little soldier crumpled instantly. Carpenter had an image of Llewellyn smoothly cycling the butter-smooth bolt, getting off three rounds with precision.

It was over in four seconds.

Carpenter stood up but remained crouched. Llewellyn was still scanning left and right, looking for additional targets. One of the scouts—Jacob, the American thought—motioned toward Carpenter's side of the trail.

Carpenter heard a rustling in the grass. *One of the other scouts,* he thought, turning toward the noise. But this man was running. Carpenter could see tall grass moving aside. He stepped back into a small clearing.

A small man in a dirty brown uniform carrying a long, bayoneted rifle burst into the clearing and abruptly stopped. For two accelerated heartbeats the astonished enemies looked at one another across five paces and two cultures. Llewellyn was shouting something behind him but Carpenter paid no attention. If extended, the long Arisaka with its two-foot bayonet would almost touch Carpenter.

The Japanese held his improbably large rifle at port arms, useless at close range. Carpenter realized that he had only to raise the pistol and execute the bedraggled soldier. Llewellyn was crashing through the brush, still yelling. "Shoot him! For God's sake, man, shoot him!"

The little soldier looked in terror, took in the big autopistol being raised toward him and, with amazing speed, brought his rifle downward. The bayonet caught Carpenter's right sleeve as the marine's finger depressed the trigger. The first round went in the dirt.

Carpenter instinctively recoiled from the thrust, tripped in a tangle of grass and went down on his back. The Japanese screamed, raised the rifle in order to thrust and Carpenter extended his arm straight outward in a terror-stricken reflex. He forgot everything he had ever been taught, forgot the sights, forgot to lock the wrist. He began mashing the trigger, losing more control each time the big Colt bucked in recoil.

The Japanese disappeared. Carpenter looked to his left, saw Llewellyn approaching, then looked right. He sat up. The little soldier's body lay almost at his feet.

"That was just a mite too close, old son." Llewellyn checked the corpse, then helped the American to his feet.

"He almost had me," Carpenter muttered. He looked at the Colt with a sense of wonder, then remembered to change magazines. "If I hadn't had this . . ."

Llewellyn gave a sardonic grin. "Actually, it wouldn't have mattered." He reached down and pointed to an entrance hole in the cadaver's right side, and a gaping exit hole in the left. "Another snap shot, though the range was close."

Carpenter's mouth felt terribly dry. He also felt something else—acute embarrassment. He checked his previous magazine. "You mean I missed four times?"

"Three times, Jamie. Look here, one of your great brutal bullets took him in the left shoulder. But he'd have skewered you just the same."

The marine inhaled as much of the humid air as his lungs could manage. "I wonder why he didn't shoot me."

Llewellyn picked up the Arisaka and handed it to Jacob, who had been making sure of the other Japanese. "Because he was as terrified of you as you were of him. Remember, your Jap-o-nese has no tradition of riflery. He's more often a sword and bayonet man. Did you know he even puts bayonet mounts on his light machine guns?"

Carpenter holstered his pistol. "You're one for the books, Llewellyn. You really are." He looked down at the dead soldier, who now seemed even smaller. "How can you preach the word of God and keep on doing . . . this?"

Llewellyn placed a hand on Carpenter's shoulder. "Ah, that's the adrenaline talking, Jamie. Besides, haven't you read the good book? 'Blessed be the Lord my strength, which teacheth my hands to war, and my fingers to fight.' Psalm 144:1, if you care to look it up."

Another scout padded up to Llewellyn and said something. The Welshman motioned for his men to regroup. "Biku says one of them got away," he explained. "They were driven this way, as planned, but apparently the missing man and your chap broke into the brush off the trail."

Llewellyn changed magazines in his Enfield, checked that he had a round chambered, then began walking eastward. He set a fast pace into the twilight.

60

TUESDAY, 22 SEPTEMBER

LIBRARY OF HAWAII

Mrs. Hedges, chief of the circulation department, called across the office to Sally. "There's a phone call for you, dear." She smiled knowingly, then left the room.

Sally thought that her superior was being unduly solicitous and wondered what it was about. She picked up the receiver, expecting a call from the Honolulu Police Department about last Saturday.

"Miss Downey speaking."

"Well, this is Mr. Rogers speaking," came the chipper reply.

She froze in place. She thought of the unfinished letter she was writing, trying to tell her man that she had almost been raped by two—what? *Not men*, she thought.

"Honey, it's Phil. I'm back!"

Sally sat down abruptly. She made a little sound that came across the line like a bird's chirp.

"Sally, are you there?" She could hear the concern in his voice.

"Oh, Phil! Yes, I'm here. I . . . I just didn't expect to hear from you again so soon." Her voice trailed off.

"Well, we . . . ah, I got back yesterday." He felt she would realize that *Saratoga* had returned to Hawaii, and that officially he could not confirm a ship movement. There was no response, so he continued. "We'll start getting leave in three days, honey. I'll call you at home tonight, okay?"

A dark thought crossed her mind like a rainstorm across the sun. "Phil, are you all right? You're not hurt, are you?" She tried to imagine any other reason why he would be back in Hawaii so soon. She held her breath.

He laughed softly into the phone. "No, I'm not hurt. In fact, I'm promoted! Some night this week you'll have to let a lieutenant, junior grade, take you to dinner."

Sally exhaled in relief. "Oh, that's wonderful." Self-consciously, she looked left and right, then loudly kissed the phone. "I love you, Phil."

"And . . . same here. I'll call you tonight."

Stung, Sally hung up the phone. Then she remembered the occasional voices she had heard in the background. *He's with his friends*, she realized. *He wouldn't say he loves me out loud.*

Mrs. Hedges walked back into the office, her footsteps louder than necessary. "Good news, dear?"

Sally looked up from the desk. "Yes. Good news."

"Then what's the matter? Are you all right?" The older woman's face and voice expressed genuine concern.

Sally raised clenched hands. "Oh . . . men!"

Mrs. Hedges laughed softly and hugged one of her favorite assistants. "I know, dear. I know."

THE FIGHTER STRIP, GUADALCANAL

A drizzling rain pattered on the canvas roof of Carpenter's tent. He lay stretched out, half-sleeping, when a familiar voice interrupted his reverie. "Anyone home?"

Carpenter sat up and swung his feet to the dirt floor. "Oh, David. Didn't expect to see you today after we got in last night."

Llewellyn pulled up a footlocker and sat down, still cradling his Enfield. "Came to say good-bye, Jamie. I'm off for home first thing in the morning."

The aviator shook his head in confusion. "Why so soon?"

"Mission accomplished, old son. I got a valuable aviator back to his airfield and I've had a discussion with the coastwatcher organization here. I'll scrounge up some supplies and be on my way."

"Well, can I help you with anything?" Carpenter smiled in the murky tent. "I have connections."

Llewellyn tugged at his hooded rainslicker. "Thanks awfully, but I'm doing fine. I'm getting some gun oil and cleaning equipment, though .303 ammunition's a bit hard to come by from you chaps. I may take some of your splendid Springfields back with me."

Carpenter thought for a moment. "Maybe I can arrange to drop some things to you later on. Give me a list."

"That's a capital idea, but we'll arrange a drop elsewhere by radio. I don't want noisy aeroplanes buzzing about over the village. Might give the Japanese the wrong impression."

Carpenter sat on his bunk and nodded. An awkward silence fell upon them as the rain intensified outside. Finally, Llewellyn said, "I'd best get back to my boys." He extended his right hand. "Take care of yourself, Jamie." Then he was gone into the wind and the rain.

Carpenter turned in early, and his fatigued body renewed itself in sleep. But late that night, during a thunderstorm, he had uneasy dreams of a sharpshooting Welsh mystic whose jungle-fevered brain conjured the demons of a hellbound self-fulfilling prophecy.

61.

THURSDAY, 24 SEPTEMBER

HONOLULU

Rogers stepped off the gray-painted navy bus and waited for the crowd of servicemen and civilians to disperse. He knew it was still early, but he sat on one of the curbside benches in case Sally was able to meet him at the bus stop. After several minutes of constantly checking his watch, he decided she would still be at the library. He hefted his bag and started walking.

The late-afternoon sunshine was pleasant, and Rogers enjoyed the breeze from the sea. He wound his way through Honolulu's pedestrian traffic, appreciatively eyeing the girls in lightweight floral prints and noting the varicolored ribbons on military blouses or tunics. He was surprised at how few of the men sported combat decorations. Rumor held that personnel who had been anywhere in the Hawaiian Islands during early June were eligible for a Midway campaign star. Lieutenant (junior grade) Rogers, with the earned arrogance of a twenty-four-year-old combat veteran, considered that policy sacrilegious.

At one intersection Rogers noted a group of men, mostly sailors, patiently standing in line under a tent canopy. Curious, he diverted to investigate the sound of hammering. One of the navy men, a third-class machinist mate, saw him coming and nudged a friend. Rogers saw that they were submariners.

"Relax," Rogers called. "I'm just curious what the line's for."

Both sailors turned sheepish grins. "Well, sir," began the third-class, "it's, ah, sort of . . ." The hammering resumed. ". . . a contest."

Rogers's face obviously betrayed confusion, as the other sailor explained. "We got nothin' much to do, Lieutenant. So we're waitin' our turn to pound the nails."

Taking a lateral step out of line, the aviator looked toward the front of the queue. Sure enough, another sailor was furiously hammering nails into a wood block while the civilian entrepreneur clocked him. "Fastest one to drive five nails wins a prize," the second-class elaborated.

Rogers shook his head in amazement. "That's the damnedest thing I ever heard of," he said softly. "Wouldn't you rather chase girls or visit the USO or go swimming or just lay on the beach?"

The two enlisted men traded looks that said it all: *Officers!* "Sir," the second-class ventured, "Joe and me just got back from our second war patrol and, believe me, we've done all that. But there ain't near enough girls to go around, and a guy can only eat so many doughnuts and swallow so much sand or saltwater."

Rogers noticed the submarine combat pins on their tunics and regarded the bored sailors with increased respect. *At least they've been shot at.* He decided to discuss the situation with his squadron's leadership to address similar concerns for the enlisted men of Bombing Three. Wishing the submariners good luck and good hunting, he continued walking.

Rounding the corner of Punchbowl, Rogers's pulse accelerated. He searched the Library of Hawaii for signs of activity. A few straggling patrons trailed down the steps as the doors closed. His heart fell. *I'm too late. She's already left.* He decided to turn around and walk the few blocks to her apartment.

Then Mary Tanaka stepped from the main entrance. Her gaze fell upon the tall, young naval officer and she smiled in recognition. She waved, ducked back inside and seconds later Sallyann Downey appeared.

Rogers dropped his bag, bounded up the steps and met Sally on the landing. She reached out to him as his arms wrapped around her and swirled her in a dizzying, joyous circle.

They walked arm in arm toward King Street, hardly speaking. She let her head rest on his shoulder part of the way, merely enjoying his presence. There would be no problem getting him into the apartment—visitors came and went frequently—but staying overnight could cause raised eyebrows. Not to mention however many following nights there may be. He had been indefinite during his subsequent phone calls.

She heard him say, "Sally, I saw the damnedest thing today. A bunch of enlisted men were actually standing in line, waiting to pound nails into a wood block." He sighed in frustration. "I can't believe the services don't do more for men on leave."

Sally shivered under her cotton dress. She unlocked the apartment door, furtively looking in each direction, and slipped inside. *This is as good a time as any,* she told herself.

She laid her purse down, then pulled him toward the sofa. He shed his cap, tie and shoes and they settled comfortably together. She stroked his hair and began. "Phil . . ." She ran out of words.

"Mmmm?" He lay with his eyes closed.

"Phil, you're right. There isn't enough for the boys to do. You know, I see a lot of them at work. They come to the library, looking for hometown newspapers or just a chance to talk to someone.

"Well, last week two sailors from the navy yard were there. They wanted me to go to some kind of party that weekend, but of course I refused."

His eyes were open and she felt him tense.

"Last Saturday evening they followed me here," she continued. "They were drunk and . . ." Her voice broke and she barely stifled a sob.

Rogers sat erect. His hands went to her shoulders and she saw the anger and the unspoken question in his eyes. For an instant she wondered if he had that same killing look when he dropped a bomb. "Did they . . ."

"Nothing happened," she hastened to add. "I mean, not much. Mr.

Tarutani, he's our neighborhood air-raid warden, and he stopped them." She leaned into him as he pulled her close.

Seconds passed before he trusted his voice. "What happened, Sally?"

She sniffed aloud and opened her mouth to gulp in air. "The authorities have them. One is still in the hospital with a fractured skull. The other's in jail. Apparently he may lose the sight of one eye."

Rogers absorbed that information. "My God! Did your Mr. Tatu—"

She managed a little giggle, then raised her head. "Yes. He's a very big man." She wiped a hand across her cheek, smearing a wet spot. "It only lasted a few seconds, but it seemed just forever."

They lay in silence for long moments, each concentrating on private thoughts. Rogers's focused on revenge. He wanted to know the sailors' names, but he knew better than to ask. *The navy values good relations with civilians*, he told himself. *They can get life in prison. But if they don't* . . .

Sally moved her head from his shoulder to his chest. "Phil, I've had the most awful thoughts. After the police and Mr. Tarutani left, I couldn't rest. I kept thinking that somehow I was being punished for . . . sleeping with you."

Rogers felt a pressure growing in his lungs until it escaped his lips in a burst of compressed air. *We're all products of our upbringing. Nice girls don't shack up with servicemen. But Sally really is a nice girl.* He could think of nothing to say that would comfort her.

She sniffed again but managed to control her voice. "I keep thinking how safe it felt back home, when I was still living with my parents. How we'd spend evenings around the radio or playing Monopoly. Or we'd invite the kids over for a jigsaw-puzzle party."

He smiled at the recollection of his own youth. She had described things familiar to most American households in the 1930s—simple activities that by themselves held little significance. Bundled together and wrapped in the rosy glow of memory, they meant Home.

"Sally, are you thinking of going back to Portland?"

She sat up and took his hands in hers. "I've thought about it, Phil. How would you feel about that?"

He shook his head. "I wouldn't like it at all. Not while I'm still here in the Pacific."

"Well, I hoped you'd feel that way. But aren't you going to have some leave on the mainland sometime?"

Rogers shrugged. "Sure, sometime. But there's no telling when that'll be, honey." He tried to think ahead. *Saratoga* was likely to be under repair for another two months, and no other carrier would be available in that time. He looked at her for a long moment. "I think we'll have some time together until November."

She quickly computed the schedule. *Five weeks, perhaps six. Maybe more, with luck.* In truth, she knew that it meant mostly one- and two-day sessions after an initial period like this, with seven to ten days' leave. But even that amounted to less actual time together because of her own work schedule.

"Well, I guess we'll just have to make the most of what time we have." She hoped her voice sounded as committed as her words.

He pulled her close again. "You bet we will, sweetheart. You bet we will."

62

MONDAY, 28 SEPTEMBER

GUADALCANAL

Jim Carpenter turned up his gunsight rheostat and mentally licked his chops. *Boy, are they going to be surprised*, he told himself. The Japanese bombers came on in typically precise fashion—nine three-plane vees, escorted by the largest swarm of fighters he had ever seen. But the coastwatchers and Cactus Radio were a well-drilled team by now. With more than enough time to respond, thirty-four marine and navy F4Fs were waiting at altitude to shred the picture-perfect enemy formations.

Looking back to double-check his division, Carpenter waggled his wings. Stankovich dipped a wingtip in response. Then, from a position ahead and to one side of the bombers, Carpenter rolled over and plunged vertically toward the Mitsubishis.

The Wildcat accelerated rapidly—so rapidly that condensation formed on the canopy and windscreen. For an instant Carpenter forgot his edginess at returning to combat as the topcover Zeros loomed in his vision. He rubbed a gloved fist on the windscreen, saw a plan view of the elegant little fighters frantically swerving to get out of the way, then he was through them. *Didn't even get a shot*, he chided himself. *Never mind—go for the bombers.*

He picked out a twin-engine shape in one of the three-plane vees and began tracking it. There was no return fire, as the enemy gunners could not bring their guns to bear. Carpenter sweetened up the sight picture and began firing earlier than he would have otherwise. From overhead he had no concern about compensating for bullet trajectory.

He fired again and knew he was getting hits. Motes of light played over the bomber's wings and upper fuselage. A white plume trailed from one wing as fuel vented into the slipstream. Just before he plunged past the formation he had the impression of the white wake turning orange-black as the fuel ignited. *Flamer!* he realized.

During debriefing, trying to sort out the claims, an intelligence officer asked why Carpenter did not make another pass. "You kidding?" came the reply. "Every time I lined up on another Jap, there were two or three more F4Fs ahead of me."

Stankovich clapped his division leader on the shoulder. "Nice shooting, Jim. How's it feel to be an ace?"

Carpenter stood in the crowded tent, coffee cup dangling in one hand, completely at a loss for words.

63.

MONDAY, 5 OCTOBER

NORTHERN SOLOMON ISLANDS

Sakaida pulled down his goggles, slid back the canopy and poked his head into the slipstream. Cold rain slammed at him as wind-driven rivulets spattered his lenses. *Outside visibility is no better than from inside the cockpit,* he realized. He reached up and backward, grasped the canopy and pulled it forward.

He had never flown in worse weather. Low, thick clouds with driving rain reduced visibility to absolute minimum, while the early morning sun added little illumination and no warmth at all. He checked his compass, saw he had drifted several degrees off course and corrected. Glancing down, he glimpsed spume from the tossing gray water and estimated a twenty-knot wind.

Sakaida remembered that he was alone. He had not seen any of Rekata Bay's other floatplane fighters since clearing Santa Isabel forty minutes before. Radio reports of American carrier planes attacking shipping off Shortland had prompted the scramble, but prospects of finding the raiders were near zero. *This is insane*, he told himself. *We may lose all our Type 2 fighters without even seeing the enemy.*

As usual, information was sketchy. There was no indication as to the Americans' approach or withdrawal routes, but the Solomons geography enabled an educated guess. If the raiders were in fact carrier-based, they probably had launched from somewhere to the north or east, beyond Choiseul. That was why Sakaida had taken a north-northwesterly course from Rekata Bay, hoping to catch some of the Americans on their egress. His squadronmates who had chosen to fly directly toward Shortland were merely wasting fuel and risking their lives to no purpose.

Sakaida had made a good guess. Given the limited range of his aircraft, it was the best one he could have made. It was also wrong.

Two hundred miles to the south, scattered elements of the *Hornet* Air Group straggled through leaden skies, seeking the only American flight deck then in Solomons waters.

GUADALCANAL

Carpenter had never felt so cold. He awoke with a deep, penetrating chill that forced him from his cot to pick up another blanket. Trembling from the icy prickling throughout his body, he returned to bed and curled into a fetal position. No matter what he did, he could not get warm.

He lay there in the dawn, alternately freezing and sweating. Eventually his teeth began chattering. He decided to wait it out, knowing that when the symptoms abated he would crawl from his cot and look up the flight surgeon. But the doctor could tell Jim Carpenter nothing he did not already know.

He had malaria.

64.

SATURDAY, 10 OCTOBER

GUADALCANAL, 0530

Major John L. Smith's hazel eyes bored into the gaunt face of First Lieutenant James Carpenter. "Are you sure you're up to this?"

Carpenter's blond head nodded slowly and, he hoped, confidently. "Yes, sir. I'll be okay."

"You know we have enough pilots for spares. Especially now that One-Twenty-One's arrived. Besides, we're leaving tomorrow."

Carpenter had seen Major Duke Davis's squadron land the day before. The outstanding character was VMF-121's executive officer—a big, confident, dark-haired captain who had pumped Carpenter's hand and drawled, "Pleased ta meet ya. I'm Joe Foss."

Secretly, Carpenter wanted to fly this mission for the adrenaline rush. He knew that the prospect of combat could supercharge his system and temporarily overcome the numbing fatigue. Sloppy thinking, perhaps, but that was how he felt. After that, he could look forward to a long rest.

"Honest, Smitty," he continued, "I'm okay to fly today. The doc gave me more pills. Besides, I'm on the schedule and I want to go." He looked directly at his CO and decided to try an unlikely approach. "Please."

Smith's level gaze swept back and forth across the lieutenant's face. Carpenter realized that the discussion had become a staring contest. If he averted his eyes, he would lose. He could sense the doubt in Smith's mind as the squadron commander weighed the risk against the benefit. In the previous six weeks, VMF-223 had lost a pilot a week killed and others wounded or evacuated with illness. Smith himself had been shot down, but showed incredible stamina for combat.

"All right, Carpenter. You can go. Just stay sharp."

Carpenter heaved a sigh of relief. The Cactus Express was running again and this was his last chance to help derail it.

REKATA BAY, 0540

Sakaida sat in his lifeless aircraft and sulked at the fates that denied him flight. He watched Kono leading another Type 2 fighter and a pair of F1M observation biplanes out into the bay for takeoff. The four floatplanes turned into the wind, slowly accelerated across the water and lifted into the air.

Lieutenant Mitaka had designated his two most experienced pilots for this morning's important mission. Providing air cover for the light cruiser *Tatsuta* and five destroyers was a critical assignment, especially since the R Area Air Force had been reduced to these few airworthy floatplanes.

The responsibility was enormous, and Sakaida felt the burden almost as much as the commissioned officers. He leaned out of the cockpit and shouted down to the two mechanics, up to their elbows in the engine accessory section. "Hey! Try again, will you?"

The mechanics exchanged expressive glances. *If this pilot is so anxious to get himself killed, let us accommodate him.* The senior man shrugged and said, "It might be the spark plugs. This engine has not had a new set in almost a hundred hours." The Japanese aircraft industry still had not been able to produce Western-quality components on a large scale. Some units resorted to scrounging plugs and other parts from downed Allied aircraft.

"We lack enough for a full change," replied the junior mechanic. "But I will get what we have."

Less than fifteen frantic minutes later Sakaida grinned a half smile and waved the men away. His Sakae engine felt and sounded like it was hitting regularly on about twelve of the fourteen cylinders, but that was good enough.

He advanced the throttle and bounced across the choppy water, hoping he was not too late for whatever was coming.

O V E R   T H E   S L O T,   0 6 4 0

The hunters found their prey between New Georgia and Santa Isabel. Looking down on the seventy-mile-wide channel, Carpenter noted the six high-speed wakes. Then he craned his neck, checking the disposition of the twenty-one navy and marine dive-bombers and torpedo planes assigned to the strike. With fifteen Wildcats and eight Airacobras to suppress the defenses, this shaped up as the largest mission yet flown by the Cactus Air Force.

Carpenter had never been this far north, roughly 175 miles from Henderson Field. The geography intrigued him—bright blue water bounding fluorescent-green islands basking in the sun's early light. The combat arena was walled by yellow-tinted cumulus clouds that hinted of rain later in the day. Then small man-made clouds punctured the air over New Georgia Sound, bursting in splotches of black, brown and gray.

With one more look around, Carpenter stuffed his nose down and dived toward the sleek, writhing shapes below.

Sakaida took one look and realized this was no place to be. An aluminum overcast of American aircraft was descending upon *Tatsuta* and her destroyers. He began wondering if his insistence on following Kono and the others had been advisable after all.

By flying directly southwest from Rekata Bay, he had made up most of the time he lost, because the escort flight had met the ships farther up the Slot. In the near distance an aircraft arced into the water, and Sakaida felt sure it was not hostile. His mind raced. *If I turn back I can say that my engine lacks power. Who will ever know?*

He shoved on full throttle as he answered his own question. *I will.*

Carpenter had been right. The sight of Japanese warships, the flak bursts, and now the peculiar little floatplanes worked their magic. His adrenaline kicked in and he forgot his sweaty chills. *There's not as many Japs airborne as we expected.*

And they were getting fewer. He witnessed Smith coolly executing a float biplane that could not get out of the way fast enough. *That's number nineteen for Smitty.*

The dive-bombing attack was well developed by now. Carpenter glimpsed white eruptions foaming the water around one of the destroyers and he knew that the TBFs—big torpedo planes resembling pregnant sharks—must be in their runs.

Carpenter swiveled his head to the left, concerned about approaching the water at such high speed. He intended to strafe a destroyer and banked in that direction, confident that Stankovich would stay with him.

Then Special Duty Ensign Yusuke Kono entered his field of vision. Carpenter remained in his turn, calculating that there was time for a quick shot at the float Zero. But the Japanese pilot was alert and skillful. He passed close to the Grumman's port wingtip, denying the American even a snap shot. Carpenter could have continued his turn but he was too smart for that. *Don't play his game, especially down low like this.* He added power and tucked the stick back in his lap, knowing his F4F could outclimb any floatplane.

Kono realized the odds were heavily against him, but if the Grumman would just remain in its turn for a few moments . . .

Loud, hard noises shattered Kono's concentration. His mind registered a variety of sensations: high-pitched *whangs* from somewhere behind the instrument panel; his canopy disappearing magically; oil clouding his windscreen.

Then came the heat, searing and overwhelming. He realized his fuel tanks were blazing. Even had he worn a parachute, he was too low to use it. Feeling his flesh begin to melt, he did the only thing he could do. He shoved the stick full forward and dived headlong into the water.

Carpenter rolled out of his climbing turn at 2,300 feet. The burning floatplane in the water was a definite kill. He keyed his microphone and called, "Nice going, Mike."

Stankovich's voice rasped back, high and elated. "Let's find another one!"

Sakaida saw the Type 2 fighter torching into the water. The sight appalled him. He saw the markings well enough to know it was his friend Kono, which was appalling in itself. The knowledge that the same fate could befall him in the next several seconds had a different effect. He felt his cheeks flush as anger replaced shock.

He had two Grummans in sight, both slightly below and ahead of him. He turned to line up the nearest one, closing from behind on the port quarter. He nudged stick and rudder, allowing for a fifteen-degree deflection shot. Then he opened up with all four guns.

Three things happened at once. Stankovich was screaming something about "behind you," red tracers flashed around Carpenter's Wildcat, and bullet impacts rang through the airframe. Without thinking, Carpenter stomped right rudder, cross-controlled and skidded to starboard.

The unwelcome sound and light show ceased. By the time Carpenter straightened out his aircraft and assessed his status, his airspeed was down to 200 knots. His zoom-climb and abrupt evasive maneuver had bled off precious airspeed.

He looked left, in the general direction of the threat, and gasped. Caught by surprise at the F4F's slewing movement, Sakaida's Type 2 sailed alongside the Grumman. For a moment the two antagonists regarded one another across the distance of less than three wingspans.

Sakaida thought fastest. He pushed over, inducing negative G, and immediately turned right. He slid under the American, knowing that for the moment the Grumman pilot would lose sight of him.

Carpenter sensed the developing situation. He calculated that the floatplane must be passing under his starboard wing. For one moment he debated whether to try to pursue, or to disengage. He decided on the latter. With his left hand shoving prop and throttle controls to the firewall, he turned forty-five degrees left to open the distance, and accelerated away from the threat. Seconds later he had the presence of mind to call his wingman. "Nail him, Mike!"

Stankovich had regained most of the altitude he had expended in flaming Kono, and was positioned to attack Sakaida from above and to one side. Eager for another victory, he nosed down, simultaneously tracking the floatplane. As he did so, he pressed the trigger. A stuttering few rounds chugged from his six guns, then lapsed into awful, embarrassing silence.

He knew what he had done. *God damn it all to hell! Fired under negative G and jammed every gun.* He aborted his attack, turned protectively behind Carpenter and tried to keep an eye on the Japanese. He leaned down in the cockpit, grasped the charging handles and pulled on the three right-hand cables in turn. Nothing. He came up for another look, saw no threat and tried the left-hand cables. He put all his fullback's brawn into the effort and one reluctantly gave way. He squirted an experimental burst. *Well, one gun's better than none.*

Big Mike Stankovich eyed the disappearing silhouette of what should have been his second victory of the day. He shook his head sadly. *You're one lucky son of a bitch.* Then he turned to follow his damaged lead aircraft back to Guadalcanal.

65.

SUNDAY, 11 OCTOBER

HENDERSON FIELD

The way home led up the boarding ladder to the dented double doors at the rear of the R4D-1. The twin-engine Douglas transport's blue-gray paint was scratched and peeling in places, but to the weary, ill survivors of VMF-223 and VMSB-232, it held the polished-aluminum glory of a peacetime DC-3 airliner.

Standing at the base of the ladder, the Skytrain's crew chief maintained a cheerful banter. "Welcome aboard, gentlemen. Watch your step. Be sure you have your boarding passes and baggage claims. Flight Two-fifty-three will be leaving shortly."

Stankovich stepped up the first rung of the ladder and stopped for a moment. The sergeant's New York accent grated on his ears, and the pilot pointedly looked down. On the ladder the height difference between the two men was amplified even more, and the crew chief felt the glare from on high. His patter abruptly ceased.

Carpenter settled onto a canvas seat beside his wingman and nudged him with an elbow. "Good work, son. If there's anything I can't stand, it's somebody who's that damn cheerful."

Twenty minutes later the R4D lifted off Henderson Field's steel-planked runway and a muted cheer arose from the pilots who were plank owners in the Cactus Air Force. As the transport banked to the south, bound for New Caledonia, many of the aviators glanced out the square windows for a last look at Guadalcanal.

Jim Carpenter sat in his uncomfortable seat, shivering beneath his jacket. He kept his eyes closed until he was sure the miserable island had fallen far, far astern.

66.

FRIDAY, 16 OCTOBER

REKATA BAY

Someone shouted a warning and another sailor began winding the crank on the hand-powered siren. But the alarm came a fraction of a minute after the bombs began falling.

Sakaida and Noichi dumped feetfirst into the noncommissioned officers' trench, followed by others. They heard the not-so-distant *caarump* of 500-pounders exploding, then the low-pitched whine of radial engines. Noichi risked a look over the lip of the trench and quickly ducked back. Wide-eyed, he exclaimed, "Grummans! They're everywhere." Another bomb detonated nearby, showering dirt, sand and chunks of palm trees upon the men huddling in the earth.

"Why don't our planes intercept the Americans?" asked a third-class petty officer.

Sakaida did not bother to respond. Rekata's dozen floatplanes had received no warning of the impending attack—not that it would have done any good. None of the floatplanes remained operational. Between battle damage and a lack of spare parts, the R Area Air Force was a military organization on paper only.

From the sound of it, this was no mere raid. It could be most of a carrier air group with bombers, attack planes and fighters. Sakaida distinctly heard the hammering of numerous machine guns as Grummans strafed the parked or moored seaplanes. He thought of the recent American strike on Shortland and his luckless hunt for the raiders. Intelligence reports indicated the carrier *Hornet* was still active in the area.

He leaned into Noichi and raised his voice above the noise. "If they're coming after us, that must mean they are finished with Buin." Noichi huddled against the trench wall, hands over his head, and nodded vaguely.

Sakaida thought back. He could recall at least four heavy raids on the Buin/Shortland area over the past three weeks. The enemy was gaining strength—no doubt about it. Boeings, Grummans, even the long-nosed Bells had appeared in the northern and central Solomons with increasing regularity. *Kono is lucky to be out of it*, he thought. Lieutenant Mitaka had received word that the special-duty ensign had been picked up by one of the destroyers six days ago. He was badly burned but would survive to sit out the war in Japan. Sakaida reflected that maybe that was no blessing to a warrior like Yusuke Kono.

The American attack seemed to be abating. Sakaida looked up, saw only blue sky and clouds, and decided on a peek. He edged his head above the trench and looked down toward the shoreline. Burning floatplanes littered the area while others sat askew on their dollies, left in the sand like discarded toys. Then he heard another staccato engine overhead.

Glancing skyward, shielding his eyes from the glare, at first he found nothing. Then he saw it—a graceful silhouette pulling vapor streamers from its rounded wingtips in the moist air. Framed by palm fronds, it was a sight Hiroyoshi Sakaida felt he would not soon forget. *A Douglas carrier bomber*, he thought. *The kind the Americans had at Midway.*

He slumped back to the bottom of the trench. The memories washed over him. Less than five months ago he had sailed in cruiser *Tone*, feeling almost carefree and full of optimism. He thought again of Azumano and Naito. *Those days are gone forever. It began with Midway.* He concentrated hard, trying to remember the name he sought. Not the manufacturer's identity most frequently used by Japanese, but the American title of the carrier bomber.

It came to him as he envisioned the palm-framed silhouette recovering from its dive. He mouthed the name. "What did you say?" Noichi asked.

Sakaida pronounced the alien word again, slowly and with difficulty. "Dauntless."

67.

SATURDAY, 17 OCTOBER

NAS PEARL HARBOR

A long line of serious-looking young men stood under the Hawaiian sky, dressed in tropical whites. As his name was announced, each in turn stepped two paces forward to be decorated. Seated in the bleachers, Sallyann Downey was primly dressed in a long dress with white gloves and a hat, holding a parasol. Despite her proper appearance, she squealed audibly when the air station commander announced, "Lieutenant, junior grade, Philip Rogers."

The awardee stepped out of rank and stood at attention as the captain intoned, "The Secretary of the Navy takes pride in conferring the Navy Cross upon Lieutenant (junior grade) Philip Rogers, U.S. Naval Reserve, for extraordinary heroism while serving as a scout-bomber pilot.

"On six June 1942, then-Ensign Rogers participated in an attack upon enemy Japanese fleet units retiring from the vicinity of Midway Island. Diving through intense and accurate antiaircraft fire, Ensign Rogers's aircraft was hit numerous times. Despite a severe leg wound from enemy action, Ensign Rogers ignored the injury and aggressively pressed his attack, obtaining a decisive hit upon a Japanese cruiser. His contribution was such that the enemy warship was sunk and another was seriously damaged.

"Demonstrating exceptional fortitude and airmanship, Ensign Rogers returned his damaged plane to the U.S. task force and successfully landed aboard. In so doing, he preserved a valuable aircraft and possibly saved the life of his radioman-gunner.

"Ensign Rogers's performance is a credit to himself and his squadronmates, and is fully in keeping with the highest traditions of the naval service."

The four-striper then pinned the medal on Rogers's chest, alongside the Distinguished Flying Cross and Purple Heart. A crisp handshake, an exchange of salutes and the rites were completed.

Sally walked to him and touched the gunmetal-bronze cross and the gold-edged heart with George Washington's profile. The Navy Cross had only recently been elevated above the Distinguished Service Medal as the service's highest decoration next to the Medal of Honor. "Oh, Phil, I'm so proud." She kissed his cheek. "And not just for the medals. But for what they stand for."

Rogers put his arms around her and hugged her briefly. Then he placed his hands on her shoulders and stood back. "Sally, you need to know something." He took a breath and plunged ahead. "The citation is wrong. It didn't happen that way."

Her brown eyes showed confusion. "But you told me when you got back . . ."

"Yeah, everything in the citation really happened. But not in the order they wrote it down. I said I dropped my bomb on that cruiser, and while pulling out of my dive I got hit. Don't you see? That switch changes everything."

Her black hair ruffled in the breeze as she shook her head. "What difference does that make?"

He felt a growing frustration. It was important to him that she understand. "Look. If I had been wounded and still bombed the cruiser, then maybe I'd deserve the Navy Cross. It's been awarded for less, believe me. But I was just doing my job like Bernie and Shawn and everybody else. I didn't get wounded until *after* I dropped my bomb."

Sally shrugged and tossed her head. "Well, it doesn't matter, Mr. Rogers." She slid her arms around him again. "You're still pretty heroic to me." She kissed him hard. "So there."

Rogers looked over her shoulder and saw Barnes standing with some of the other aircrewmen who had just been decorated. The gunner winked at his pilot and beamed a male-bonding grin as Rogers felt his cheeks redden with the onset of an embarrassed blush. *There's no use ignoring it,* he decided. He took Sally's elbow. "Come on, there's somebody I want you to meet."

Barnes stood proudly erect as the couple approached. He looked recruiting-poster perfect in his starched whites with a row of ribbons adding a splash of color below his silver aircrew wings. He also wore the Distinguished Flying Cross with a cluster for the second award of that medal.

Rogers tried to remember the protocol. *The lady is presented to the man, I think.* "Barnes, I'd like to introduce Miss Sallyann Downey, my . . . ah, friend." His cheeks reddened some more. "Sally, this is Radioman Second Class Bill Barnes, who's flown with me since before Midway."

Sally extended her gloved hand and Barnes grasped a bit too hard, bowing slightly. "I'm sure pleased to meet you, ma'am."

The pressure of Barnes's grip and the same white sailor's uniform from the library incident sent a little electric shock through Sally's body. For an instant she wanted to turn toward Rogers for support. She told herself, *That's stupid. Phil said this boy probably saved his life.* It occurred to her that they were three young people, all in their early twenties, playing at being adults in a social situation. "Well, I'm certainly glad to meet *you*, Mr. Barnes. Phil told me what you've done. Congratulations on your medal." Belatedly, she wondered if she should have called him something other than "Mr. Barnes." *To hell with it. I'm not in the navy, they are.*

The aircrewman looked down at the red, white and blue ribbon with the stylized propeller pendant. He grinned self-consciously. "Thanks, ma'am. But I think most of the guys have 'em by now."

Rogers interrupted. "That's not so. Bill has shot down two Jap planes and not many gunners can say that. It's why I think he's going to be accepted for flight training."

Sally turned back toward the gangly young Montanan. "Why, that's wonderful. Maybe you and Phil will end up flying together again."

Barnes radiated enthusiasm. "That'd be something, wouldn't it, Mr. Rogers? Me flyin' your wing!" Both men knew that the odds were infinitesimal. "Do you know where you'll be goin', sir?"

Rogers shook his head. "Not yet. I told the detailer that after getting torpedoed three times, I don't like submarines very much. Maybe I'll wind up in one of the escort squadrons being formed to hunt subs." He extended his hand and they shook. "You keep in touch with me, now. That's an order." His voice was stern, his smile wide and genuine.

"Aye, aye, sir!"

Watching Barnes rejoin his friends, Sally leaned against Rogers's arm. "I'm glad you did that, Phil. I needed to be reminded that most sailors aren't like . . ." She sought the word. ". . . some."

Rogers gave her a quick hug. As they walked toward Burnett, Murtagh and the others, his mind turned to the future. He fingered his Navy Cross and silently cursed to himself. *Now I have to earn this damn thing.*

68.

SUNDAY, 1 NOVEMBER

OVERLOOKING KAWAILOA BEACH

Rogers sat with his back against a palm tree, a three-day-old newspaper folded in his hands. Sally lay on their blanket with her head resting on his leg. He scanned the headlines once more.

NAVAL, LAND BATTLE RAGES IN SOLOMONS

He put the paper down. Reading between the lines, it was apparent that another carrier battle had been fought during the 26th or 27th.

That means the Enterprise *and* Hornet *are involved.* To Phil Rogers, it meant not ships and squadrons, but friends. Frank DiBella, Bucky Petersen, undoubtedly several others. *At least Sunny Jim's back from Guadalcanal,* he thought. *But he's changed.* Rogers silently chided himself. *Hell, we've all changed.* He looked down at the young woman dozing in his lap. *Including you.*

He ran a hand across Sally's forehead and she opened her eyes. "The bus will be here in about half an hour," he said.

She nodded, reached up and clasped her hands behind his neck. Still sitting under their palm tree, wrapped around one another, they watched the blood-red sunset on the oceanic expanse that men still called Pacific.

EPILOGUE

"[The Dauntless] was the only U.S. aircraft to participate in all five naval engagements fought exclusively between carriers, and deficiencies notwithstanding, it emerged with an almost legendary reputation as the most successful shipboard dive-bomber of all time—albeit success that perhaps owed more to the crews that flew it in truly *dauntless* fashion than to the intrinsic qualities of the aeroplane itself."

CAPTAIN ERIC M. BROWN,
ROYAL NAVY (RETIRED)
Wings of the Navy

Bombing Squadron Three returned to the United States in August 1943, re-formed with Curtiss Helldivers and logged another combat tour from the second *Yorktown* (CV-10) in 1944–45. Despite two postwar redesignations (Attack Squadron 3A and -35) the unit retained its identity as the Panthers, flying the AD-1 Skyraider—another legendary Douglas product—from USS *Leyte* (CV-32) in the Korean War. The Panthers were still flying Skyraiders a generation later when they transitioned to Grumman's jet A-6A Intruder in 1965. Over the next eight years VA-35 logged four more combat tours from the new *Enterprise* (CVAN-65), *Coral Sea* (CVA-43) and *America* (CVA-66).

In 1991 the Panthers flew their A-6Es on overland air strikes deep into Iraq from the second *Saratoga* (CV-60). With combat deployments from nine carriers in four major wars, VA-35 remains the senior attack squadron in the U.S. Navy and the second-oldest of all carrier squadrons.

Of the *Yorktown* squadron commanders who led their aircrews into combat in June 1942, none remain. Lance Massey perished at the head of Torpedo Three. Wally Short died in 1979, Jimmy Thach in 1981, and Max Leslie in 1985. Leslie's successor, Dave Shumway, was killed in a flying accident nine years after the war. Syd Bottomley, the squadron's next senior aviator, became the skipper in 1943 and succumbed to cancer in 1990.

The fate of "Wayne Wik" was not known until 1947, when war-crimes investigators tracked down the story. The murder ship, IJNS *Arashi*, lost a night torpedo duel with American destroyers in the Solomon Islands during 1943. Her captain at Midway, Commander Watanabe, died later that year; the division commander, Captain Ariga, was killed in action off Okinawa in 1945. Identity of the actual executioner never was firmly established.

As for what became of Phil Rogers, Sallyann Downey, Bernie Burnett, Jim Carpenter and Hiroyoshi Sakaida—that's another story.

American Aircraft Types

SBD-3 Dauntless. Single-engine, two-seat carrier scout-bomber built by Douglas Aircraft. The most successful Allied dive-bomber of WW II. Top speed in level flight: 250 mph/218 knots.

SB2U-3 Vindicator. Single-engine, two-seat scout-bomber built by Vought Aircraft. Obsolete by WW II, largely restricted to land-based and Marine Corps use. Top speed: 243 mph/211 knots.

TBD-1 Devastator. Single-engine, three-seat carrier torpedo plane built by Douglas. Three TBD squadrons sustained crippling casualties at Midway and the type was withdrawn from fleet service. Top speed: 206 mph/179 knots.

TBF-1 Avenger. Single-engine, four-seat carrier torpedo plane built by Grumman Aircraft. Larger, faster replacement for the TBD-1. Top speed: 271 mph/236 knots.

F2A-3 Buffalo. Single-engine, single-seat carrier fighter built by Brewster Aircraft. Largely relegated to Marine Corps use early in the war, its only combat was flown from Midway. Top speed: 321 mph/279 knots.

F4F-3/4 Wildcat. Single-engine, single-seat carrier fighter built by Grumman. Replaced the F2A both in carrier- and land-based squadrons. The F4F-4 variant had folding wings and six versus four guns. Top speed of the F4F-4: 312 mph/271 knots.

PBY-5/5A Catalina. Twin-engine, long-range patrol bomber built by Consolidated Aircraft; the U.S. Navy's premier flying boat of WW II. The amphibian PBY-5A version could operate from land or water. Top speed of the PBY-5A: 179 mph/156 knots.

R4D-1 Skytrain. Military transport version of the Douglas DC-3 twin-engine airliner, modified with large cargo doors. Top speed: 225 mph/196 knots.

B-17E Flying Fortress. Four-engine bomber built by Boeing Aircraft. Employed by the U.S. Army early in the Pacific war, it was more valued for its range than for its success against shipping. Top speed: 317 mph/275 knots.

B-26 Marauder. Fast, twin-engine medium bomber built by Martin Aircraft. Occasionally armed with torpedoes for shipping attacks by U.S. Army units. Top speed: 315 mph/274 knots.

P-400 Airacobra. Single-engine, single-seat export version of Bell Aircraft's P-39 Army Air Force fighter. Unsuited to aerial combat but effective in ground support missions. Top speed: 355 mph/309 knots.

Japanese Aircraft Types

A6M2 Type Zero Carrier Fighter. Single-engine, single-seat carrier fighter built by Mitsubishi. Commonly called "Zero" but later code-named Zeke by Allied intelligence. Top speed: 331 mph/288 knots.

A6M2-N Type Two Sea Fighter. Floatplane version of the Zero fighter, built by Nakajima. Later code-named Rufe. Top speed: 270 mph/235 knots.

B5N2 Type 97 Carrier Attack Aircraft. Single-engine, three-seat carrier torpedo plane built by Nakajima. Later code-named Kate. Top speed: 229 mph/199 knots.

D3A1 Type 99 Carrier Bomber. Single-engine, two-seat carrier dive-bomber built by Aichi. Later code-named Val. Top speed: 240 mph/209 knots.

D4Y1-C Type 2 Carrier Reconnaissance Plane. Scouting variant of the single-engine, two-seat dive-bomber built by Yokosuka. Two prototypes were both lost at Midway. Later code-named Judy. Top speed: 343 mph/298 knots.

E13A1 Type Zero Reconnaissance Seaplane. Single-engine, three-seat floatplane launched from battleships and cruisers, built by Aichi. Later code-named Jake. Top speed: 234 mph/203 knots.

F1M2 Type Zero Observation Seaplane. Single-engine, two-seat float biplane built by Mitsubishi. Later code-named Pete. Top speed: 230 mph/200 knots.

G4M1 Type One Attack Bomber. Twin-engine naval land-based bomber built by Mitsubishi. Later code-named Betty. Top speed: 266 mph/231 knots.

H6K2 Type 97 Flying Boat. Four-engine, parasol-wing seaplane built by Kawanishi. Later code-named Mavis. Top speed: 206 mph/179 knots.

H8K1 Type 2 Flying Boat. Four-engine, long-range seaplane built by Kawanishi; perhaps the finest flying boat produced during WW II. Later code-named Emily. Top speed: 269 mph/234 knots.

DAUNTLESS GLOSSARY

AirPac	(Commander) Aircraft, Pacific Fleet
AirSols	(Commander) Aircraft, Solomon Islands
BuAer	Bureau of Aeronautics
BuPers	Bureau of Personnel
CAG	Commander of Air Group
CAVU	Ceiling And Visibility Unlimited
CinC	Commander-in-Chief
CO	Commanding Officer
DCA	Damage Control Assistant
DFC	Distinguished Flying Cross

MCAS	Marine Corps Air Station
NAS	Naval Air Station
SNAFU	WW II slang: Situation Normal, All Fouled Up
VB	Navy bombing squadron
VF	Navy fighting squadron
VP	Navy patrol squadron
VS	Navy scouting squadron
VT	Navy torpedo squadron
VMF	Marine fighting squadron
VMSB	Marine scout-bomber squadron

BIBLIOGRAPHY

Cressman, Robert J. *That Gallant Ship*. Missoula: Pictorial Histories, 1985.

Cressman, Robert J., and Steve Ewing, et al. *A Glorious Page in Our History*. Missoula: Pictorial Histories, 1990.

Douglas Aircraft Company. *Pilot's Handbook for SBD-5 Aircraft*, 1943.

Dull, Paul S. *A Battle History of the Imperial Japanese Navy*. Annapolis: Naval Institute Press, 1978.

Fahey, James C. *The Ships and Aircraft of the U.S. Fleet, Victory Edition*. Annapolis: Naval Institute Press, 1978.

Francillon, René J. *Japanese Aircraft of the Pacific War*. London: Putnam and Company, 1970.

Frank, Pat, and J.D. Harrington. *Rendezvous at Midway.* New York: Warner Paperback Library, 1968.

Heinl, Robert D. *Marines at Midway.* Washington: U.S. Marine Corps, 1948.

Lord, Walter. *Incredible Victory.* New York: Harper & Row, 1967.

Ludstrom, John B. *The First Team.* Annapolis: Naval Institute Press, 1984.

Prange, Gordon W., ct al. *Miracle at Midway.* New York: McGraw-Hill, 1983.

Tillman, Barrett. *The Dauntless Dive Bomber of WW II.* Annapolis: Naval Institute Press, 1976.

U.S. Navy. Action Reports and War Diary of Bombing Squadron Three, 1942.

———. Action Reports for USS *Yorktown* (CV-5), 1942.

———. *Articles for the Government of the Navy,* 1937.

Watts, A.J. *Japanese Warships of WW II.* Garden City: Doubleday and Co., 1970.

ABOUT THE AUTHOR

Former managing editor of *The Hook*, the journal of carrier aviation, Barrett Tillman has won writing awards from the American Aviation Historical Society, the Air Force Historical Foundation and the North American Institute of Oceanographic History. With his father, a World War II navy-trained pilot, he restored and flew a Dauntless dive-bomber in 1971–74. That experience inspired his first book, an operational history of the SBD, leading to six subsequent nonfiction volumes and two previous Bantam novels: *Warriors* and *The Sixth Battle*. Among other pursuits, Tillman serves as executive secretary of the American Fighter Aces Association in Mesa, Arizona, and is a rangemaster and special deputy sheriff in his native Umatilla County, Oregon. He is currently at work on the sequel to *Dauntless*, another "retro" techno-thriller set in World War II.